The Jeffries Affair

John Sherwood

First published by Dog Ear Publishing
4011 Vincennes Rd
Indianapolis, IN 46268
www.dogearpublishing.net

ISBN: 978-1-4575-5560-2

This book is printed on acid-free paper.

Printed in the United States of America

"**M**att DiGrande's office, may I help you?"

"But of course. Is Mr. DiGrande in?"

"Whom may I ask is calling?"

"That's a very interesting question. On one hand I could say a fellow business executive with a desire to discuss an opportunity of mutual interest. On the other, I could simply say an old friend, a childhood friend to be exact."

"That sounds intriguing. One minute please."

The phone went blank for a nanosecond and then some spasmodic new-age music hovering somewhere between mild irritation and utter annoyance rang steadfastly over the line. Bryan listened with mixed emotions. He had rehearsed his re-introduction to Matt DiGrande a thousand times and was still not sure at what emotional or intellectual level he would respond to hearing his voice. The Bryan Jeffries from long ago might emerge suddenly with quixotic retorts reminiscent of the '70's or the Bryan Jeffries of recent professional years might immediately wrestle control of the dialogue with business like precision. No matter how he rehearsed the scene, his odds one way were only even with the other. In other words, he didn't have a clue.

"This is Matt DiGrande. How may I help you?"

Silence clung to the moment like a cat clawing air before falling earthward and then Bryan, in more 70's speak than current vintage, uttered "Wild Man, its Jeffries. Long time no talk. I thought it might be right to rectify that wrong."

"Bryan Jeffries. Oh my God! I think of you often but never thought I'd hear from you. I've followed your career and have been undeniably humbled by your success. Mr. WorldSupplî CTO, what an accomplishment!"

"Give me a break Matt! Editor in Chief of Chicago's only worthwhile rag? Like that's something to sneeze at? You're one of the most talked about people in circles that matter."

"Very flattering Bri, but the sword I carry has two edges, if you know what I mean. Sometimes the sword is wielded upward in victory, but it also comes down, and when it does it's with the force of gravity on Jupiter."

"Oh I know exactly what you mean. No matter how high you climb there's always someone above you. Someone that you have to report to. Someone that thinks they're better than you. Someone with the power to end your career with a wink. Doesn't matter if it's some ass-hole on the board of directors or a major shareholder. The minute they spout some uneducated, inanely sophomoric dribble that would make a layman look smart, it becomes gospel, immediately. The world is full of assholes... Good God! What am I saying? Enough of this already, I haven't talked to you in over 20 years! How the hell are you anyway? How's the wife? And kids? We have to catch up. We can't let the fun we shared as kids lie dormant forever! I want to reminisce. I want rekindle the exuberance of our youth."

"Wow. That's certainly a mouthful, but you always were the talker. Direct, but not to the point of arrogance. Flowery, but with firm petals. OK Bri, we can catch up, but not now. I've got a major presentation with the owners coming up and have no time at the moment. How about sometime next week? Dinner one night?"

"Great I'll call your assistant to lock an opening in your schedule. That work for you Wild Man?"

"Yeah that works fine. And Bri, I haven't been called Wild Man in a long time. It sounds good."

Matt sat still after their brief conversation, his mind flooded with memories both grand and poor. The thought of thinking about the past was as overwhelming as a village elder facing a tsunami. Terrifying but unavoidable. Scary but exciting. He had to let the wave pass through him and ebb completely before returning to the reality of his present. Bryan fucking Jeffries! The greatest times, the wildest times, but a life-time ago. Was this random contact to be taken at face value or could that crazy man be carrying some other agenda? The idea of his random con-tact after so many years didn't feel right. Too late to worry about that now and no time in any case. Back to work ol' boy. You need to dazzle the chieftains one more time, DiGrande thought.

Jeffries was left with a fermenting brew of strange emotions after his brief conversation with Matt. So many years had passed that the idea of a reunion seemed surreal. DiGrande was, by his looks in the papers, in shape and wearing his age well. Rumor had it that his marriage was truly successful too, the all American family - kids, dog, great house - the works.

A panoramic view of downtown Chicago on an early Monday morning in the midst of spring finds the city rapidly awakening from its Sunday evening nap. The eastern skyline shows promise of a warming sun, though a major chill still lingers in the air from the breeze off Lake Michigan. Trees are just starting to bud, a sure sign that nature has again made it through the harshness of winter, and while people remain wrapped in heavy clothing to stave off penetration of the cold there is an abundance of cheer in the air in expectation of summer days to come.

Street vendors, newspaper stands, coffee houses, breakfast shops are all busy readying themselves for a day of solid revenues, portended by their internal glow and the growing globe of gold from the east. Sausages are steaming to life from the stand on the corner of Main and Commonwealth, while their master sips from a freshly made cup of Starbucks. Gena's Breakfast Knuk has just rolled back her iron gate and unleashed her OPEN sign to the joy of some hungry regulars. Newspapers have been delivered outside Ken's Daily News Stand and Ken, while sucking on the remnants of yesterday's cigar, hums as he organizes his brothel of paraphernalia.

But not all is totally rosy in Chicago. The allure of the waterfront, with its' multimillion dollar high-rise condos, fancy four star restaurants and bars for the young and glamorous, fade from view, and mind, in the distance of just a few blocks. As one move's into the depths of the city, from river front toward Wrigley field, the demeanor of morning activities transitions from eager ambition to mandatory compliance. Instead of embracing the beauty of the new spring day, people are gathering their energies to face another difficult week. Their motions are constrained and deliberate; their faces taught in anticipation of the stresses they will encounter. In rapid pace, with coats drawn tight, heads bowed slightly and faces set with determination, they march toward their inevitable encounter with their professional destination, where they will don smart, encouraging faces and muster the best of their morning graces.

Still further in our city, tucked away on the seventh floor of a modest apartment building, in a comfortable, but disheveled dwelling, is the residence of Charles Prescott. Charles, who jokingly is referred to as

Charlie Chip and wants to be known as Chad, remains asleep as the morning din rises around him. Charles is not the neatest guy in the world. His bedroom looks like a hurricane passed through it sometime last year and his closet door, blocked by mounds of half used clothes, hasn't been opened in months for fear of the avalanche coiled within. His dressers gather no dust for they are blind to the light of day and while Chad is sound asleep, his bed is covered in boxes full of books - books mainly on music. From the history of classical orchestra to engineering of the moog synthesizer, from the life and times of Bach and Baez to theory on sound, lie hundreds of books where one would expect to find a person.

As nasty as this bedroom appears, a path to the outer world has been maintained. The Oriental rug beneath speaks only where holes exist between the array of obstacles that litter the floor. From guitar picks to ties, old magazines and clothes, barely more than a footpath marks the area reserved for the feet of Chad. By the bedroom door, held ajar in a fashion similar to the closet, stands a threshold into another world, a world in which Chad is sound asleep.

Chad's other world is a living room, in the broadest sense of the term. It is rectangular for functionality, has a full kitchen and eating area behind a counter-height bar and an integral area for lounging and social engagement. With a normal occupant the place would have the wherewith-all to be fashioned in a quaintly appealing manner, but Chad is not of that ilk. And, where the bedroom reflects the necessities of ordinary activity, the living room shares no such suggestion. Chad's small TV and couch, his only "home-like" possessions are dwarfed by sets of computers, printers, other electronic gadgets and several keyboards. On a small but sturdy table in the center of the room, neatly and with purpose, are stacked rows of different papers all with a common format. It is music-sheets of written music.

Overtly evident from the surroundings is Chad's passion for music; so extensive that one would correctly surmise that his main ambition in life is the creation of poetry through sound. He is equipped with all the latest music making instrumentation and music writing software. His

daily routine normally involves hours of writing and for this he has con-
structed his own special chair, the chair where he is sleeping. Chad is
slumped over his favorite keyboard with his latest creation still looming
on the CRT overhead. His face, turned starboard and planted in the keys,
is placid and at ease. His slightly open rounded mouth has mined a vein
of drool that puddles slowly on the flat white surface while it generates
an almost appealing snoring sound. While Chad generally sleeps on the
sofa, it is not unusual for him to depart from consciousness while still in
his chair - for a few minutes, if not for a several hours.

Suddenly, the piercing sound of an angry horn sends shock waves
through the apartment and in an instant Chad is snatched from his deep
comfortable sleep. His eyes light up and his torso twists into its normal
sitting position as his brain drinks in the reality of Monday. Seven fifteen - twelve minutes to get out of the apartment in time to catch the bus.

"Damn! I did it again!" Chad screams as he wipes his mouth,
jumps from his chair and bolts toward the bathroom. While in flight his
clothes start peeling themselves from his body, landing hap-hazardously
on clothes met by a similar fate on similar days in the past. In minutes
his shower is complete, his teeth are brushed, some wrinkled clothes are
arranged to resemble the shape of the torso within and a mismatched,
saved from extinction tie, is noosed into position in close proximity to a
fold pretending to be his collar. Launching a comb through the wet
entanglement of his thick chestnut hair is all it takes to complete the finishing touches of morning hygiene.

With three minutes left Chad has plenty of time for his usual breakfast - a candy bar and a bottle of Mango Madness. He yanks open the
door of the frig exposing a world laden with a variety of unique aromas
which collectively remain overwhelmed by the milk-turned-yogurt a few
weeks past. Fortunately the bottom row, reserved for Mango Madness, is
not yet bare and the Snicker's box on the counter still has a 2.07 ouncer
for the uptake. With both in left hand, and briefcase in right, Chad bolts
for the exit and the bus stop six blocks south. But just as quickly as he
leaves, he stops, spins around and bolts back into the apartment. In
three leaps he is tight to his keyboard staring at the silent poetry of last

nights' effort. One quick change and a glimmer of satisfaction later Chad bolts again from the apartment hopeful to get a seat on the bus.

Getting to ground level is a simple and fun task for Chad and one he looks forward to most days. With no love of idleness, for even a minute, Chad foregoes every attempt at using the elevator opting instead to skip as quickly as possible down the stairs to the street-level door below. He is expert at the process, hitting every step in quick succession on one floor, jumping two and three steps at a time on the next, and tapping in rhythmic harmony on another. The resonating echoes of his office shoes on the con-crete slabs produce a melody that Chad calls Chicago aboriginal. On the landing by the street-level door Chad slows a bit, collects himself in prepa-ration for his entry into his other reality and emerges faceless to blend seamlessly into the crowded morning street.

With a hundred feet to go Chad peers at the bus-stop to gage the nature of the competition for space. A crowd of twenty or so is seen jock-eying into position on a small patch of cracked sidewalk. A rotund fel-low in the middle has established first position, eyeing the others in his midst like a Sumo wrestler readying for take down. An older women stands directly behind him knowing well that he will suit as the blocker for this morning's play off tackle, while the others mill about in a state of anxious denial like guppies in a bowl with Piranha. The sight is all too common and the results too predictable. When the bus finally pulls to a halt there is barely enough room for the driver to flick open the door, and when the door shuts, there is more total occupied space than there is air left available to breathe.

Chad finds his way into the bus from the entrance in the rear. The standing crowd grimaces as each new entrant forces them to huddle more closely together. About five feet to the fore Chad finds a square foot of floor on which to plant his feet and a seat-back on which to place a steadying hand. A normal start in his daily routine – a necessity that is by no means voluntary.

The bus ride takes about twenty minutes and if it is on time so too will Chad. Business hours begin at eight and while the company is somewhat lenient with morning punctuality, abuse is not tolerated for very long. Chad has already consumed his share of tardiness tickets and is hopeful for an on-time arrival to forego an ass-chewing as kick off to his week. The bus lurches forward as his mind begins to recollect the open issues left looming from Friday last. As technical assistant of information systems there is no end to the variety of issues in need of constant attention. His involvement runs the complete spectrum of the technical maze, from training no-minds in PC applications to supporting a cloud based business system.

Without fully acknowledging the distasteful surroundings of the morning sojourn, but simply existing through it, his bus stop at last arrives where the five minute walk to his building will be the only peace he has for the balance of the day. Chad completes the trek each and every day in ceremonial death-march fashion in observation of his feelings for the inevitable that lies ahead. In fact, his marching game ends each morning with a quick, sharply performed immediate right hand turn exactly at the bottom center of the front entry steps. He then resumes a more normal posture to enter the lions' mouth with the best mindset he can muster where, immediately on his arrival, there will be a few quick system checks to be certain that the weekend back-ups were completed without a hitch. Then he will make his way to his office where the war games begin.

"Good morning Chippie! Have a nice weekend? What enchanting activity did you undertake during your leave from prison? Write a couple of programs to pass the time, or maybe IM yourself from different screen names?" It was Fred. Sales manager of aftermarket services, the worst conceivable person to encounter first thing on any day, let alone Monday. Fred was the type of guy that guys like Chad hated most and Chad truly hated Fred. Fred was a shallow, hollow person, but Fred was somewhat popular because he was able to regurgitate on demand every joke he was ever told. Fortunately for Fred most people never got beyond his jokes because what remained was nothing but laughable for all the wrong reasons. Chad could never figure out if Fred intentionally kept people out of his nothingness or if his nothingness, by design, voided entry like an exit turnstile.

"Morning Fred. My weekend was great. Thanks for asking. I wore another quarter inch into my floor pacing around with nothing to do. Thank the Lord for Monday. It's so good to be back here." Chad chirped back at his compatriot. Unfortunately, Chad was not given to quick wit, normally finding snappy retorts emerging only after time and distance had rendered them moot to bother uttering aloud. So, as he smelled his way to his cheese at the end of the cubicle maze, he was thinking about ways to upstage good ol' Fred and his sarcastic dribble. Unfortunately, as hard as he tried, no better comeback could be marshaled for the cause.

"Heh Chippie! How's the world of techno babble these days? Have any new bytes to share?" uttered Susan. "Listen, my computer keeps locking up on me. I thought you said you fixed it. You are responsible for keeping them in working order aren't you? When can I expect you to get it operating again? It's such a nuisance, you know. I'm really busy right now and every time it locks up I lose quite a few minutes, not to speak of the work that I've lost, or the effect that the interruption has on my train of thought. It's simply unacceptable to have an unreliable PC. They're like phones these days – you need to have them constantly and they have to work without fail. All my friends have PC's that work fine, why can't you get mine working right? Well?"

"Well, what?" Chad replied.

"Well when will you fix it?" Susan demanded.

"I don't know Susan, I just got here. Give me a minute to check my email and I'll see when I might be free to look at it." Chad said reluctantly. Every other day was the same with Susan. Her PC kept crashing and it was never her fault. Never mind the fact that she overloaded her ram with multiple open applications while downloading Internet spam and emailing her friends. Never mind the constant change in screen savers and banners that she somehow found time in her busy schedule to be constantly toying with. Never mind how she was always doing stupid things to her task bar and start-up menu and messing around with unnecessary features in her configuration. She had a tendency to close her virus utility and donned an excruciatingly belligerent attitude towards learning when given the chance. No, Susan made no mistakes and whenever anything went wrong someone, or something, else was "obviously" the cause. The fact is, she was such an ignoramus that she didn't even know what an ignoramus she was. She could be pigheaded enough to drop a charging bore in its tracks, but the guys in the office tolerated her annoying personality because it was offset by a rather impressive set of antlers that Susan flaunted with pride.

Chad finally wound his way to his office, if you want to call it that. It was more like a cage than an office; maybe pit would be a better descriptor. Several years prior the company hired a productivity specialist to study the operation and recommend changes to foster improvements in the bottom line. Included in the various inane suggestions was a standardized seating format. A specialist determined that a position-based office system would create an environment that eliminated barriers between management and the rank-and-file. Without barriers, communication was bound to improve and with improved communication employees were apt to make fewer errors, and, since errors cost money, the result would be a significant improvement in the companys' bottom line. Company headlines "New chairs save company!" The executives were enchanted with the idea, so they tossed out the old and brought in the new transforming what was a comfortable workplace with a soft feel into a sterile plastic maze. Every position was given a grade and every grade was authorized a specific number, size and arrangement of panels. Grade six got a two by two with five short panels, one tall panel, one chair, one ell shaped desk, two bottom drawers and one top cabinet. Grade seven got a two by three, and so on. There were no exceptions, including the disdain it aroused in the employees.

Just after Chad crossed the threshold of his two-by-three, a nearby face popped over the wall, invading the space held by policy, exclusively for Chad. It was Paul, Paul Landau. A nice guy, the only person Chad could consider a friend.

"Morning Chad. What's up? Good weekend?"

"Not bad, went by too fast as always. How about you?" Chad answered as his PC booted into action.

"Pretty good. Got outside for a change. Felt good to breathe some real air. 'Bout time we had some decent weather. What's on the plate this week?"

"Same stuff. I've got to fix Susan's PC again and there are a few in the cage that need some work. There's always plenty of programming work to do. Give the bosses an hour and they'll create a new emergency in need of a report. You know how it is."

"Guess what?" Paul inquired.

"Guess what? Did you say guess what? If you said 'guess what' then something big must have happened. You never say guess what. You haven't offered anything that approaches personal information in ages. So if you said 'guess what' it means you must have bought a new car, moved into a new apartment or met a girl that you figure could turn out to be like your Mother."

"Wise ass. Never mind. I don't know why I waste my time. I get better feedback from an over-amped woofer. You talk about me not wanting to share my life? What about you? When was the last time you had anything to tell anyone? I bet you call your Mother and read her the newspaper to keep the conversation going and she's the closest thing you'll ever have to female companionship."

"Oh don't get so trumped up. You know I was only kidding, so what's the big news anyway?"

Paul hesitated a moment before replying. Chad could tell that he wasn't sure, after their last round of sparring, if he still wanted to give Chad the gory details. Chad told himself that whatever the news, he would be kind and supportive, happy while not jocular, interested without appearing as if he were merely mollifying. Paul was the kind of guy that nobody paid much attention to. Bland like peanut butter on white bread. Open like a blank journal. A thick cooked steak, that when sliced, had only one pinkish brown color from top to bottom. Not too loud, not too witty but very, very bright. Not mister personality but still somewhat good looking. One could look at Paul and see a cup half empty, on the other hand, what if the cup were really half full? Chad had always thought of Paul as a cup half full. A nice, honest, hard working Christian boy with a value system as true as the National Institute of Standards and Technology. Paul was the kind of guy that would elicit questionable remarks from Mom when first brought home to her after some dates. Paul was also the kind of guy that Mom would spoil with relish after the fifth. A true small town good guy, an unassuming gentleman without spite.

"I met a lady friend over the weekend. It wasn't your normal encounter, you know, the bar scene with all the noise and artificiality. I was walking by the lake and there were a ton of Geese on the lawn, so I decided to chase them. Some of the mother Geese took unkindly to my charade and started getting on their high horse. Have you ever seen a Goose rear up in protest? It was funny. She stood erect, stretched her neck and opened her wings to make herself look like a dragon or something. Then she started to hiss. I could only imagine her trying to belch some fire, which struck me as funny, so I started to mimic her myself."

"Oh great! I can see it now! I'll bet you were wearing a long dark raincoat and you opened it up to mimic her wings and all of the sudden you looked down, noticed that you failed to get dressed and started imagining that your hooter was her neck belching forth fire from the pits of hell."

"Asshole. That's not what happened. I was wearing a windbreaker and I started flapping my arms and squawking. It was nothing like that!" Paul shouted with exasperation.

"You were flapping your arms and squawking? Is that what attracted this newfound love in your direction? Does she find flapping squawking men somehow romantically appealing? How did she approach you, in a goose-like mating ritual?" Chad said as he realized, too late, that he had broken his promise to be nice.

"No, as a matter of fact she came upon me rather abruptly from the rear and gave me a good stiff tap on the shoulder. She was annoyed at me for picking on the poor mother goose and gave me a tongue lashing that only a card-carrying member of Green Peace, Audubon Society and ASPCA could muster. I'm telling you she had every angle covered. She read me the riot act like she was unveiling a State of the Union address.

Before I knew it, I was back peddling from her to keep from getting spit on, if not bitten and wham, it happened. I tripped over a piece of crap on the ground and went down in a patch of goose shit covered grass. I ended up with more goose shit stuck to my clothes than sheep have wool in winter. And she started laughing, hysterically."

"What did you do, throw some goose-shit pate' her way to seal the romance?"

"No actually, I just sat there. I was overwhelmed with an immediate feeling of dejection, so I just stared at the ground and starting cleaning my hands on the best spot of clothing I could find. I kept rubbing them for a while and when I looked up she was still there, standing akimbo, and then held out her hand to help me up" Paul said in a somewhat meekish tone.

"So you grabbed her hand and pulled her down into Chicago's' finest quagmire and lived there, together, happily ever after. You're right, that's not a normal encounter."

"Actually, I looked at her without expression and after a couple seconds pulled myself to my feet on my own. She dropped her hand and said 'I'm so sorry; I had no intention of causing you to fall. I really was only kidding. I thought you were funny playing with the goose and so I thought I would play with you. I'm terribly sorry. The whole Mother Nature routine was meant to be a joke. I'm not at all a bleeding liberal, far from it. Listen, I've got some hand towels in the bag on my bike, come on over and at least I can get your hands clean.' She immediately started walking to her bike and didn't even look back, like she knew I would obey and didn't need any reassurance. It was weird, but I did follow her, and she did clean my hands."

"Sounds like you found a real winner! Did you get her phone number, or what?" Chad inquired, with a bit of newly found interest echoing from the tone in his voice. Chad hadn't been on a date in quite some time, in fact, Chad hadn't been on a real date in over a year. Sure, he had some blind dates organized by friends that felt sorry for him, but a real date with a real girl that he liked and that liked him? Not in a very long while. Chad wasn't the type to go out too often and he certainly wasn't

007 when he did. He found the bar scene impossible for social engagement, not only due to the phony social setting it provided but also because he was unwilling to stress his vocal chords to the degree needed to carry on even the most basic of conversations. While Chad enjoyed listening to the joy of his comrade, he was also feeling a twinge of jealousy and a heightened awareness of his own loneliness. All he could think of to shun the ill feelings garnered by Paul's obvious ecstasy was his joy in his music. Thank God for my music, Chad thought.

"You gonna fix my computer before it snows again?" Susan jeered. "I could hear you two social cowards baying at each other for the last twenty feet and while I find your discourse truly enlightening, it isn't getting my PC fixed. How about it Chippie? Gonna stand there and dream about Paul's goose egg or you gonna fix my computer?"

"I guess I better go" Chad said to Paul. "It would better serve us both if I repair the PC of madam maharini before she calls the royal guard! Sorry about teasing you. What about lunch? I'd like to hear the rest of your story."

"I'll catch up to you later Chad, I can't do lunch. I'm meeting Janice. She's at a meeting nearby and thought it would be nice to try Samali's. Maybe tomorrow OK?" Paul said as Chad disappeared unwillingly in the wake of maharini Susan.

"**M**y goodness Chippie, sounds like your buddy has planted an Ali knockout punch. Now there's no-one left with whom you can share the anguish of your oneness any longer. Must make you feel even more like sun baked mayo, huh? What a shame. Maybe Paul's new suitor, Janice is it, can find you the love of your life! Hey, you never know!" Susan said curtly.

"Susan, you haven't a clue. You have no idea what kind of life I lead, or Paul. Why you, or any of your other heinous friends bother, I'll never know, and quite frankly I'll never care. I'm just sick of hearing the same monotonous dribble from all of you mindless grubs. It's amazing that you have nothing better to do than belittle people who despise your idea of fun." Chad blunted in exasperation.

"Oh, and what do you suppose IS my idea of fun?" Susan shrieked with an air of superiority.

"I don't know for certain Susan, but judging from the hallway gossip it must have something to do with getting drunk, picking up guys and apologizing all weekend for your behavior. Now why don't we see what's wrong with your PC before I completely lose control of my desire to render it functionless? Okay?"

"No problem, techno geek, but don't let your jealousy spread lies that you'll regret. Better have your facts straight before you dust off your mouth. Misunderstood hearsay can be dangerous if used in a maligning or accusatory manner. Be careful what Morse code you start barking to your dogs in Baskerville, understand?" Susan said in a tone so threatening that it bordered on inhuman.

Instead of continuing, Chad gave up the battle and started to tend to her PC. As always, there wasn't really anything wrong. By changing a few programs in her startup menu and rendering a few features inactive and reducing her admin rights, Chad was able to bring the system resources back to a level where functionality was assured. It only took a few minutes, but it seemed like hours because Susan just stood there, glaring over his shoulder, as if in kinship with some unseen poltergeist in the keyboard.

Chad could tell that Susan was mad as hell about his accusations and he was sure she would find some way to administer payback, particularly because his comments contained more truth than fiction. Susan had a history of failed relationships, each of several months' duration. She always allowed her initial infatuation with a new male partner to overwhelm her, continually misconstruing lust for love, and falling headlong into a one sided affair. According to her, every man she touched was finally Mr. Right and every time she touched one she was convinced that he would be her last. Susan went after these poor hormone-crazed guys with the strength of a category five hurricane and in the process drove them away like a trailer park in the height of the storm. The scenario was always the same. On a Monday following her discovery of the next Mr. Right, she would show up for work a tad early, with a little extra bounce in her step and lift in her brazier. For the next couple of weeks she would tuck Madame Maharini in her hip pocket and pull out Madame Mellifluous. The change in her personality was similar to a three-year-old before and after a much-needed nap. Everyone loved the little angel when her courtship was on track, for she truly reflected a spirit anointed. She would bounce around the office on light feet with an upbeat attitude and an appearance of shear joy. No task was too big nor too little and no request inappropriate. Her good days were so good that during them Susan she could ask for a raise but unfortunately, what goes up must come down, and in Susan's case with the vengeance of an experienced bull newly castrated.

With his weekly Susan sojourn complete, time was now available to get back to the routine tasks at hand so Chad bee-lined for the mainframe to pick up the Monday morning reports. On entering the room his eyes were immediately affixed on the mound of computer paper in the dot matrix tray. The weight of the reports by themselves was enough to tell Chad that all was well with the system, so he simply snapped them up, reeled around, and made a hasty departure. As he fought his way back to his 2 by 3, he began to peruse the reports while thinking about the priority of each program request in his backlog of open activities. His mind got so wrapped up in the process that he forgot to look where he was going and walked directly into Fred, who was having a conversation with Pat, the marketing guru.

Whap! Chad hit Fred's backside with the impact of a frontal lobotomy, the collision vaulting Fred's freshly filled mug of Java in an elliptical arc about four feet long while Fred, himself, lurched a few feet to keep from going over. Fortunately for all concerned, the airborne blob of warm brown fluid found a new home only when contact was made with the side of a panel from a nearby cubicle and the compatriot with whom Fred was engaged suffered only the type of momentary increase in heart rate that a near miss can cause. While the incident was recorded in a fraction of a second it felt as if it lasted for a minute, providing a clear demonstration in the theory of relativity. But rather than revel in the splendor of what was obviously a mind expanding experience, Pat the Marketing Guru, chose to freak out in an unseemly and inappropriate way.

While jumping violently away from the flood to his left, Pat started to yell. "What the hell are you doing you mental midget? Who let you out of your cage? For Christ sake, it's barely after nine and you've already created a bigger mess than Mayor Daley. Do you read when you drive? What makes you think it's OK to read to when you walk? You have enough trouble walking and chewing gum at the same time so maybe you should save your excitement about last weeks computer stats until you get back to your cage."

"Sorry, Pat. Sorry Fred. I got a little wrapped up in my thoughts and forgot to look where I was going. You guys just continue along, I'll clean up the mess. I'm just glad you didn't get wet."

"You mean lucky. You're damned lucky we aren't wet. Get your act together Chippie. We both took showers before we got to work and have no intention of taking another right now" snorted Fred. "Let's go Pat, before the wizard of techno-magic decides to launch another volley. We've got to get ready for the forecasting meeting anyway."

Chad felt an insatiable urge to continue the banter, but refrained. While Fred and Pat walked away Chad had all he could do to quell the growing hatred inside. He wanted to wage a war of words, to unravel a string of adjectives long enough to tie a noose with but decency prevailed and in silence Chad turned toward the men's room to grab some paper towels. The room was empty when he got there, so Chad put his coffee cup and the computer reports on the counter between two sinks and went for the paper towels. The dispenser was jammed. Wadded, wrinkled paper could be seen at the discharge rollers and the star wheel wouldn't turn. Chad yanked, pulled and twisted every moving part without a fraction of success. He whacked on the sides, pried on the lock and finally inserted his favorite pen to use as a crow bar, for it only to be broken under the stress. It was a pen that Chad used religiously for years, becoming much more like a partner in his quest to create, a special agent for transmitting thought to paper, than merely an implement. The loss of such a confidant was difficult to bear and it thrust Chad into a worse state of mind. The morning was yet infant but already circumstances were giving rise to angst and Chad could only imagine more of the same as the day progressed.

Abandoning all hope for dispensed paper, Chad hurried from the men's room to the luncheon area. As he rounded the corner by the entrance he saw a mixed group of animated co-workers sharing weekend stories and questioning the nature of certain ongoing political posturing within the organization. They were bees busily diffusing information into the rumor mill like spam across an unguarded monitor. They were so engaged with themselves that they failed to notice Chad as he entered the room.

Chad scurried to the paper towel rack overhearing the conversation du jour. One of the females was addressing an enraptured audience about something she heard from someone who heard something from somebody else. The topic seemed to involve Susan and one of her panic stricken attempts to find love in all the wrong places. While Chad despised the scene in its entirety he was unable to suppress a burst of yearning for each sordid detail about Susan, so he slowed his pace in an attempt to capture the story.

"We were out on the strip with a gang of old friends doing a little bar hopping after dinner and as I rounded the corner near DeJa Who? I saw Susan getting into a cab with Fred. She was all smiles and her gaze was fixed on Fred and he had his hand on her ass. He was patting her like he was checking some fresh dough to see if it was rising correctly. When they got into the cab they started clinging to each other like Velcro laced with superglue. I had all I could do to keep from laughing 'cause the second I saw them an image of them together popped into my head. I saw Fred on top of Susan engaged in wild sex and at the peak of her excitement Fred starts telling one of his ultra-nasty jokes. Susan, did you ever hear the one about the one …?" Chad overheard as he amassed an ample supply of towels and exited the room. He had heard enough.

Susan apparently had had a fling with Fred.

Chad is considered a techno-geek by most of the no-minds that he supports; a reputation that earned him the water cooler knick name of Charlie Chip. He isn't exactly climbing rungs on the ladder of social success, in fact, he probably isn't even on a rung at all, and to Chad the workplace is nothing more than an ugly necessity in the road to other endeavors.

He would best be described as pleasant but private, competent yet modest, supportive but unenthusiastic. Unfortunately, he tends to be depicted by his peers as a disheveled goofball, a sort of social baboon. People who do not know Chad think him a techno-wizard of wacko proportions immersed in a sea of ones and zeros, a nerd-brain capable only of retaining the electro-jargon that others strive with veracity to dispel. People that get to know Chad tend to react in one of two specific ways. They either walk silently away shaking their heads in disbelief, or they laugh hysterically at the utterly incongruous nature that he is. Unfortunately, Chad isn't like that at all, he simply has no interest in playing by the rules of the office culture. If he could find the means to live without such a time consuming, demanding job, maybe he could finish his music and sell some copy instead.

With paper towels in hand Chad returned to the brown stain he created and began to sop it up in the midst of rising activity. The muted color of the cubicle fabric made it an easy task to clean and with only a few swipes the splotch was sufficiently removed as to be unnoticeable by the casual passerby. It therefore didn't take Chad long return to his cube to resume his review of the morning printout.

After quickly shedding loafers and assuming a comfortable posture Chad opened the lengthy report and began to scan the contents. These were system reports that provided data on activity by user, the status of resource utilization and the status of routine system diagnostics. On a normal weekday resource utilization ran somewhere around 60 percent of full capacity, a level that assured effective operation of the network with reliability and speed. On weekends capacity levels were normally lower, generally around 45%, reflective only of the CPU required to run routine weekly activity, which was constituted of full backups, system scans, security scans and updates. Chad was an unusually cautious system administrator and reviewed the reports with a fine-toothed-comb religiously every Monday. Several reasons drove Chad to operate in this manner. First, after receiving a thorough ass-chewing early on in his tenure, Chad vowed never to be caught unaware of matters falling within his jurisdiction. Second, Chad was by nature a person who valued attention to detail no matter how mundane. For these reasons Chad made it a habit to set aside an hour each Monday to read the computer reports, almost on a line by line basis. He had gotten so used to the data and all of its corresponding entries that deviations stood out like a fat girl in a bikini contest and even though this week's report had every sign of exhibiting normalcy, when Chad got into the details there was another imbedded report that was laden with one fat girl after another. Chad had a really hard time with what he was seeing. It was as if someone were running a completely different set of books only they messed up quite dramatically in the process. The evidence reeked of intrusion, corruption or falsification and Chad couldn't quite grasp the meaning of what he was seeing. He thought that perhaps someone had hacked into the system but nothing in the data indicated a virus, worm or Trojan. Thinking instead that there must have been a glitch in the system when the report was scheduled to run Chad instinctively decided to run another set and headed for the computer room with the original in tow. Just as the second set printed Alan Chandler, company CEO, whooshed into the room along with Bryan Jeffries the Chief Technology Officer. Never in Chad's time at the company, now a little over two years, had either of these two executives set foot in the computer room. Their presence took Chad totally by surprise.

"Excuse me but can you tell me if the weekend printouts have been run yet?" Alan inquired.

"Yes, they run automatically and are available for review when I arrive first thing every Monday. I was just getting ready to take a look at them." Chad answered. "This is the report right here Mr. Chandler." Chad said holding the thicket of computer paper up to Alan. "Would you like to look at it?"

"Actually, we'd like to review it in detail" Bryan answered. "We haven't had a chance to look at the system's statistics in quite a while and would like to brush up on our skills. You don't mind if we take these do you?"

"Not at all. I already, um, have plenty of other work to do anyway." Chad mumbled as he handed them the report. He almost began to tell them that he had run an extra set when for some reason a rare inkling of precaution caused him to stop mid-sentence, and continue with a redirect instead. The odd report and their appearance out of nowhere could not have been a coincidence. Chad purposely continued to look directly at both executives as they began to switch the conversation to normal pleasantries. He was hoping that they wouldn't notice the extra report in the hopper to their left.

"Thank you son. What's your name anyway?" asked Alan.

"Chad, sir. Chad Preston. System Administrator. Been here a little over two years now."

"Well Chad, you must be doing a great job because we never have reason to question operation of the system. Mr. Jeffries just thought it would be a good idea for us to get – you know – reacquainted with some of the details of the system. Thanks for your help Chad."

"Any time Mr. Chandler." Chad said as the two executives turned in unison and fled from the room. Now Chad was really perplexed. What could all this mean? What should he do with the duplicate report? Was it a duplicate report?

Chad looked to see that he was alone and then ran to the hopper to retrieve the duplicate. He quickly opened it to page 56 to see if it contained the same data as the first copy and sure enough, the fat girls were still in their bikinis. Chad decided that it would be in his best interest to keep the entire matter quiet while he ushered the duplicate data out of the building to a safe holding spot. He decided to sneak the report to his apartment at the end of the day so he bundled it up and headed back to his office wondering with utmost concern if he had done something wrong, if the system had been breached, if the company needed to restore data from last week and why Chandler and Jeffries had departed so hastily when they could have, should have, asked Chad about the mysterious nature of the weekend activity.

With haste and concern Chad proceeded forthwith back to his cubicle to bury himself in work until the whistle at five. He needed to be alone to review the report with the scrutiny it was going to take. He wanted desperately for the anomalies to disappear and never return, but he knew that that was out of the question. He hoped beyond hope that he could find a simple explanation for the evidence in front of him and to be quickly rid of this unexpected turn of events. But that would have to wait until he was home. That would have to wait until he had a chance to reflect on the strange circumstances before him and make some sense out of them. That chance would only be available when Chad returned to his private sanctuary by Harrison Park.

Fred's morning was as action packed as always. In his job as sales associate he was responsible for handling all front line communications with his customers. Every minute of his day was loaded with something in need of resolution or someone for whom his charm was the miracle worker in restoring customer confidence in World Supplî. His demeanor was as amply amicable with his customers as it was obnoxious to his office compatriots and they never failed, for reasons unknown to all including Fred, to trust him when he promised them the moon. He had an innate talent that could carry him far in life if only he also had the perceptivity to understand it and the insight to keep it under control. Unfortunately, having neither, he walked through life oblivious of his double edged strength, failing entirely to see that the second edge could just as easily become his undoing.

By lunchtime Fred was hungrier than a junkyard dog and in need of a break from the constant strain of appealing to difficult customer requests. As he walked down the hall to meet Susan he was thinking, "The customer's always right - my ass. The customer is usually a stupid pain in the ass. If I tell them I'm doing everything I can it means I'm doing everything I can. I'm sick of hearing that my best is just not good enough. Why does everyone think that by dragging me into their pain it will somehow improve my ability to reduce a lead time or shave my price? I don't want to hear your GD life story to expedite a shipment, OK?"

"Fred. Fred! What are you doing?" It was Susan. She left her cubicle to greet him but he failed to notice her until she was almost on top of him. "Your mouth was moving and you were shaking your head and looking at the floor. Are you delusional or something? What's the matter?"

"Nothing, just another typically hopeless morning of trying to placate the implacable. How's your day going?"

"OK I guess. Same ol' stuff. Approving expense reports, arranging travel itineraries, answering phones, you know the routine. Ready for another gourmet meal at the caf'?"

"I'm starving and the caf's not so bad in case you were being Ms. Sarcastic again."

"I know. It's actually pretty good. I'm just getting bored with it. Hey look – there's Chippie all by himself, poor fella. Should we go say hello?"

"Why not? I could use an easy target to prey on right about now. Without it I might not be ready for the onslaught of abuse I'll have to take this afternoon."

Fred made his way to the Sandwich Shoppe where a helper make him roast beast on rye with Swiss cheese, tomato, red onion and a hefty portion of mayo. Susan went to the salad bar and built herself a nice mix of greens with a variety of cut veggies, some shredded Colby and a low fat French dressing. They met again at the cashier's station and inconspicuously meandered by Chad after settling their tabs.

"Hey Chippie. What're you reading? Bits and bytes for digit heads?"

Chad looked up devoid of a change in facial expression and stared at them without reply. He was determined not to let them get under his skin.

"Is that a local rag? The Southtown Star? Oh I forgot you're in love with music aren't you? Anything of interest going on?"

"Actually, there is. The Forty G's are playing downtown this week and I'm planning on seeing them this Thursday. Now if you don't mind, I'd like to finish my lunch in private please."

"In private. Is that the way you attend those wonderful concerts too? In private? Must be fun to sit there all by yourself - no one to distract you from your love affair with your music. Only love affair you'll ever have Chippie ol' pal! Just you and your musicians making beautiful music together. Ain't that sweet Susie Q?"

"It's just ducky Fred. A vision so sweet it gives me goose pimples just thinking about it."

Chad should have ignored the two morons but they got where he promised they wouldn't, under his skin, way under his skin. "You two assholes need each other more than flies need shit so go find some shit and fly away."

"Chippie, that's not nice. We were just teasing you. No need to get nasty. Why don't you let me find you a girl? I know some street corners where a couple of real beauties tend to hang out."

"Funny, real funny. If you must know I have a date on Thursday, so there." He lied. "Sorry to ruin your image of the perfect nerd."

"Well I'll be damned. Chippie has a date. Must be the first time since the senior prom. That's it. You called up your personal little prom queen to go with you. That's it, isn't it? Chippie and his prom queen, president of the math club and inventor of the plastic pen pocket protector. What a pair."

"Drop dead Fred."

"Come on Fred, let's get going, I'm hungry." As the two walked away satisfied with the outcome of their bout, Susan asked, "So tell me Fred, what, exactly, is it that you know about street corner beauties?"

Susan led the way to a table by the window and sat down. Fred chose a seat next to her that gave him a view of the goings on in the caf' and took a big bite from his sandwich. Without bothering to wait until he swallowed, he asked, "Do you really think Chippie has a date? It would be kind of fun to spy on him. A bunch of us could go to the show on Thursday to take a sneek peak at Chippies gal. What'da think?"

"I think it's cruel but I'm not necessarily ruling it out."

Alan Chandler became the head of operations of WorldSupplî in August of 2001 at the tender age of 43. This made Chandler a relative new born in the world of multibillion dollar enterprise managers and the subject of much conversation in Wall Street and internally with senior management. Chandler made his way to the top of the organization in only seven years with the company, having started as divisional vice president in charge of international business development. His climb to the top was rumored to be the result of happenstance rather than skill because shortly after joining there was an enormous development in China that doubled international sales in less than two years. Whether it was skill or "being in the right place at the right time" or a combination of both, mattered not to Chandler. His only goal was increased power and authority; his only ambition wealth, and his desire for ever greater heights always ample justification for the ends regardless of the means.

Chandler's professional career was earmarked with one success after another and in some circles the reputation that preceded him was considered stellar. A graduate in economics with an executive MBA and a hopper of experience with different employers from a variety of industries made Chandler's past reek with capability. But for those who knew the details, the reality of Chandler's escapades was vastly different. Nothing ever stuck to him and, conversely, he never stuck to anything. He was a master at identifying circumstances for elevating his self-worth and a genius at their exploitation. Chandler was an opportunist in the truest sense of the word, viewing himself as his most important opportunity and one that he fancied merchandising without restraint.

World Supplî, a multinational corporation with a mix of manufacturing and distribution businesses, was in the midst of its second re-invention when disaster struck the World Trade Center buildings. Several tangential acquisitions that closed late in 2000 were destined to push WorldSupplî over the three billion mark in 2001 and Chandler felt certain that this benchmark would generate positive speculation from Wall Street and a corresponding spike in stock price. Attitudes were positive in the halls of senior management; an observation attested to by arms dangling helplessly, like a boxer in late rounds, from patting each other too much on the back. Unfortunately, the post-911 economy showed swiftly its impact on World Supplî's growth when orders came to an abrupt halt, inventory levels skyrocketed and open purchase orders, many with multiple releases, could not be halted in time to mitigate its impact on cash flow. Managing an economic downturn from feast to famine is hard enough in normal times, but the accelerated nature of the post-911 drop was cause for even more serious concern.

From Chandler's point of view the timing of 911 couldn't have been worse. It caused WorldSupplî to shift focus from the joy of bottom line growth to the mundane details of balance sheet maintenance. The board was instantly focused on maintaining positive cash flow and demanded a full accounting of all actions being undertaken to reduce payables, collect receivables and cut expenses. They were ruthless, expecting an almost instantaneous change of course that was synony-mous with stopping a mega-freighter at 12 knots in less than 500 nauti-cal yards. While an essential activity, especially given the circumstances, it was none-the-less a fate worse to Chandler than losing a finger, maybe even a hand. Chandler only relished those activities that carried with them magnanimously positive press that carried a zeal only for unveiling never before seen synergistic strategies, new global organizational initia-tives, or unexpectedly inordinate m-and-a announcements. The idea that he might have to hold a press conference to discuss cost cutting measures for bolstering shareholder confidence was about as much fun as having to tell Olympic athletes that America wasn't going to compete. It simply had the appeal of a dirty diaper and nothing more, and the look on Chandler's face was as if that diaper were permanently draped in front of his nose.

Like it or not, Chandler went dutifully to his staff and began to seek their input on the best ways to meet the directives from the board. They held several breakout sessions and conducted a few focus group meet-ings on specific items and then issued an action report for the board's approval. The action report was immediately given the go-ahead albeit with the caveat that further changes should be expected in the future.

The action plan spanned every conceivable domain, from elimination of variable costs to refinancing and was akin to making the decision to pull your mother from life support because their decisions would irreversibly alter the atmosphere at World Supplî.

Chandler came to WorldSupplî with several compatriots from his professional past with the exception of his newly trusted CFO Bryan Jeffries. Chandler didn't know it and wouldn't acknowledge it if he did, but without Jeffries, Chandler the renowned business person wouldn't be as renowned. Jeffries was the one who gave Chandler the data, tools, insight and observations that he needed to look like an effective leader. He provided both the brains and the brawn for the organization, while Chandler only the bravado. Jeffries was one of those rare individuals with the ability to see clarity in situations where others only saw haze. He was a genius with computers and data and possessed an uncommonly strong, common sense oriented, business acumen. Jeffries could listen to the concepts and ideas of others in the midst of a commotion packed conversation and convert them into a cohesive product. And Jeffries maintained, by choice but not by nature, a private and soft spoken demeanor; he presented an individual who preferred a low profile to public speaking because he found people, in general, to be annoying and oft times indolent. His disdain for the masses gave him and Chandler incredibly complimentary profiles, and it was Jeffries who understood this and protected it.

Bryan Jeffries began his association with Alan Chandler in early 2000 when the two met at a business conference on global supply chain management. Chandler, keynote speaker at a breakout session in the conference, masterfully delivered a speech on globalization and the role of technology that mirrored Jeffries' thoughts to the last detail. Jeffries immediately thought they were kindred spirits and decided to forge a friendship that he hoped would lead to greater things in the future. At the conclusion of the session Jeffries cornered Chandler to birth his intentions by starting a discussion with him on the notion of borderless marketing. While Jeffries' strengths were most profound in computer system architecture, he was none-the-less capable of creating visionary strategies, generating unique marketing campaigns and synthesizing abstract concepts into concrete programs. In the matter of just a few minutes Jeffries and Chandler were involved in such a deeply animated discussion that it looked as though they worked together for years and it didn't take Chandler long to know that he needed the skills he was being held witness to. One week after the conference, having done enough of a background investigation to confirm Jeffries legitimacy, Chandler was on the phone making him an offer he couldn't refuse. The two became an inseparable tag team from that point forward, earning a reputation for hard work and even harder play that preceded them wherever they went.

"Thank God we got the report before that techie did. How the hell did that data get into the weekly stats report?" Chandler asked excitedly, but with a look of relief when they were safely back in his office. "That was way too close for my taste."

"I think I mistakenly queued the data into a system call routine that I setup a long time ago. It was a back door application that I developed to process reports without anyone knowing. It must have cross linked with the stats report when I used it in some analysis work that I was doing last week. Don't worry; I caught the problem first thing this morning when I couldn't find the data. I've checked the system to see if the file was used over the weekend, it wasn't, and I've closed the door permanently so it can't happen again."

"You're certain? One mishap like that could create a whole shitload of unnecessary chaos before we have a chance to figure out what's going on."

"Nothing is going on, Chandler. Let me show you the figures and you'll see for yourself. We have a completely explainable gap in our profit margin at the volume of revenue reported through 6 months. It can all be explained by mix – our sales have been more heavily skewed to product lines that generate lower net margins. The analysis is all here."

"Fine. Let me look at the numbers and I'll get back to you if I have any questions. Does this contain a variance analysis?"

"Of course, the variance is where our shortfall is best explained."

Jeffries left the office of Alan Chandler convinced that he had once again successfully snowed the young CEO. What looked like the possibility of exposure was now cunningly disguised in a bogus product line profitability report that no one had the ability to unravel, let alone dispute. Jeffries was convinced that his bogus report would answer all the questions about the drop in profit that WorldSupplî had to disclose during the upcoming midyear directors meeting. Jeffries was so pleased with his artfulness that his fear of exposure was replaced with jubilation. He felt so brilliant at manipulating facts and figures that he thought himself unconquerable, omnipotent.

The indefatigable charisma of Alan Chandler was the carrot that originally brought Jeffries to World Supplî. At first glance Chandler appeared to be the next breakthrough leader, a Jack Welch, or Lee Iacocca in the making. So when Jeffries joined World Supplî' he made study of the emerging global business leader's passion, placing all focus on the various aspects of his style and the application of his skill set. Unfortunately on inspection, Jeffries found a leader vastly different from the one seen in the public eye. He found a vain self-absorbed person whose only specialty was the ability to surround himself with the excellence of others. He found a person who thrived on claiming the rich ideas and successes of his staff as his own and was cheap to grant praise in public. It didn't take long for Jeffries' initial enthusiasm to turn to silent disdain and his focus to turn to the weaknesses of World Supplî's new leader.

In short order Jeffries had found two weaknesses in Chandler - his lack of attention to detail and his blind faith in trusted subordinates – which together provided him a clear path for illicit exploitation. A CEO that took everything at face value without question made it easy for Jeffries to devise the perfect money laundering scheme; all he needed was an accomplice, and none could be better than his estranged life-long friend, Matt DiGrande. DiGrande, as Editor in Chief of the Chicago Tribute, was loaded with ties to the banking industry. DiGrande was the perfect "silent partner" and DiGrande couldn't afford to say no. Bryan knew there must have been a good reason for that tragic, tragic event in Miami so many years ago, but only in this most recent scheme, did he know what it was.

In 1976 Matt DiGrande was a sick-of-high-school high school senior. Even with the advanced classes and extracurricular activities it was just too boring for him, so he was constantly on the lookout for screwball ways to break the rules with his lifelong best friend Bryan Jeffries. Both were popular despite their patrician arrogance and brutish demeanor because their rebelliousness had not yet tarnished their reputations; they were still considered "nice boys" within the community. As is the case with coins they also had two sides, but so far heads was the only one to turn up, at least publically.

Their friendship dated back to Kindergarten class when Bryan was sent into the corner one morning after forcing the girls to feel his muscles. From his perch in the rear row Matt witnessed such anger and defiance when Bryan was quarantined that his interest in Bryan piqued and he decided to introduce himself. On the playground the next day Matt approached Bryan and Bryan began to stare him down with a bravado that was already branded into him. Matt looked back at Bryan calmly and without fear and a little later, when his initial reaction to prepare a defense had subsided, started to laugh and they shook hands. That moment cemented a lifelong relationship and the two became each other's shadows from that point forward. They were inseparable during their free time and where other kids were dabbling with electric games and other mindless activities, Matt and Bryan were constantly outdoors creating their own world, one devoid of social mores, parental control and other constraints. In their world they were always the victors, slaying whatever unfortunate creature or thing that became their fictitious enemy du jour. Grasshoppers stuck to pine pitch laden boards were witches in disguise and had to be burned. Frogs caught in the swamp were evil princes hung from tree branches until they converted to their human forms or were taken by dehydration. Chickadees slain by BB guns were sacrifices to the god of the wood and their feet were saved as evidence of their forfeiture.

Time passed, activities changed and before long their focus was converted to a new world where girls ruled and contact sports were the way to rule girls. Pop Warner football in the fall and Major League baseball in the spring became their passion, not so much for each sport itself, but for the way their athletic notoriety drew groupies to them. There was nothing better than twelve year old girls in tank tops and tight cutoff shorts to drive the pre-pubescent male into feats of physical mastery on the sports field. Nor was anything a more potent attraction to the girls than the sweat-soaked blood stained uniform of the post-game gladiator. Matt and Bryan set their other world aside to conquer the new one that was enveloping them and in the process discovered an uncanny capacity for manipulation and control.

Time passed further and with it came new worlds, not so much with other focal points but with a variety of different means from which to achieve their ends. Chief amongst these were the benefits provided by mobility and money and it was equipped with these that their ultimate shapes took form. In the ninth grade they befriended high school seniors who owned cars and were quick to use them as chauffeurs and couriers. With this mobility came exposure to different people and places and soon they had contacts with nefarious businessmen. And with these contacts came the opportunity to earn money by running numbers and selling black market merchandise. Before long both Matt and Bryan were rolling in dough, always running a lark, and constantly exploiting some unfortunate person, place or thing. They were ruthless in their pursuit of money and felt the means of their pursuit always justified, becoming street bred capitalists who learned from the start to stay completely in control of their endeavors and to never bend, regardless of the circumstances.

By eleventh grade Matt and Bryan were on top of their game. Both were driving cars that they earned from what they called their "sharking" business and both had lines of girls waiting for a chance in their spotlight. Theirs was not a typical high school existence. While most of their peers exaggerated their sexual encounters and understated their intake of controlled substances, Matt and Bryan lied about abstaining from drugs and kept their sexual exploits largely to themselves. Other than an occasional beer neither had any interest in getting high or spending weekends wasted, instead, they spent countless hours in pursuit of their two, and only, most valued occupations – earning money and exploiting girls - and they were naturals at both.

In twelfth grade thoughts of the future loomed so large that they took a hiatus from their business ventures to have lengthy discussions about their options going forward. It took countless hours for them to examine the myriad different directions with interest enough for discussion, but when it was done they both agreed on the same next step. Neither of them was content to stay in the local racket as a small time entrepreneur/businessman because it was simply not challenging or rewarding enough. Wild ass options like going into the military held romantic position but in reality they agreed that neither were suited to take orders or follow leaders with less intellect than they. Heading out into the sunset to see where it fell also held no interest for, regardless of their outlandish local stature, they were members of a community and couldn't fathom the lack of essence that a nomadic lifestyle would bring. So with no options left and no desire to face adulthood both agreed that college was the only way for them to defer the inevitable while also continuing to grow.

With this decision firmly entrenched they were forced to make the most gut wrenching choice in their lives - should they attend the same university or go their ways separately? With exception of the unusual family vacation, over the past twelve years they were together almost daily so they really had no idea what life would be like in each other's absence. As a tag-team they were largely incomparable in their exploits but as individuals their capabilities were virtually unknown, because they shared every idea and launched all of their adventures jointly for more than a decade.

Both agreed that it would be fun to continue the tag team in a new environment with new clientele and a wholly different set of expectations but both knew too that continuance would be all consuming and would limit their experience else wise. Both also agreed that while separation represented a huge step into the unknown, this new "unknown" was exactly what each needed, so regardless of their trepidation there was also a feeling of excitement brought on by the thought of independent pursuit of the future. In essence, it was time to cut the umbilical cord for momma was ready to deliver.

By March of their senior year college enrollment letters had been signed and returned and their fate was thus sealed for the next four years. Matt got accepted into Boston College as a business student while Bryan opted for Stanford to focus on technology. No one could believe their choices. People were stunned by the geographic separation, and stupefied beyond belief by their chosen courses of study. Everyone expected both of them to pick curricula that supported a playboy life style, not ones that required focus on studies, and bets were out that the two would be back in town running their next crazy scheme within a year.

S enior itch is that uncontrollable inability to not give one shit about the last few months of school. Its impact is universal across all types of students - the fit and not-so-fit, the geeky and the popular, and the serious and gooky types as well. The effect of a nearing graduation is pervasive enough to create in all seniors a unique sense of commonality, one that transcends past grievances and forgives indiscretions. A senior in waiting is like an unrestrained puppy – largely out of control but not in an overtly malicious or unsavory way. Senioritis makes seniors become less socially conscientious too. The girl that you liked from a distance is no longer threatening enough to avoid, the math genius in calc no longer has the degrees of separation that were present all year long and the gangs of ruffians no longer hold others differing behavior hostage when in their presence. It's a time when students exhibit a heightened level of maturity while at the same time demonstrating their naiveté in new and different ways. They feel all grown up but have no idea what it means or how it should manifest itself. The maturity thing peaks on graduation day during the valedictorian speech and then disappears from view as soon as the caps are launched skyward in unison.

Senior itch definitely had its effect on Matt and Bryan. They found themselves constantly guessing the course of things to come, lost focus on new business and completely stopped caring about grades. Instead they spent time tying up lose matters, shoring up banks accounts and collecting old debts so they could take the summer off unencumbered.

"Hey wild-man, we've got a couple of months before heading off to school so why don't we go on some kind of an adventure?" Bryan asked frankly one afternoon.

"Sounds good to me. It's about time we got out of Cincinnati. What do you have in mind? Where would you like to go?"

"Well, you're heading east so we don't want to go east and I'm heading west so we don't want to go west. What about south? Why not road trip to Florida? We should have enough money if we camp along the way. We could take like six weeks if we want to. Jack Kerouac and Tom Sawyer rolled into one."

"Deal, but we have to take my car, more room, and better stereo. We also have to go to Miami Beach; I hear the girls are amazing; it's time to seek out some new females anyway." Matt said with bravado.

"Graduation is only a couple of weeks away, so let's get this thing planned. We have to make sure the car is up for a 5K, we have to map the places we want to visit along the way and decide what we need to pack. I'll start a list and you start a list and then we can compare and combine them. OK?" Bryan said with an exuberance matched only by the splendor of graduation itself.

The graduation ceremony was held on a sunny Saturday morning at an amphitheater style town park and by evening the hundreds of graduation parties started to blend into one another. Matt and Bryan had had enough of "where are you going?" and "what are you doing?" and "best of luck" and "I can't believe it's over" so around ten thirty they decided to dump the bicentennial class of 1976 and rack some pool balls to end the night. Over eight ball and sodas they finalized their trip. Tomorrow would be family day and Monday morning the ship would set sail. They would make their way quickly to Florida and then move slowly south along the east coast until they got to Miami, so their route would take them through Knoxville and then Atlanta before heading east to Jacksonville just south of Valdosta. From Jacksonville it was route 95 all the way, with stops in St. Augustine, Daytona Beach, and Cape Canaveral. Then it would be on to West Palm, Lauderdale and finally Miami.

"We better get a little sleep in the next two days 'cause the next six weeks are going to be crazy." Matt said when their planning discussions were complete. "Let's hit the road."

They left the pool hall shortly thereafter, each in his car, with the promise of immeasurable excitement burning in their heads.

Monday came quickly and with the first muted yellows of dawn Matt was fully revved and packing the car. By seven he was on the short jaunt to Bryan's and as his house came into view so did the mountain of gear that Bryan's Dad helped organize. A tent, some sleeping bags, a good sized cooler, a box with cookery and utensils, another with dry goods, another for cleaning aids and making fires. Neither graduate had imagined the plethora of 'stuff' that was needed to be a successful camper and Matt had to pull his belongings and repack the car to get everything smartly inside.

Matt's car was a pretty decent looking, but older, Volvo 144S and they hit the road fully loaded with fresh oil, a full tank of gas and a new Rand McNally as their only guide. On 75 just south of Cinci Bryan surprised Matt with a couple of Montecristos.

"What the hell are those?"

"Cigars wild-man. We're cage free animals. We can do whatever we want, so let's light 'em up, roll down the windows and get the hell outta dodge. What better way to demonstrate manhood? The open road is in front of us, time on our side, and we have no responsibilities. So toke away my friend." And with that proclamation a Zippo magically appeared and with a click of the lid and a flick of the flint there was fire, and where there is fire there is smoke. Bryan handed the lit cigar to Matt who, with astonishment, grabbed it, stared at it, rolled it around in his fingers, said 'what the hell' and took a drag. Five minutes later as highway scenery flowed beautifully by, Matt and Bryan were on top of the world merrily sucking on their cigars and life could not be better. In another five minutes their car was in the breakdown lane and both of them, green and puking, was in the ditch re-evaluating manhood.

"Oh my God I think I'm going to die." Matt moaned.

"Shut up, you're making my head hurt." Came a muted reply.

Just then a cop car pulled up and two officers got out, hands to the ready. They sauntered over to evaluate the situation and were surprised when neither of the boys so much as acknowledged their presence, let alone stood up to greet them.

"What's goin' on boys? Don't look like a car problem or your heads would be under the hood, not underground." One officer said. "You in some kind of trouble?"

"No sir." Bryan barely offered as a reply. "We're just learnin' one of life's lessons the hard way. Inhaled a bit too much from a cigar."

"Looks like that car is pretty loaded down with stuff" the other cop said circling it like a bird of prey. "Where'd you boys git all that stuff?"

"From home" Bryan said, now sitting Indian style in a little less agony.

"What'dya mean from home? You got your own home or somethin'? Don't look like your old enough to drive let alone be leaving town with all that loot. Lemme see your driver's license."

"Not my car. Get his instead."

"I asked for yours wise ass. Don't recall saying nothin' 'bout the car, so just do as your told boy."

Bryan pulled out his license and handed it over to the officer who stared at it silently for a few seconds with the dull confused, expression of a bull staring down a matador's cape.

"Bryan Jeffries from Cincinnati. Where you headed Bryan?"

"Florida."

"Florida huh? Maybe. Then again maybe not. Could be you boys stole this vehicle and all the stuff in it. Could take us a while to figure out the truth, but that's what we got to do now isn't it?"

"Excuse me officer." Matt said. "The car is mine; I have a copy of the title in the glove compartment. The goods inside all came from the Jeffries household and Mr. Jeffries would be glad to vouch for the fact that none of them are stolen. He helped us pack the car and can describe in detail the family gear we are using. You won't find any drugs or alcohol inside either. They don't interest us. So please proceed as you see fit, but your actions will only confirm my statements and the fact that we have done nothing wrong and have nothing to hide."

"Show me your driver's license, insurance card and the title and if I'm satisfied then I might let you continue on your journey." The other cop shouted.

Matt silently dragged his sour stomached body to the car to get the title and as he opened the door the cop yelled "Don't move. Hands on your head. Face the car and don't say a word, smart ass."

Dumbfounded, Matt did as told and the cop shoved him to the ground and handcuffed him. "This is how I see fit to proceed boy. Understand? Don't you try smart talking me! I gotta see for myself that you ain't no thief and unfortunately for you, that means that I gotta do what I gotta do, no matter what your punk ass thinks. Now you just stay still while I do a little inspectin' on my own."

Matt lay there motionless, in a state of such humiliation that he was close to tears. The cop started poking around in the car and then opened the trunk to see what was there. His head was under the lid for a couple of minutes during which time Matt imagined slamming it shut on the fucker.

"They're clean Fred. Stuff's all marked with the Jeffries family name. We gotta let 'em go" the cop said reluctantly, and turning to Matt and Bryan said "Now you listen boys. Don't even think of doing anything even close to bad or some really mean cops will come along and plant on you a life's lesson you do NOT want to get. And stay away from cigars. Not get out of here."

Steaming, fuming, heart racing and just plain mad as hell they got into the car and drove cautiously away. Both were too pissed and still too shell shocked to talk to each for several minutes, but when they did the expletives were famous.

The cops drove away in a slow, deliberate and satisfied fashion and when they got out of sight started laughing hysterically.

"I'll call Mr. Jeffries to let him know that we had the little chat with the boys that he wanted. He won't have to worry any longer about their behavior during the road trip. I think we scared them enough to assure him of that. Wait 'till he hears about the cigars!"

I t took about thirty minutes for Matt and Bryan to recover from the self-imposed smoke attack on their bodies and the bazaar encounter with the cops. When impact from the combo punch had finally subsided their road trip thrills returned and before long the radio was blaring and the two were once again enthralled by the idea of their independence and the open road ahead.

"Holy shit man. That was not a good start to our journey. If we hadn't smoked those dumb cigars none of this would have happened. But screw it, it's over now and we're back in action" Bryan said with conviction.

"Back in action and almost back to normal. My stomach is still a bit queasy and my head is not yet clear. But give me a couple more minutes and I'll be there. What's the plan anyway?'

Bryan opened the atlas and found their first destination. It was only a couple hours away, Laurel River Lake in Daniel Boone National Forest. A quick stop there for some site seeing and an already prepared lunch and after that it was down through Knoxville and finally to Chattanooga where they would overnight at Harrison Bay State Park.

When eventually they arrived at the park the few hours of sunlight left in the beautiful summer day helped them to relish the job of establishing camp. It was a first. Even though they were teenage entrepreneurs extraordinaire, for the first time in their lives they had to tend to the basics of food, clothing and shelter without parental support and while they didn't recognize it, it was their first exposure to the essence of Maslow's hierarchy of needs. But with the pleasantly warm afternoon sun and the splendor of nature at arm's length, fulfilling the first rung on the hierarchical ladder never made their list of considerations.

Bryan was more than animated at their current state. "Let's go for a swim and then we can set up camp. What'da think?"

"Sounds good to me. Last one in is a rotten egg."

Without further word both were tearing into their bags to don swimming trunks and sandals, and grab towels for the beach. Ready and in the rare form that only teenage boys can muster, they drove off to the beach each overwhelmed by the cacophony of different thoughts flitting through their brains. Matt was still somewhat perturbed by the encounter with law enforcement and while far from the most active of his brain waves it was none-the-less a constant presence. Bryan was hoping for a beach crowded with virile felines in scant bikinis and swelling young breasts and both were also ruminating randomly about the vagaries of the future that the rite of graduation had imposed on them and their classmates.

The beach sand was still warm from a day in full sun, although it was sparsely populated because the campers were mostly busy tending to early evening pleasantries like ice cold beer and nice red wine with some appetizers al naturale. Not affected by the lack of female scenery, Bryan hastily shed sandals and towel and started running to the water. Matt followed suit, behind but just barely.

"You're the rotten egg wild-man." Bryan announced plunging into the shallow waters with a half twist and hands firing fake pistols back at Matt. Matt followed suit but less flamboyantly and, after several seconds of an underwater dart, both emerged like dolphins having narrowly escaped the clutches of a killer whale. The water was pleasant and relaxing and at a temperature that made one appreciate the warmth in the air but not at the expense of comfort. It was as damned close to perfect as one could imagine and the boys stayed in it to be embalmed by its glory until dusk overtook them.

"Wow, wild-man we'd better high tail it back to our spot and set up camp before it gets too dark. We have a tent to pitch and food to cook, so let's get going. What'dya say?'

"Absolutely, I'm starving. Nothing better than food cooked in the great outdoors. Everything tastes better. Even cheap hotdogs pass the test of gourmet cuisine. Let's get going and pig out as soon as possible."

Together they trudged out of the water, lumbering in long slow strides with bent swinging arms urging them forward until the water sank to below their knees. From there ensued a race to the towels and the car where Ol' Faithful waited patiently to be called again into service.

Minutes later, after passing a couple of lavatory/shower facilities and a number of camp sites labeled by yellow painted lettering on brown Cyprus posts, they pulled into A34, their designated site. It was designed for tenting only, so beyond the parking spot was a flat for the tent, wooden picnic table and block fireplace nestled under a mixed forest of sinewy pines and broadleaf oaks.

"Hey wild-man, why not back in so the trunk is closer to the campsite? We're gonna need all the help we can get. There's only about 20 minutes of daylight left." So Matt yanked the Volvo around, pitched the gears into reverse and zipped it back into the site, right up to the flat for the tent. Hey scrambled out, popped the trunk and looked in bewilderment at all the stuff, not knowing quite where to start.

"OK. The tent is important and so is some food. I'll grab the tent and you start unloading the coolers and cooking stuff. Have you ever put this baby up before?"

"I watched my father do it. It looked easy enough, so we shouldn't have any problems." Bryan said as he hoisted a cooler from the back seat and placed it on the table.

Matt grabbed the bag with the tent, splayed open the top, dumped all of the contents on the ground and stared down at the ensemble of parts, which looked like pick-up sticks in a pile of dirty laundry. There were ropes, poles, stakes, stringers, mats, covers and barely visible within it all, the tent itself. With a bit of common sense as guidance Matt began to separate the pieces into items of like geometry and after a couple of minutes had four distinct piles. From the pile of assorted materials he pulled the ground cloth and quickly spread it on the flat. Next he grabbed the tent and from the outline of the ground cloth was able to discern which part was the floor. It lay with ease on top of the ground cloth but the balance of tent material was an unruly mess from which no configurable orientation could be had.

"Bryan, give me a hand. I don't have a clue how this thing goes together. We don't even have a picture to guide us." Bryan stopped unpacking their kitchen to come to the rescue and gaped at what could have been a parachute as easily as a tent.

"Man, it's getting' dark and I'm starving. Why don't we eat first and then figure this out. We can grill some hot dogs and heat up some water for soup. I've got a package of chicken noodle out and the stove is on the table."

The stove was a vintage three burner green Coleman with one burner that doubled as a grill. It had an empty cylindrical fuel tank in front that needed white gas to operate so Matt opened the knurled aluminum cap to pour in gas from the red and silver Coleman container. With fuel all set the only need was fire so he grabbed a wooden match from the box of Strike Anywhere Diamonds and swept it briskly across a nearby rock. The match made a snapping noise that was immediately followed by an explosion of sparks, then flame, and two very self-assured grins.

"Open the valve when I hold this over the burner." Bryan did as Matt suggested and though the match was more than an adequate pilot, it lit nothing and proceeded to burn itself out. Both stared dumbly at the barely visible charred remains as dusk closed in quickly under the forest canopy.

"I'll get the flashlight and then we'll figure this out. It won't take but a second." Bryan said while sauntering to the Volvo. "You have any idea where the flashlight is?"

"I remember seeing it in the Clorox box in the trunk. It's red."

"Got it." Bryan turned back towards the table clicking the switch with no response from the flashlight. "Damn. It's not working. Get a match so I can see what's wrong."

Matt snapped another match to life and in Bryan's hands both saw two rusted, leaking D sized batteries whose life was obviously spent years ago.

"Shit Bry, when was the last time you guys used this?"

"I dunno. Must have been a long time ago. Now that I think about it, my father told me to get new batteries."

"Which, of course, didn't happen. So what now? It's dark, we have no light, the stove isn't working, and we can't figure out how to pitch the tent."

"Let's turn the car around and use the headlights for a while." So Matt reversed his campsite parking job then shut the Volvo down but kept the lights burning. Their campsite was awash when they returned to diagnose the stove.

"What's this knob for? I can pull it out and push it in. Maybe it's a pump. I'm going to pump it and you try lighting the burner."

Matt grabbed another match and shoved it into the burner as he opened the valve. When the match got close a flame miraculously surrounded the burner tip, producing a shape that looked like a giant blue zinnia.

"Hallelujah! We have fire. I think you can stop pumping now. Get the wieners and let's get roasting!"

Bryan cycled the pump one last time and went to get the hot dogs from the cooler. When he returned the big blue zinnia had dwindled to a little yellow pansy and a few seconds later it abruptly went out. Two more identical light-off attempts produced the same result and neither could fathom the cause.

"Man, I can't believe this. So close but yet so far. I'm starving and I can't wait any longer. I'm eating my hotdogs cold."

"You can't do that."

"Why not? They're cooked. They'll just be cold."

"Yeah but they'll taste like shit."

"And at this point I'll eat shit. Better that than nothing."

Matt reluctantly agreed to abandon the stove and a few minutes later both were seated at a paper plate laden table adorned with four cold dogs in buns and heaps of potato chips. At the top of each plate were ice cold 16 ounce Cokes and at center stage were ketchup, relish and mustard. The table would have been totally silent throughout their dinner if it weren't for the noise of high energy mandibles working so hard that they drowned out the sound of every nearby insect. Neither boy came up for air until his plate was clear of the gourmet spread, and satiated, was ready to sit back for final sips from his soda.

"That wasn't so bad." Matt blurted while burping boisterously.

"Better than I expected. Guess the ol' adage is true; there is nothing better than food in the great outdoors."

"Yeah, especially if it were cooked." Both laughed out loud and Bryan smacked the table as if it too were part of the joke.

"I guess it's time to tackle the tent. We need somewhere safe to sleep and the car just won't cut the mustard."

"Agreed. I guarantee that we can get that puppy raised, I'm certain of it."

Somewhat amply fed and once again raring to go, both set off to conquer the mass of material heaped on the ground. They started tugging and pulling edges, sides and corners and inspected zippers to find the entrance and while so doing failed to notice that the brightness of the car headlights was dimming, and dimming quickly. Before they had time to insert a single pole the lights had faded to the point where even their engrossed focus on the tent was finally penetrated.

"Holy shit." Matt yelled as he ran to the car. "I've got turn off the headlights immediately. We're losing the battery! We'll never get it started in the morning. Jesus! What else can go wrong?" And with that their surroundings, disheveled and unfinished, were bathed in darkness.

"Listen. Let's just go to bed. We can put our pads on top of the tent and climb in for the night. I'm making my way to the table right now. Are the matches on top?"

"Yeah, get one lit and I'll find the sleeping gear. I'm more tired than I thought anyway."

A few matches later the boys were snuggled in their bags and while somewhat fearful of their exposure managed to relax and settle down - that is - until the mosquitoes came buzzing on a blood sucking mission of 'til death-do-us-part and thank God there were no mirrors because when they awoke in the early skylight of dawn they looked like a set of twins with a bad case of the measles.

M att rolled over and sat up inside his sleeping bag. His senses were just beginning to wake up as his eyes adjusted to the thin morning light. When his nerve endings fired up they detected, and then reacted to, a surface invasion of the major itch kind.

"Jesus my face itches. Oh my God, I have bumps all over. What the heck happened?"

Bryan sat up rubbing his eyes and blinked a few times to get them into focus. Then the boys looked at each other. Shock is insufficient to describe the delayed response each had to the other's face.

"You look like shit. It almost looks like you have acne on acne."

"Look who's talking. Your face looks like a mine field."

"Doesn't feel much better either. God I itch. Did we bring anything that resembles a first aid kit?"

"I don't think so. I mean, I don't have any anti-itch cream or anything like that. We're gonna have to live with this until we can get to a pharmacy."

"Why don't you try to start the car? We might as well see how bad things are."

Moments later both emerged in their skibbies and threw on yesterday's outfits. Matt moseyed with trepidation over to ol' not-so-faithful to see if she had any life left in her. He sat for a quiet moment with the key in the ignition and head bowed forward into the steering wheel as if willing her to start on her own. With his silent moment of truth complete and a twist of the wrist they had their answer. Wroom, wroom, wroom the starter slowly turned the engine - and then stopped. He tried it again and there was no response at all. They were stranded. Matt yanked open the door, charged out, slammed it shut and yelled, "Damn."

Ed Moses was walking down the road past A34 just as Matt slammed the door. He was kind-of whistling silently as he went having showered and shaved immediately after delivering a top ten turd of the year – no better way to start the day. Seeing the boys gave him a chuckle while at the same time, for reasons unknown, making him feel proud and somewhat nostalgic.

"What seems to be the trouble boys?"

46

"Our battery died. We had to use the lights last night to set up camp and left them on a little too long."

"No problem. I'll come back in a minute with my jumper cables and we'll have you going in no time. Already got your tent down I see. Planning on movin' out early this morning?"

"Actually, we never got it pitched. Had a little trouble understanding what goes where."

"Tell you what, when I get back I'll show you how to pitch the tent and you can ask me any other questions you want as well. See you in say, about five minutes? Oh, I'll bring you some Benadryl for those nasty mosquito bites too." Ed said as he left.

"That would be terrific, sir. Thank you so much." Both shouted in unison with a note of utter relief. A couple high fives and "Thank God's" later, Bryan dug out the OJ, milk and cereal and, as with the ritual from the evening before, they began in silence and without pause to devour their breakfast.

When Ed returned he threw them a bottle of Benadryl, quickly showed them the tricks to erecting the tent and, being a father himself (but alas only with girls), was savvy enough to disassemble it and make the boys pitch it on their own. While they tended to their lesson Ed inquired them about their trek and in the process also learned of their saga with the cold hotdogs.

"Well, you got it about 70% right. That knob you shoved in and out is a pump. It develops pressure in the fuel tank so the fuel will flow when you open the valve to a burner. But see here? This is a vent and its part way open. So as you pumped, you developed some pressure but it quickly escaped through the vent and the flame went out. Just close the vent and then pump and you will be all set. But remember to relieve the pressure before you store the stove, just to be safe. You don't happen to have a Coleman lantern as well do you? It works the same way, so be sure that the vent is closed when you pump it and open it back up again when you are done. Now let's get that car jumped."

A few minutes later the car was running and what started as a calamitous day was immediately transformed into a new opportunity of intrigue and adventure, care of Ed. The boys thanked him profusely for the help he provided, as they ought to, not realizing how Ed's involvement in their predicament actually made Ed's day as much as it made their own.

"Time for me to go fishin' boys. You have a great trip and be careful."

After packing Matt jockeyed Ol' Faithful into reverse and gently nudged her onto the gravel campsite road. He shifted into drive and off they went while waving to Ed, whom they vowed they would never forget.

They got quickly back on route 75 heading south to Atlanta, figuring it would be in their sights in around three hours. Both decided that Atlanta would be a nice place for a short stop to check out the downtown area around Georgia Tech and then head east to Stone Mountain for a late lunch and a little hike.

As they approached Atlanta the jammed freeways became more daunting than pleasurable so they skipped the downtown aspect of their plans in favor of more time at Stone Mountain. Stone Mountain is just that – a big stone - a really big stone. It's more than 800 feet high and covers more than 500 acres. The park boasts, among other things, an enormous adventure course, a tram ride to the top and a wildly large carving of Jefferson Davis, Robert E. Lee and "Stonewall" Jackson seated on steeds so tremendous it makes one wonder how the south lost the war.

The late June day was famously warm; humid to the point where being scantily clad in tee shirts, shorts and flip-flops was inadequate to ward off the overwhelming feeling of damp dish rags. Sweat was more common among the vacationers than salt on French fries but despite the difficulty in remaining comfortable, spirits everywhere were keen. Matt and Bryan got instantly caught up in the atmosphere, being aided by the plethora of tight tees sculpted to the chests of daddy's little girls. The eye candy was a better driver for their exuberance than stream water to a parched camper and they decided, after their previous day filled with debacle, to stay the evening to get their road trip back on track. An hour later their tent site looked as well sculpted as a veteran camper's and they headed off to the campground pool where sunbathing beauties lay in waiting for their rescue from boredom.

Matt tossed his towel to Bryan and immediately jumped into the cool clean water. Bryan circled the area for a spot with the best available vantage point and after eyeing it laid out the towels, shed his tee and started to catch some rays. A few minutes later he was baked into the kind of sleep that only a hot sun can trigger, sweating profusely and drooling on the towel while the heat toyed psychedelically with his dreams.

The pool, while not crowded to the point where attempts at swimming were fruitless, was none-the-less well enjoyed when Matt took his plunge. Typical of pools everywhere in the country it was used by all except the female contingent between ages 16 and 35, whose presence was exclusively reserved for viewing while working on their tans. It didn't take Matt long to tire of the endless energy of the predominantly preteen bathers so after about fifteen minutes of breast strokes and surface dives he emerged refreshed to go find Bryan.

"Nice picture Bri. You're not even a sight for sore eyes. How do you expect to meet any girls with towel marks and dribble all over your face?"

"Leave me alone. I need to take a short nap. I didn't sleep a wink last night."

Matt sat quietly on his sun drenched towel to air dry while he scoped the surroundings. He spotted a group of cute teenage girls making their way to the snack shack. Dressed in halter tops and jean shorts over bikinis, they moved in unison to get diet cokes like a herd of does entering a grassy knoll. He was mesmerized by the commonality in their behaviors. In the midst of nonstop chatter they kept looking awkwardly about their surroundings while repeatedly tucking their long straight hair behind their ears. They walked slightly slouched as if height were a thing to fear and were quick to jab each other gingerly and giggle when their conversation peaked. The site of their innocence gave Matt a rise and he was quick to start scheming the best way to capture their attention. Bryan was still sleeping so Matt, who wasn't prone to missing an opportunity, decided to venture out on his own. His approach would be simple, he decided, just meet them at the snack shack and ask them for advice on what to eat.

"Good afternoon ladies. How are you all doing this fine afternoon? I just arrived from Chattanooga and I'm famished. Any idea if anything here is worth ordering?"

The girls stared at him for a few seconds before uttering a garbled group response, and finally one at the back of the pack got bold enough to speak up – the team representative. "Nothing's great, but nothing's all that bad either. I kind of like the corn dogs, and they make a decent fish sandwich too."

"Thanks for the advice. I think I'll have a corn dog and a pop when you ladies are done ordering. Where're you from anyway?"

The representative maintained her position as spokesperson, "We're all from a small town at the outskirts of Birmingham. Our families have been coming here since we were really little. It used to be lots of fun but now it's kind of boring."

"I've never been to Birmingham. I'm from Cincinnati. My name is Matt." He said holding his hand out for salutations.

"Sharon." She replied while accepting Matt's greeting. "I thought you said you were from Chattanooga."

Her handshake was firm and left a feeling of confidence in its wake that took Matt enough by surprise to cause him to look at the source. Her fingers were long, slender and perfectly manicured and her wrist was petit but not fragile. On it was one simple handmade braided bracelet. It was the perfect garnish to the perfect wrist – an accent rather than a piece of jewelry – destined forever to be rightfully overshadowed by the jewel it adorned. Matt had never seen anything quite so graceful and it moved him in a new and mysterious way. Suddenly his urge to captivate these girls was reduced to the single desire to hold Sharon's hand and when he looked up he was fearful that his blushed face would be a dead give-away.

"Actually my friend and I are from Cincinnati. We camped in Chattanooga last night. It was the first night of our journey to Miami Beach and things didn't go well so we decided take it easy today instead of driving down to Jacksonville."

"You're here alone without your family? With just a friend?"

"That's right. My friend Bryan and I are taking about six weeks to tour the south, and intend to spend most of our time touring the east coast of Florida. We just graduated and are taking this trip as a farewell before heading off to college."

"Wow. That's so cool. My parents would never let me do anything like that and I just graduated too."

"Well, right or wrong, I guess parents treat girls a little differently. I mean, they assume that you aren't capable of defending yourself and make decisions about what you can and can't do to protect you. Maybe it's not right, but wanting to protect you is not a bad thing."

"It's hard to argue with that logic, as much as I would like to. Where are you going to college?"

"Boston. Boston College actually. How about you? What are you doing now that you're free?"

"Boston College, huh? That's pretty impressive. It's supposed to be a great school. I was actually thinking about going there, but Northeastern gave me a deal that I couldn't refuse."

"You mean we're going to be neighbors? Isn't Northeastern right by Fenway Park? Where the Red Sox play?"

"I wouldn't know about that, but it is in downtown Boston and I think it's pretty close to BC."

"Well isn't this amazing. We haven't even gotten there yet and now we each know someone in the area. We'll have to get together there, just to sanctify our acquaintance here."

Just then a smack on the shoulder told Matt that Bryan had emerged from his slumber. Bryan could smell a cute girl against a strong headwind from over a mile and arrived refreshed and full of smiles.

"Wild-man. What's goin' on? Who are your friends?"

"Bryan – meet Sharon. The rest of the gang I have yet to be introduced to."

"Pleasure to meet you. What do you girls think about going on a hike? We've never been here before and can't leave without seeing the view from the top. What do you think? Interested?"

The girls looked at each other in silence to assess the group opinion and from facial gestures alone arrived at an affirmative quorum in no time. Sharon replied for the group.

"It's pretty hot, so why don't we take the tram to the top and walk down from there?"

"Great idea. You lead the way."

The group to the top totaled seven and it didn't take long to complete the introductions. Two of the girls were sisters, two of the girls had just graduated, two of them were to be seniors in the fall and one a junior. The girls all went to the same school and had grown up together although they weren't classically "the best of friends". Their parents were the ones that hung out with each other, so their friendship developed through family ties and not through school. The result was a wonderful kinship, but one that was largely isolated to family events that had transpired over the fourteen years since its inception.

Matt continued to talk to Sharon about their college plans while Bryan, in heaven and at the top of his game, entertained the remaining foursome. He loved to draw attention to himself and had a natural charisma that warmed those in its presence. Before long the four girls were hanging on every word like band groupies after a concert and soon their shy posturing was replaced by a competitive boldness that even they found foreign. Bryan was an equal opportunity kind-of guy and shared himself with all the girls even though he had his eye on Barb, the older of the two Patten sisters. While he continued to wow them, he slowly withdrew a bit of his attention from Barb, hoping to prompt a rise in her yearning for him. This well-orchestrated move was all about paying dividends later that evening when, if the opportunity presented itself, he would play the second inning of his shrewd game. Bryan was a matador with many spears of which his bull had received just one.

At the same time Sharon and Matt found each other so engrossed in their constant stream of dialog that the other five members of their clan were nothing more than a distant memory. They found an instant easiness in each other that felt good yet unsettling. The more Matt talked to, looked at and assessed Sharon the happier he was that she would be close come fall. His only hope was that she felt the same.

The top of Stone Mountain is higher than the surrounding land so the vista reaches tens of miles in all directions. It's a nice view albeit not as spectacular as one might think, with the main attraction being a distant view of the city skyline. The clan reached the top without incident and spent about half an hour tooling around before starting their decent.

The way down was fairly easy and the group had fun the entire way. They told each other stories of their most outlandish childhood exploits, embellishing each beyond truth like a politician making promises on the

campaign trail. The laughter was infectious and the teasing dispropor-
tionate to the newness of their acquaintances.

The trail was too well groomed to be adventurous so when an
option was presented for them to take a road less traveled there was
nothing to consider and off they went. In a few turns the terrain got
steeper and pocked with boulders.

"Here, let me help you." Matt said offering an outstretched hand to
Sharon. "We don't need an accident to be the cause of meeting your
families. Better that something more positive take its place."

"I'm fine, really I can manage." But she took his hand anyway and to
Matt's delight held it firmly. Matt couldn't believe his good fortune. His
head was swimming as they descended the rock, so much so that it was he,
more than Sharon, who needed the support. Matt had had plenty of
episodes with girls in a degree of different circumstances and in a variety of
settings, and he never failed to be the one in control. But with Sharon it was
different. There was no need for control, no need for pomposity and no
requirement to be the entertainer. He was able to just be himself - no – he
wanted to just be himself and to allow his true essence to steer their fate.

When they got to the bottom the girls decided that it was time to
check in with their parents; a bogus need they used as a pretext for getting off alone to talk about the boys.

"Guys, we're gonna go see if our families are doing anything that
requires our help. What if we catch up with you later?" Barb said as
Bryan feigned a momentary breach of attentiveness.

"What? Uh, oh yeah. No problem. Where do you want to meet?
We're in B64. Want to stop by our place after dinner?"

"Sounds good to me. You guys want to stop by their place after dinner?" Barb said to the girls. They were quick to nod an affirmation of the
idea, muttered a bunch of "OK" and "sure" comments and started to
again move in unison as they departed.

"Sharon!" Matt called. Do you have your college address yet? If
you do bring it with you, I mean, if you want to."

"I'd love to but I don't have it yet. All I know is that I'll be in one
of the freshman girls' dorms."

The girls moved quickly out of hearing range and begin an animated discourse of their encounter. Barb was the first to let loose.

"What do you think of those guys? What about that Bryan anyway? What a smooth talker. He's destined to be a success. He just has that way about him."

"He's alright but a little too smooth for me. He just might be a tiger in waiting instead of a diamond in the rough, if you know what I mean."

"Oh he's a diamond for sure and not so rough either. Those dimples just about kill me. I want to stick my tongue in his dimples and slobber wet kisses all over that handsome face."

"Eewwww. That's disgusting." They all echoed together.

"Well it doesn't matter anyway because I'm not so sure he likes me. He seems to be paying more attention to you girls than me."

"That might be, but not Matt. He's all eyes for Sharon and none for anyone else. I think he has a crush on her. You better be careful not to lead him on. He seems like a nice guy and you shouldn't hurt him."

"You mean the way I hurt all the other boys? Well maybe this one is different!" Sharon defended herself.

"You mean you like him? Maybe you even have a crush on him!"

"No. I just mean that he's a nice guy and could be a good friend and since he's going to college nearby and since I might need someone sometime to help me, or whatever, I thought I should make sure that we at least part friends."

"So you want to keep him in your hip pocket in case you get lonely or desperate? Have an escape plan in the event that things don't go quite your way? That's real sweet, Sharon."

"That's not what I meant. I like him, but let's face it, what does that matter? We had a nice conversation for a few hours and he's leaving in the morning."

"Don't be so certain. That boy has more than just eyes for you. He seems to have a hankerin' to be close to you and not just for sex either. He's smitten beyond repair in my opinion. Play your cards right and he's all but wrapped around any finger you choose."

"I don't want him wrapped around any finger, now or in the future. He's his own man and needs to stay that way. And I'm not about to give up any of the freedoms coming my way either, for him or anyone else for that matter. Barb and I are just about to be cut loose from the noose and the worst thing either of us could do is to limit our exposure to the experiences we have coming."

"I agree. There's a big world out there that we don't know anything about and I too am not going to let something stupid like a boy get in the way of my explorations. I'd rather they be part of them. And as far as Bryan goes, if he wants to be part of my explorations that would be just fine by me!"

"What are you saying? That you're gonna let him have his way with you? You're nuts. You don't even know the guy."

"Let's just say that if he wants to do a little kissin' and a little pettin' I could be persuaded. It would make this evening more enjoyable than the last couple have been."

"I think you're getting experimentation confused with exploration. We were talking about exploring, not experimenting. You explore the world; you experiment with boys, but only with boys that you know and like. Not with strangers. If you want to experiment with Bryan, go ahead, but I'm warning you, this is not a guy you should be toying with. He'll eat you up and spit you out. You're a lot more innocent than you let on to be. So be careful, if you intend to do anything with him."

"We'll see." Barb said, donning a grin more mischievous than the Cheshire Cat.

"What's up with you, Wild Man? I've never seen you in such a daze before. You couldn't take your eyes off that Sharon girl. Holding hands on the trail – great move! Looks like the chivalry tactic is working pretty well with that one! Keep it up and maybe we'll both score some tonight!" Bryan said while smacking Matt on the shoulder for emphasis. "I'm pretty sure that Barb is all hot and bothered too, probably wondering why I'm not swooning over her like a puppy trying to suckle its momma's teat. I can't wait to put some more moves on that one. I'll have her panting so bad she won't know what hit her!"

Suddenly Matt started to see Bryan in a different light and the bravado in his great friend changed instantly from something to admire and revel in to something distasteful. Instead of being funny and hip Bryan's preoccupation with himself felt more like a smoke screen of insecurity and low self-esteem than strength in his character. Matt always thought Bryan's need to be in control and to dominate was a sign of leadership, but now it looked more like cowardice and felt more like being used than being a partner. The thought that his friend had flaws made him angry.

"Bri, I'm not going to hit on Sharon. I like her and I want her to respect me so I'm going to act accordingly, like a gentleman should. I don't know why I feel the way I do, but there's definitely something different with this girl. Maybe that saying about chemistry is real. Maybe we have chemistry. I don't know, but I'm not going to jeopardize finding out 'cause I've never had any feelings like this before."

"Holy cow Wild Man! Me thinks you're in love. Matt and Sharon. Sounds great together. Good for you Wild Man. You go find true love, but me, I'm still just the conqueror and that's all I want to be. So tonight I'm polishing up my best moves for Barb and we'll see how far I can get."

"Don't be an embarrassment. And don't do anything that will cause a problem. I don't want to get kicked out of this place and I do want to spend more time with Sharon."

"Don't worry Wild Man." Bryan said with a smile that only the Grinch could duplicate. "Now let's go cook some dinner and freshen up for the post meal festivities!"

Bran's Dad had stocked the cooler pretty nicely so Matt and Bryan had the pick of several different prepared dishes and some meats for their evening meal. After a glutinous rampage involving potato salad, New York strip and some Cokes, their picnic table looked like the food scene from Tom Jones and they were so sated with good food that their issues with sustenance from the day before felt like another world. Matt toasted, "Here's to Ed Moses. Thanks Ed for all you did."

"Hear, hear. Now let's get some wood, take a shower and start the fire."

An hour later dusk was waning; a cool breeze swept through the campground and the fire was catching in small wisps of flame that kept creeping steadily higher through the tinder and into the logs. Just then a bobbing flashlight affront a din of high pitched whispers broke the silence and evening greetings were quick to replace hypnotic stares into the dancing yellow flames. Only four of the girls had returned; the youngest being confined unhappily to the home site with Moms, Dads and other youngsters. The boys only had two chairs so they jockeyed the picnic table around to make a place for all to sit in comfortable view of the fire. Matt and Sharon were side by side on the bench with the two other girls while Bryan and Barb sat next to each other in the chairs.

The evening conversation started slowly and with a bit of awkwardness but gained momentum like a loaded freight train leaving the depot. Once up to speed there was no stopping it but when it reached full bore it suddenly bifurcated into two distinct one-on-one discussions that left the two junior bench players sitting idle. They listened for a few minutes quietly poking the fire and then excused themselves, leaving the couples on their own.

Bryan sat angled toward Barb, this time making her his only focal point. He spoke in a deliberate but soft tone, keeping frequent eye contact and softly stroking her hair. His head routinely ventured downward to hold fast an obvious fix on her breasts. It was a process that Matt had seen many times before, with varying degrees of success.

Barb simply loved the attention and each time Bryan looked down at her chest she felt a surge of perkiness in her nipples. He definitely had her aroused. With artfulness belying his years Bryan shifted his hand from stroking her hair to rubbing her back and shoulders, placed his other on her knee and moved in closer to speak in intimate whispers. His style was not to strike like a Cobra but to wrap like a Python and his prey was nearing the point of no safe escape. Then, when he knew her body was yearning for a kiss to release its passions, he sat back abruptly and feigned to tend to the fire. Now she would have to come to him.

Sharon's appeal was so wonderfully enhanced by the tones of the firelight that Matt could barely keep his eyes from drowning in her splendor. In daylight her hair was down and unadorned but this evening she had it fixed to one side and curled over her shoulder. Her faintly floral scent boasted of nature, as if passing a honeysuckle in the height of spring and her exposed ear modeled a simple earring that dangled from a perfect lobe and glistened in the reflected firelight, as if beckoning only sweet sounds to pass through it.

Her legs were strong without being sinewy, lean without losing their softness and her arms were of a thinness whose proportions were matched flawlessly to her supple torso. When she spoke her voice carried strength but was still strikingly female and musical. Matt could just as easily imagine her singing as delivering a powerful speech and felt so enriched when she spoke that he would have recorded their conversation if he could.

They talked about a range of different subjects from Watergate to the Olympics in Montreal and lots of others in between. They shared memories of their life experiences from their first kiss to the senior prom. Matt never felt so at ease with a girl before and Sharon seemed to be equally at ease with Matt.

While they talked Barb nestled up to Bryan and took lead role as courtier. She started massaging his shoulder to regain his attention but he remained focused on rekindling the fire. At first he kept jostling the logs and paid her no attention, but after a few minutes he leaned into her, affirming his pleasure with her rubdown, and kissed her briskly on the cheek. Her response was as expected, turning toward Bryan in anticipation of kisses that would linger and grow in intensity and Bryan was not to disappoint. He moved his chair to face her, placed both hands on her knees, and then leaned in slowly with lightly pressed lips to brush hers with a bogus innocence that he mastered from experience. This followed with a roll of the head that found his hair in contact with her cheek, his nose in contact with the nape of her neck and then his half opened mouth, ready to suckle softly like a baby drawing milk from the breast, found a spot behind her cheek and below her ear to work its magic.

Before long Bryan and Barb were in locked arms with lips on lips sharing every aspect of the fluids that lingered within. She showed no sign of hesitation with Bryan's advances so he began to grope her breasts and through her shirt felt her nipples become erect in response. It was the exact reaction that he hoped he would witness and it, by itself, was cause for his arousal, not the potential for intimate contact with a desirable young female, but the control that he knew he was exerting. His plan was working, in his estimation with divinity, and now the time was right to carry it to its successful conclusion. He gently placed his hand below her right breast, grasping her side with just enough force to slightly interlace his fingers in her rib cage, and leaned close to her ear to coo her pleasure into a state of final submittal.

"Barb. Why don't we get more comfortable? You'd be surprised by the comfort that my air mattress provides and instead of kissing in this awkward position we could cuddle a bit in comfort. Want to go lie with me for a few minutes?"

"Okay, as long as you promise to be a good boy and behave yourself."

"Oh I promise. Scouts honor. Actually I never was a Scout, but Scout's honor anyway."

They stood together hand in hand and quietly slipped into the tent. Matt and Sharon paid no heed as their enraptured conversation held no opening for foreign participation, no intervention in any form. Once safely inside the tent Bryan grabbed Barb around the waist, dragged to her knees and kissed her savagely with a new level of force and brutality that, while not waking the cautions laden on her from parental guidance, did generate a modicum of hesitance.

Moments later Bryan was holding Barb on the air mattress with legs intertwined and arms enfolding her like a vine sucking the life from a tree. He rolled over her and began to covet her with false pretentions so obvious that Barb was instantly awoken from her journey in Wonderland.

"Whoa, Big Boy. Whoa. Take it easy. Can we just talk a minute?"

Bryan answered her with nothing more than the quiet grind of his hips into her crotch.

"Hey there. Take it easy. Cool down a minute." She said while pushing him with a force that was pronounced yet not explosive. "I need a breather."

Her attempts to gain control of the situation were in vain as Bryan continued to unleash his adolescent storm. He held her fast despite her attempts to wriggle out from under, deftly slipping his hand under her shirt and bra to the soft and indescribably irresistible tissues of her firm young breast. When he touched it, it created an explosion. His cupped hand around her splendor unleashed in him an alternate life form whose existence was predicated on imbibing the flesh of young females. His normal state was succumbed by a primordial one that was intently preoccupied with domination, physical. One purpose. One goal. One finish line.

"Bryan. Stop. Please stop. Bryan. Come on. I can't do this. I don't want to do this. Please stop." Barb called firmly but gently.

The response she received was an acceleration of the same controlling behavior. Bryan pulled her bra above both breasts, yanked open her blouse, and began to devour her breasts like the homeless devour soup. Her placid white skin played candy to the flickers from the firelight while her deep pink nipples were frosting to an addict of sugar. Bryan loved sugar and started to suck sumptuously.

"Stop. Please. This is wrong. Bryan, please stop. This is not what I wanted."

"No?" he asked vengefully. "You've been swooning over me all day and now that I give you the things you've fantasized about and got wet over you want to discard them? Throw them aside? Why? Because you have some dogma derived notion of acceptable behavior? Because you fear your parents more than you fear your fantasies?   No Barb. I shouldn't relent. You want this. You want me."

"I don't. No, I don't. This is a mistake. I made a mistake if I led you on. I'm not ready for sex Bryan. Please let me go."

"Your body language all day was saying 'take me, take me' and now I'm gonna take you. So ready or not here I come."

In less than a second Barb's mind's eye reeled off a thirty minute video of her being raped by Bryan. The image was so frightening and distasteful that it immediately piqued her survival instincts and she started kicking, screaming, biting and scratching. Her defense was unleashed so fast that Bryan was forced to recoil in protection of his valued assets, freeing Barbs thrashing legs to do damage in unintended places as she scrambled from his clutches. With no concern for her image she emerged from the tent with breasts exposed and blouse a shambles like a scuba diver gasping for air from a malfunctioned tank.

"Barb, what's wrong? What's going on?" Sharon screeched.

"He, he's trying to rape me. I tried to stop him, but he wouldn't listen. I've got to get out of here now. I've got to leave. I'm going right now. I can't wait. I'll go alone. You don't have to come. But I'm leaving. He's crazy. Jane tried to warn me, but I didn't listen. Sharon, I'm so sorry but I can't think. I have to go."

Barb was so visibly shaken, shaken to the core of her essence, that Sharon had no choice but to get up and join her as she made her hasty exit. The whole escapade lasted no more than a few seconds and before Matt had time to register the circumstances both girls were hundreds of feet down the road swiftly making tracks. Matt stood motionless in a state of confusion trying in vain to synthesize the turn of events. Seconds ago he was enraptured by the splendor of a woman without equal in his world and now she was gone without a trace, under circumstances that conceivably had negated all possibility for a future encounter.

The girl's voices faded from hearing as their flashlight beam faded from view and with the ensuing silence Matt could hear an eerie noise escaping through the door of the tent. Bryan, still largely motionless on the air mattress with shirt unbuttoned, left hand rubbing his chest while right stroked his unkempt hair, was snickering like Wylie Coyote after devising a new plot to capture Roadrunner. He was staring at the tent ceiling made strangely opaque from the remaining campfire flames, with his head gently swaying and giggling every few seconds like a kid that just ate a stolen candy bar. Matt stormed the entrance crouched with the intent of a tiger springing on unknowing prey.

"What the hell was that? What the hell were you doing?"

"Oh give it a break Wild Man. I was just teaching the pretty young thing to be a bit more careful with her flirtations. That's all."

"She accused you trying to rape her. Why did push so hard? You scared her to death."

"Yeah, and now she won't go around leading guys on anymore."

"You're an asshole. You not only knew that you were abusing an innocent girl, but in the process you cost me an opportunity with some-one that I really started to like. What the hell is wrong with you?"

"I'm a free bird Wild Man. No parents to rein me in. On this trip there aren't any chains. Just the rules of road and they change just as much as it twists and turns."

"What the hell does that mean? Because we're traveling you're allowed to throw decency out the window, act like an animal without the benefit of your moral upbringing?"

"Wild Man, my dad was constantly knocking me all over the place, trying to keep me in line based on his rules. Not anymore. I'm making my own rules from now on and this is as good a time as any to put 'em to the test."

"That's total bullshit Bri. We're in this together and until we sepa-rate you've got to stop acting like a demented child and behave yourself."

"Aye Aye captain."

Bryan started to get up, making his intentions to exit the tent as plain as the sarcasm in his tone. Matt was taken, totally taken, and with-out further words they sat in the silence of their own thoughts, staring at the remains of a dying, devilish fire that a moment before was a source of inspiration. For the first time in over a decade they didn't share what the other was thinking, didn't meld their minds into one as had become their custom.

"We better leave first thing in the morning, Wild Man, in case Barb tries to make more out of this than it is. I don't need a confrontation with her parents right now."

"We're gonna leave first thing in the morning alright, 'cause I'm too embarrassed to see Sharon again, and God knows I want to."

"Sorry Wild Man. I didn't realize what you had going. I'll be more careful next time."

Matt got up still raging at the loss that Bryan caused and went to bed. Bryan followed suit a few minutes later when the last embers were safely below the point of flaring. Both stared at the ceiling for what seemed like hours, before settling to sleep, Matt's deep but troubled, Bryan's excited and erotic.

D awn came early with blue-grey hues and a chill in the air befitting of the feelings between Matt and Bryan. Their spat left them without the ability to enjoy the splendor of nature that was so eagerly awaiting anyone breathing and conscious. If they were inclined they would have listened to the day graciously revealing the first page of its book; it's opening paragraph a cacophony of bird songs, frog calls and breezes rustling through trees as if their leaves were hair in need of a comb and nothing more - not a sound from the highway, not a lawn being mowed or an outside intrusion from mankind, anywhere. But Matt's distress over losing Sharon pre-occupied every thought other than the perfunctory ones needed for collection of the gear, so he saw nothing beautiful and heard no music. At the same time Bryan's thoughts of freedom from the clutches of home were so pervasive that he also was blind to the splendor that dawn was unwrapping.

Breakfast came to nothing more than a thirty second gulping of OJ and a leftover donut and by half past six the camp was packed and they were ready to depart Stone Mountain, ready to leave their troubles behind. Today they would venture forward into Florida where they vowed to use their first dip in the Atlantic as a christening, a renewal. Some scant research led them to choose the waves at Villano Beach in St. Augustine for their baptism and when they arrived the early afternoon sun was so strong that the sky teemed with its brightness, forcing the normal blue hues of summer to fade from sight like a child hiding from the boogie man.

"The Atlantic, Wild Man. We're here. Smell that insane ocean scent. Listen to the sounds of the surf. Suck it all in Wild Man, for this is why we ventured forth. Sun. Sand. Surf. Bikinis! First stop on the love train Wild Man and I'm hittin' the waves."

Matt parked Ol' Faithful and they headed toward the beach in cut-offs, sneaks and tees, each with a towel draped keenly over strong young shoulders. Bryan punched Matt's arm in a playful and somewhat apologetic gesture and Matt responded with a slightly more intense whack that told Bryan all was forgiven. In seconds they were wrestling for first position to the beach, pushing, shoving, and tussling with each other like lion cubs winning the battle for momma's teat.

"Bring it on Atlantic Ocean!" Matt yelled as he plunged into the frothy-cool blue-green surf made choppy by a steady westward breeze. "This is the life Bri. I could die tomorrow and be a happy man. We're land lubbers no more my friend."

"Got that right Wild Man. Surfs up and life is great. I want this to soak in so deeply that the feeling never leaves my soul. It can occupy me forever, if it wants."

They wrestled with the waves for hours before relenting to the need for nourishment. When thirst finally overtook their glee each emerged from the water seeking a beverage stand from which to relinquish their salt extracted dryness.

"I need a Pop."

"I need three Pops."

"Three Pops and a pickle."

"Three Pops, a pickle and a potato chip."

"Three Pops, a poop, a potato chip and a popsicle."

"Three Pops, a pickle, a potato chip, a popsicle and some pussy."

Their game continued to the edge of a local stand where they were greeted by a resident summer helper who happened to be a quietly cute and nicely endowed teenage girl with a southern twist as sweet as a Georgia peach.

"Hi guys. How can I help you?"

"Three Pops and a peach, please." Bryan said laughing.

"I'm so sorry, we don't have any peaches."

"Well you're certainly a peach so why can't I just have you?'

"I don't think that would work; you'll have to settle for a soda."

"Alrighty then. I'll have a Mountain Dew for starts. How about you Wild Man?"

"Same for me but add a fish sandwich and some onion rings please."

"That sounds good. Make it two orders, but we're really thirsty so can we have the Pops now?"

"Coming right up. Will that be all?"

"That's all for now sweetheart. That is, until you get off work and we go for a stroll on the beach."

"Sorry boys, I'm busy all summer long, if you know what I mean. That'll be $15.20."

Matt forked over the money, gulped down the Dew in one long satisfying pull and ordered another. A minute later they were sitting at a table in the shade and, while waiting anxiously to fill their bellies, started planning their St. Augustine stay.

"We're gonna have to get to a KOA pretty soon to set up camp unless you want to get a hotel room tonight. KOA works fine for me."

"How long are we staying here? If we're leaving in the morning maybe it's easier to get a cheap room."

"We can stay here another day or so. There's supposed to be a nice historic section in town and there are other beaches in the area as well."

"Sold. Let's get a campsite for two nights, do some site seeing and plan our next few stops. We need to get a little more organized anyway, so we can use this time to figure out our stays at Cape Canaveral and Cocoa Beach and stuff like that."

They inhaled lunch like a ShopVac sucks up sawdust, searched a phone book for a local campground, made reservations, and then cranked up Ol' Faithful for the ride to their next make-shift home. It was a strange little KOA right in St. Augustine with barren camp sites, a swimming pool and little more privacy than that provided by the wall of their tent. If camping was meant to have a population density of Harlem, then this was camping at its finest.

St. Augustine proved to be historically interesting and quaintly appealing. The boys played tourist in the morning and went to the beach in the afternoon but Bryan's only interest lay in the seductive provocation of teenage girls given momentary straying rights from their parents. The fanatical manner with which he hit on young chicks was akin to the unexplainable inevitability of a tornado destroying a mobile home park, with pretty much the same results. Try as he might to overwhelm some innocent thing with his polished bravado Bryan continued to come close, but failed to score any points, for he never quite realized the degree of arm's length flirtation being played by his intended partners. And try as he might to ignore Bryan's bazaar behavior, the brashness of his escapades kept leaving Matt with a queasy, somewhat dirty feeling, especially when he thought about Sharon.

They left St. Augustine the next day without fanfare and headed south to the balance of their agreed destinations. After a number of similar stops along the way, six days later, browned from head to toe and appearing rustic but rested, they arrived in Miami Beach to start the pinnacle of their extended vacation.

Their journey took them just beforehand into Daytona where they headed as far east as one can drive – to the edge of the Atlantic ocean. It ended with them literally driving on the beach amongst a mass of sun crazed beach lovers parading their sculpted bodies like models on a runway. Everywhere the eye could reach beach cars packed with revelers edged ritualistically along the sandy trail, to see and to be seen. Girls in the latest scantily designed, ultra expensive swimwear were so prevalent that the eye could barely distinguish one piece of candy from another, while the guys played a mixed variety of guy games or drove souped-up rigs in demonstration of their masculine superiority.

Matt found a sweet place to park when an open topped Jeep with massive, blaring speakers pulled into the meandering stream of vehicles. Pumped to check out the scene in its entirety but too hot, they took a dip before strolling along the beach.

"This is absolute heaven. Hello sweetheart! Come sail away with me." Bryan started singing.

"Can't you let just a couple of chicks walk by without going gaga?"

"Wild Man, the boys are back in town and schools out for the summer, so I feel like makin' love and it's more than a feeling, it's time to be runnin' with the devil."

"Cut the song crap Bri."

"Can't, cause one way or another, I'm gonna get back in the saddle on my stairway to heaven, even if I have to wade through smoke on the water to get a girl under my wheels. Hah, how was that one?'

"Oh God! You're gonna turn me into a psycho killer, qu'est que c'est."

"Its radar love, baby."

"OK, enough or you're gonna have to go your own way," Matt said getting into the game. "Hey – look at that girl over there, doesn't she look like Sharon?"

"Stuck on her aren't you Wild Man? Don't worry. She'll be around come fall, so tuck her away for a while 'cause it's time for dirty deeds done dirt cheap!"

"You know, you might actually get lucky if you showed these girls some respect. I don't get what's come over you. It's like you just want to screw every girl you see."

"Not sure Wild Man. This freedom thing's gone to my head. I'm having a hard time controlling myself. The idea that I no longer have to report to my father has made me a changed man."

"Well I'm not so sure it's the change you need Bri. Just try takin' it easy for a while OK?"

"Sure thing Wild Man."

M iami Beach is the palm treed art deco capital of the world. Its inoffensive architecture along Ocean Drive is bathed in soft pastels that complement the intricate colors one finds in sand and shells, making it the perfect balance between man and sea. Even the beachside walkways, built with gently sweeping curves of inlaid stone, feel in harmony with their surroundings, at peace with their role as an artery bringing human life to the ocean.

The water in Miami Beach is always comfortable and its color must have inspired Crayola when they released their popular sea green crayon. The array of sidewalk bars and cafes present no end in style or atmosphere and the eclectic mix of neo Latin cuisine, with sundry other gourmet specialties, makes eating an experience that starts with pleasure and ends in ecstasy.

When Matt and Bryan arrived they were instantly aware that this was something different. It was as if they crossed an invisible international border only to land in a country where beauty and art were far more powerful than business or money, where time was wasted only when governed by haste.

"I had no idea that saving the best for last would be this good." Matt exclaimed. "Let's stay here a week."

"This place rocks Wild Man. It's beautiful. We're gonna see if we can rent a small place for the week; a place where we can party and entertain chicks. But I'm starving so let's go get some lunch first."

Matt drove to the south end of the beach and paid to park the car. The attendant told them to head north about 4 blocks and they would see a bunch of casual open-air eateries. Bryan chose their lunch spot du jour without hesitation; the one with waitresses dressed in bikini tops and hip wraps.

"Wild Man, this calls for a celebration. How about a beer?"

"Sounds good to me."

When the waitress arrived they ordered a couple of long neck buds and talked while they began to peruse the menu.

"OK, so we stay here a week or so and then head back to Cinci. Sound like a plan?"

"Absolutely, but it would be nice if we could get a small efficiency for the week instead of tenting. A week in this hot humid air without any air conditioning will probably kill us."

"I agree. We need to get a place. Maybe we should ask the waitress if she knows where to look."

When the waitress returned with their beers Matt asked her if she knew of any low cost one week rental places.

"I don't know any, but I think the cook might have some ideas. I'll ask him. You guys ready to order?"

The waitress recommended a grouper sandwich with fries and coleslaw that sounded perfect to both boys and a few minutes after she left with their order one of the cooks stopped by the table.

"Mandy said you guys were looking to rent a place for a week or so. I think I know a place if you're interested. It's pretty basic, but it should do. A friend of mine runs an apartment building that's mostly for low income families, but he keeps a few apartments available for weekly renters."

"Sounds great. How do we check it out?"

"I'll call him right now and let you know."

In the middle of their lunch a stranger approached the table and sat down. He was a short thick man with dark hair and a permanent five o'clock shadow. He was wearing a tee shirt stretched thin from over-sized, hairy, and poorly tattooed limbs and spoke with a heavy accent that reminded the boys of Juan Valdez on the coffee commercials. He said he had an apartment that they could rent for the week for $200.00. If they were interested he could show it to them right now.

Without ordering or saying a word to anyone Mandy arrived with a Dos Equis in one hand and a glass with lime in the other. The men made no gesture on receiving the beer but poured it and pulled half in one swallow. Bryan was thrilled by the idea of renting and told the man straight away that the boys were interested. Matt on the other hand had an uneasy feeling about the whole event and felt that Bryan was being remarkably naive. Nonetheless it was decided that they would go see the place after they settled their bill.

The man showed them his car and told them to follow. It was an old Ford F150 that looked like it belonged to the locals in Deliverance. The tailgate was missing, there were no hubcaps on any wheels and both fenders were so distorted from unintended contact that their attachment to the truck defied gravity. But when the man fired up the junk heap the boys were surprised, for it came to life in an instant, purred like a kitten in idle and came wonderfully alive when revved.

They followed the man west over the causeway and into Miami. About ten minutes later he veered right and then right again into the parking lot of a small apartment complex. It held one plain faced three story brick building with simple iron railings on cement walkways and stairs at each end. Every story had ten doors spaced evenly across the front and between each was a plain window below which creaked and leaked their attendant air conditioners. The parking lot was largely empty so it was easy to see the full Monty with one quick glance. It was totally basic, as advertised, but for some reason also oddly comfortable because it was spotlessly clean.

The man explained that he bought the place about five years ago. It was then a vacant hotel overrun by drug lords and prostitutes who used it as home base for running their illicit activities. With the help of local authorities he drove off the druggies and their entourage of petty criminals and then began the painful process of restoration, all of which he did by himself. He explained that while there were thirty doors, there were only 15 apartments, because he combined two rooms into one bedroom suites, using the second room for a small kitchen and sitting area. His explanation was delivered in broken English that made its understanding difficult though the pride in his accomplishment was as apparent as the air was clear.

Since the boys thought themselves entrepreneurs extraordinaire, they spent a good half hour talking to the man named Carlo about his amazing efforts. Carlo immigrated to America from Nicaragua in 1965 with the shirt on his back and a few hundred bucks in his pocket that he immediately exhausted on Bellisimo, his beloved truck. Bellisimo, Carlo explained, provided him the means for work in those difficult first days by unselfishly transporting him to odd jobs for middle class double income families with no free time for the regimen that home upkeep demands. Within a matter of months he developed a loyal stream of customers that kept him busy seven days a week all year long, making enough money to expand his repertoire of services with the purchase of some critically needed tools. Bellisimo, he added, was always there to carry him and care for him, without complaint, without expectations, and for that reason she was something he never wanted to lose, for in her banged up, cobbled together appearance was held the tether to Carlo's past that kept him a humble, giving man.

"Carlo," Matt inquired, "How come the waitress brought you a beer without you ordering one?"

"They know me there. I am friend of the owner and do work for him."

With that explanation the boys were satisfied and decided to take the apartment. A few minutes later they sealed a deal with Carlo for ten days of occupancy at the $200.00 weekly rate that he originally offered, and paid him in cash.

"Wild Man, this is truly amazing, just what we need to finish our trip in style."

"Absolutely. A furnished apartment to call home base just a few minutes from beautiful Miami Beach."

"Yes sir, and ladies galore. Everywhere you look there are wonderful young things offering their physiques like gourmet food on a platter. This is going to be like taking candy from the mouths of babes, only the mouths that I'm talking about are the mouths of sweet young virgins with soft pink tongues, supple and ready for just the kind of suckling that only I can provide."

"Bryan - you're nuts. Keep your libido behind bars for the next ten days, OK? We don't need any more problems like we had at Stone Mountain."

"Not to worry Wild Man. I'll stay cool."

The next ten days sped by like a downhill racer. Each was similar to the last but each was also different. If parents asked how their time was occupied the answer would be mornings in bed, afternoons on the beach and evenings hopping bars - a suitable answer, but one that failed to reveal a fraction of the real story. If friends were to ask the same question their answer would be entirely different, entailing hours of detailed stories with lavish embellishments of escapades that existed, but not quite as fantastically as delivered.

Throughout it all Bryan continued to hound women with the kind of irritation that a horse fly generates on a beach full of dozing sun bathers. He remained thrilled by the goal of conquest, was consumed by its achievement and stopped at nothing even when engaging with parties most obviously disinterested. He also developed a new found liking for the effects produced by massive quantities of beer. Being away from the strong arm of home unleashed in Bryan something heretofore nonexistent, a behavior that Matt found foreign and disturbing, conduct that was unreasonable and uncompromising. Bryan simultaneously became a slovenly joker and an unleashed tiger on the prowl, flip-flopping between the two in an instant, in the fashion of Jekyll and Hyde.

When they went to the bars Matt would quietly veer off when Bryan found a target of his liking, caring instead of partaking, to watch his charade from a distance. The modus operandi was always the same. Jekyll the joker was first on the scene with bright smiles, trite witticisms and haughty laughter. Then Hyde would lurch from the crouch, when his victims' interest either waned or piqued, to finish the kill or be killed himself. To the subject of waning interest was given a "what-the-hell" invitation for casual sex - quick success or, at least, a minimum of lost prowl time. To the interested subject was given the softer, more intimate approach of dreamy-eyed cooing and innocent touching, a tiger playing, rather than pouncing.

Tonight was their last before heading home and as fun as the whole adventure was, Matt had had enough. He was ready to go. Ready to prepare for college and what lay ahead. Hoping to see Sharon again and hoping that Bryan would stay away from trouble for one more night.

"Wild Man, tonight's our last and final. We gotta make the best of it. We gotta do something special. Go out in style. How much money do we have left? Enough to go someplace fancy?"

"I think so. At least we do if we take it easy on the way back home."

"Then take it easy it is 'cause there's nothing like Miami Beach on the way home. What'd you think we should do?"

"I don't know. Go to a nice restaurant, I'm starving. Then maybe a club instead of a bar?"

"We can have both in one spot if we go to Penrods. It's supposed to be the best night club in Miami. That's what we'll do. We'll go top shelf tonight at Penrods, so wear your best duds my man."

Situated on the beach with a palm tree laden terrace and a multitude of bars made Penrods an unparalleled South Beach tradition. Its location at One Ocean Drive afforded it access to the best of the best in clientele, especially when it came to the hordes of college-age girls whose penultimate desire was to be seen. It goes without saying that where the girls are, so too are the guys and Penrods, packed to the gills with muscular suntanned physiques, was no exception.

Penrods was also a full service establishment. It offered access to sun, sand and waves, and beachside refreshments served from easy access cabanas were more plentiful than the flowering bougainvillea scattered throughout the grounds.

Matt and Bryan arrived just before nine for their last Miami feast. A mixed crowd of younger couples and early evening revelers greeted them on arrival - busy, but not yet booming. The hostess asked them for ten minutes while a table was prepared so they cruised to the bar and ordered a couple of beers.

"Here's to us Wild Man." Bryan proclaimed, pitching an open Corona for a hearty toast. "It's been a hell of a ride so far Matt. All the things we've done over the years, all the fun we've had on this trip. Here's to the future. May we never lose our friendship and may our separation be measured only by the miles in between."

"Hear hear. To mastering college and moving on, without losing sight of where we've been." Matt consummated the toast with a chink of their bottles.

"Well said. Bottoms up." Four and half seconds later air replaced the golden liquid in Bryans' bottle and he readily opted for another round. It came without much delay, as did the hostess, who announced that a table was ready for their dining pleasure.

The restaurant at Penrods was on the second floor and the boys were seated at a table by an eastern window that overlooked the growing crowd beneath. The atmosphere was comfortably elegant, but with not a hint of pretentiousness, an appeal to the serious side of Miami with appropriate limits.

The menu was rich with choice and broad in spectrum. Seafood, steaks, pasta, light fare, salads, house specialties and over 50 different types of beer adorned their eyes and whet their appetites. Most of their meals had thus far come from quick roadside stops and street vendors, so this was an extravaganza extraordinaire in the realm of their culinary experience.

When the waitress arrived both boys nearly fell off their seats. Matt was left speechless and Bryan had difficulty assimilating enough coherent thought to utter even a simple salutation.

She was dressed in a conservative black skirt with a simple white blouse and red sash, as were her colleagues, but on her it looked like a top model in designer clothes on a NY fashion runway. To start with she had unbelievably unique strawberry blond hair that fell across her shoulders with a curl that had both purpose and appeal. Her eyes were brilliant green, made even more so by unblemished opaque skin graced gently with an array of make-up that only Cosmopolitan could duplicate. Her lips were painted the red of her sash, providing balance while accentuating the thick sensuous appeal of her richly flawless mouth. The beautiful package that was her face came together like a well wrapped gift through her nose, a delicate bow giving synergy to all its surrounding parts. She was gorgeous, drop dead gorgeous.

Her body was an easy fix in a mind's eye too, for each item of cloth that adorned her suppleness fit in the manner envisioned by the most exacting tailor. Strong round shoulders ended in line with sexy curvaceous hips that together took proportion to a new height of perfection.

Firm broad breasts promised some lucky fellow the treat of a life time and legs – her fabulous legs – were so alluring that kissing them could only lead to the most majestic area of all. Her nametag said Diane.

"Hi Guys. My name is Diane and I'll be taking care of you tonight. Need a refresher before you order?"

"Diane. Yes. Certainly. Please bring us each a Corona while we glance over the menu." Bryan spoke in an uncharacteristically respectful manner, an obvious reaction to her overwhelming presence.

When she left he continued, "Wild Man, she's the most perfect thing I ever laid eyes on. If ever there were a dream come true she is it. Did you see that? She's the definition of perfection."

"I'm still rebounding Bri. I can't seem to get my jaw off the floor or my mind back in gear. It's like I'm drugged or something. She walked away with my self-control. That's how bad it is."

"I know what you mean Wild Man. There's not a guy in the world that would pass on an opportunity with her."

"Girls. Don't they just drive you crazy? The pretty ones can turn you into a fool faster than a door slamming in a hard wind. I wish I understood them a little better."

"Don't we all. They can be so crass. I mean, they love to play with your emotions, make you think that you're special and all that stuff when all the time they're just leading you on. I've been gettin' that treatment all week and you know what, I don't give a shit. At least I make my intentions known. And someday I'm going to get a girl that wants what I want - raw, unadulterated sex."

They stopped talking when Diane approached the table with their beers. Matt looked at her and then glanced down, but Bryan held his gaze.

"Thanks Diane. Been working here long?"

"Just this summer. I'm a student at U of M and this is my summer job. You guys from around here?"

"Nah, up north. We're vacationing before heading off to school. I'm heading west and he's heading east. Stanford and Boston College."

"Wow. That's impressive. Couple of high school genius's huh? What are you going to study?"

"Actually neither of us knows for sure. We're hoping that our first year will help us craft a decision."

"I know what you mean. It's difficult. I just finished my freshman year and I still don't know."

Miami must be a pretty crazy party school."

"Oh yeah, it's a party school alright, but there are a lot of serious students as well. Listen, good luck to you both, I gotta go. Customer service if you know what I mean."

"Believe me, we know. We'll see you later."

As Diane left Bri couldn't help thinking how wonderfully sincere she appeared. She didn't carry an air about her like most other girls. Could she really be approachable or did he need to be on guard? Stupid thinking, no matter what. She was just doing her job.

Diane returned a few minutes later to recite the daily specials and answer any questions they might have. She recommended the grouper because it was caught fresh that morning and it was also her favorite fish. Her endorsement was so appealing that not even a steak and potatoes guy could say no, not to mention two fixated males drooling over every word.

"The party outside is gaining momentum Wild Man. Look at all the people. We should have come here before tonight."

"Is that a fashion show out there or what? Look at those girls; they must have spent hours getting ready. We lucked out with this table too. The whole scene is our oyster baby. Not bad; not bad at all."

"We should plan our attack over dinner. We can see where the best opportunities lie from here and scope our approach. This is going to be really fun."

A few minutes later Diane brought their dinner and another round of beers. The table fell silent immediately as they down shifted focus to the food on the table. The grouper was filleted and served in a light cream sauce with some shredded crab and shrimp. It came with lightly seasoned fingerling potatoes and an okra stew that nicely complimented the flavors of the fish. It was good enough, and they were hungry enough, for ingestion to divert their libidos until the last morsel was captured with a final bit of French bread.

"Damn, that was fantastic. Why didn't we treat ourselves earlier?"

"Because that food likes us more than our wallets like that food."

"I guess you're right. Anyway, it certainly was a great way to start our last night."

Just then Diane appeared and turned topsy-turvy the warm drowsy feeling that was brought on by their gluttony. It was as if a shining light appeared in a densely foggy night, like she was the only three dimensional object in an otherwise planar world.

"Take your plates guys? I don't need to ask if you're through. How about some desert? Coffee perhaps?"

"Diane. Thanks for recommending the Grouper. It was outstanding."

"Glad you liked it."

"I think we're gonna pass on desert and coffee. It's time for a beer in the great outdoors and a look at the sights.'

"Oh? Gonna hang out for a while and check out the girls huh? It's a popular pastime at Penrods."

"Well, if you must know, yes, we're gonna try to meet some young ladies. That's why they're here isn't it?"

"I'm not so sure. I think it's more about being seen holding someone hostage then actually meeting someone that could become a friend."

"That's well said. I like the way you phrased that. I think I get it now - it's more about elevating position in the eyes of your peers than it is about an experience with a new person. It's more about showing your friends who you can blow off so they'll continue to think you're cool."

"I never looked at it quite that way, but yeah, that pretty much describes what I see here most nights. Some poor guy, whether genuine or just a dopey predator, ends up forlorn over some selfish girl who used him to feel good about herself."

"Sounds like you're talking about me." Bryan said with a hint of despondency. "I'm batting a thousand in that baseball game."

"Well don't feel bad, you're not alone. And if the rejection doesn't get to you, what have you got to lose?" She said unflappably and then followed, "If there's nothing else I'll get your checks. OK?"

"That would be perfect, and again, thanks for a wonderful dinner."

M att kept thinking about Diane's comments as they made their way onto the terrace. Maybe she was right. Why not go for the gusto, he thought. I may not have a lot of respect for Bryan's style, but what the hell; at least he's out there trying. Why am I so afraid of rejection all the sudden? It never bothered me before, was never even a consideration. Is unfamiliar territory causing me to lose my courage? Is courage the right word or is it confidence, or comfort factor? Does it matter? The worst thing that can happen is for a stranger to tell me to get lost. So what? That's no reason to get embarrassed. Just say piss off and move on. What have I got to lose? Nothing. Absolutely nothing. It's time I re-emerge from my shell – like right now!

As they exited the restaurant, a cool breeze swept across them awakening them anew. At the same time their auditory senses were overwhelmed by a myriad mix of sounds from loud voices and DJ music to the clapping of windblown palm fronds and gentle breakers. The party was in full swing; the place packed with every type of young person imaginable. Small groups of spontaneous dancing broke out when, and where, the spirit hit them. Dotting the landscape everywhere were tight clusters of friends engaged in animated conversation interspersed with random fits of wild laughter. In the quieter corners clutching couples were seen passing special moments in kiss laden embraces while scores of awkward young ladies stood queerly, searching for their pet of the evening.

The boys grabbed a couple beers from a buxom gal selling nothing but from a big, round, ice-filled cooler and then went off to take in all that Penrods had to offer. Before long Bryan gave Matt a gentle whack on the arm, nodding enthusiastically at a giggling group of sun affected girls turned beet red from too many hours of screen-free bathing. Matt could tell immediately the one that Bryan would approach. He liked the bigger more curvaceous girls that carried a hint of baby fat over otherwise leanish frames. This one had a medium build, stood about five six and had a roundish face with large full breasts and ample buttock. She was the obvious ring leader of the group; vivacious, quick eyed, witty.

"Evening ladies. You gotta watch this Florida sun. It'll fry you like an egg on hot skillet 'fore you have time to hop from the pan. Hope the sunburn doesn't hurt you as much as looking at it hurts me."

"What kind of stupid thing is that to say? We're just a little red, that's all." An underling of the boss piped up.

"Don't mean to offend ladies, but it seems as though 'a little red' has taken on a new definition. Let's face it; a baked lobster could hide on you better than camouflage fatigues in a rain forest. Be careful you don't get sun poisoned and have to spend your vacation inside. Be a shame if no one could see those pretty little faces on the beach."

"Like my friend Bryan here said," Matt interrupted, "it would be a shame if you got too sun burned, so please be careful. But like he also said, we don't mean to offend, so we'll just say 'have a nice evening" and be on our way. Come on Bri."

"So you're gonna drop his name and leave without telling yours?" The ringleader almost interrupted. "That doesn't seem right. Maybe your friend is a bit too forward. And maybe his opening line just plain sucked but I kind of liked the lobster comment. It was pretty quick. So what's your name anyway? Hit an' run?"

"Well that depends, if I'm hit an' run, you must be hit below the belt. Then again, if you go by another name, I could go by Matt." He replied with hand extended in friendship.

"No touching just yet Mr. Matt." The ringleader said with arms raised in surrender. "I haven't finished sizing you boys up. A name is an introduction not a friendship. Now a good conversation - that might qualify as an opening for friendship. Are you boys capable of good conversation Mr. Matt? Can you be an entertaining sort? "

"Do bears shit in the woods? Do women expect the toilet seat down? Do guys enjoy a good beer piss? Do parents expect a call at midnight? Do girls spend too much time on make-up? Do I need to continue?"

"Not if you're trying to be entertaining you don't. That'll require a different approach, Mr. Matt, one with a bit more tact. But I'm sure you're capable of shifting gears. By the way, my name's Bonnie."

"Well Bonnie." Bryan started in. "You certainly seem to enjoy a bit of bantering. I'm used to the games people play in these situations and I must say yours is certainly unique. If this were a chess game I'm not sure if you would choose to be the king or the queen."

"Oh definitely the queen, Mr. Bryan. The king is absolutely worthless, a little side stepping here or there, but basically powerless. The queen, on the other hand, can do whatever she wants, go wherever she wants and is the key to victory. Oh yes, the queen is definitely my space."

"Ah yes, but the king is the key to continuity. Without the king there's no need for a bishop, knight, rook, pawn or even queen for that matter. And what of the mobility the queen possesses? It's merely physical while the king is mindful. The king can sit back and take leave of daily ins and outs while quietly keeping control over his dominion. King is definitely the space to be."

"Well Mr. Bryan, we'll just have to agree to disagree on that score now won't we?"

"I guess we will Ms. Bonnie. I guess we will."

"Where are you from anyway? All this formality must have something to do with a southern upbringing, but yet you don't quite sound like a real southerner. You actually sound like more of a northerner."

"Very observant Mr. Bryan. Very observant indeed. When in Rome do as the Roman's do, I always say, so when in the south do as the southerners do, and that Mr. Bryan, is to administer a bit of southern charm, a bit of authentically administered faux charm from a silly northern girl took temporarily southern."

"I see Ms. Bonnie, indeed I do. Much more enjoyable an occasion for clever scheming when two partake of the exercise, don't you think?"

"I do, Mr. Bryan. Yes, I do. It would be worlds of fun to flitter about this evening as plantation born aristocrats in search of other landed gentry. Care to join me in my bazaar fantasy Mr. Bryan? Care to indulge in the mind of the spoiled southern land owner for a while?" Bonnie said with a deepened southern drawl.

"Don't mind if I do, Ms. Bonnie. Shall we?" And Bryan extended a gentleman's elbow to seal their fate as accomplices in their harmless escapade.

The two immediately set off in search of victims likely to embrace their silly mindedness while Matt shifted focus to the three remaining red beacons. They seemed at ease with Matt, exchanging pleasantries without hesitation and were soon lost in boundless conversation. It was fun. It was friendly, made more so by the familiarity of like backgrounds absent of the tension that some "chemistry" tends to foster.

Bryan and Bonnie took their role playing to every corner of Penrods and had a blast in the process. They found couples who willingly devised outlandish play-a-long characters and others whose response drew no more than a glazed-over look of dumbfoundedness. Despite the response theirs was always effervescent. Despite some rolling eyes their behavior remained raucous, laughter filled, comedic. It was the best night of the trip for Bryan, with Bonnie becoming his kindred spirit, and he hers. Bryan never applied his typical attempts at garnering interest in sex and for some strange reason its absence felt right.

An hour or so into their beer infested merriment, Bryan leaned into Bonnie with casual grace and gave her a quick kiss on the lips. It was over and gone before his brain had it registered and Bonnie made no mention either. It passed as naturally as a setting sun.

"My dear young lady you look famished. Can I interest you in a choice cold beverage?"

"Well certainly sir. I thought you'd never ask. This lady is plainly in need of refreshment. I think too that a little touch of tequila will set well with that cold beverage you so kindly offered."

Bryan got the idea and ordered two beers and couple of shots of Cuervo Gold. They were fast to complete the ceremonial placement of salt and lime and with a quick clink of glasses the traditional lick-chug-suck progression of downing their shots was over. Both stood staring at the other with lips puckered tight from the tartness of the lime. Bryan felt a warmth in his midsection as the tequila spread through his stomach and Bonnie got a special sparkle in her eye from the extra tearing that it caused.

"So where are you and Matt staying?" Bonnie asked dropping her southern façade.

"We rented a small apartment on the other side of the causeway. How about you?"

"A couple of rooms in a hotel a few blocks from here. It's not great, but it's not bad either. We're only there to sleep anyway, so it really doesn't matter."

"I know what you mean – sleep, get ready, go out to play. Start the process again the next day."

"Yeah, sleep past noon, party till dawn. It's crazy but it's fun."

"You want to get away from here? Go for a walk on the beach where it's a little quieter?"

"Sure." She said taking his hand and turning to the ocean.

They walked in silence from the mob at Penrods until the cacophony of sounds faded to a dull white noise. The beach greeted them with a warm breeze at low tide and they walked barefoot in the shallow remnants of dying waves, reaching out for their last few inches of life. The blackness from a moon absent in the cloudless sky was offset only by lights from shoreline windows. They seemed blinding in one direction and surreal in the other, casting an eastward hue that left faint shadows of palms in their wake.

Bonnie stopped without cause and looked to the light, her face made especially seductive from the soft reflections of pink and yellow and copper. Bryan turned to query her pause and found her staring into his face. Her lips were parted slightly, and were wet, and she flipped her hair back and swelled her breasts. He stood motionless gazing at her splendor before closing the narrow gap between them, his member becoming wildly rigid and aching. He placed his hands carefully on her alluring hips, slid them around her waist and then leaned slowly into her uplifted face to devour her anxious quivering lips.

Locked, grappling passionate kisses sent ripples of ecstasy through them, their racing hearts beating in unison. Bonnie's breathing became deliciously labored as he held her neck and bathed her face with his lips. Then she pulled Bryans face into her breasts and his hand caught a firm protruding nipple, erect beneath a braless top. His touch of her tender caused her to shudder and reel and he responded with brisk clean kisses from breast to nape to ear.

Bonnie lowered her hand to his groin and her touch overloaded Bryan's senses, sending spasms of release from his nerves. Her fingers started dabbling with the sides of his manhood, as if she were mapping the surface of a sculpture, her touch elevating Bryans heightened excitement to the brink of explosion. He responded instinctively by grabbing her and squeezing her plump lithe roundness as together they tried to pour each other's bodies into one unified mold.

"Bryan, come back to my place with me. Let me touch you some more." She whispered.

"Show me the way, Bonnie. Just show me the way."

Matt continued a long conversation with the three shining beacons albeit with a roving eye for more alluring alternatives. Several times when on the cusp of leaving to meet another new acquaintance his intended target became occupied by competition, so opportunities found became dead ends before the car got out of park. It was then that he spotted Diane and politely excused himself.

She had changed clothes before leaving work and was now dressed casually in a skort with a modest blouse and sandals. Her simple dress gave her the innocence one ascribes to the farmer's daughter and it worked better for Matt than anything so far that evening.

She was walking with purpose toward the rear of the place as if hastening departure from a spot lost to endearment. Matt had almost to jog to catch her.

"Diane. Hi. Just get out work?"

"Oh. Hi. Yes, I'm on my way home. How goes the search for miss right?"

"Good conversations, but no chemistry. I'll have to keep looking."

"Well this place doesn't close until sunrise, so you've got plenty of time to continue your search."

"But my searching led me to you. Can I buy you a drink?"

"Listen." She paused.

"It's Matt."

"Listen, Matt. It's really not a good idea for me to hang out with customers after work. Management kind of frowns on it. I'm sure you understand."

"I understand that you're rush to get out of here that has nothing to do with me. Is something wrong?"

"It's been a long day and I just need to get away. That's all."

"What if I escort you?" Matt said almost jogging to stay alongside. "I'll just make sure you get safely where you're going. I'm getting a little tired of this scene anyway."

Diane stopped abruptly and gazed at Matt. "Look, Matt, nothing against you, you seem like a nice guy, but you should turn around now and walk away. I'm not someone you want to be seen with. Not now."

"What the hell does that mean?"

"It means I have a jealous boyfriend, ex-boyfriend actually, who's as crazy as they get. He swears he'll kill any guy who even looks at me. He's one of those obsessive possessive types and he's just about insane enough to do something really stupid."

"If that's true then you need someone to protect you more than the other way around."

"I'm fine. You don't have to worry about me."

"If he's crazy enough to do something stupid to me then he's also capable of hurting you. What makes you think he's going to leave you alone? I bet he's been harassing you. He's probably threatened you too."

Diane stayed put and stared at the ground. Matt could tell that she was scared. A moment later she looked up with a tear stained face.

"Go away. I don't want you or anyone else with me. Please, just leave me alone."

She turned and immediately resumed the quick march of British light infantry. Dumbfounded, Matt watched her lovely petite figure fade into the evening. Then, without thinking, without reason or under-standing, he opted for pursuit – not to catch up to her and try to dissuade her, but to keep a distant eye just in case.

Diane reached the ocean front and headed north along the coast at a pace that caused Matt's breathing to accelerate. She passed the palms of South Beach Park without breaking stride, looking excitely from side to side the entire way. At Fourth Street she headed west, turning the cor-ner a few hundred yards in front of Matt, her shadow temporarily fading from view. When Matt rounded the same corner moments later he ran smack into a wall – a wall of human flesh.

"Asshole, why are you following my girl?" Fumes of hard liquor filled the air and massive tattooed arms began shoving Matt back against the wall.

"Whoa. What are you crazy? I don't know what you're talking about. Leave me alone."

"Lying pig. I saw you talking to my girl and I see you following after her like a dog in heat. Filthy fuckin' pig. I'm gonna fuck you up big, you fuckin' asshole."

"I don't know what you're talking about."

"Oh no, and I'm Mr. Stupid too. Jack ass. This here's a taste of what's coming fuck face." And he slammed Matt hard in the rib cage.

Bryan left Bonnie's hotel a satisfied man. She was a great lover, leaving little to doubt. When they got to her room she yanked off her top, pulled off Bryan's shirt and guided him to an unmade bed. Her breasts were full and supple with large deep pink nipples. Their gorgeous pert shape was accentuated by a crisply delicious tan line from a bikini that revealed much, without stealing the joy of imagination. They lay on the bed kissing and caressing and before long were completely naked and raging in a torrid rushed desire for climax.

Bryan swept his hand across the baby smooth skin of her buttock and into the warm abyss between her legs. His fingers were instantly greeted by the sweet moisture of her shaven femininity, his explorations welcomed by passionate whimpers and hip thrusts that would kill a belly dancer. She grabbed his member and pulled it firmly to her sweetness and he responded in missionary position to let her gently guide the trip home.

Bryan penetrated slowly, in part from resistance born from the abruptness of the coitus, in part from the hand that remained wrapped around the balance of his exposed shaft. His eyes were closed to focus on the millions of nerves tingling with the power of concentrated starlight, in anticipation of being engulfed by the warmth of her soft womb.

Full penetration left no dream unfilled. Bonnie's sweetness responded to Bryan's rhythms with the harmony of a tropical waterfall in a virgin forest. His climax was so complete that it sent ribbons of ecstasy through his loins, up his back and into his shoulders. He made shot multiple times while thrusting his member deeply into Bonnie's house, bringing to her new pinnacles of pleasure that culminated in repeat vaginal orgasms that rocked with the syncopated rhythm of the Grateful Dead.

Bryan walked down Ocean Drive with his head in the clouds reliving the moments just past, shaking his head in disbelief. He wasn't a virgin at the start of the encounter, but his previous escapades had been timid and reserved. This was a completely new experience that heightened his appreciation for the joy of sex, one that resulted in the best orgasm of his young life, more far reaching by far than any experience to date.

As he neared Fourth Street an oddly disturbing noise filled his ears. He could have sworn that he heard Matt's voice crying out in fear, parting the early morning stillness with the shrill call of a person in shear torment.

He looked down the lane and in an instant his hair-raised reaction to the cry was confirmed. A big bleached blond surfer boy was pummeling Matt with both fists. The dull thud of blows to the midsection and ribs reverberated down the empty street with sickening frequency. Bryan sprinted to Matt's aid and tackled the blond freak with all his linebacker skills, coiled tight like a steel spring. The guy went down hard on the pavement but the impact only pissed him off and he jumped to his feet before Bryan could get fully erect.

The first blow from the beach bum landed on Bryan's temple while he was still on his hands and knees. It sent him reeling to the ground on his stomach, clutching his head in the process. The man was powerful and quick and turned Bryan onto his back before the first blow was fully registered. Then he bounced on Bryan's midsection, forcing the air from his lungs, taking aim at his face. He let the next blow fly, smashing his fist into Bryans eye and then another into his nose. Bryan was able to get his arms free and block the next volley of shots, but a few more would disfigure him completely, perhaps with permanent damage.

Matt saw the carnage with immeasurable rage as his aching breath began to recover from the onslaught. What took only seconds to occur felt like hours, his brain registering data at rates ten thousand times faster than normal. One thought that was locked and fused was the ensuing fate of his best friend. If he didn't find a means to alter the current situation Bryan would be dead in minutes. He had to put the bum to a stop and he had to do it now.

Matt leaped to his feet still somewhat shaky from the blows he received. He looked at Bryan getting pounded and then quickly scanned his surroundings. He spotted something that might help. Just ten feet away was an empty half gallon bottle of Gallo Hearty Burgundy. He leaped at the bottle, grabbed it and in the same motion ran wildly at the crazed beach bum while he swung it with all his might. The bottle connected with enormous velocity on the side of his head, just below and behind his right ear. It shattered on impact, leaving the jagged remains of the neck in Matt's hand.

The change of venue was instant as the bum went limp at impact and keeled over in silence. His big body fell sideways and lay completely motionless except for the pulses of splattering blood that popped from his neck with each beat of this heart. Bryan and Matt collected their wits and checked each other out as they stood over the man assessing the situation. The blood kept coming in pulses as they watched, but the volume lessened and the time between spurts grew longer. It was obvious that the man was dying right in front of their eyes.

Matt looked down at the dismembered end of the bottle neck that stayed tightly gripped in his hand. While the body of the bottle shattered into hundreds of tiny pieces the neck was broken into the shape of a clef with a sharp curved leading edge. It was obvious that the curved shard had severed an artery as the bottle's trajectory passed the point of implosion and at that realization Matt threw the neck hard against the building wall, dusting it in the process.

The boys looked at each other again in silence still so completely stupefied by the turn of events that neither could muster a word. Matt's stomach and sides began to ache like hell as his adrenaline rush abated and Bryan's face, swelling fast enough to see the change, was becoming lopsided and turning color.

They glanced again at their assailant. The pulsing blood stream had slowed. A minute later the pulsing stopped and the man was dead.

"We gotta get out of here. We gotta get the hell out of Miami like right now." Bryan yelled.

"No Bri, we gotta call the police. We gotta let them know this was self-defense."

"Oh yeah, right, and get some empathetic cops like the ones we ran into on the way down? No way Wild Man, you just killed a guy."

"You know I had no choice."

"I know, but try to prove it. At a minimum you're looking at manslaughter. Matt, it's late and it's dark and there's no one around. We got lucky; we don't even have any of his blood on us. We can get away. We have to get away. Our lives are just beginning. College, remember?

Matt looked down in thought, the first real thought he had since the incursion. He knew it wasn't right to leave the scene of the crime but the idea of putting his life indefinitely on hold as the police, and perhaps the court, sorted out this mess – it was just too much.

"Matt, come on. Let's get out of here."

"Ok." And they both began to run.

Ol' Faithful was about ten blocks away on a narrow side street. They reached her without incident and without passing any late night partiers in the process. Matt started the engine, threw her into reverse and eased out of the lot.

"Come on, Wild Man. Get this bucket moving. We gotta get out of here."

"I know, but I don't want to risk drawing attention. We have to go easy like nothing's happened. No one can stop us or we're screwed. They'll see your face and question us immediately. And even if they let us go, they'll have a record of us fleeing when the body is discovered."

"You're right. We have to take it easy. Take it easy. Take it slow. Calm down. Calm down. Oh my God, what the fuck just happened? Jesus Christ, what the hell was that? Who was that guy? Why was he beating on you?" Bryan asked as reality began to replace his ebbing panic.

"Diane's jealous ex-boyfriend." Matt said slowly, and told Bryan the rest of the story.

Matt and Bryan maintained an extremely low profile on their way back to Cincinnati. They spoke little of the incident on Fourth Street, with the exception of getting daily newspapers to see if homicide had developed any leads. There were several stories on the death in the first few days, but additional articles dwindled quickly with time. In none was there mention of a suspect or even a lead and the boys began to feel a bit more relaxed with each day.

urned to work after reviewing the mysterious report with
,h trepidation that he feared acting strangely and getting
unusual behavior. He got to work on time and was first to
c.. Paul enroute to his cube. He was glad that neither Fred nor
Susan was anywhere to be seen and he relaxed a bit in Paul's consistently
predictable presence.

"Morning Paul. How was your night?"

Good morning Chad. It sucked, but thanks for asking. I usually
come to work rested and ready to throw my brain cells at the next problem du jour, but today I arrive a tired sleepless man."

"Couldn't get Janice off your mind, huh?"

"Correct, compadre. I'm hopeless."

"Well at least you have something new and exciting in your life."

"Yeah, but I'm not too sure how to play the next step. I don't want
to appear too aggressive, but I don't want to seem disinterested either. If
I had my way I would have placed a wakeup call to her this morning to
whisper sweet nothings in her ear."

"Why not call her today for a date at the end of the week? That way
you won't look over anxious and at the same time you can make it
apparent that you are respectful of the fact that she has a life of her own."

"Great idea. I'll try that and see what happens."

"Remember yesterday I asked what you were doing after work? I
told you that I had something I wanted to show you. Remember?"

"Oh yeah, I forgot. What is it? Some new music that you wrote,
that you actually like for a change?"

"No, nothing like that but I am in the middle of a new piece that
I'm pretty happy with. Anyway, want to catch something simple tonight
for dinner? How about Giordano's, at the downtown location?"

"OK. Pizza and a few beers sound pretty good to me. How about
6:30?"

"Excellent. See you then."

Giordano's is home of Chicago's famous deep-dish double-crusted
pizza and is one of the area's most popular places for excellent, light Italian fare. It was started by two immigrants that came to America in the

late 60's armed with a set of family recipes whose excellence evolved from generations of food loving relatives. Their outstanding cuisine was first offered in the 70's in a casual atmosphere accented by excellent service that quickly became a Chicago tradition, by all Chicago definitions.

Chad was first to arrive. He was early enough that a table was available, but he asked for a booth instead. After being seated he ordered a Peroni while he waited for Paul. If anyone could understand the implications of the data that Chad stumbled upon, it was Paul. His job put him in touch with a number of the company's product streams so he had more than just a grasp of the product portfolios, their cost basis, the involved manufacturing processes, etc. etc. He also was really quick at deciphering reams of data.

"Hey old buddy, where's my beer?" Paul said effervescently on arrival.

"Here as soon as you order it, my friend. Have a seat."

"Listen to this. I called Janice like you suggested and asked her if she wanted to get together Friday night."

"Waitress." Paul interrupted. "A beer for my friend here please. Same thing. Thanks."

"Anyway, you know what she said? She asked me why I wanted to wait until Friday. Can you believe that? She suggested we do something tomorrow night and Friday too."

"That's tremendous Paul. You 'da man." Chad said longingly.

"This is what I wanted to talk to you about. On Monday when I picked up the weekend runs I found this set of data included in my system status report. It's not like anything that I've ever seen before and it doesn't make any sense to me. It looks like someone, I think its Chandler and Jeffries, is trying to explain the reasons for a year-to-date shortfall in profit. But I've never seen the company present data in this manner before so it automatically looked suspicious to me. I usually see information presented by line item with columns of actual versus budget so variances stick out like sore thumbs. This material makes it impossible to know the actual location of the differences, because it rationalizes the shortfalls by changes in volume and mix by product line vs. the plan. I want to show you the report to get your read on it. Am I just a paranoid idiot or do you think something funny is going on?"

"Whoa, that's a lot to digest. First of all, you probably weren't supposed to see this information and should probably destroy it. Second of all, there are all sorts of ways to slice and dice data and I know that volume, mix and inflation are common factors that some companies use to look at year on year change, so it definitely could be legitimate. Third and last, you came this close", Paul said holding two fingers together; "to indicting our two top executives for something like fraud or theft. That's really frightening and perhaps a bit over reactionary, if not actually psychotic."

"OK. I understand. But do me a favor. Look at it. If you think there's nothing unusual in this then just throw it out. But if you think there is something weird here then let me know. By the way, Chandler and Jeffries were both in the computer room retrieving this report when I got there. They got the second copy I printed out and don't know that there was a first. They both looked like kids caught with their pants down when I walked in. Nervous, and eager to get out of there. Maybe that's why I'm so suspicious."

"I don't know if I'll be able to make heads or tails of this data, but get it to me and I'll give it a whirl. Don't be surprised if it's in the trash the next morning."

"Thanks buddy."

At that point their pizza arrived and the conversation changed to their newly disparate social lives while their meat lovers special began to disappear.

"You know, I'm actually jealous of you, you pain in my arse. One day you're as miserable and lonely as I am and the next your knee deep in raw emotion.

P aul Landau came to WorldSupplî from Cornell University after he successfully completed a grueling four year mechanical engineering program with a minor in computer science. Cornell, the wonderfully beautiful university high above Cayuga's waters affectionately known as Corn-smell, is a perfect place for developing intelligent young minds into obnoxiously self-assured professionals. It boasts a myriad of different colleges that range from a world class hotel school to architecture and everything in between, including one of the world's largest private engineering colleges, the halls of which were practically home for Paul during his four years there.

Cornell attracts some of the brightest minds in the world, from all over the world and as such hosts an incredibly unique, albeit unusually artificial student environment. Cliques of ultra-competitive students from like nationalities scurry about the campus with the single minded goal of maximizing study time utility to maintain straight 4.0's. Equal and opposite are the scores of frat boys who fit class and study into an otherwise busy social life that they share with their neighboring sorority girls. Unique in its own right is the culture found in the college of engineering where the mix of warped brilliance is surpassed only by an overbearing fear of failure, the result of which is manifested in lit hallways, occupied labs and overheated computing centers on a 24-7 basis.

Paul liked Cornell for its diversity and the natural beauty afforded it by the glacier generated hillsides and stream-cut gorges, but he didn't find the all-pervasive focus on individual achievement to his liking, so when the stress of pending exams loomed too large it was a hike through the gorges that became his elixir. Paul, while a good student, was not crazed enough by the Cornell ethos to lose sight of the need for balance and normally dedicated time on weekends for some relaxation and quiet partying. But he was somewhat of a misfit. He didn't join a fraternity, opting instead to live in an apartment off campus with three other engineers of differing backgrounds. The net result of his decision was a pretty weak social network that tended over time to render Paul more and more reclusive at a time when social development is equally as important as scholastic achievement, so by the time of graduation he was more than ready to shed himself of the snowy hills of central New York.

Paul's Ivy League degree had grades that secured a Summa Cum Laude diploma and this, together with a particularly strong market at graduation, provided Paul with a plethora of differing employment options. The employment decision was a tough one, but it was the special courting effort by WorldSupplî that ultimately made the difference when Paul decided to sign on as a process engineer. Process engineering in WorldSupplî is a discipline focused on systemic productivity. It associates itself with evaluating, testing and implementing process changes that optimize work flow, which roughly translates into a focus on getting more bang for your buck. Paul demonstrated a keen and observant eye and Boo Koo amounts of common sense so in his first year he was able to make a significant contribution to productivity and was quickly heralded "Process Paul", a label given totally out of respect.

Now in his fourth year, after several promotions and special assignments, Paul held the newly created position of Productivity Coordinator; a position that he postulated and convinced management would remove a process gap that caused missed deliveries, late shipments and elevated rework costs. It was an experiment that had started only recently and, true to form, appeared to be generating payback. Paul enjoyed the challenge of fixing complex business problems with simple solutions, solutions that inspired people to ask 'why didn't I think of that?' The problem solving process is itself complex, starting with the often over looked or incorrectly assessed root cause identification, culminating in an often inappropriately applied change whose intensions to eliminate problem from re-occurring never materialize.

Paul has a test to determine if his solutions have merit, an easy test at that. If, after the effort of distilling figures and facts and formulating an administrable change, the solution stands up and smacks you with its simplicity, then the solution must be right, otherwise there is bound to be a flaw of some unknown origin and the solution process must begin anew.

Right now the issue on his plate was an inordinately high order entry cost, in both time per transaction and the level of returns that resulted from shipping mistakes. The problem was not yet identified, in fact the data that was needed to isolate the problem was not yet identified, so as Paul walked to Samali's to meet Janice for again lunch, he was formulating an approach to identify the data sets that he needed to isolate the problem that thus far had manifested itself as high order entry cost.

Paul spotted Janice as he rounded the corner about a block from Samali's. His first reaction was one of sheer joy and his first impulse was to yell out to her to capture her attention but something restrained him and he stood there instead watching her with utmost satisfaction. Janice was tall and fit, not petit or attractive in the sense of glamorous cover-girl models, but she carried with her an aura of peace that itself was extremely beautiful. As he stood there watching her a sense of calm imbued his psyche causing even his subconscious tensions to be lifted away like a waking baby returning to the warmth of a mothers carry. It was such an exhilarating feeling that it also brought on a sense of fear. I just met this girl, he thought to himself. We barely know each other. Am I nuts to have these feelings? She's probably just trying to make up for knocking me into the mud.

At that moment Janice spotted Paul and waved with an enthusiastic flair that looked genuine and content, satisfied, and as she ended her distant greeting her hand went habitually to her hair where she neatly tucked some stray brown strands behind a sumptuous, loop decorated ear. The smile that ensued was more captivating than a cloud laden sunset and the hug that she extended at their physical greeting left Paul speechless for more.

"How are you?" she asked. "It's nice to see you."

"It is?"

"Of course crazy. How about some goose liver pate?" she laughed, snaking her arm in his as naturally as water flowing through the path of least resistance.

"Certainly! Let's go." Paul said and they turned towards Samali's each smiling silently, each consumed by the strange yet pleasant events that brought them to this point.

Samali's sported a sound reputation for really good food and the crowd reflected the certainty of its popularity as well. It was an unusual place, with an eclectic mix of furnishings that summed into an atmosphere suitable for a scene from Casablanca, which given its Mediterranean tapas-style cuisine, was comfortably fitting. When Paul and Janice arrived the place was already vibrating at high frequency but was not yet fully occupied and they found a table for two at the front window overlooking the street. Immediately after being seated a waitress in a long flowery skirt with naturally curly unkempt hair garnished their table with hummus and flat bread and Janice readily broke bread and dipped, proclaiming simultaneously how famished she was.

Shortly thereafter the waitress re-appeared with two glasses of lemon enhanced water and some menus. After a quick sip of water, each scooped up their menu and began to peruse the available selections.

"Seems like we've eaten here before?" Paul inquired. "I really like their cuisine and there are so many items I can hardly tell what to order."

"I have eaten here quite a few times so I'm quite familiar with the menu. Perhaps I can give you some suggestions."

"I'm really not a picky eater, so why don't you just order for us both."

"Happy to. They boast some outstanding salads and a variety of other bean dishes and curried foods, so if that sounds appetizing, I'll just get us a mix and we can share." And with that Janice ordered a number of small plates, each with its own unique presentation and each more delicious than the last.

The luncheon conversation that followed ordering was endlessly free flowing and multi-faceted and before either realized it the lunch hour had passed and it was back to other matters. Paul at least now knew that Janice was a banker of some form, dealing in commercial lending, but she was scant on furthering a description of her curriculum vitae preferring instead to talk about personal things.

Janice described herself as a student of the world, somewhat in jest but not entirely, because she was a consummate reader with the uncanny ability to retain a tremendous amount of the detail she consumed. She was also one of those unusual persons who felt a bond with artistry, defining its realm as anything from gourmet cooking to interior design to the more creative side, which spanned the likes of painting, sculpting, gardening, dancing and more. Her current subject of focus was associated with the unseemingly glutinous zeal of modern day political cronyism and as she explained herself Paul remembered the basket on her bike that held the towel he used to dry his hands, recollecting that in it too were several books.

Janice was also a lover of the outdoors and spent as much time as possible staying in touch with nature by simply keeping in physical contact with its mother. She routinely went for bike rides along quiet park roadways and practiced yoga many days in secluded areas where the sounds of wind and insects provided the music through which to stretch, reflect and relax. The results of her efforts were acutely evident in both her physical appearance and behavioral norms. Her body was supple and lean in a strong and sinewy way that was something to admire for the accomplishment itself as well as for the gritty sexual appeal that it radiated. Her approach to matters was open, intelligent and honest and while extremely well versed she none-the-less maintained a searchingly inquisitive outlook, even though a know-it-all position would not have been construed as arrogant.

Paul was so enraptured by Janice that his body shook in mixed emotion as he walked back to work. On one hand he couldn't believe his good fortune in finding what felt like a soul mate, on the other some consternation weighed heavily with the abruptness, and risk, of the circumstances. Which hand to play? The one that held his heart or the one that held his fear of it being broken? When he reached his desk the answer was clear and he immediately rang her number.

"Hi Janice, its Paul. I was wondering if I could see you again."

"Of course crazy. Anytime."

P aul returned from lunch intending to immerse himself with the details of his latest project but his luncheon engagement continued to serve distraction sufficient to render this goal impossible. So rather than waste the afternoon with his thoughts oscillating in and out focus he opted instead to go see Chad, without first thinking of the pretense associated with his interlude.

"What's up Chad? Busy?"

"Normal stuff, you know the routine. Just checking some reports and working on an upgrade to our order entry system. Some idiot sold the idea of read forward in all the fields. Some sort of productivity based thing. I assume that you had your hand in this." Chad said jokingly. "And to what purpose do I owe this visit? You never stop by in the afternoon."

"I might have a small amount of my hand in that "productivity thing" you're working on. More important than the order entry time savings is the number of typos that will be eliminated. Do you have any idea how many repeat customers we have under different corporate names? Our ability to database is ruined by stupid order entry issues. This change should significantly drive up our level of consistency."

"Give me a break man; you know that I know the value of this project. That's not why you're here. So how was lunch anyway?"

"You think I'm here to talk to you about my lunch date? Sorry, but I didn't come here to serve up a bunch of gory details for you to regurgitate back to me bastardized by your infamous sarcasm. But since you asked - it was okay."

"But since I asked, it was okay?" Paul repeated. "If that doesn't reek of 'ask me more because I'm dying to tell you the whole naked truth' then I don't know what does. Let me guess. You find her so alluring that you can't stop thinking about her and the distraction is so great that "Mr. Productivity" has lost his ability to be productive and it's killing you. Is that it? It is, isn't it?"

"I admit she's on my mind. It was weird. Lunch was relaxing. I'm able to just be me around Janice and that in itself is foreign enough to be as disconcerting as a Taliban leader at a Bar mitzvah. One day you're all alone, feeling unfulfilled and the next a brand new friend has entered your realm and totally shaken up the definition of your existence. I mean, it's like the dimensions of my life have just been tremendously altered and I'm scared shitless."

"Why scared?"

"I don't know. I just met her and I think I like her. In fact I might like her a lot and nothing like this has happened to me since about eighth grade. So I'm perplexed. She may just think of me as a nice guy, you know, someone to fill in the gaps when nothing else is available. I really don't have a clue."

"What difference does it make? You're obviously more attracted to her than stink on stink so just go with it. What's the worst case scenario? I'll tell you. You eventually let her know how you feel and if you're misreading the situation then she'll respond in a way that makes you feel like an ass. Your ego will be bruised. Your confidence will be temporarily shattered. Big deal. On the other hand, what if she is the real deal? You gonna give up an opportunity to see if you two were made for each other simply because you're afraid of rejection? That's so idiotic, so preposterous, that it isn't worth the cost of entry to a show with free admission. Come on Paul, go get her and if it doesn't work, then it wasn't meant to be in the first place."

"Your platitudes might help me make my decision but they won't make my nerves any less jumpy. Jesus Chad, what if I'm in love?"

"Then you have reached a goal you've dreamed of now for about five years and you should relish the opportunity to nurture the feelings that come with it. Do yourself a favor. Let your emotions dictate the way forward and set caution aside. Pursue her with the zeal that you pursue your gains in productivity and have faith that the result will be in your best interest no matter what the outcome. You gonna see her again?"

"Tell you the truth, I already called her to ask if I could and she said yes."

"Way to go! You see, you've already made your decision, so stop second guessing yourself." Chad paused. "Listen, on another matter.

103

What are doing after work tonight? There's something I want to show you."

"Actually, tonight doesn't work very well. I have a pile of things I need to do. Old bills, stale clothes, rotting food, full garbage cans. Standard bachelorhood fare – I've let things go to the point where I can't stand it any longer and have resigned myself to an evening in purgatory setting my place straight. Tomorrow works. What's up anyway?"

"Nothing major. I just want to show you the report that I mentioned. Tomorrow works fine." Chad replied with relief. "Now that you mention it, I should clean up my act too and tonight might actually be just the right night to do it. After a momentary silence Chad continued, "Listen Paul, seriously, have fun with this new gal of yours. Don't get trapped by some fear of failure thing. You're a decent enough guy to deserve some nookie every once in a while."

"Thanks for the compliment; your support is about as heartwarming as a burp with bile in it. For the record, I haven't thought of Janice in sexual terms yet and I'm in no rush either. This thing needs to percolate slowly, if it's going to percolate at all."

"Hundred bucks say's you're wrong." Chad blurted as Paul began his exit. "Hundred bucks say's you're in the sack within two weeks."

Paul could be heard muttering an indistinguishable string of random dom expletives as he left Chad's cube to return to his role as Productivity Coordinator. Chad was largely relieved that Paul couldn't come over that evening because it would give him time to digest the unusual report that he had hidden in his laptop case. It would also give him time to organize his apartment enough for Paul to have a place to sit when he arrived the following evening.

Chad spent the balance of Monday wrestling with the numerous sundry issues that routinely happened to land on his desk. While many were actually associated with his job there were always an equal amount that had nothing, whatsoever, to do with the reason he was hired. They became his responsibility by default anyway because he had a knack for finding a speedy fix and most Mondays passed quickly as, for some unknown reason, there were always the issues that weekend gremlins imparted to laptops that ventured homeward during the two day respite. This particular Monday was pretty average in that regard, but it nonetheless passed more slowly than refrigerated molasses through an eyedropper from the weight of the unseemly report stowed securely in Chad's briefcase.

Chad wanted to get up and bolt when the 5 o'clock whistle finally blew but as he started on that course a cautious sensation crept from his subconscious and caused him to leave calmly and with as much normalcy as he could muster. The sun was mostly gone when he exited WorldSupplî but the clear evening sky provided a pleasant twilight that promised to linger until he reached home. Some twenty minutes later, after lucking into a ready bus at the workplace stop, Chad made eye contact with his domicile and was immediately overwhelmed by a sense of gloom, for there was simply nothing therein on which to dine and no one therein from which to be joyfully received. Oh well, Chad thought, some Moo Goo Gai Pan and a bottle of Chardonnay will make it easier to swallow this evenings' detective work, so he sauntered down Marquette in quest of his two oft frequented establishments.

Chad's apartment was just as he left it ten plus hours ago, so when he returned with his fodder he first had need to scrape free a bare spot on the table before shedding his load. Now seated comfortably with a still hot dish of decent Chinese food and a chilled glass of adequate (cheap) wine Chad decided it was time to peruse the morning report. In somewhat of a wary state he grabbed his briefcase and, hefting the poison from within, entered unknowingly into an irreversible course of matters with profound consequence.

The report was in every respect just like all the others that he reviewed for the past 100 or so Monday's, until he got to page 56 where an entirely new set of data loomed large before his eyes. The new data began with a banner that for all practical purposes was sufficient in itself to give cause for alarm for it read, "Confidential classified financial information, system call #6 – Product Line data."

"Product Line data? I've never seen any kind of breakout like this before." Thought Chad, as he began to digest the information it contained.

What Chad saw was truly unconventional. It was a reconciliation report of the current years' cash flow and income statement by a totally new set of identification codes. It was only a few pages in length and it was only five columns wide, but it inferred, if he was reading it correctly, that somehow, somewhere about 3% of the company's EBITDA had mysteriously disappeared. Chad was only able to understand what he was reading because he fully intended on becoming a CPA, and had gotten mostly there, before his strength with computers derailed his accounting ambitions.

It appeared that this report was an attempt at reconciling the reasons for the loss in profit. It broke the variances into four categories – volume, price, inflation and productivity – to identify from where the losses were originating. The result of the analysis was an exercise in confusion. In some product lines volume was up but according to the analysis inflation outstripped the increase in volume so net profit was down. In other cases product line volume was flat but price per unit was lower and improvements in productivity were insufficient to offset the negative pressure on price. When all the product line changes were pulled together the result showed a significant change in product mix at a volume that equated to a drop in net profit of about 3% of plan.

The data compelled Chad to do a little math to see what the losses could mean, despite not having a clue what might have caused them.

If every invoice had excess costs equal to one tenth of one percent of invoice value then with total annual income of $3.8 billion the amount that would accrue to the overcharge would be a drop of $3.8M from the bottom line. Since the company reported 6% EBITDA* the amount of the overage would equate to a 2% drop in EBITDA and, since the value of EBITDA on stock price is roughly $4 per share per percent of EBITDA, this loss would mean a lessening of company capitalization of $800 million because there were roughly 2 billion shares outstanding. The implications were staggering. With so many millions of transactions if some scheme were enacted to extract just a minor amount per transaction the aggregated value could be huge and very difficult to pinpoint. Was something awry with the book keeping? Was management making bad decisions that were leading to a loss of profit? Chad had no idea but what he did understand, was the importance.

"This is pretty significant. Something is just not right. A strange report and an odd encounter with the big boys. Does anyone know what's really going on?" He thought silently.

* EBITDA = Earnings before Interest Taxes Depreciation and Amortization

Georgette Cummings was really feeling her oats. Her first year in the Windy City had been a disaster. Nothing seemed to go right, there was never enough time to get ahead, and meeting decent people was as impossible as keeping your hair on your head when walking east on Congress. To make a long story short – she was miserable. The adjustment from being a small town/small college heroine to a cosmopolitan queen was simply not what she expected. Was she crazy to chase her dreams? Everyday made attainment of her aspirations feel more and more futile; everyday another roadblock seemed to be placed in the way of her ambitions.

Until Georgette moved to Chicago her life was nothing but a bowl of cherries. She was popular in high school, had a number of good friends, lived in a stable middle-class home with a couple of rival siblings and carried a perpetual smile. Her friends all called her Gette, a name she grew to admire after everyone in the talent show audience cheered her for an encore performance during a standing ovation.

Gette not only had a great singing voice, she had a voice that carried dimension, like the best of the best in the world of TV commentators. No matter when she spoke people would stop to listen because her voice had an unusual capacity to carry an aura of crisp perfection. It was this, prompted by constant feedback from every conceivable source, that gave Gette her confidence and determination to pursue a communications degree at a local university. She graduated with honors, enjoyed every moment of her collegiate life and left the university convinced that there was nothing she couldn't accomplish. As far as she was concerned life had already thrown a multitude of challenges across her path and none were so foreboding as to cause even the least bit of consternation. On graduation day Gette was certain of just about everything, especially her decision to move to Chicago.

Chicago, for those hapless souls whom by fate were calved and weaned in the blah of a small mid-west town, was nothing less than the ultimate destiny. Any move away from Lacklusterville was considered a step in the right direction, but a move to Chicago was envy in such proportion that it carried gossip on every street corner, for at least a season.

When the star of the football team found a home on the roster at North-western the local paper doubled in size for a month. Every detail of every major play throughout his four-year stint on varsity was magnified to Heisman caliber, like the fisherman whose meager catch grows to trophy proportion by the fifth version of the story. Not to be outdone by competition with greater circulation, the paper ran a series of lifetime stories on the boy-turned-man and featured numerous editorials on the unparalleled talent marinating within. Every trip home turned into such a homecoming event that after the first year he came home no more.

For Gette, the hype was no different. Her talents were well recorded and the heights to which they would catapult her were invented beyond all proportion. Editorials, articles, bio's and more depicted her as a sure fire success among the best of the best. When her decision to move to Chicago was made public (a happenstance not to her liking) the local blab had her winning a Grammy within a year. Everywhere she went people would stop her to ask how her career was blossoming when in truth it hadn't even started. While Gette went largely unscathed by the attention it became a growing nuisance none-the-less, making her more than eager to pack up and high-tail it outta' Dodge.

In the year that followed her departure there were no developments in her singing career and the hype from Lacklusterville waned out of existence. Gette was no longer a conversation piece among the local elite and her failure to reach the artificial expectations levied on her had somehow become her own fault. The fact that she was working at the Chicago Tribune, as an assistant to the one of the editors, was a miserable failure to those who committed the entirety of their emotional essence to someday knowing a famous person. Their pain became as deeply rooted as was their assuredness of her being an unequalled success. Gette now walked cautiously in her old hometown for what was once an embracing community was now a disgruntled set of peoples whose sensitivities were lost.

Rising in a fit of doom in the darkness before daybreak was becoming too much for Gette to bear so when her alarm began pounding tidal waves of shock into her skull sharply at five the thought of rallying to the call made Gette cringe and coil into a fetal position. Drawing herself near gave Gette a feeling of control that made her better able to cope with her Monday morning ritual, one that began by pressing the snooze bar twice, each time providing nine wonderful minutes of last minute bliss. At eighteen after the fated hour, Gette rose cautiously from her bed, slid on a pair of puffy down slippers, grabbed her robe and wandered into the kitchen. Gette was a fanatic about morning coffee, so without even sidelining into the bathroom for some much needed relief, she made way to a terra cotta container in the frig teeming with the best deep roasted Italian gourmet that money can buy. Only with her coffee system brewing would Gette allow herself the luxury of an empty bladder and a splash of cool water on her face.

Still donned matronly in a white fleece robe, Gette made her way to the sets of locks on her front door to retrieve, with much ambivalence, a copy of the Tribute lying brashly on the other side. Even after a year in her apartment Gette found it awkward and annoying to need so many locks and to have to constantly be wary of her surroundings. The small town girl locked away in the big city apartment, the small town girl swallowed up by the ruthless style of big city life, was still a small town girl – naïve, forthright and incapable of deceit. Her exposure to the newspaper world was a shock and the reality of it wrenched her with incredulity. She believed deeply in freedom of speech and defended ardently the right of the press, assuming beyond question that reporters give nobly their best possible version of the truth. Now a member of that nobility she continually found herself shocked at the twists and spins that journalists took to generate a slant on an issue in hope of increasing its attractiveness. While the journalists she came to know were cautious in their prose, they were none-the-less liberal in edging a story to greatest appeal. Their take on every issue was first guided by the means through which it would sell, second by the information in its raw, unadulterated form. She could never be a reporter, she told herself. As an assistant editor she was offering an informed opinion and her work was presented in that light. Her bias was expected, not contrived, and she could live with that.

Monday mornings' are tough enough without any unforeseen stress and if Monday's are bad everywhere, they're horrible at the Tribute and worst for the editorial staff. Every Monday begins the same way when, sharply at eight, the entire editorial staff gathers in the executive conference room for a feedback session. The editors in chief sit in front on an elevated platform behind a heavy Mission Oak desk and review, line by line, every comment they received on the editorials released to print only hours before. While favorable reviews do sometimes warrant comment, it is seldom and generally brief. Most of the hour is spent defending a well-researched and clearly developed position against an inane, arcane and insane counter position written hastily by a misinformed miscreant who happens to subscribe to the paper merely for the pleasure of hating every word posted. Without forewarning and with not a second to think, the assistants responsible for a given piece are expected to elucidate an elaborate defense against any and all retort, regardless of its validity, pertinence or accuracy. The format is a killer. Imagine shedding your weekend cobwebs while all the bosses, in front of everyone, nit-pick every word in your work. Just when you feel good about a piece, and expect a little notoriety, they beat it, and you, unmercifully into a sea of broken vowels. Soggy alphabet soup has more zeal than the editorial staff following a Monday review session.

The morning paper was rather blaze , having only the usual rash of violent weekend crime, sports wrap-ups and activities of political posturing plastered across the front page. Gette was glad for the lack of allure, but it meant a tough week ahead for everyone. The search for exciting news would be excruciating and the pressure would be felt throughout the halls. This only meant that Monday morning's grit session would be harsher than normal, a thought that didn't exactly hasten Gette to the door. After a quick but placidly completed cup of coffee it was off to the shower and office-face preparation time. Gette's appearance was handsome, if not pleasing. Her tall angular body and flowing dark brown hair gave her an elegant, inviting appearance even without the highlights of make-up. Her modesty and upbringing would never allow Gette to think of herself as an attractive woman instead, on a good day, she might think herself not un-attractive. Gette wasn't the type of beauty that turned heads at first glance but she carried with her a type of wholesome attractiveness that left the detailed observer with an appreciation for the fineness in her features. Her co-workers described her as pretty but her personality appeared guarded to them and their relationship was largely superficial as a result. Gette was certainly friendly and participatory but her upbringing was less flamboyant than most in the office so she felt uneasy with the quickness in the Chicago social scene. Besides, she was consumed by her desire to become a singer and spent most of her free time practicing and familiarizing herself with the Chicago nightclubs.

After a moderately long hot-as-Hades shower it was time to kick things into first gear. Gette always determined what to wear while being massaged by the fine, sharp streams at the tail end of her pleasure, emerging from it psychologically energized, ready to tackle the day. Today she would don a smart black outfit befitting of the funereal atmosphere that she anticipated. A little heavy on the eyeliner, a bit thicker with the mascara and her costume was complete – serious, focused, determined, firm. With a second cup of Italian roast now drained from her favorite mug all that remained was to scour gleaming her straight white teeth and to collect her outer gear for departure. Today a hat and gloves were not needed so coat, purse and laptop were the only adornments used to complete the ritual before Gette launched herself into the Chicago morning air.

The sun, still low in an early sky, was bouncing spectrums of light off distant wispy clouds. Glass in buildings reflected its splendor as if attempting to mimic it, like young children who proudly imitate their parents. The air was crisp in the shade of western walls while quick to spread warmth in their absence. It was a glorious morning regardless of what the future held and it gave Gette a renewed feeling of belief in her ambitions. Something in the air awakened her sense of self-esteem causing her, completely beneath her psyche, to take a deep breath of satisfaction which when exhaled, left Gette more certain of her ambitions than she had been in months. She told herself that things were going to change, that she was going to change. As she winged her way to the bus-stop a metamorphosis was already underway. The girl who found her-self temporarily caught in a trap of self-pity was emerging from her confines like a hatchling pecking its way out of its shell. How could she have allowed the city to envelop her dreams like leaden smog? Not any longer. The old Gette, young and courageous, cautious but fearless, had somehow found herself again. It took the vigor of spring to land a knockout punch on pessimism, but what a punch it was!

The bus arrived loaded with the usual somber crowd, but today it held no negative affect on Gette. She was no longer an outsider immersed in a sea of hardened salty faces, but a member among fellow workers making their way through each day with the happiness from loved ones urging them on. In the past when her eyes happened to fall upon another the images registered were full of wrinkles, stubble and blemishes. But today for some strange reason, when Gette gazed upon the faces of her fellow riders, she saw worlds of experience registered in their eyes, she saw compassion lodged inside their tough exteriors and expressions that bordered, she thought, on contentment. The man to her right held a steady gaze through a sidewalk-facing window. His eyes reflected an aura that was solemn and at ease, no doubt digesting the warmth of breakfast tendered lovingly by his most cherished compan-ion. A woman nearby, when caught glancing at fellow passengers held a welcoming smile for all who cared to partake. Realizing that her out-look had just been inverted from cynic to idealist, with nothing to pin-point for cause, gave Gette reason for a momentary shudder, just as the bus itself shuddered to a halt at the stop by the entrance of the Tribute.

Gette bounded up the granite steps and through the ornate brass doors to the main foyer. It was only 7:30 so she had time to boot up her PC and get the neurons firing before the review meeting began. There weren't many people at the paper on Monday mornings and Gette was happy to arrive at her office without having to exchange morning salu-tations. Email was always the first application to open and she found 15 new messages ready for the uptake. Many of them were sent to an unnecessarily broad distribution and were of little, if any, value. One of them was from Meghan, the office assistant that Gette and others relied on to keep their schedules straight and their assignments on target. Gette and Meghan respected each other, worked well with each other and were confidants in the realm of office politics. Gette opened the email from Meghan and read.

"Hey Gette. I'm gonna be late tomorrow (Monday) so I wanted to wish you luck in the review meeting. I just finished reading your editorial on the plight of our inner city homeless and it was great! I love the way you show compassion and support without blaming "society" as the agent for all of their un-doings. Way to go girl! Keep the faith – you're an insightful writer. Don't let the bastards wear you down."

The note from Meghan was just what Gette needed. It helped her prepare mentally for the anguish at eight. After scanning a few more emails it was time to head to the executive conference room and her weekly ration of pinpricks. Gette whisked herself away from the monitor and headed to the dungeon. She wasn't sure how bad the meeting would be and for the first time didn't care; instead of being consumed with trepidation she had an unusual feeling of aloofness. The fear that normally engulfed her was replaced with a moderate level of irreverence and she found herself practicing some artful dodging from a bombardment of made-up attacks. Before she knew it she was at the conference room door where ten or so of her peers were milling about. The routine was always the same. The executives were already inside preparing their assault, and when readied, an assistant would be hastened to open the door. She would push it completely against the outside wall and then use her body for a door stop as the group began their awkward shuffle inside. Gette, who was normally a shuffler in hiding amongst her peers near the rear, decided instead to go first and sauntered boldly into the room.

The review room was used for a variety of business matters ranging from major press releases to the most mundane and trite conversations imaginable. It was equipped with every conceivable high tech gadget, from internet video and teleconferencing to pre-programmed ambience settings for optimal meeting effectiveness. Unfortunately there was only one setting for the Monday review sessions, a setting endearingly known amongst its victims as "death by suffocation". Gette had never been first to enter the room and the aura of it presented to her empty was an entirely new experience. At the front on this particular morning sat three executives, each shrouded in a shaft of ethereal light that evoked eminence from their beings. Each shaft was strategically located to accentuate power and control, to create a separation between bosses and subordinates big enough to fly a plane through. For some strange reason it reminded Gette of the one time she had to visit the principal's office in ninth grade. She and her best friend Sarah were going through a period of boy craziness and couldn't stop passing notes back and forth with vivid descriptions of their intent for each of the hulks of their passion. Their desire to outdo each other got the best of their imagination and their profundities became profanities about the same time that their algebra teacher had enough and intervened. He feigned shock to keep from laughing and immediately sent Gette and Sarah to see the principal. Gette was the first one to enter the interrogation room where the principal, sitting boldly behind his marred wooden desk, tried affably to shed seriousness over the matter. Unfortunately, he wasn't able to maintain his role as commander in chief and soon the tone of his lecture softened and his steadfast and stern gaze converted into a smile. "Oh Gette, get out of here, but don't let it happen again!" He said while removing his glasses to wipe the wetness of laughter from his eyes. The thought of it made Gette laugh out loud and what previously was a deafeningly silent room seemed to erupt when her brief laughter pierced the air.

"Something funny Ms. Cummings?" Mr. DiGrande queried. "Can I assume that your laughter has something to do with the quality of your work? Perhaps your work is a laughing matter but take it from me our desire for journalistic excellence at the Tribute isn't a laughing matter at all. Please take a seat so perhaps you can begin to learn something of value about the art of the editorial."

Gette wanted to speak back but didn't. Instead she quietly took a seat front and center at a location never before even remotely considered, let alone occupied. Her renewal of her faith in herself unconsciously took control of her body and she seated herself dead center before rendering a thought about what she had done. Several rows behind Gette seats began to fill without any sound other than the dragging of feet and an occasional stifled cough. Sitting by herself caused Gette to reflect on the absurdity of the situation and the repugnant arrogance that management had come to think was their birthright. No longer would she allow herself to let their demeanor give her cause to cower or feel of lesser import. No, Gette thought, their management style was not something to behold, or revere, its merit was instead something to question and Gette was feeling unusually inquisitive.

"Let's get started, we have a long day ahead of us and no time to waste." Matt DiGrande, a lifelong Tribute devotee, bellowed. "We need to keep this meeting on track because there are a variety of issues we need to cover and we really can't afford to be here to begin with. The editorials printed yesterday were met with such outrage that I am certain it will be reflected in our circulation next week. You are paid to provide editorial content that is provocative yet appealing, interesting but not offensive. Apparently this message has not been adequately communicated, though I feel more like a broken record with each passing week. I can't imagine doing your jobs the way you are doing them. There are hundreds of different subjects and angles on issues that our public would love to digest, why can't you find one? I am tired of leading you to water and now it appears that I have to force you to drink as well." DiGrande barked. "It seems that our readers are sick of hearing about the blight of the inner city homeless. They've been bombarded for years with issues of the homeless and must by now feel beaten into a coma on the matter. Not one response was generated from yesterday's editorial. Why did we spend so much space on a subject of no apparent interest? Do we study the marketability of a subject before venturing out? Georgette, this is your piece isn't it?"

"It is." Georgette said with panache. "And I thought it was a good piece and I'm sorry that none of our readers commented on it. But, I think it was just last week during a review that you said no news is normally good news. So, I'm sorry, but I'm at a loss to know how to respond. Do we desire readership feedback or not? What is the right barometer of a successful story? I'm not trying to sound smug, but I'm not sure I know what, exactly, it is you are looking for."

"I'm looking for our editorials to provoke thought in our readership, thought that evokes an intellectually based and interesting response."

"I think you give our readership too much credit. People in this city aren't sitting around waiting for our editorials to stimulate their intellectual prowess. They read them and move on and the ones that don't are the eccentric weirdo's that thrive on conspiracy theory and feel compelled set the world straight. Frankly, I think the paper gives their opinions too much credence." Gette pronounced boldly.

"Oh, you do, do you? Well Ms. Self-appointed-spokesperson-of-the-day, what do you suggest? Care to enlighten us? Care to cough up some phlegm of change? Or would you rather step down from your spokesperson appointment and let us conduct this meeting as was originally planned?"

"Was that a rhetorical question or do I get a real opportunity to respond? I'll assume it was an invitation for dialog, and I'll assume that we all agree that this is an important subject and I'll gladly 'cough up' some suggestions." Gette said excitedly. "Instead of publishing the common responses and beating us to death with the ones most outlandish, I think we need to spotlight the zany characters in our midst. I think we should take the craziest stuff we get and analyze it and its authors and use it to show our readers exactly how insane some of those amongst us truly are. Rather than hide the fact that we are constantly bombarded with insanity we should spotlight it to reveal the true risks that freedom of speech implies. In fact, we could create a column called "Freedomly Speaking."

"Ms. Cummings, I appreciate your enthusiasm, but rest assured ideas as mundane as these have been tried many times over without success or notoriety. Stick to improving your basic skills and perhaps you will someday be a solid contributor. Now," DiGrande shouted quickly, "if the diatribe has ended perhaps I can continue chairing this session."

With that pronouncement DiGrande wrested back control of the meeting, moving thankfully past Gette and on to other hapless victims. Gette wasn't certain what to make of the exchange, but it was the first time she ever approached DiGrande with authority and regardless of the outcome, she felt good about herself. More importantly, she felt good about her idea. Why not exploit those who choose to disrespect the freedoms they were granted as Americans? Why not expose the risk that our noble bill of rights has granted? A liberal paper like the Tribute should capitalize on out-to-lunch opinions that demonstrate the vulnerability that freedom of speech proffers, and in the process reinforce a commitment to our Constitution. Wow, thought Gette, why not?

The meeting ended as ten was drawing near - almost two hours of constant bombardment. Not one accolade for any of the hard work was provided and rather than inspire the audience to seek higher pastures it resulted in lowering self-esteem into valleys of quagmire. Talented but dejected hardworking professionals returned to their hectic week with the additional burden of questioned self-worth to overcome. Gette decided that next week she would offer some praise on her own if, she thought, there was a next week.

Meghan was so busy working on ad insertions she barely noticed when Gette returned from the Monday morning monstrosity. That was just like Meghan. She would get into creative streaks that consumed her so completely that she would actually stop breathing if it weren't involuntary. Her focus when so consumed was sufficiently all encompassing that fellow employees' could talk about her within earshot and not worry one iota about censoring their comments. Meghan would explain that her thoughts were as loud to her as a minds' eye has perfect vision and that all other sound was totally imperceptible when she was in the groove. Gette could tell as she neared that Meg was in one of her grooves, recalling a time when even the ring of her phone was beyond her cognitive realm, and paused to marvel at the anomaly that currently defined her, in her workplace. After a few long and idle seconds Meg recognized the sensation cast by Gette's presence and emerged from her world to deliver Gette a genuinely warm greeting.

"Good morning Ms. Cummings. I see you made it through another lovely round of Monday morning bash-and-dash. Did you get my message?" Meghan asked cheerfully from the random mix of items on her desk.

"Got it and thanks. It was just the perk-up that I needed. I don't know what came over me this morning but I participated in the meeting, I didn't just sit there and cower. I actually tried to hold a conversation with DiGrande. It didn't go very well, so I wouldn't be surprised if I'm looking for new employment soon."

"What happened?"

"I just got sick of being on the receiving end of a very long and negative stick and interjected a few comments about some changes we might make to improve things. DiGrande didn't like losing control of the meeting and dismissed my idea without thought or consideration. But you know what? It felt good anyway."

With that Gette recounted her idea for the paper and without even recognizing it the two were instantly embroiled in a brainstorming session. At the conclusion Gette had Meghan more excited than a concert conductor at the crescendo of a featured piece and promised to further their discussion by developing it into a campaign with some specifics and more structure.

Gette returned to her office to check emails before digging into her next assignment and noticed that her message light was blinking. She normally had plenty of messages and dialed her mailbox without hesitation until she heard DiGrande's secretary in her voicemail tell her to call immediately to schedule a meeting. Her first reaction was not a pretty one and her blood froze from fear. "Do they want to get rid of me that bad? Was I so out of line that they're going to fire me already?" she thought. Moments later her fear unwittingly converted to anger and where seconds before there were frozen veins was now a vascular system ready to boil. Without thinking, she dialed DiGrande.

"This is Georgette Cummings. I'm responding to your message about a meeting with Mr. DiGrande."

"Yes Ms. Cummings. Mr. DiGrande would like to see you at your earliest convenience. Are you available now?"

"I assume that Mr. DiGrande is not used to waiting, so yes, I am available."

"Very well, I'll tell him that you will meet him within the next five minutes then." And she hung up with further comment.

"Dear God." Gette thought as she started walking slowly toward DiGrande's office. "What have I done? I should at least have taken enough time to decouple my emotions from the business side of things before subjecting myself to the wrath of DiGrande. OK Gette, get hold of yourself and get through this with dignity. Walk proudly and don't let him sense the fear in your eyes." She said to herself half nervously.

DiGrande's office was one of several in a sequestered area reserved only for executives. It was totally different than the balance of occupied space at the Tribute, having plush oriental throw rugs on top of oak flooring and classical hardwood paneled walls. It looked and smelled stately and had a soft balanced resonance that was unique to it as well. After checking in with the secretary, Gette was told proceed to Mr. DiGrande's office. She knocked on the partially open door when she arrived and without seeing DiGrande heard him quickly snort "Come In".

Gette entered and turned to her left to view the spacious and opulently adorned office where DiGrande sat behind a neatly organized modern cherry desk crafted for access to, and adorned with, multiple computer screens.

He appeared to be in the middle of creating an email and did not look up when she entered. After a few keystrokes he hit the enter button with undue emphasis and gazed at Gette in complete silence. His stare held an x-ray like pierce but contained no sexual malice or hatred. It was more like an assessment of a revered enemy than the critique of an insolent underling, more like a sizing up than a dressing down, and it immediately elevated Gette's self-confidence.

"Ms. Cummings, please sit down. Aside from some of your work and the boldness you exhibited this morning, I have little knowledge of your capabilities, so I'm not sure why I am doing this, but I have a special project that needs attention and I'm wondering if you are interested."

Registering his comments sent flutters of varied emotion through Gette's body and with no outward display of their being received Gette took the chair he offered with relief. She looked through him for a minute deciding how to respond and said, "I thought you were going to fire me."

"What makes you think that? We are publishing your work aren't we? You need to worry about your job when we no longer decide that you can generate prose worthy of our readership. Unless that happens, as long as our circulation levels remain, you needn't worry about anything but continual improvement. In our industry, more so than all others, you must be focused on what you can do for me today and tomorrow, for what you already did is history and history does not make news or sell papers."

"I understand. So what's this special project? And why me?"

"Let me start with the why me question. There is no answer to the why you. I've been looking for someone who stands out a bit to run this project and you decided to stand out at the right time. Quite frankly I have my reservations, but I can also see benefits. Someone newer to the industry will by default employ different tactics during the investigations and that may end up a plus in the end. Also, in some cases women can more easily get information than men and this may be one of those circumstances, so why not hedge it?"

"OK, so I may succeed and I may fail and if I succeed it will be good for the paper and if I fail the damage with a newbie like me is minimal. In other words, I'm low risk. Is that it?"

"Interesting observation. I didn't look at it that way, but your observation is not easy to refute. Perhaps it's more of an indirect circumstance than a primary consideration, however true it might appear. Ready to listen now?"

"Ready." Gette said after a slight delay.

"I want you to study World Supplî. Find out who they are, what they sell, where they sell, how they manage, who does the managing, what their financials look like, what their culture is like. Get into the bowels of their operation and determine for yourself, are they the type of large publicly traded corporation that we should revere, are they a company that deserves to be discredited or are they somewhere in between. Be open. Be neutral. Be factual, specific and detailed. And then, and only then, render an opinion. Interested?"

"I'm not sure. What's up with World Supplî?"

"I don't really know. We're hearing that something is going on and don't know what. If you take this assignment you aren't to speak of it directly to anyone and you are to report only to me and only when and as I dictate. Do you understand?"

"Not really. I mean, I've never been asked to perform in this manner before, have no idea if it's common practice for special assignments or why this assignment needs that level of secrecy."

"It doesn't. It's just that this is my baby and I want to keep it close to vest. The decision to allow you the freedom to explore WorldSupplî is entirely mine, although my staff concurs with the investment. Ready to start?"

Gette wasn't sure what to make of the strangeness of the situation. She hadn't been given any really important assignments and wasn't sure she could trust the reasoning behind the offer to work this one. On the other hand, she felt ready for something with meat in it so why not? She knew she was ready for a breakout assignment and perhaps this was how they were made. When it came down to it, what did she have to lose? She wasn't happy writing drab editorials and regardless of how this panned out, she needed a change and this could be the change that she needed.

"I'm ready. When do I start?"

"You just did." DiGrande said dismissively.

After a little further debriefing Gette left DiGrande's office immersed in an array of emotions foreign enough to render the current world surreal. The effect produced in her a mental haze so overpowering that function beyond the involuntary was temporarily obviated from existence. She walked from the executive offices in a trance-like state, as if surrounded by a cloud thick enough to shunt visibility in a matter of feet. Then, as reality re-sculpted itself her world changed for reasons unknown to a new, different and scary place, with a fear not unlike a mother who loses sight of her child.

Gette needed to understand the nature of this new assignment. What possibly could be the reason for this absurd change? It was too out of character, too spontaneous, too random. She needed badly to get away and think; to triangulate on the potential for unspoken purpose. Better yet, she needed to discuss it with someone, but DiGrande wanted it kept silent. Why? None of it made sense.

L ater that week Gette decided to reward herself with an evening of good music at a local jazz club. It wasn't Gette's normal thing to travel unaccompanied to such places, but tonight's solo appearance was purposeful simply for the pleasure of the anticipated sound for the band that was readying to play, the Forty G's, had become a recent favorite. They held an ensemble of instruments and a set of skilled musicians that allowed them to play anything from Stanley Turrentine to Cole Porter, with a mix of Chick Corea and Miles Davis in between.

She entered the club cautiously and stood in the doorway to allow her eyes to adjust to the muted surroundings of the bar. It was a pretty typical jazz place with a booze wall along one side, a miss-mash of small tables strewn across the floor and a raised platform in the corner for the band du jour. It was big enough to hold a good crowd, but small enough to be guaranteed astonishingly loud when fully in swing.

As Gette entered she became accustomed not only to the light but also to the pervasive crowd noise and as her hearing adapted she became acutely aware of a small group of people snickering from a corner to her immediate right. It was hard not to overhear them. In fact it was down-right impossible because they were sneering and jeering about some poor guy from their office. It didn't take long for Gette to get the picture. The guy who was the victim of their diatribe was some misfit from their IT department who apparently lacked the where-with-all, or confidence, or both, to be socially active.

"Chippie, oh Chippie, where for art thou Chippie?" she heard the boisterous one yell. "Hey Chippie aren't you supposed to be on that big date tonight? What happened? Did she stand you up?" He continued. And then, after a long pull on his draught, he sauntered over to a small floor table in the center of the bar, about 2/3 of the way toward the back, and without hesitation slapped a lone young man on the back of the head, presumably "Chippie".

"Hey Chippie! You know that date you were bragging about? Well we all wanted to meet her so we decided to come and introduce our-selves. So where is she? What's her name?" spat Fred with freshly lath-ered beer breath. "I'll bet she's a no show. No, I'll bet she doesn't even exist! A thing imagined from deep within your loneliness. A creature created to lessen the pain of your lonely, boring life!" Fred spat as he turned to face his peer group for accolades.

Gette, always a quick thinker and an individual given to support the downtrodden, digested the situation in a flash when "Chippie's" downturned face turned crimson. It was obvious that Fred's barrage had left him decimated; perhaps because Fred's message had an unsavory ring of truth to it. Gette immediately assumed the worst case scenario on behalf of their victim and feeling instantly irritated decided to be a remedy to the situation. In a flash she whipped off her coat and with a lovely beaming smile ran to over to "Chippie's" table. Leaning into him from behind Gette planted a casual kiss on his cheek and said, "Hi honey, sorry I'm late. Got caught up at the paper again." Then, without a moment's hesitation turned to Fred with outstretched hand and beamed "Hello there. Georgette. Are you a friend from the office?"

The speed with which the tables had turned was too much for Chad and way too much for Fred, who stood there for a moment dumbfounded beyond belief. Fred couldn't fathom the idea that Chippie actually had a date, and to make matters worse, that his date was a knockout. Rebounding from his initial shock while starting to drink in the splendor of the image before him Fred meekly replied, "Uh, yeah, a friend from the office, name's Fred. Nice to meet ya." Then, as Fred took Gette's outstretched hand he turned to Chad and said, "Gotta go Chad, have a nice evening", and departed, hastily, with the look of a deer caught in headlights.

As Fred floated disbelievingly back to his bullying cohorts Gette made her way to the chair opposite Chad where she slid confidently into the seat and said "Look up and smile and your friends will continue to think this is real. I overheard them as I walked in. I think I know what's going on. If I'm wrong, I apologize and will leave immediately."

With that Chad looked up and for the first time saw what had planted the sweetest, most gentle kiss, he had ever felt. She was beautiful, beautiful in a wholesome, intelligent and healthy way. Her skin was absolute, pore less, smooth, without flaws of any kind. Her nose was long and slender and regal and her eyes glistened in the reflected light like the moon on a still pond. Chad found himself staring at her and was speechless, but not totally incapacitated, and with an ingratiating smile slowly slid an outstretched hand across the top of the table as he again cast his look downward and away.

Gette wasn't sure what to make of this initial contact, but construing the outreach as a gesture of thankfulness, surprised herself by returning it and placed her hand on top of his. Though Chad was a stranger in the most prolific sense of the word, his powerful fingers did not feel uninviting when she touched them. They were long and lean and to her surprise fit perfectly as hers were conjoined in his. This was the most unusual of circumstances; two nameless, faceless strangers touching hands; yet a casual observer would undoubtedly conclude that here there was love, here there was something unique.

When Gette touched his hand Chad glanced over at his co-workers and to his dismay the mocking revelry was absent. In its place were silent stares, open mouths and stilled drinks. Where once stood a cocky insubordinate clique of upwardly handicapped professionals was now a humbled jealous group of disbelieving children and the site of it put immediate perspective on Chad's life. He was not the only one wrought with insecurity, fighting feelings of malcontent. He simply didn't mask it with an abundance of alcohol and the strong doses of intimidation as, apparently, did some of his peers.

"Hello." Chad said softly but not with a hint of cowardice. "My name is Charles, but my friends call me Chad and for what you have done, I think I should call you Saint Georgette."

"It's nothing. I can't stand people like that. Further still, I can't believe people from your office would be so callous. I'm glad I could be of help, but I'll stay here only as long as I feel it appropriate and then I'll take my leave. And by the way, my friends call me Gette." She said as her hand withdrew from the table.

At that moment the waitress came by and without a word Chad and Gette said in unison, "Grey Goose with a splash of soda and a twist please" and both promptly began to laugh. While Chad continued to laugh, Gette registered a handsome, unassuming smile that emerged from Chad's otherwise somber face. It cast Chad's demeanor in a light of decency and immediately put Gette at ease, despite the bizarre circumstances.

"Drink's on me." Chad said as the waitress was leaving. "How did you know that I didn't really have a date? Is it that obvious?"

"Not at all. I had no idea who your cohorts were talking about when I overheard the conversation and then, when that idiot came over and whacked you on the head, I put two and two together."

"Well you must be a rather quick thinker because you summed up the situation and made the decision to be my heroine in record time. I'm not so sure I would have done the same if circumstances were reversed. First of all, I would not have synthesized the situation in time to react and secondly, when I did, I would start thinking about all the potential outcomes of my actions before I initiated them. Net result – once I understood the circumstances, it would probably be too late."

"In any case, Gette, I'm don't really know how to react to you. You really turned this situation upside-down and while I appreciate what you did, I don't feel comfortable with someone else taking pity on me."

"Someone else? You mean you take pity on yourself enough that no one else should bother?" Gette looked incredulous after the comment and muttered "Pompous ass."

"What was that?" questioned Chad.

"I said pompous ass. I didn't do what I did out of pity. I did it out of disdain. I didn't do it to save you," she said while gesturing quotation marks with her hands. "I did it to stop them. I did it because I believe in the golden rule. Maybe I was a bit too forward but believe me, this small town girl has her values in order and isn't afraid to admit it," she finished as the drinks arrived. "Thanks for the drink. It looks as though your friends might be leaving, so perhaps I should too." Gette said as she stood and started to saunter away.

"Hey," Chad muttered "I'm sorry. Please wait a minute. I'm feeling really awkward at the moment; it's not every day that a beautiful woman comes to my rescue. This isn't a situation that I have any experience with and I don't know how to react, so unless you're meeting someone and really have to go, I would welcome your company for as long as you care to share it. I came here alone to see The Forty G's, something I do more than I care to admit, because they're one of my favorites; unfortunately, I made the mistake of telling that crew from the office that I had a date. I had no idea that they knew it wasn't true or that they would make a mockery of it."

Gette stopped to listen without turning fully around and when Chad finished talking continued to stand motionless for a few extra seconds while she contemplated her alternatives. Common sense told her to simply wish Chad an enjoyable evening and find a suitable place to watch the show, but instinct meandered away from her subconscious and overruled common sense for one of the few times in her life. In a matter of seconds, without realizing the speed or insightfulness with which thought had already altered her direction, Gette decided to stay and as she reversed course the thoughts that preceded her decision slowly became apparent. She too had come alone to watch the Forty G's and she too was devoid of anything approaching an adequate social life, just like Chad. And while the idea of watching the show by herself did not present itself as totally unacceptable, the idea of at least sitting with someone else had more appeal than the image she saw of her pathetic little self trying to look comfortable as a loner.

"I guess I can sit with you for awhile, anyone who likes the Forty G's as much as I do can't be all bad." Gette said with gesture of surprise. "When did you start listening to them?" she asked as Chad readied her chair.

"Not too long ago, actually. I'm pretty new to the area. When I first got here I tried to learn something about the Chicago nightlife by reading local rags like the Chicago Reader and the Southtown Star. One of them had a review of local bands in the region that impressed me, especially the mix of talented jazz players, so I decided to learn more about them by going to gigs. That's how I came to like the Forty G's."

"I saw them a few months ago for the first time and was really impressed. Not only with the array of instruments that they use, but also their voices. I think they produce some exceptional sound and have some really unique vocal arrangements too. A very skilled set of musicians who play the offbeat stuff that I like to hear."

"So you're a music buff, then? Perhaps we at least have that in common. I'm somewhat of a crazy person when it comes to music, for me it's more than just an interest, its part of me; I'm hopelessly hooked. "

We may have more in common than you imagine Gette thought as the band struck their first chords of the evening. The bar, instantly awash with melody, changed from a commonplace gathering site to a spectacle of astonishing sound and Chad and Gette became immediately immersed in the experience. Gette gazed at Chad part way through the first piece and the person she saw was entirely different than just minutes before. Chad's once solemn face was animated and intense and his otherwise placid eyes were sparkling and full of vigor. His feet were tapping perfectly to the rhythm of the beat and his hands were miming the chords from the piano as if their delivery were his personal responsibility. He was a beacon of concentration aimed totally at the sound, the site of which gave Gette an unexpected feeling of calm and she decided to settle in for the evening.

Fred didn't stop staring at Chad and Gette, didn't even blink, until the band started its first set. "Let's get out of here" he commanded his troops. "Can't stand this music anyway and the site of lover-boy with his nanny is too much for me to handle. Deco' Dan's is within walking distance. What'd ya say?"

With that pronouncement Fred's crew quickly washed down their drinks, donned whatever outside apparel they had thought fit to wear, and scurried from the crowded room. Breaking into the silence of the chilly evening air gave them opportunity to exchange observations and they did so with hoots and hollers and lots of "Oh my God's" and "Holy Shits". When things calmed a little Susan whacked Fred upside the head and promptly started to bore a new hole into his skull.

"What the frig man?" she shouted. "Did you get some bad intel or what? I thought Chippie was supposed to be lying! He didn't look very alone to me; in fact I'd say he was far from it. You better find someone else to pick on before people start picking on you."

Fred stared at Susan and didn't utter a word. He couldn't get the image of Chippie and Georgette out of his head. Something about it just wasn't right; something wasn't kosher. Fred met Chad the first day of Chad's employ and Chad had never ventured socially beyond his planar interactions with Paul, who was another quasi misfit as far as Fred was concerned. How could such a dish-pan end up with a girl like that?

"I don't get it." Fred stated blankly. "There's no way that Chippie is dating that woman. His idea of a date is a pitted candied fruit. The guy has the social skill set of Quasimodo and the libido of a snail darter. I can't imagine him spending an ounce of energy on the dating scene let alone the effort needed to land a chick like that. No, something is amiss, that must be his sister, or his cousin, or someone from his high school chess club."

They walked the rest of the way to Deco Dan's in silence; each hunkered down within his or her own thoughts on the matter of their unexpected interchange with Chad. When they got there the body language emanating between Fred and Susan was so sexually obvious that the others decided to call it a night and hailed a cab. Fred was eyeing Susan like a rabid pit bull ready for a takedown while Susan unabashedly devoured Fred with a wanton piercing stare. They entered Deco Dan's in an embrace that turned into a tongue swallowing display of uncontrollable lust, not fit for public consumption in any place or under any circumstance. Oblivious to the affect that their entanglement had on other patrons, they made their way to a small table at the far reaches of the front left corner.

"Susan, we gotta find out what's going on with Chippie. This doesn't make any sense. A guy like that just doesn't all-of-the-sudden end up with a girl like that. We have to devise a plan to get to the bottom of this. I think we should spy on the little bugger until the truth comes out."

"Fred, just drop it. Let's have a drink and then go to my place. OK?"

Chad and Gette had a couple drinks while the band kept playing but otherwise engaged in little else due to the fact that talking above the noise was nearly impossible. About the only exchanges were brief awkward glances and a few nervous smiles. When the first show ended things lightened up a little, the place quieted just enough for a smidgen of verbal exchange and Chad, not liking to yell in order to be heard, asked Gette if she wanted to go someplace quiet for coffee or a drink.

"Coffee would be just great." Gette said. "There's a little shop about a mile from here that makes the best Italian espresso in Chicago. Interested?"

"That sounds wonderful about now. Should I follow you in my car?"

"Not unless you want to watch me walking or try to keep up with one of the local cabbies."

"Of course I'd be happy to drive you there, but I would also understand if you weren't comfortable with that."

"I think by now I've come to realize that you're harmless so, yes, I'll let you drive, but I must warn you, I'm a black belt in case you have any evil intentions."

"Are you really?"

"That's for you to find out." Gette smiled as she stood, donned her coat and readied the rest of her gear for a hasty exit. The bar was still crowded so Chad placed his hand on her back to guide her to the door. The force of the crowd pressed him into Gette as they inched their way forward and he caught a glimpse of the sweet scent of her hair on the way. It reminded him of the time he slow danced at the seventh grade prom, coiled neck in neck with his love of the week, when he noticed for the first time in his life the subtle pleasures that a woman can hold. The thought of it lingered as they walked in silence to Chad's car.

"So where is this place anyway?" Chad asked as they buckled up.

"Take a left at that light and then a right in about three blocks. I'll let you know when we get there."

"How did you like the show? It was pretty similar to the last one I saw but nonetheless inspiring as far as I am concerned."

"I thought it was great. My real interest in life, although I work at the Tribute, is to be a singer. I like to see shows with offbeat vocals and unique delivery. It's as much fun for me to get exposure to new ways of looking at old material as it is to experience original composition. That's one of the reasons why I like the Forty G's. They remix songs really well, their new compositions are usually very creative and when they replay a golden oldie it has a lot of character."

"I like them pretty much for the same reason, but I tend to focus more on the instrumentals than the lyrics. They're great at weaving solo elements with different accents into their riffs and using syncopated rhythms to create new feelings."

"Well, don't you sound like a musicology student! Should I be impressed?"

"No, no, no. Not really. I mean, I haven't published anything yet, I've written a bunch of stuff, but I haven't published anything."

"What are you waiting for? You won't know what you've got 'til someone else has the chance to hear it, to work with it. You're not afraid of failure are you?"

"Failure? No. There's no reason to fear what you've already achieved, failure that is. I guess when it comes to music I tend to be a perfectionist and since there's no such thing as perfection it's hard to know when enough is good enough. You can always make your material just a little bit better and in my case as long as I feel like it can be better, I let it sit until the next round of inspiration prompts a rewrite. I find myself rewriting quite a bit."

At that moment Chad spotted Espresso Alley a few buildings down and, with amazing luck also noticed the reversing lights of a car parked just ahead. He slowed quickly to see if the driver was leaving and when the left blinker came on knew immediately that fortune had found him a great parking spot. Moments later Chad was holding the door to Espresso Alley for Gette. It was a small and very Spartan place that overwhelmed its patrons with the wonderfully distinctive aroma of fresh ground coffee, and nothing more.

Gette motioned Chad to a small wrought iron table with a mosaic tile top near the stores' front counter. A small Eurasian woman with straight black hair and honey accented skin came promptly to take their order. Chad ordered a double espresso with lemon and Gette a mocha latté.

"So," Gette continued after ordering, "so far you're nothing but a failure, is that it? Is that why your office picks on you?"

"I don't really consider myself a failure, let's just say that my five year plan looks like it's going to take longer than I envisioned. No matter how much I try, I can't seem to get beyond a paycheck to paycheck existence so my time to compose is somewhat limited. And as far as my office is concerned, their world doesn't interest me. Office politics, water cooler gossip, finger pointing, sucking up to the boss, all that stuff – it's for others, not for me."

"I can't say that I disagree, but the fact remains that those elements of the office environment exist and are real. Most of us are powerless to change them, so the best thing is to deal with them and in my opinion, ignoring them is not dealing with them."

"What are you saying?"

"That perhaps you need to confront those appalling circumstances when you find yourself the target of office shenanigans. Maybe then things like tonight won't happen any longer. If you ignore people completely you set yourself up for abuse, you become an easy target, and that guy Fred looks like just the type to prey on easy targets."

"It just seems easier to ignore everyone. What about you? What's your office like?"

"Oh, it has issues, just like yours." And Gette began to explain the nature of the pressure cooker environment that consumed her on a daily basis. Discussing it with Chad was a whole new venue for her. Explaining her circumstances to him, as an outside neutral party looking in, forced Gette to express herself in an entirely new way and she found as she talked to Chad a greater degree of clarity develop than ever before. At the same time Chad had his first real opportunity to study his bazaar latté lapping acquaintance, guessing that beneath the tough faux exterior was a sweetheart dying to emerge. She certainly was pleasant to look at and to be with, but maybe, Chad thought, she just might be a bit too much on the clutch. The level of her self-assuredness held the swagger of a cowboy after four seconds on a bronco and her tendency to correctly complete his sentences before he uttered not even half of his thought left him feeling intellectually marginal. Then why was he wishing that the night would never end? Was it something magnetic or just the reprieve from his otherwise melancholy pastime?

Only when Gette found herself looking at the bottom of her empty latté did she give moment to stop talking and reflect on the past twenty minutes. It went by in a flash because, for some strange reason, her words came as easily with Chad as they did with anyone. She reeled off an in depth analysis of the culture at the Tribute, with some criticisms and psycho-analyzing of her peers and superiors thrown into the mix. She lambasted the pervasive arrogant style of the management team and emoted dramatically when disclosing her deep dismay with the paper's push for volume over their push for accuracy. Gette had not recently allowed her pent up emotions to convert from subliminal thought to an articulated position and found the process rather cathartic. When she concluded her speech a sense of wellbeing enveloped her that was sufficiently weighty to feel physically present. It was so healthy that her posture felt rejuvenated as if her weight, though unchanged, could now be much more easily managed.

"That's some pressure cooker you work in. I certainly have days when the demands placed upon me outstrip my capacity to supply, but it's nothing like that." Chad said empathetically. "My problem is really pretty simple, I just don't like what I do that much and don't really want to be there. At least you have challenges that require creativity and thought; I only have variations on the same stupid theme and it tends to get boring."

At that moment both fell silent while looking into each others' eyes. It was comfortable, and each knew it, so mention was not needed.

"Well this certainly has been a most unusual evening. I'm glad I helped you out of your tight spot. I had a good time. I mean, it was different. I normally have to fend off the jerky testosterone driven guys that want to get lucky. It was nice to be able to relax for a change."

"I enjoyed it too. I was ready for a hasty exit when Fred whacked me. This was a much better outcome. Thanks."

"You're welcome. And now it's getting late so I better head for home. And no, you can't drive me, I'll hail a taxi."

"You're sure? I thought I was deemed safe passage. Did you change your mind?"

"No. I know you're safe. But I would be breaking one of my cardinal rules if I let you drop me off and I am not willing to do that."

Gette stood and Chad grabbed her coat and held it open for her in hope that this last display of chivalry would serve as retribution for her earlier kindness. After she slipped comfortably into it he flipped a few bucks on the table for a tip and they walked silently from Espresso Alley to hail a cab. It wasn't long before an empty Yellow pulled to the curb and Chad was forced to quickly configure an appropriate good-night.

"Um, thanks for everything Georgette. It takes a very special person to do what you did and I'm grateful. It was a pleasure to meet you."

"And you. Good luck with your music. I hope to hear your compositions on the radio some day." And with that Gette slid into the back of the cab and was off. The sight of the vanishing cab, and the realization that with it went the most special person Chad had met since coming to Chicago, left Chad in such a state of confusion that all he could do was stare stupidly as it rounded the nearby corner.

"What the hell had just happened? Where was my brain? That was such a dumb goodbye. Why didn't I ask for her phone number? I could have seen if she was interested in going to another show or asked to repay her kindness with an elegant dinner. But I didn't. I didn't even think about it. No wonder I don't meet women, I'm such a dumb ass." Chad thought dejectedly.

Where minutes ago existed a warm internal glow was now an overwhelming feeling of lonely destitution and as Chad turned toward his car it was with the despondence of a newly made widower.

"Shit." he muttered.

At work Georgette instantly immersed herself in the quest to understand WorldSupplî and found the task incredibly daunting due to the complexity that is typical of large multinational conglomerates. WorldSupplî was an entangled and layered mix of about 100 corporations that spanned a number of industries and geographic domains. The mechanics for consolidation of financial statements alone were so convoluted that it was impossible to understand how, in the post Sarbanes-Oxley era, sufficient checks and balances could be instituted to give the CEO disclosure certainty adequate to bear his signature.

Gette found herself overwhelmed by the lexicon that surrounds corporate jargon, coming quickly to understand her need to pull all-nighters to acquire, at a minimum, a basic capture of business administration. It was a new and difficult world for her, but she took an instant liking because it somehow made sense as it revealed to her the real-world aspects of the accounting 101 course she took sophomore year. In a few weeks she understood enough about WorldSupplî to feel capable of discussing the company with DiGrande and arranged for a meeting.

"I was wondering if I was ever going to hear from you Ms. Cummings. What do you have for me?"

"Nothing earth shattering that's for sure. Everything with the company seems to be on the up and up. No questionable acquisitions. No particular change in their R&D activities or funding. No change in corporate governance, board of directors, charitable contributions, trade show activity, marketing direction or anything like that. And nothing noteworthy on capex or depreciation either."

"That's it? Two weeks of digging and you recite their income statement and balance sheet? Surely you found out more than that."

"Well, there is one trend that I think I need to study. That's why I asked for this meeting, to get your opinion."

"OK. What is it?"

"It seems that a few years ago, Alan Chandler came to meet some hot shot by the name of Bryan Jeffries and hired him immediately as his CTO. Jeffries invested in a number of new systems; upgraded internal security and pretty much revamped the financial consolidation platform in the process."

"Oh? And just how did you learn about that?"

"Actually, I found a place where a bunch of WorldSupplî middle managers go to lunch and all I had to do was be there and listen. You wouldn't believe the things they complain about. They make it seem like a horrible place to work."

"Go on."

"A few days ago I overheard a conversation, more of bitch session actually, where some people from an accounting department were literally screaming about some type of new process that was making their jobs impossible. They indicated that not only were activities more difficult but the value for the effort just wasn't there. I guess you could say that they just didn't get it and this guy Jeffries name kept coming up over and over again."

"Jeffries huh? So I assume that you started to investigate him. Did you find anything interesting?"

"Actually I haven't investigated him yet at all but I did take a look at the performance of the business since he came on board and about a year after he was hired profit margins began to slip. Now I'm no business major, mind you, but sales stayed pretty strong so you would think that volume alone would allow profit to drop to the bottom line at a higher rate of return, not the other way around."

"Pretty astute observation for a communications major. You're right, when sales increase without adding manufacturing capacity or overhead the profit on the incremental sales should be at a much higher rate. What makes you think that Jeffries has anything to do with that? He's the Technology Officer, right? Maybe it's as simple as competition forcing downward pressure on price."

"I thought about that so I did a quick assessment of the pier companies in their industries so see if the trends were similar. They're not. WorldSupplî has lost ground, relatively speaking, and there isn't any apparent reason other than mismanagement."

"The CTO doesn't normally make decisions that have that much influence on the bottom line. That's more a function of purchasing, and manufacturing, and marketing. Have you taken a look at any supply chain issues? Is there any evidence of a change in their marketing strategy? Are there any reported problems with product recalls or cost of quality? Those are the kind of things that can really hurt a company."

"Yes and no. I mean, I've started to look in those areas, but only briefly, and so far nothing major has surfaced. I need to keep digging, but first I wanted your input on the direction I should take."

"OK, I think you're telling me, without telling me, that your gut has a thing for this Jeffries guy. And if I understand the makeup of a reporter, your gut thing will get in the way unless it's ruled out, so go ahead and investigate your Jeffries feeling before looking further into the company per se."

"OK but I don't know where to start. Should I check out where he grew up and went to college and that kind of thing to get a better feeling for his personality traits?"

"No. I don't think that's necessary. Let's analyze him from the other direction. Take a look at his recent employment record to see if any similar trends unfold. See if there are any correlations available to strengthen the conjecture you may have about him. If there are, then we dig. If not, we'll go back to the fundamentals. WorldSupplî is a big company and it will be hard to know if something is awry. Use your luncheon location to get to know some people. Pry a little deeper into the culture there so we can get a pulse on the work environment. World-Supplî employees will be your best sources of unwritten information. They'll tell you whether the company needs investigation or not."

"OK. I'll get started right away."

"Good, now out of my office. I've got real work to do."

With that Gette got up and headed for the door. Just as she reached for the knob DiGrande spoke up.

"Georgette, I know you've been working hard on this. You've learned a great deal in a short period and it's appreciated. Just don't tell anyone I said so, or you'll blow my cover."

Gette stood motionless in a fit of bewilderment with her hand on the knob and the door cracked a few inches while she let the complement sink in. Then she turned to DiGrande and said, "You got it boss" and left the room. DiGrande liked her reply. It was much more intelligent than it appeared on the surface and he smiled, slightly, for the first time in days.

Gette left DiGrande's office with a new spring in her step. Amazing, she thought, how one well-placed sentence could alter the entire disposition of a person. She felt renewed and invigorated and starting thinking of clever ways to get the private information she needed for her assessment of Jeffries. She was glad that DiGrande had picked up on her suspicions; it felt somehow like a sign of trust from a boss that was otherwise a tyrant. She vowed to determine if Jeffries was in some way responsible and to do it quickly.

B ryan left for Stanford a few days after the boys had returned from Florida. He left without fanfare, leaving just a simple message with Matt's mother that he was off. Anything less than that would have drawn suspicion and anything more an unwanted resurrection of memories trying desperately to stay hidden.

Matt had about a week to kill before heading to Boston. It was difficult under the circumstances to muster an appropriate degree of enthusiasm, blaming his aloofness on some pre-departure trepidation and general anxiety over the unknowns that lay ahead. When the day finally did arrive his car was prepped for the long journey and loaded with all the important things in his life – his new HP calculator, his turntable, amp, speakers and milk crates full of LP's. A duffle bag of clothes and some toiletries sealed the deal for his life as a dorm rat.

The drive would take him about 12 hours and he intended to do it all in one day, so he spent hours and hours copying to cassette every "favorite" LP in his vast repertoire. Now his Pioneer tape deck would be able to blast a different song the whole way there and he chose Led Zeppelin 2 as the premier entrée for the journey.

Cincinnati to Boston is just one straight shot east. I-90 through Ohio and Pennsylvania is flat and boring, as is the stretch in NY from Buffalo to Albany. The Mass Pike is a little more refreshing as the climb through the Berkshires provides a pleasant panorama of folding hills and plush forestry. Just past Lee in eastern Massachusetts, on an outcropping of rock cut for passage of the thru-way, stood one lone buck with a huge rack of stately antlers. His graceful bold stance spoke of mastery over the harsh mountain environment and it emblazoned in Matt's mind the goal that he had set for himself. The buck triggered a set of emotions so foreign to Matt that his arm hair stood on end. It was as if he were placed there to grant Matt passage from adolescence and at that moment a new clarity of purpose formed in Matt's mind. It was so pronounced that he silenced Skynrd and pulled off the road to let the moment gel.

He was off to college. The direction for the rest of his life was a decision now in his grasp, within his reach. In a few days he would select courses, pick new friends and choose the social fabric within which his personality would mould into an adult. He started thinking about the person he wanted to be. His professional self. His social self. The image that others would carry of him. He wanted to be a leader in his college and academic excellence, though a must, was only one element in the complex mix of success. He decided that he would always stay clean shaven and well dressed. That he would present himself to others and not wait for others to address him. That he would seek out relations with upper classmen in leadership roles and join those societies where influence was greatest. At that moment, sitting silent alongside the Mass Pike, Matt formulated the process he would use to develop into the being that he envisioned himself becoming, and only when it had morphed into a plan did he restart the engine in Ol' Faithful.

Matt's mind kept simulating new and different scenarios as he sped past Springfield and further eastward. His thoughts continued to generate arbitrary situation after situation so he could test his retort and shore up his skills. In the random mix were preposterous circumstances that required him to artfully and successfully pay homage to beauties of the opposite sex and from this dream world wrested a fabulous memory of Sharon hiking up Stone Mountain, an image that brought simultaneously both excitement and calm. Sharon, he hoped, was on her way to Northeastern having perhaps thoughts not that different from his own. Did she ever think about him? Should he try to contact her? He decided he would, not in the first few days, but definitely within the first few weeks.

Soon the bustle of metropolitan traffic gave evidence to the proximity of Matt's quest, in fact his exit was just a few miles away and it conjured up another round of butterflies and wonderment. With utmost caution, he followed a string of cars up Commonwealth where finally he reached a parking area near enough to begin unloading, so he stopped the car and emerged for his first taste of terra firma ala Boston College.

The area was awash with cars in temporary parking locations and people of all types were steadfastly focused on the same ambitious exercise of transporting goods to readied dorm rooms. Matt decided to lock the car and get oriented before delving into the tasks ahead. He quickly located his building and, mounting stairs double fold, came to his floor and found his room in no time. The hallway outside was littered with boxes indicating that he was far from the first to arrive and wondered if his roommate was already there. The door was open.

Inside sitting cross legged on a bed was a lanky guy in torn blue jeans and Grateful Dead tee shirt with a thick shoulder length head of toe colored hair. His first impression was mixed.

"Hey. How's it goin? I'm Tom and you must be my roomie."

"Yeah, I guess so. My name is Matt. Been here long?"

"Just finished unloading and decided to take a break. Where's your stuff?"

"Still in the car. I guess I should start to unload."

"I'll give you hand. Where you from anyway?"

"Cincinnati and you?"

"Upstate N.Y. Saratoga. Ever heard of it?"

"Of course – famous horse racing locale. I heard it really rocks in August. Isn't there a big concert place there too?" He asked as they walked.

Yeah. SPAC. Saratoga Performing Arts Center. Has great concerts. The Who, The Dead, Crosby Stills Nash and Young. I've seen them and lots more too. It's an amphitheatre style place. You can buy lawn seat tickets pretty cheap, smoke some j's and have a blast hangin' out with friends."

"Sounds great. Here's my car, Tom meet Ol' Faithful, 'Ol Faithful this is Tom."

"Good wheels man. I like Volvo's. You keeping it here?"

"Yup. Not sure where the parking is or anything yet, but I'll find out."

The two continued their piece-meal conversation while emptying the car and got to know a bit about each other in the process. Tom seemed to be a nice guy, but perhaps not Matt's type since his priority in life was partying and rock-n-roll ahead of everything else. Matt was familiar with the type from high school but it wasn't ever his scene.

A few hours later they had their room all set, Matt on one side and Tom on the other. Tom was really impressed with Matt's stereo and took control of spinning some LP's while they organized their drawers, desk tops and closets. Matt's walls were rather barren since he failed to bring any personal items while Tom's were adorned with posters of all his favorite bands. The Yes poster was pretty cool and Matt vowed to make his puke-tan walls disappear under posters of his own.

The first days of freshman life are akin to the first time you ride a major rollercoaster. Everything is all upside down and the world passes by at the speed of light. As each minute of the day unfolds it presents a virgin experience to deal with, from your first exposure to the college book store to your first cafeteria meal. Every person you see is also new and unique, so a silent current that runs throughout the entire freshman population cradles you as an unspoken compatriot, a BC'er, an Eagle, and the notion of it automatically creates an unexplainable yet tangible bond.

Matt was totally spent after setting up his room and cashed in early. When he woke it was just after dawn and he rose in eagerness to spend much of next day walking, investigating, orienting. He checked his route to classes, to the athletic fields and campus stores. The layout of various quads and eating locales. The girl's dorms and the newly controversial co-ed one. He took it all in and had the general scope of BC under control by mid-afternoon on Thursday. Tomorrow there was a formal orientation meeting and a freshman welcoming party, but the weekend was free and because Monday was Labor Day, classes didn't start until Tuesday.

After preparing for class to the extent possible, which eventuated late on Friday afternoon, it was time to relax and meet some fellow students so Matt ventured along rows of college affiliated housing to check out the doings of the upper classmen. Everywhere he went there were parties and with each party were dozens of kegs, hundreds of plastered students and thousands of plastic cups, lying about in every imaginable state. Music blaring from over-woofed stereos could barely be heard above the vocal chaos of each environ. Pockets of students catching up from their summer hiatus were seen routinely chugging 16 ounce beers followed by several series of over emphatic belches and bouts of raucous laughter. As Matt strolled by in awe of the carefree abandon, he spotted one house where the atmosphere was more reserved, but still open and casual, and hastened in that direction for introductions.

What Matt found was an energetic group of student scholars that were the life blood of the Boston College Chronicle, the school newspaper. The conservations in each cluster varied greatly in content but not in zeal, each being animated to the level of a debate, whether it involved the national scandal du jour or coverage of the next Women's Field Hockey game. Before Matt knew what happened he was knee deep in dialogue on the US presence in Vietnam, voicing adamantly his objections to a war without purpose. He spoke with enough panache and fluidity that before long a bystander asked him if he was interested in expanding his sphere of influence.

"I'm not sure I know what you mean."

"I'm saying that you need to do something more with your opinions than to simply broadcast them to nearby ears." He said waving his arms at the small group.

"How exactly do I do that?"

"Well, you can start by working with us on the paper. Interested?"

When Matt left the group later that evening he was a full-fledged member of the newspaper gang and even had an assignment. He was asked, as a member of the freshman class, to write a brief article on the helpfulness of the orientation meeting – what was good about it, how it could be better. If it had a noteworthy feel, then they would print it in the next release.

S aturday morning arrived quickly and after Tom and Matt ate break-fast together Matt decided to draft his newspaper article. He began with an outline that logged the meeting topics and quickly tossed it aside. Then he listed the strengths and weaknesses of the presented material and again felt it too mundane. Finally, he personalized a list of things he wanted to know about and found that much of it was absent from the meeting material, so he focused on augmenting the meeting with answers to the questions that remained. Unfortunately, the questions were social in character and subjective in nature and demanded research to be answered with any semblance of knowing. What Matt thought was an easy exercise was just made into a quick study of underground BC and shortly after lunch he hastened to begin finding answers to his queue of difficult questions.

Matt's mission proved valuable in many respects. Because he needed input from a multitude of tenured students he made acquaintances with a variety of people whom otherwise he would never have met. And, since many thought his article worthwhile, gave openly their own list of lessons learned and things "they wish they knew". The result was a gold mine of unusual BC student trivia that ranged from the best times, places and methods for meeting the opposite sex, to the best laundry mats and uses of public transportation, and many things in between.

In the process Matt developed a sense for extracting the right knowledge from the right people by asking open ended questions and guiding (or halting) the response. He quickly learned that when he asked "what's the one thing you know now that you wish you knew as a freshman?" the response was both immediate and effervescent or required examples to elicit the right memories. Matt discovered that he possessed a here-to-for unknown gift for getting people to talk by simply being an open, caring and inquisitive person. He collected more material than he knew how to manage and by Monday afternoon distilled it into a witty and eye catching piece of sound journalism with innuendo sufficient to render it folklore. The staff loved it too for it personified every facet of BC life, presenting reflections of valuable daily routines that oft went unnoticed, and they ran it as the front page in the Autumn opener.

The article gave Matt notoriety in his circles on par with the stars of the football team and his acceptance as a writer opened avenues with those involved with the paper that were normally closed to freshman. Within weeks he developed a routine with classes, exercise and working on articles that left him consumed but happy.

"Hey man, you need to take a break. Too much work is going to drive you crazy. Gotta take it easy once in awhile. Smell the roses. Know what I mean?" Tom said one Friday afternoon.

"Yeah, I know what you mean. I like being busy but you're right, I need to relax, which is what I'm planning to do this weekend." Matt replied.

"That's good to hear. There's a lot going on. Parties all over campus, a pep rally tonight, a great football game tomorrow and then you can always go downtown to the Combat Zone if you really need a change."

"I don't think the Zone is for me. I'll just stick around here. First I've got to do some laundry. Care to join me?"

"It's Friday afternoon man. I'd rather have a root canal. Sunday is my day for laundry. Laundry and the books – they go together a lot better than the beers I'm thinkin' about."

"OK. But the laundry mats are empty now so I'm gonna get my clothes done and then head out for some partying. See you later."

"Later. We're headed to Crossroads if you care to join us."

With that Matt grabbed his duffle bag and headed to Ol' Faithful for a ride to the laundry reckoned best by the interviews he conducted for the article. Why not be true to his written word? Best to live by the sword so you won't die by it.

When Matt got to Ol' Faithful he noticed some paper under the driver's side wiper. It was too large to be a ticket, so thinking it an advert he began to crumple it for chucking just when he noticed that it was handwritten. Someone placed a note on his windshield? That's odd, must have been a prank from one of the newspaper guys. He decided to go along with the prank and straightened the crumpled mess for reading.

"Dear Matt – I think this is your car, at least it looks like the one I remember from Stone Mountain. How are things? I'm fine and school is going great. I happened to be at BC today with a friend for a party and as we passed this car I absolutely freaked out. What a coincidence, huh? Look me up sometime at Northeastern. Sharon."

Matt couldn't believe his eyes. A note from Sharon? A note from Sharon! The idea was beyond belief, and he became immediately consumed by the possibility of her being in close proximity. Without realizing it he began to scan the area in case she left it just minutes earlier. No dice, price. She was not to be seen.

Not knowing what to do or how to respond Matt took Ol' Faithful to his appointed destination and began to cram laundry into every available corner of several empty machines. His mind was so preoccupied that the doors were closed, the money was inserted and the machines were spinning before he realized his failure to administer soap. Damn! Now what? The machines won't open once they've started so Matt was afraid that he would have to do each load twice and waste an extra hour or so. Just then the store manager sauntered past.

"Hey Mister, excuse me. I messed up and started these machines before I remembered to add the soap. Is there any way to stop them so I can add it?

"Yeah there is, just give me a minute. Happens more often than you think. I just need to trip them at the breaker and reset the breakers after you add the soap. I'll go back and trip them. When they stop, add the soap, close the doors and holler at me so I know when it's safe for them to restart."

Matt felt instantly relieved. Sharon was at BC and he had to scour the grounds to find what party she was attending. While the wash washed, he conjured up a method for covering the maximum amount of real estate in the shortest period of time and when the dryer cycle finally spun to a halt Matt grabbed the clothing within, jammed it into the duffle and raced from the establishment. He still needed to shower and dress before embarking on his search and wanted to do so as quickly as possible. He knew that several notorious parties were planned for this evening and was determined to visit each until he found and got to embrace that lovely morsel of femininity. Sharon's image burned bright in his mind's eye and consumed his being from head to toe. Why hadn't he contacted her earlier?

First stop on his journey was a group of apartments on Beacon Street followed by a swing through the dorms off Hammond and then on to the bars on Commonwealth. Going on foot was the only way to make tracks sufficient to the task and Matt made his tracks at a pace like the trotters at Churchill Downs. He met several friends along the way and stopped briefly at one point to down a beer while he scanned the patrons for signs of his quest. No sight of her in the first group of parties.

The dorms were going crazy on this particular night. Psyched up from a pep rally held earlier overly jacked-up party animals were stacked everywhere imbibing everything from light beer to Ever Clear. Some guys were still tossing footballs in the grass while scores of nicely clad girls ferreted about on the outskirts. Dorm room windows, open to the evening air, were stuffed with KHL model 17's or equivalent, each beating vibrantly to the heartbeat of their master's music. The cacophony of overlapping sound was so pervasive that it faded to white in the distant air.

Finding Sharon in this madhouse was akin to finding Jimmy Hoffa at a police convention. Only lady luck could yield a positive result and that lady was off duty tonight, so Matt headed for Commonwealth.

The bars were all jammed. The Texas Longhorns were in town for the football game and the place was so crazy that finding someone you intended to meet was next to impossible, let alone someone whose whereabouts was unknown and was not on the lookout. In despair Matt decided to give up the search and instead, stop at Crossover's for a beer. As he entered he couldn't believe his eyes. Sharon was sitting at a table in the corner. But it wasn't even close to the way he dreamed it to be. Instead of a demure setting where each find simultaneously the twinkle in each other's eyes and run to greet warmly like lovers lost from raging storms, there sat Sharon enraptured in conversation with a tall handsomely dressed and obviously rich college male. It was entirely wrong. It was a journey doomed from the onset. It was a balloon popped.

Matt's emotions changed instantly from conquistador of love to purveyor of doubt. Who the hell did he think he was? He met this girl once, and only briefly and now he acted like he owned her, like there was some form of unwritten but understood commitment or bond? What a fool. She had no obligation to him. What did he think? That she was just sitting around waiting for him to mysteriously show up? They really weren't even friends; only acquaintances. The emotional 180 that enveloped Matt caused him to undertake a physical one as well, and he exited Crossroads just seconds after his arrival.

The cool evening air allowed Matt to once again breathe, quelling a few of the emotional peaks within. In front of him lay a honky-tonk bar that seemed his best bet for a friend so he sauntered across Commonwealth determined there to quench his fire with some libation. When he entered a group of served revelers scampered away from the bar leaving in their wake a stool devoid of patron so Matt was quick to saddle up and order a double Jack on the rocks.

"Here you go fella. Double Jack. Bottoms up and good health."

"Thanks pal. I need it." Matt said while hoisting the swill for fast, full delivery. He wasn't much of a drinker and it formed a burning path from lips to groin that felt like a lava flow on Big Island as it went down. It took a minute for focus to return to normal and for the lava to go from burn to smolder to glow. When the shock to the midsection subsided and was replaced with a buzz to the brain, Matt gladly ordered another. The second went down quickly as well but with less of the abuse sustained from the first and the third was consumed at a more normal pace.

In short order Matt was feeling no pain and he exchanged his failure to secure time with Sharon with "saving the world from itself" talk that only random bar conversations can muster. It was one of those evenings where brilliant and elaborately enumerated mind-blowing solutions to global problems fail to re-materialize on awakening in the morn, having emanated from a swirling carousel of euphoric brain waves, delivered through slurring speech that garbled from its circumference.

In no time Matt turned from down trodden mess to enlightened reveler, becoming rapidly verbose, and loud to the border of belligerence. The alcohol was working its magic, but his pace of consumption was far greater than the rate of absorption and as time marched on its toll became evermore evident. He was drunk before he knew it and the bar went from friend to foe as it decided to spin out of control. Matt tried to get hold of himself but stumbled in his attempt and almost fell down, a lucky hand plant on a nearby table serving barely to keep him off all fours. He knew only one thing - he had to get out of there.

Matt made cautiously for the door, stepping with slow deliberate strides and using props along the way to stay somewhat erect. He made the door just as some people were entering and slipped through without having to open it himself. A God send.

The street lights were blinding as he made his way back, the night air providing just enough of a revival to keep him in motion. He didn't realize the danger that he presented to himself as his staggering took him off the sidewalk and into the street. Several cars honked and jeers levied from open car windows failed to register with Matt at all. At that moment Sharon and her girlfriend were driving by enroute to another party and saw Matt as he stumbled and fell beside the road.

"Man, that guy is really in trouble. Someone's going to run him over."

"I couldn't agree more. Turn around. We'd better help him before it's too late."

With that Sharon's girlfriend quickly hung a left into a nearby parking lot and was able to swing back onto Commonwealth heading the other direction. They pulled up alongside the felled student to protect him from traffic and got out to size up the situation. Matt was almost unconscious.

"Oh my God!" Sharon shouted. "I know this guy. He's the one I was telling you about. The one on whose car we left the note."

"Matt, wake up. It's Sharon. Matt, are you OK?"

Sharon started pummeling Matt's arm and shoulder to roust him from his stupor and he responded by rolling over and puking in the gutter. The puke kept coming until the heaves were dry and Matt was exhausted. He lay back down and tried to fall asleep as a cop car pulled up behind them and the officer got out.

"Seems to be the problem ladies?"

"Nothing officer. We saw this guy on the ground and came back to see if he was OK. It looks like he's going to live, just needs a ride home. Can you help us get him in the car?"

"You gonna take a stranger home?"

"It's a funny story, sir, but he's not a stranger. I met him this summer in Georgia while on vacation and . ."

"Alright, alright. I don't have time for the story. This evening is full of trouble. I'll help you get him in the car but you go straight home and don't try any more partying. Got it?"

"Yes sir, no problem."

With that they dragged Matt's lifeless, puke stained body into the back seat and with all the windows cranked down and the fan on high, headed towards Matt's car. They found it a few minutes later and Sharon fished through his pockets for the keys. Together they managed to wrestle him into the backseat and he lay there sound asleep with drool puddling beneath his chin, reeking of alcohol.

"I can't just leave him like this. What should we do?"

"He'll be fine. I think we should head back home. Let him sleep it off. He won't remember anything anyway."

"OK. But I should at least leave him a note."

"Are you nuts? The bum just about ruined our evening. You must really like this guy or something. What gives?"

"I know this sounds crazy, but there's something special about this boy. Someday I hope you get the chance to see." Sharon said scribbling briefly on a notepad. Then, they locked Matt in his car with his keys and headed for home.

The sun shone early through the cracked windows in Matt's Volvo wresting him from the unfit sleep through which his night passed. As his world returned to the present so did his lack of understanding. He had no idea why his neck ached so badly, how he ended up in Ol' Faithful, or why the windows were sweating with the water his breathe had thereon condensed. He did know that his mouth was dryer than cotton on a desert ground, that the taste in it held the essence of bile and that his bladder was on a crash course for rupture. He sat up abruptly and in the process awakened hurting brain cells that revolted by giving him more spinnies. The day was not going to start easily.

In a sufficient but quasi state of consciousness Matt finally managed to get focus of his surroundings. On the floor at his feet were his keys and a note.

"Dear Matt, finally we meet again. Perhaps not in the best of circumstances. You probably won't even remember. Give me a call and I'll fill you in. Sharon."

"What the hell?" thought Matt. "I saw Sharon last night? Oh, shit! She saw me and I must have been blitzed at the time. I don't even remember. Now what do I do?"

He instantly got in a fit of anger over the stupidity of his drunkenness and in the process felt an overwhelming urge to puke again. Not only did he lose his chance to spend time with Sharon, but he felt like hell and had dug himself into a deep hole on top of it all.

"Now what idiot?" he thought.

After a shower, chocolate milk ala Tom's recommendation and plenty of Excedrin, Matt restored himself to about 50% of capacity, enough to start his recovery plan with Sharon. He went through a number of elaborate scenarios before realizing that an apology was the only sensible one so he dressed, found a florist, bought a dozen roses and headed to Northeastern.

Northeastern is located closer to downtown just a bit south of Fenway Park in a part of Boston entirely different from the bountiful area around BC. It's definitely in a more city style environment, but just a short jaunt north of Huntington Ave there are some really great city parks and the Charles River if you need to get away from the congestion and chaos.

Matt parked near campus and started strolling the area for signs of dorm life, or an admin building, – anything that might help to guide him to Sharon. He ran into some students at a coffee house and, after asking how he might find the dorm room or phone number of a freshman, they directed him to a student housing facility.

Since it was Saturday the place was pretty much vacant. Fortunately, an RA from one dorm was in checking the bulletin board for updates on assignments and other stuff and Matt, after giving her a brief rendition of his plight, got her to check the dorm listings for Sharon's whereabouts.

"I'm breaking all the rules by doing this you know. In fact, I can't give you her room number. The best I can do is ask you to wait nearby and I'll go to her room and let her know that you're here, that is, if she's in."

"That sounds wonderful. Thank you so much. It's more than gracious of you."

They walked out in silence and took a left towards a group of fairly plain 4 story buildings that were obviously dorms. In the middle of the quad the RA stopped with Matt alongside her.

"You better wait here." She said.

"That won't be necessary." Matt said as he spotted Sharon exiting a nearby door. "Sharon's right there and I think she sees me. Here," Matt said drawing a rose for the RA. "Thanks so much for you help."

Sharon stopped so abruptly when she saw Matt that her hair flipped slightly and she had to straighten it. Then a radiant smile filled her beautiful face and Matt laughed, improving slightly his state of nervous anxiety.

"Hey." Matt said sheepishly.

"Hey to you too. How are you feeling?"

"Foolish. Stupid. And worst of all blank. I don't remember a thing so I don't even know how to start apologizing."

"What've you got there?" Sharon said pointing at the roses.

"Oh, here. I bought these for you. There were a dozen but I gave one to the RA that helped me."

"Eleven roses huh? Well that's a start." Sharon said laughing. "Let's get these in some water and then we can talk." With that she took Matt's hand and in silence started for her room.

When they got there Sharon put the roses in a tall coffee mug and Matt said "Sharon, I have to tell you what happened last night. The whole truth and nothing but the truth. It's embarrassing so please don't laugh, but first I have to know how you ran into me and how I ended up in the back seat of my car."

Sharon gave an elaborate and intentionally lavish account of their chance encounter with Matt. As she described the event Matt kept looking down and shaking his head in total embarrassment.

"Picture of the perfect student, huh? Well, first off thank you for saving my life, or at least keeping me from doing myself further harm. Second, I just want to say how nice it is to see you again and how happy I am to be with you."

"Thank you."

"Now I have a confession to make. I got your note yesterday afternoon just as I was getting ready to do some laundry and as I did the laundry I made my mind up to scour the campus in search of you. I was kicking myself for not getting in touch earlier and was determined to find you and spend some time if that were possible. I went practically everywhere I could think of and didn't see you until I ventured into Crossroads later that evening. That's when I saw you, paying rather close attention to that handsome and well dressed guy. It made me crazy. Instead of acting like someone with an ounce of maturity and coming over to say hello, I got instantly angry."

"Don't you mean jealous?" she interrupted.

"Yeah, I guess so. I was jealous; an emotion that I, admittedly, had no right to have. Anyway, I got upset enough that I decided to look for friendship in a bottle of Jack Daniels. A bit too much Jack to be sure."

"To be sure, you dope."

"I am a dope and I'm sorry. I'm an idiot and I figured the best I could do was to level with you and apologize." Matt said passionately.

The few seconds of silence that followed his delivery felt like hours. He was looking at Sharon and her at him, neither with a word, thinking that she was ready to dismiss him forever. Then Sharon said calmly "What are doing this afternoon? Want to go for a walk?"

The sense of relief her words gave Matt were more profound than anything he had ever experienced. He fell back on her bed like a sack of potatoes and stared at the ceiling silently giving thanks.

"What's the matter?"

"Nothing. Absolutely nothing. I was afraid that I had completely blown any chance I may have had to be your friend and I'm just relieved, that's all."

Sharon quickly bent over, pecked him on the cheek and with a yank to his feet guided Matt into the hall for their walk.

"Hey, I said I was relieved. I didn't say I was going for a walk with you."

And she punched his arm and took his hand in hers.

That afternoon with Sharon proved to be a life changing event. Before she entered his life Matt was consumed but far from fulfilled. Now he felt an indescribably pervasive wholeness. In her presence the world was a wondrous place, perfect in every sense. Sharon gave him support, strength, encouragement. She gave him empathy, camaraderie, laughter. She extended to him as much intimacy in each everyday kiss as she did when they were ravishing each other's nakedness. It all rolled up into that one big unbelievable word – love.

They quickly became an inseparable couple and all the joy that Sharon gave Matt he gave her in return. Their relationship was truly healthy. Neither found cause for pretense in the presence of the other, both being equally at ease when silent as when captivated in an intense discussion.

Time flew at an unprecedented rate, first freshman year, then years two and three, and before they knew it they were seniors looking at each other and wondering what was next. By then it was unspoken, but understood, that they would spend their lives together.

"Hey sport. We graduate in another semester. So what should we do? Stay here and go to grad school? Get jobs and start our careers? Join the Peace Corp? What do you think?"

"Are we doing this as a team or going it alone?"

"As a team, of course. Or at least, I thought of course."

"Then isn't there something else to consider?"

"There are lots of things to consider. That's why I'm bringing it up."

"Don't you think you need to consider making me an honest woman?"

"You are honest. You're the most honest person I know."

"That's not what I meant."

"Perhaps you should be more specific then."

"Perhaps you should stop being a horse's ass."

"What do you mean? What'd I do?"

"You know exactly what I mean and what you're doing. What are you afraid of?"

"Hold it right there woman. I start a civil conversation about the future and within a minute you get all huffy and call me a horse's ass. What's that all about?"

"It's about you being a pigheaded male idiot. Plain and simple."

"You think it's plain and simple, huh? Well take a look at this and tell me what's plain and simple." And with that Matt opened a stunning, antique style, 4 pronged diamond engagement ring and showed Sharon that he knew exactly what she meant. He got on his knees with the ring in his hand and said "Sharon, you are the love of my life. I knew it the minute I laid eyes on you at Stone Mountain. I've been a happy and fulfilled person every second since you entered it and my most important aspiration is to humbly grow old and wise in your presence. Please, Sharon, will you be my wife?"

Sharon sat silently so fully aglow that a radiant shield of energy cast a halo shaped aura around her presence. She held her hand askance with fingers extended and Matt slid the diamond perfectly on her ring finger. It was simple and stately and beautiful and elevated her elegant hand from a thing of watchful grace to a masterpiece of art.

After staring at the ring for a minute in awestricken silence she said "All you want to do is grow old with me? You better want to make some money too!" And she threw herself into Matt's arms, wetting the front of his shirt with tears of happiness.

From that moment their conversations were refocused from the day's challenges to their vision of a future together. Both agreed that they needed a change from college life and elected to start investigating careers. The process was simple for Matt. Throughout his four years at BC he continued to be a force on the school newspaper and felt desperately ready to move into the ranks of the profession. He had already amassed a stunning resumé with excellent grades, a plethora of student activities, summer internships with local rags, and awards from his work on the BC Chronicle. In short, he was very marketable at the tender age of 22 and on graduation had landed an excellent starting job with the Chicago Tribute. So in June of graduation year, as an engaged couple, they made their way to the windy city in Ol' Faithful to start their new life together.

B ryan's trip to Stanford was filled with a mixed bag of emotions that ran wider and deeper than the Grand Canyon. At their depths, when thoughts of the Miami fiasco loomed pervasive, they ran cold and violent like the Colorado River. At their heights they were as rapturous as the splendor of sun painted hues on eastern canyon walls, especially when his thoughts veered to a mind's eye creation of California coeds gracing the lawns at Stanford. But the highs and lows, though new and unusual experiences, were nothing compared to the blank empty feeling Bryan got when he thought about Matt. No matter how hard he tried Bryan was unable to break through the raster screen blocking his thoughts of Matt and their ruined friendship. What weeks before was certain to be a lifelong brotherhood was already reduced to something surreal and distant and by the time Stanford came into view he locked it there, seemingly forever.

Being alone was never Bryan's strong suite so after settling in and going on a brief exploratory jaunt across campus, he decided to grab some beers and a towel to sun in Oval Park. When he arrived there were plenty of students of various sorts doing everything from Frisbee football to blowing joints to practicing yoga. The spectrum of diversity was like nothing he had ever witnessed and neither were the girls. Tall, lean athletic hippie-clad women with braided headbands, tie dye tees and hole-laden jeans intermixed comfortably with sorority sisters clad in conservative blouses and slacks. Many were strolling in a manner that bespoke of relaxed randomness so Bryan thought best to sit and let them pass than travel and gawk.

When one trio of suntanned beauties ventured past a third time Bryan immediately decided to bestow upon them his first "college try."

"Ladies, care for a cold beverage? Just happen to have a few cold Coors left for someone with a hankering for a good brew. Name's Bryan. From out east. Where are you gals from?"

"I could use a sip, Bryan, beer boy from back east. I hear you can't get Coors there. Is it true?" Their leader said with the panache befitting a lifelong tenant of opulence.

"That is true, yes; they don't truck any of this lovely Banquet beer east of the Mississippi, so getting your hands on one is something really special. They don't brew young ladies like you back there either."

"Is that right? So does that mean that getting your hands on one of us would be really something special as well? Nice pick-up line Back East Bryan. I think I'll just pick up this special beer and keep on walking. Thanks." She said while stooping to grab a cold one.

"Wait a minute Special! Don't I at least get a thank you kiss for the beer? I'm alone and thousands of miles from home for the first time in my life and all I want to do is make new friends. What'd ya say?" Bryan said as he got to his feet.

Without a word Special looked straight into Bryan's eyes and with surgical precision cupped her hand gently under his chin. Then ever so slowly she closed the gap between their lips and opened her mouth slightly to let linger one expertly executed tongue moistened smooch that made happy loins in Bryan's midriff. "That should be payment adequate to the gift, Back East Bryan." She said, as she turned abruptly and sauntered off with her two companions laughing in unison.

Bryan was dumbfounded to be beaten at his own game. What a girl this "Special", he thought, and popped another Banquet before settling back for more grazing.

Within no time Bryan established himself as the grand master of bullshit, developing in the process acquaintances from all over campus. He studied just enough to keep his averages around B, spending all other time networking with wealthy studs to build his image and flirting with pretty girls to feed his libido, which demanded two women a week and one new one each month. With California being the free love leader in the country, and San Francisco its capital, finding a willing partner was ultimately not that difficult, just time consuming. In a few months Bryan had a repertoire of girls he could call on to feed his endless hunger, but too much was never enough and the more he fucked the more he wanted to. Each day the thought of the ultimate smell, the fullest breast, the sweetest pussy and most supple ass consumed each stray thought. Every girl he passed while walking to class was immediately undressed and converted to a fantastic image of naked sexuality. Bryan was a sex maniac with no known capacity to be satiated, like a Roman emperor feasting, retching and feasting some more.

By Bryan's junior year his experiments with sex left him a reputation that preceded him like the dust from Pig Pen's clothing. Even freshman girls, within weeks of arrival, were warned of Bryan's obsession and were quick to throw up defenses when he approached. Sex was still available but only with the wild girls who were loose or obsessed themselves and after time even his games of bondage and sadism no longer gave cause for the continuous hours of arousal that he lived for. With pleasure from new young bodies faded like a distant train Bryan took to masturbation for his primary release, ejaculating into a mirror four or more times a day until his penis ached and could accept no more. And when he frequented bars his purpose was to drink and think – to drink beyond coherence – to think of how fun it would be to hurt some unsuspecting coed with the thrust of his shaft.

In February of his senior year he attended a job fair where the realization of life beyond graduation opened a window in his brain, awakening a new reality. Life is more than just chasing pussy and satisfying the moment. Life has to be given serious thought. Life needs foresight to be guided to a fruitful conclusion and foresight, to be valuable, requires purposeful application of intellect, an attribute that Bryan had thus far stuffed away as if asleep.

The recognition that in a few months he need be gainfully employed snapped Bryan back into the mode of old when he and Matt fervently planned alike their business and social endeavors both. The effect created a focus for Bryan sufficiently consuming that it crowned the chase to satiate his libido and within days Bryan's demeanor changed from raging sex maniac to consummate business professional.

The metamorphosis was all encompassing. Not only was his mental state of mind radicalized but also his dress, grooming, posture and personality - revamped to the role of a hungry emerging graduate inspired to climb the corporate ladder. Before long he had arranged a number of interviews, mostly with emerging tech companies focused on computer technologies, and they resulted in two job offers available on graduation.

The effort he expended to secure a post-graduation place in the world was uncanny and with it came into existence a new Bryan dedicated to controlling every aspect of the world within his sphere of influence. Early into his first job Bryon learned that power was granted to he whom assumed it and that increased power came by virtue of an increasing sphere of influence.

He was quick to study the behaviors of senior management and young fast-trackers alike and soon found himself capable of manipulating those around him for his own gain without their knowledge or understanding. For Bryan, the capacity to control without being in control was an art that he studied fervently, like the Dojo Master studies his trade. His innate understanding of computers, in conjunction with his newly developed business acumen, gained Bryon notoriety across a wide array of influential people who granted him responsibilities that belied his years.

Power was Bryon's ultimate end and money, Bryon fast learned, was the means. So he studied business accounting, secured a CPA degree, and applied himself to learning the details of his firm's chart of accounts. He now knew every aspect of the company books, from the debits and credits in the account ledger system to the process for rolling up the corporate income statement and balance sheet. He felt invincible yet still somewhat empty, as if something were missing. His efforts left him feeling vague and tangential because he wasn't pulling any strings, just learning all the strings to be pulled, and found little satisfaction in life without overall control.

So he decided to exercise his newly acquired knowledge in his own way, on his own, independent from all others. It didn't take long before he was able to find an artful means for modifying account entries and moving small items on the income statement and balance sheet of his division. He studied ways to manipulate numbers and create false entries, only to reverse them before the next month's closing.

It was the start of an elaborate master plan that ultimately would materialize when Bryan became disenfranchised with WorldSupplî.

B ryan wondered how Matt would respond to his proposal during their upcoming dinner. He sincerely hoped that the need for leveraging the past would stay dormant, but he seriously doubted it. Using DiGrande as an intermediary was the only way he could think of to safely launder the money he was collecting. DiGrande had all the right banking connections and added that important invisible layer to the tangled web he needed to weave, to make the scheme foolproof in its transparency.

He managed to reserve hump-day night the week following their brief phone conversation for a reunion dinner and couldn't stop thinking about it. The scene had to be perfect, comfortable but not stuffy, private but not isolated, good nouveau cuisine with artistic appeal that wasn't just artistic and a great wine list, so he chose Charlie Trotter's, at seven, for two.

Matt called Bryan beforehand to confirm the dinner and asked if they should head there together.

"Great idea Wild Man, but I'm on the west side making my way towards the city, so it's probably easier to just meet at the restaurant."

"That's fine with me, see you at seven."

Matt decided to take a cab and as he was settling the fee glanced westward up Armitage and spotted Bryan. Bryan hadn't changed a bit. He was dressed in designer clothes fitted to perfection with a lightweight dress coat draped loosely over one arm. His other hand held a phone to his ear and it was obvious by the excitement in his conversation that it was something of importance, at least to him. As Bryan approached Trotter's he stopped to conclude his call and with a snap of the phone lid held a long, deep smile while searching Matt's face before speaking.

"Wild Man! How the hell are you? You look tremendous. Just like you did more than 20 years ago. I can't believe my eyes! What a specimen of middle age. Still a lady killer! Even now you must have to beat 'em away, you ol' dog."

"Well, if it isn't Bryan Jeffries, world famous playboy and all-round wheeler dealer of the 21st century. You're looking great yourself, young man. Come here and give me a hug, you a-hole."

The ensuing embrace was like a time machine, their presence together conjuring up multitudes of dust laden memories as clear as if they were thoughts rendered last before bed the previous evening. They broke and headed toward the restaurant wondering while they walked where the evening's conversation would take them, which path of the past it would open.

"Bryan, party of two for dinner."

"Welcome. Your table is ready. Right this way sir."

They were seated in the second of four elegant dining rooms adjacent to a window. A privacy wall on one side gave them ample opportunity to speak freely and with discretion.

"Thank you my dear. This will work fine. Drink wine Matt, or would you like something else?"

"I love wine. Perhaps too much. A nice bottle of red suits me. Your pick."

"Hard to beat California for good wines. I went through a period where I experimented with California reds from a number of different regions, just to get a feel for their differences, and their strengths by varietal. Then I decided to develop a taste for wines from Spain, Portugal and Argentina and afterwards France and Italy. Now I bounce around depending on how I feel and tonight I feel like rejoicing, so it's either a Chateauneuf du Pape or an Amarone. Any preference?"

"None whatsoever. Both are fabulous."

"Then we'll do French tonight. Their Amarone's not one of the best anyway."

An endless and bountiful conversation followed their perusal of the menu; it continued unbroken for over an hour without straying from countless anecdotes of yore told with all the fervor, zeal and boisterousness that accompanied their return to adolescent personalities. They were 18 again.

"Remember the time I had a run in with that stupid bookie? He didn't know what hit him. He started out wanting to beat my ass and before we ended the argument I had him working for us."

"Oh my God that was hilarious. What a set of brass balls we had! Funniest part of all is how well that relationship worked out. Guy made us a ton of money."

"Remember what studs we were our senior year? Every girl in the class had a crush on us. Hell, we were passing second base as freshmen and routinely hit home runs as seniors. Those were the days my friend." Bri boasted.

"I remember alright and with fondness too, but perhaps with a bit of guilt as well."

"Nothing to be guilty about Wild Man. We were just young that's all. Just young."

They refilled their glasses to bridge the momentary silence that enveloped the table after mention was made of guilt, and then the conservation swayed to queries of present day life, both personal and professional.

Bryan gave a quick rendition of the steps he took to his current position as Chief Technology Officer at WorldSupplî. He also sailed through the foibles of his many female companions and conquests, stopping only briefly to mention that marriage was never amongst them. Now in his forties, lonely and without immediate family, he questioned the intelligence of his decisions and the paradox that was his life.

Matt, who was more apt to shy from discussions of self, mumbled sheepishly and without flamboyance the anthology of his career ladder. He also mentioned quickly the circumstances surrounding his contact with Sharon at Boston College and how they instantly became friends and lovers. This was the one area of Matt's life that he spoke of openly and with a pride that he couldn't help, for as hard as he tried, he couldn't hide the importance, or the value, that his wife and family meant to him.

"Wild Man, I too, at least for a fleeting moment, well more than a fleeting moment, had that same great feeling of love. Unfortunately, I guess it was infatuation disguised as love because now after little more than two years of living with the same girl I've got to get back to my old way of life, as a bachelor, yes as a hound dog, but a successful one, even now in my forties."

"You've been living with someone for the last couple years? Why didn't you mention it?"

"Well, as Ronald Reagan used to begin every statement, because it's partly the reason why I wanted to get in touch with you. You see, I've come into a lot of money and this girl and I have been together long enough that common law gives her rights to my estate. Rights that I just can't bear to see exercised. I've got to find a way to rid myself of my estate value before I make her my ex-girlfriend."

"OK. But I don't see how that has anything to do with me."

"Well, it does and it doesn't. I need to hide a bunch of money and I need to have a path to a numbered account that makes the connection impossible to trace. That's where you fit in. Since we haven't seen or heard from each other in over 20 years no one in their right mind would ever think that you could be part of my scheme. And I know that you have plenty of the right connections in the banking industry." Bryan said while refilling their glasses from the second bottle of Pape.

"What's this all about? You mean you contacted me and set up this dinner under the pretense of reliving old times when actually it was all about involving me in a ponzi scheme? I can't believe this. No, actually I can believe this. My gut told me there was more to this reunion than a few innocent laughs."

"I'm sorry you feel that way. It's not altogether true. I've thought of you often over the years and only now did I muster the courage to establish contact. And yes, I'm sure that my current situation helped remove whatever final obstacle may have been in the way. Matt, we were young and scared, and parted company hastily in the only way we thought we could. I lost my best friend, one of my only friends, and certainly the only one that I ever considered my brother."

"I can't break the law on your behalf."

"I'm not asking you to break the law. Just hear me out. It might be bending it a little, that's all. The money is mine and I should have the right to do with it as I see fit, even if the motive is back handed. I worked hard for that money and I'll be damned if I should be required to give it up because of some stupid ill-conceived law."

"You're going to have to find some other way to deal with your issues. I'm not getting involved. My life is too complicated without having it mottled in your quagmire. Excuse me; I've got to use the men's room."

When Matt got up Bryan immediately summonsed the waitress for their bill, handing her more than enough cash to cover it with an excellent tip to boot. Now the only record of their visit to Trotter's was a reservation for Bryan, however they determined to spell it. Bryan knew too well, regardless of the evening's outcome that every track had to be covered, every movement a controlled articulation, now and from this point forward.

Matt returned looking a little less troubled but none-the-less disheveled. He used the few minutes in the bathroom to shake away the pleasant glow that wine, food and laughter had extemporaneously overshadowed from the reality of Bryan's message. The effect was sobering enough to make a priest on call for last rites refuse even the purest soul his ear on final breath.

"Bri, I'm gonna leave now. I loved the laughter. I loved the reminiscing. But I can't let you tie any strings to me. I have a life that is open and honest and I can't jeopardize my values or what I have accomplished to support your petty angst. I'm gonna thank you for dinner now and take my leave."

"Wild Man. Please. You're over-reacting. I need your help. I know it's no small favor, but I have nowhere else to turn. I need you and your connections to create an irrevocably untraceable route to hide my money. I'm being honest. Too honest. If I were being deceitful that would be one thing. But I'm leveling with you. I'm telling the truth. I have millions that I have to hide and I don't want to get caught. The only way I know to keep from getting caught is with you as my partner, like in the old days, back in Cincinnati. If I had any other recourse I would take it. But I don't."

"Great speech Bri, but I'm not buying. I won't be a middle man to hide your wealth. It's just not me, not now, not ever."

Out of the blue Bryan snapped, "I thought that's what you would say; in fact I knew that's how you would react. You're Mister Perfect.

Haven't missed a beat in over 20 years. Life's just a bowl of sweet unblemished cherries, isn't it? The all-American dream boy." Then Bryan started singing "With two cats in the yard, life used to be so hard, now everything is easy 'cause of you." Then suddenly fell silent, but only for a moment.

"Remember when we used to play the song game Wild Man? Remember when we stuck together come thick or thin no matter what? We were an inseparable team! Remember the road trip to Florida my friend? It was our first real journey as men, away from home on the open road. Remember how I got the shit kicked out of me for saving your life in Miami? Remember how you murdered that guy? And after all we shared together you callously turn away from me in my time of need?"

"It was a life time ago Bri. I moved on. You moved on. And we did so without each other. Without owing each other anything more than to keep the pact that we made when we parted."

"You were stalking that girl and you murdered her boyfriend. Murder has no statute of limitations. Remember my friend, my perfect friend, whose life has been nothing but a symbolic bowl of cherries that I can turn those cherries from sweet to sour with the snap of a finger. So don't be so hasty to refuse my request."

"Are you blackmailing me you son of a bitch?"

"I told you I need your help and have no other place to turn. I didn't want it to come to this Matt, but you leave me no choice. Don't fuck with me. I have an air tight plan that will net me several million more dollars than if I just roll over and play dead. I've worked nonstop since college to get to this point and won't, I repeat won't, let this ruin my estate. If I have to threaten you to get where I'm going then so be it. It's not as big a deal as you are making it and just remember it's not by choice."

"Yes it is. It's totally by choice. You chose to make my life a living hell because you are choosing to leverage that unfortunate incident for your own selfish wellbeing. And now I have no idea how to react. I entered this evening with enough consternation at just the mention of

Miami and now you not only mention it, you use it as ammunition to black mail me. I have to digest this Bri. I have let the essence of this encounter sink beyond the level of my emotions before I can even fathom the consequences. Call me Friday morning. I need a full day to get used to the notion that my childhood best friend just decided that he had no other way to deal with his issues than this. Good night Bri. Call me Friday."

Matt downed the remainder of his wine, threw down his napkin, snapped back his chair and promptly exited the establishment, blazing with anger and confusion. Could this be real? Do I really have to confront this? Oh my God. I always knew that Miami was a hidden wound that could be reopened like the gangrenous mess that it was. I always felt it lingering beneath the surface, waiting to emerge as a source of major pain. But not like this. Not like this.

Bryan sat quietly savoring the balance of his splendid wine while contemplating the evening's performance with mixed reviews that ranged from stellar to horrific. Matt couldn't have been more damaged if a truck had run over his foot but unfortunately his vehement reaction to the mere suggestion of "questionable" support forced Bryan to let loose his rehearsed course of bribery, and while it wasn't desired, the results were more than acceptable. Matt was shaken to the core and in his moment of instability hadn't so much as uttered even an innocuous question challenging the story driving the request. So Bryan ranked high his strategy to go instantly from pleading friend to knockout foe, for in his quick about face he left Matt with no time to think, only to react, and it worked perfectly. Matt was now going to start figuring out how to minimize the damage, just like Bryan thought he would.

M att normally woke up feeling refreshed and ready to rock but today was entirely different because his rendezvous with Bryan loomed larger in his mind than the national debt. Sometime today he had to confront the situation and there was no way to avoid it. His attempts to forge a defense in advance of their meeting were all in vain for no matter how hard he tried to conjure a scheme to protect himself they always came back to satisfying the maniac's demands, which he knew were going to present themselves in very short order.

He got to the office a bit earlier than normal to check his calendar and settle in as best possible. There were no scheduling conflicts to further confound his already heightened state of anxiety, just the routine review of final submittals and layouts for the weekend publications. Bryan called around ten on an unknown number and Matt took the call when his secretary said that a business acquaintance wished to speak with him.

"This is Matt DiGrande."

"Matt. It's Bryan, calling you as requested the other night. Why don't we meet for lunch?"

"OK Bri. Same place?"

"No. I'll set something up nearby and give you a call."

As time was closing on noon Bryan called and asked Matt to meet him just a few blocks from the office at an upscale diner reputed to have good home style food offered with an abruptness that bordered on pushy. When Matt arrived Bryan was already seated in a corner booth.

"Hey Wild Man. I took the liberty of ordering a couple of lunch plate specials. Hope you don't mind."

"That's fine. Food's not on the top of my list right now. Anything will do."

"Great. Let's eat quickly and then take a walk so I can lay out the details of my plan and what I need from you. I've tried in every way conceivable to keep you as much at arm's length as possible. Your role is really quite minor, albeit important. You'll see, and when you do I hope you feel better about all this."

Matt didn't respond. The food came and they ate in silence. The bill came, Bryan paid it in cash and they left in silence. Matt was thinking what a fool he was. Every step with Bryan was untraceable and he didn't even think to bring a recording device, let alone hiring a snoop to take pictures. He had failed himself miserably and now walked in a state of heretofore unknown dejection, for a mental failure like this was never before a condition that he had brought upon himself.

"Let's go over here and talk." Bryan said sitting on a stone wall. "I've got to take some time transferring the money so it doesn't generate too much attention. Ultimately I will have it deposited in numbered accounts in the Cayman Islands. It will go from me in the name of a paper company to you and then to a secured account at the bank of your choice. From there the money will be automatically swept to a bank in Zurich and from there I will take care of getting it transferred to the Cayman Islands. All I need you to do is talk to your most trusted banker friend and convince him to open an account for you that you are using to tuck away some retirement funds outside of government control. Just tell him that it has already been taxed and you simply wish to avoid any further erosion of your wealth because you fear that government greed will institute new inheritance tax legislation that will destroy your ability to pass on your wealth to your kids. Once the account is set up I will give you the details on how it's to be swept, but you have to tell your banker friend upfront, and I don't ever want to know his name, that you are authorizing a daily sweep into an offshore account because it has better interest bearing returns. I will give you the details on the offshore account; all I need from you is the ABA routing number on the account you create. It's that easy." Bryan stopped for a minute to take a breath before continuing.

"When this is done there is nothing further for you to do. The money is post tax so there are no IRS implications. The money will be deposited in small amounts and swept daily so there won't be any flags to prompt a securities investigation. The money will be outside of US jurisdiction immediately so the feds can't do a thing about it. And it will be forwarded to a nameless account that is accessible by a code known only to the owner, which is yours truly. Kapish?"

"You make this sound so easy I question why I need to be involved. Why can't you create the account yourself?"

"I have to liquidate the money and then relieve myself of it first to be sure that it won't be considered part of my estate. Without a third party that's just not possible. Having you involved is the only way."

"Well thanks a fucking bunch. Since I have no choice and since this is going to eat away at me until I get it done and get you out of my existence, I'll look into it immediately. I should have something for you by the middle of next week. Don't contact me. I'll contact you. And after this is over, I don't expect to hear from you again, ever."

"I'm really sorry to hear that Wild Man, your reaction is way over the hill, but your wish is my command, so here is my contact information." Bryan said dryly as he handed Matt a business card. "All of the information on this card is secure, so don't worry about using it." And Bryan thought "Don't plan on it helping you in the future either."

P aul left Giordano's so overstuffed with pizza and beer that he felt as bloated as a blowfish in danger, not realizing that the danger he held had nothing to do with the past 40 minutes of gluttony, but everything to do with the report from hell tucked under his arm. It had been a long day and that, coupled with too much blood to the midsection, left him feeling groggy and ready to collapse on the couch in a state of semi consciousness. When at last he reached his apartment and was emerging from his digestion coma his thoughts drifted to Janice and their time together. Thoughts of her became forefront in his mind, renewing his state of mental alertness, and while it pleased him, it was also unnerving and he found himself pacing the room, unable to settle down, absorbed in various role playing scenarios.

Finally, after acting out several painstakingly detailed scenes of stupendous valor conducted on behalf of wooing Janice, and feeling stupid in the process, he decided to peruse the infamous WorldSupplî report rather than further his thespian quest. Perhaps, he thought, it would give him cause to relax so he opened it and just as Chad mentioned found the report structured in a totally alien format. It contained a set of product line breakouts with product line profitability stated in terms of deviations from plan and while the sources of those deviations appeared to be varied and random, the results were the same – profit was down and a cause was hard to pinpoint. Paul sat staring at the figures trying to rationalize application of the data and whether it could rightfully be used to address corrective actions accurately. He wasn't able to make any positive determination, considering rather, that the breakouts were more a smoke screen than an evaluation of discrete issues decipherable into potential remedies. He kept looking at the data and getting nowhere, finally deciding that the question was not what the data meant or how to interpret it, but how, or whether, he should dig into its origin sufficiently to generate his own understanding. After mulling over the details and comparing what he was seeing with what he knew about the financials of the corporation he decided, unwillingly but from a position of duty to his employer, that he would reconcile the mess in front of him. The question now was how and after much deliberation he ultimately settled on creating a list of the fundamentals of the business' cost structure to develop his own comparison. Before he knew it time had flown well past midnight, but he was intrigued by the potential of foul play and went to bed only after he had a game plan to study the matter further.

Paul's on-time arrival at work the next day started with placing a phone message to his buddy Chad. "Morning Chad. Appears the shark may have teeth after all. Want to get a bite at lunch time? Give me a call." After, Paul started work on a detailed query that he would then ask Chad to compile and export into a spreadsheet. It took Paul most of the morning to select the data fields and organize the array that would give him the easiest method for conducting his analysis. By then Chad had agreed to meet him off site at The Shoppe for a quick bite and brief discussion. Chad arrived first and waited at the door for Paul.

"Hey." Chad said when he saw Paul bounding toward The Shoppe. "How's it going? Did you figure it out yet?"

"No way Jose. Let's order lunch and then we can talk."

The two went immediately inside where the warm air, moist from fresh baked bread, welcomed their senses with alacrity. The Shoppe was notorious for making artisan breads that approached those which can only be bought on the streets of Paris, with airy dough and a leathery crust that was tough but welcomingly chewy. They also provided a range of gourmet spreads, organic meats and great veggies that gave no end to the variety of sandwiches one could build. The day was warm enough for the winter-acclimated body to feel fine in the brisk air, because of the bright sun and mild breeze, so they sat outside, coats still on but unbuttoned.

"OK Chad, here's what I know and what I don't know and what I don't know tops the list by over ten fold. I spent several hours last night looking at that stupid report and I can't understand it. I mean, I understand the data and what's its intimating but I don't understand how it can be useful because it doesn't give enough detail. So, what I know is that it's a strange report and I agree to evaluate it further. I agree because the circumstances under which you discovered this are weird and as a professional committed to this company I believe it my duty to investigate."

"So I'm not crazy?"

"You're still crazy - this has nothing to do with that – chances are that everything is fine and we just don't understand the rationale for this exhibit. But I think I've figured out how to assess it further. Here, take this thumb drive. On it you'll find an array of data that I need to be able to do some comparative analyses. Get me year to date and prior year to date in the format that I've specified so I can draw my own conclusions. Can you find a way to do it under the radar?"

"Yeah, I can log on to another computer as administrator and take a couple hops with remote desktop to make my path difficult to trace. Shouldn't be too hard. I'll try to get to it this afternoon."

"OK, sounds good. Now here's what I don't know. I don't know why the corporation is using this new format. I don't know if circumstances beyond management control are at fault for the decline in performance. I don't know, or suspect, foul play and I don't know if there is even any need for alarm. So don't be surprised if we run the query I just gave you and end up laughing at ourselves when we see the results."

"That would be just fine by me. I wish I never saw the stupid thing. Can we change the subject now?"

"Not soon enough amigo! You're all the talk around the water cooler. I heard you had a wild date the other night with a really hot young lady and you didn't even bother to mention it to me! What the heck?"

"What was that you said?"

"You had a date, fool. I'm filling my bottle at the water cooler and Fred and Susan were there leading the gossip club in a round of other people's business when your name came up. Fred said he went to give you shit at some jazz bar because you were bragging about having a date and they followed you there on a hunch that it was all bullshit. He said he couldn't believe the hot young lady that graced your table that night. So, what's the story?"

Chad reluctantly recounted the events from that evening, thinking how ironic it was to be on the receiving end of criticism from someone like Paul. But true to form, Paul didn't judge, he simply started laughing with an hysteria that Chad never before knew existed.

"What the hell are you laughing about?"

"Only you could dig yourself a hole to China, fall into it, come out the other side of the world and end up smelling like roses. It absolutely cracks me up. An unknown girl comes to the rescue of the consummate social inebriate in the face of the worst enemy onslaught to date, with the timing of a gold medalist, the grace of Ginger Rogers, and pulls it off like a heist planned by Walter Shaw with the savior-faire of Einstein. So who's your savior, what's her story?

"She," Chad said while dismally facing the floor beneath their table "is no one. I mean, I don't know who she is. We had an evening without comparison and when it was time to say good night I completely screwed up. I didn't ask her for her number, or get her full name or anything. I acted like an eighth grader with a crush on a senior cheerleader. While my gut said yes to every aspect of our encounter my emotions got tied up in knots so tight that I couldn't even choke out an appropriate closing, let alone attempt at asking for another. She rocked my world Paul, and now it's over before it even began."

"You must know something about her. What's her name? Where does she work? I'm sure you can find her."

"Maybe, but I don't think I want to, because if I did do you know how desperate and lonely my actions would appear? I can't go groveling over some chick that I fell for under these fairytale circumstances. It just doesn't work like that."

"Yes it does. Look at the circumstances that surround my finding Janice. They were unusual to say the least and now we're pursuing each other with what feels like a vengeance. I have no idea where it will lead but it's a shitload better than the options."

"Yeah. You're lucky. I can't tell you how much I envy your situation, but mine is not like that."

"For Christ's sake stop wallowing in your pity pile. Tell me her name and where she works and I'll get you her number."

"Her name is Georgette something and she works at the Tribute and I'm sure you can get some information on her, but I fail to see how that changes things. I'm not about to be humiliated by her rejection. I won't contact her regardless of what you find. I can't."

"Man, listen to you, all mouth and no balls. You preach to me about how to deal with Janice and then cop out on your own advice when it comes to this Georgette girl. Fucking hypocrite."

"You're right. I am. I'm chicken shit when it comes to women. Don't know why. I'm fine with them when the conversation is casual and noncommittal, but the minute it turns towards something else I can't deal. I run like Roadrunner from Wylie Coyote and don't know why. I must have the worst rejection complex in the world."

"Fear of rejection my butt! You're just hiding from your emotions. I hate to tell you but it's time to grow up and face them, learn how to overcome your fears and move into the realm of the socially active. I know I'm no role model, and I'll admit I got lucky, but this thing with Janice has been an awakening. We have attributes man, attributes that intelligent women want – we have promising careers, we're stable people, we can converse on an intelligible level, we're not ugly or physically unappealing, we're college educated, healthy. Need I go on? Yeah we're not the ultra-sexy glamour-model type, or the knock-your-socks-off humorous type, but we're solid man, we're solid. I've come to realize that we need to remember how solid we are and if we get rejected it's no big deal because any woman who doesn't think we're worthy of some time with her is not worthy of us, and that's a fact!"

"Wow, you sound like a new man. Have we really been as pathetic as you make me feel we've been?"

"Yeah Dude, we have and that's the bad news. The good news is that it's not too late. Now finish up; we need to get back to work."

Paul left Chad back at the office thinking about their conversation. It was the first time they had had a discussion that crossed the line on personal matters. It was well overdue and he decided to bring Chad's dilemma up with Janice.

Chad grabbed a mug of fresh ground Columbian to spring feed his metabolism back into a state of mental acuity. He logged onto the IT maintenance computer as Admin, enabled one of the USB ports, installed the thumb drive and then went back to his cubicle. When he got there it was only a matter of seconds for him to establish two hops through remote desktop to find and operate the PC with Paul's thumb drive. He quickly opened it and began writing the query that Paul had asked for. Several hours later Chad was able to successfully run Paul's query, so he saved the results on Paul's thumb drive, disabled the USB and terminated his remote desktop connections. With his pathway safely dissolved he made haste to the maintenance PC to snap up the thumb drive before anyone stumbled upon it.

"Paul, its Chad. Want to meet after work for a minute? I've got the shark's tooth you asked for."

"Sure, corner bar at five o'clock. Okay?"

"See you there."

The day closed quickly without event and shortly after the whistle blew Chad made haste to the corner bar. The place generally drew a large array of WorldSuppli's younger employees, the single ones with carefree lifestyles and itchy libidos. Tonight was no exception; in fact as Chad entered he was quick to spot Fred ogling Susan at a small table directly in front of him.

"Chippie, welcome ol' pal. Come have a drink and do share all the sordid details of your love life. We're just dying to learn your secrets. Even the Kama Sutra would be impressed."

"Thanks, but maybe some other time. You're doing well enough without discussing the banality of my existence. In fact, you two have taken lead role in the water fountain gossip column."

"You don't say? Well what have you heard? Tell us, dear Chippie."

Fred continued to ramble as Chad strode past to order a beer.

"Get one for me as well good buddy." Paul bellowed as he slapped Chad on the shoulder. "Today flew by and I've worked up quite a thirst. How about an IPA to start the party?"

Chad ordered the beers and then managed to find a corner where they could discuss their tryst more quietly. After glancing about for onlookers he furtively slipped Paul the thumb drive and then proceeded to describe the tactics he employed in generating the query. The exchange did not go unnoticed though, as Fred, nosiest of the nosy, remained fixated on Chad as the two friends began their conversation.

"Did you see that?" He whispered to Susan. "Chad just handed Paul a thumb drive. And he looked guilty when he did it. What do you think is going on?"

Susan looked at Fred with questioning eyes, sipped a portion of her libation and said coldly, "Who gives a shit. Those guys, they're probably swapping stolen copies of Madd magazine. They can't be involved in anything. They're too – too pure to do anything stupid."

Wednesday night couldn't come fast enough for Paul. He made plans to meet Janice at a quaint tapas style restaurant for a "get more acquainted" evening that was slated to encompass nothing but long volleys of Q and A. When Paul called to secure the dinner engagement it was she who suggested that the evening be prescribed to follow an information gathering format and Paul gladly agreed. So now they were going to ferret out each other in game like fashion, so to speak, with the most bazaar string of open ended questions each could muster to throw the other off. It was a challenge Paul knew he would lose handily but it didn't matter for he also knew that the format would inspire conversation otherwise left unsaid and the novelty of it rang like a perfectly tuned middle C.

Their reservation was early enough for each to meet directly after work. Paul arrived first and sat in eager anticipation of Janice's arrival. About five minutes later she bounded through the door and on a quick scan of the place spotted Paul sitting meekly at a table for two.

"Hey there Crazy! It's nice to see you. I've so wanted to try this place. I can't wait. Have you ordered anything? I'm famished." She said quickly while leaning over to plant European style air kisses on each of Paul's cheeks.

"Nice to see you too and no, I haven't ordered yet. I've just been sitting here using the time to amass a queue of knock out questions for this evening's volleys. Want something to drink?"

"Absolutely. I think a nice bottle of wine is in order. You do like wine don't you?"

"Definitely, but I'm no connoisseur so perhaps you'd better make the selection.

"Happy to. Red or white?"

"That depends on what we want to order doesn't it?"

"It does, but I'm in the mood for a nice Chardonnay. Does that sound OK?"

"Great by me."

The waiter came, Janice ordered wine, Paul ordered a couple of light appetizers and with that their evening's journey was launched. Janice was quick to start.

"OK, I'll start with an easy one. Where were you born?"

"Wilkes Barre. Where were you born?"

"San Diego and you should have asked me a harder question because your grace period just ended. Who was your first girl friend, how did you meet and why were you in love with her?"

"What makes you think I was in love with her?"

"You just were, so answer the question Crazy."

"OK but that's a hard one to answer. If by girlfriend you mean a relationship with a mutually reciprocal set of feelings then the answer becomes virtually vacuous. It might be more appropriate to let you know the first girl that crushed me because of my crush on her. Once in high school, eleventh grade, I became friendly with a girl in my class. We started spending a bunch of time together during school, you know, study halls, lunch, stuff like that, and I made the dumb assumption that she "liked" me and asked her if she thought of us as going steady."

"Going steady! Now that's a term I haven't heard in ages. I love it; it's so wonderfully naïve, so pristine."

"It sure didn't feel that way to me. She got instantly embarrassed by the mere suggestion and said that we were more like study partners, not really even friends. It killed me. One second I thought of her as my girl-friend, the next she acted like we didn't know each other. We stopped talking completely. That experience alone shaped the way I deal with women."

"She didn't handle it very well, but that's what happens when you're young. You don't know any better and hurt people when you didn't really have any intention to. I don't think people become socially mature until well into their twenties and even then we tend to make lots of mistakes."

"I agree completely and now it's your turn. Tell me all about your early lovers."

"Plural huh? OK let me count." She said while looking skyward with fingers on one hand tapping the other. "First there was Johnny on the base-ball team. Then there was Frank, captain of the football team, and Andrew, the dreamy singer in our glee club. And then in high school . . ."

"Maybe this isn't such a good question." Paul interrupted.

"Why not? We have to know more about each other to know if we're compatible don't we? Sex is a big part of that equation don't you think?"

"I guess so. But maybe it should wait until we know if it could be important."

"I was pulling your leg, Crazy." Janice said with a devilishly coy smile. "Fact is I'm a neophyte when it comes to boyfriends. I mean, I've always had lots of boys that were my friends, but I hardly got beyond that stage. None interested me enough to venture past the platonic until college. And you know what college is like - that artificial environment where the mind ventures into differing scenarios of utopia. I found my 'utopia guy' alright. An incredibly talented art student. A visionary. Knocked me off my feet until reality picked me back up again. And when it did Mr. Utopia went from wonderful visionary to insane maniac. I broke up with him when he started describing his vision of life because his picture had no semblance of mine."

"It must have been a good experience. I mean, at least you got a chance to learn what it means to have a relationship. That hasn't happened for me yet. Who knows, maybe it never will."

"Oh it will, don't worry about that."

"I'm a bit young to worry, but that doesn't stop the desire to fall in love, if you know what I mean."

"Sure do."

"Speaking of falling in love, I've got this friend at the office who's even worse than me when it comes to women. He met this girl, or rather she met him, and now he's refusing to follow-up." With that Paul elaborated for Janice the bazaar details of Chad's chance encounter with Georgette at the Jazz club.

"What if we intervene on his behalf?" Janice said. "I can easily find her office number and give her a call to see if she wants to see him again."

"That's a great idea. If she's interested then I can tell Chad that I want him to meet you and we can arrange for Georgette to come too. Sort of a blind date with eyes, if you get my gist."

"I love it, and it's not a gist, it's a play on words, Crazy."

The rest of their evening passed with timeless conversation that stopped only when the lights in the restaurant were dimmed at closing. The ease with which they fell into each other's persona was beguiling to both, more compatible than peanut butter and chocolate, more refreshing than a cold beer after a hot workout.

"Oh my goodness, it's after ten. Time to head home so we can be our best in the morning." Janice said with a contrary smirk.

"I feel like I could talk all night, but I guess you're right, we'd better head home."

Paul paid the bill after a minor debate about cost sharing and they headed for the door. Janice interlaced her arm in his, snuggled closer as they exited and stopped for their parting words. She looked up and directly into Paul's eyes with oceans of depth teeming from her baby blues. She so entranced Paul that he didn't realize the kiss that followed until the soft parting of her warm lush lips overloaded his senses. They held each other closely for a few minutes each exploring the other with nippy pecks and gentle nuzzles, intensifying their desires to the point where each heart banged against the other like a hammer striking an anvil.

"Janice, I am so glad I met you."

"Me too Crazy. See you Friday!"

"**G**ood Morning. This is Georgette Cummings. Can I help you?"

"Hello Georgette. My name is Janice. I was wondering if you have a few minutes."

"I'm sorry I don't take sales calls at the office."

"Forgive me for not being clearer, this isn't a sales call. It's a personal call; a rather unusual one at that."

"Do I know you?"

"No, you don't. But I know a little about you. You see, I'm calling to ask if you would be interested in seeing Charles Prescott again."

"Charles Prescott? I don't understand."

"Again, I'm sorry. You probably only know him as Chad, the guy at the blues club."

"You mean the guy I saved from a ridiculously callous bit of office shenanigans?"

"That's the one. Nice guy, but too easy to walk all over if I understand things correctly. I haven't actually met him myself."

After a moment's pause Gette replied in amazement, "Let me get this straight. I save a stranger from embarrassment in a night club and then get a call from someone who has never met him to see if we should meet again? This is a bit preposterous don't you think?

"Oh absolutely. It's ridiculously bazaar, so much so that the story has to be worth listening too."

"Nice reply. That's about the only answer you could have given to keep me from hanging up, so go ahead, dazzle me. I'll give you a minute."

"Thanks, but a minute only affords me the opportunity to give you an abbreviated version. If after that you're interested in hearing more we can talk in detail. OK?"

"Clock's ticking."

"I recently met a guy named Paul who is Chad's best friend at work. Paul and I have just started seeing each other. It's casual at this point, but we seem to get along really well. Anyway, last night Paul told me about your encounter with Chad and he also told me that Chad refuses to contact you out of embarrassment over the situation, even though he's nuts about you. So we decided to see if you have any interest in Chad and if you do we want to arrange a date. Paul is going to ask Chad to join us for a drink so he can meet me, and we thought we would get you to come along. Care to work out the details?"

"That's about the craziest thing I've ever heard. You've got guts Janice, and I like that, so maybe we can work something out. But I don't have time right now. Do you work in the city?"

"Yeah. Not too far from you actually."

"Oh really? Where do you work?"

"Chicago National Bank. Downtown branch, in commercial lending."

"Nice. You know the Greek place on the corner of Clark and Adams?"

"Sure. Great Gyros."

"Want to meet for a bite? Say one o'clock?"

"Wonderful. What am I looking for?"

"A befuddled female." Gette said in jest.

Janice spotted Georgette the minute she entered the eatery. Her look of determination was sufficient enough to distinguish her from the more casual patrons who were swarming the place merely for gastric gratification. Janice was impressed by her presence. She appeared strong and confident, and carried herself with a regal level of self assurance.

"Georgette. Over here." Janice yelled from a nearby corner. "Have a seat."

Gette strode over to the small table and extended her hand. "You look just like your voice leads one to believe. A pleasant happenstance given the fact that this encounter already has surprise sufficient to kill the lighthearted. Have you ordered yet?"

"No, but I'm ready to. I like to eat; I eat more than most women do and I'm not shy about it. I'm lucky because it doesn't stay on me the way it seems to on some females."

"You must have quite an active metabolism then."

"I guess. I stay pretty active. I love the outdoors and spend as much time as possible staying in touch with nature. I like yoga and meditating, things like that. How about you?"

"I'm just a simple small town girl lost in the throes of the big city. Came here a few years ago to seek my fame and fortune and got sucked into a 9 to 5 existence to pay the rent. Same as most young people these days. Big on expectation, short on money."

"Somehow I don't quite believe everything you just said. We all struggle with our disposable income, but aside from that there are all sorts of personal avenues to explore. Seems to me you were exploring one of yours when you bumped into Chad."

"As a matter of fact I was. I love the lead singer in the band that was playing. She has an amazing voice and knows how to use it. I like to sing so I appreciate talent when I run into it."

"So what do think about a rendezvous with us this Friday?"

"Let's order first and talk a little more, and then we can see about Friday. OK?"

Both girls ordered a lamb gyro, curly fries and an herbal iced tea while engaging in a casual conversation about each other to get more acquainted. It wasn't long before stories of high school proclivities and college experiences had each laughing with the hysteria of a small child being tickled by a parent. Gette felt a warmth spread through her being that had been missing since leaving home. She hadn't realized how much she missed having a girlfriend, someone of the same sex to share feelings with, to emote with and conjoin with, spiritually.

At the end of their hour Janice changed the subject. "Gette, whether you join us or not, I'd really like to stay in touch. I've enjoyed meeting you and I feel like we could become good friends."

"Thank you for being so frank. I've also enjoyed our conversation and mimic your feelings. I think Friday might be a good way to see what develops."

With that they shared cell numbers, made lose plans for Friday and set their future in motion, with the first action slated for the ambush of Chad.

riday came fast to Paul and Chad because work was unusually busy. Neither had time to talk let alone make social plans or to discuss Paul's research into the mysteries of the company. In the middle of the afternoon Paul realized that he hadn't yet gotten a commitment from Chad for the evening's chicanery, so he gave him a call.

"Chad, its Paul."

"Hey what's up?"

"I'm going out after work with Janice for a couple of drinks and I want you to join us."

"I don't think so. I'm pretty tired and would just be in the way."

"It's important to me. I want you to meet her. I don't want to go gaga over this girl without an unbiased opinion; you know some third party input.

"Paul that's crazy. Just follow your heart like we talked about and stop worrying."

"I will once I have your input. Come on man, I really want you to meet her and she wants to meet you too."

"Where are you going?"

"Some small place on Rush Street. According to Janice it's not that popular so it shouldn't be insane."

"What time are you meeting?"

"Anywhere between 5 and 6. We're meeting directly after work. Come for a quick drink and if you're still feeling like the social retard that you are, then leave."

"Gee that was ingratiating. Really helps me make a decision in your favor. Know what I mean?"

"I was kidding ass. Come on. OK?"

"OK. I'll stop by for a while. I'll meet you there."

"No way. We'll go together. See you downstairs at 5." And Paul hung up.

The bar was adorned with traditional English pub woodwork that looked to be at least one hundred years old. It was darkened beyond the original color from the years before smoking was banned, which, without the updated lighted, would have left it looking dingy and depressing.

Fortunately, without being overly ornate, the eclectic mix of new decorations with old gave the place a quaintness that was oddly appealing.

Paul and Chad arrived around half past and ordered a couple of beers. There was no sign of Janice or Georgette, in fact Paul wasn't even certain what scheme the two had cooked up for their rendezvous. They got a booth alongside the bar and waited, Chad somewhat patiently, Paul like a fully wound spring.

"What's the matter? You're all pent up. Chill out fella, she'll be here."

Just then Janice walked in and in nanoseconds of seeing her Paul uncoiled to go greet. Instead of air kisses this time their salutation was more intimate and Chad looked on impressed and a bit jealous. When they turned towards the booth he got his first chance to process the whole of her and his impression left him in wonder. Janice was a perfect fit for Paul, slightly shorter with a matching stride that made them appear hinged, like two sides of a singular device, matched plates of a well machined tool. Their easy hand clasped gait held an aura of compatibility that outstripped their time as a couple, as the radiance of their combined energies pulsed positively into nearby surroundings. Paul had never looked happier or more complete.

"Chad, I'd like you to meet Janice, the girl I've been telling you about."

"He's been talking about me behind my back already, huh? Well, we'll have to see about that mister." She said with a mocking sweetness.

"It's a pleasure to meet you Janice. Don't worry about Paul's comments, he doesn't often say mean things about people and he's a pretty private person as well, so you really have no reason for concern."

"That's good to know, but I think I already suspected as much." She said as Paul guided her into the booth and snugged closely, but not uncomfortably, next to her.

"He's just a good old boy from small town USA with too much intelligence for the average person to handle. I can only handle him because I don't have enough intelligence to know better."

"That's not what I hear. Paul said you have all sorts of hidden talents waiting to surface, especially in music. By the way, I've invited a friend of mine to join us this evening. I hope you guys don't mind."

"The more the merrier." Paul said without hesitation. It was a bit too quick a response for Chad and he looked at him queerly to gauge the authenticity of his remark. Paul was not one given to comfort with strangers and the tone in his brief response rang alarm-like in Chads mind.

"Not to worry in any case. She's a wonderful person and a music lover as well. I'm sure you'll both enjoy her company."

The waitress brought Janice a beer and they settled into a relaxed round of casual conversation. Janice was easy to like and even easier to be around. She possessed the gift of being naturally ingratiating while exuding a profound love of life and the capacity to live in the moment. Chad liked her instantly and it made his thoughts wander to his recently escaped heroine, just when Gette stepped into the bar.

Gette immediately spotted the threesome. They were in an animated discussion that allowed her to regard the surroundings and gather her thoughts before taking the Nestea plunge that was waiting.

As Gette approached the booth Paul looked up and almost pissed his pants. His face instantly took on the notorious deer-in-the-headlights expression - a person shaken so greatly by an earthmoving event that all but involuntary reflex become trapped in a state of temporary paralysis - while Gette, at the same time, looked directly at Janice to continue feigning the truth of their encounter.

"Hi Janice. I hope I'm not too late."

"Not at all Gette. Why don't you have a seat next to Chad?" Janice said while offering the vacancy to her with an earnest dignity that only a lasting friendship could command. "Chad, slide over."

In the few seconds since Gette had arrived Chad's brain processed more transactions than in an entire week and the toll on his mind had not yet let it come back to the moment. The escaped heroine that captured his thoughts just moments ago was now in the process of sitting next to him. The girl he fell for in a single outing, who was errantly shed from his life, had re-appeared from nowhere and was now seated on his right hand side. Her presence was more than he could manage. Could Georgette and Janice really be friends? How was he supposed to handle this coincidence? How was he to save face? More importantly, could he further his relationship with this wonderful woman?

"Charles is that you? I can't believe it. What a small world!"

"You two know each other?" Janice inquired with amazement.

"We do. Charles and I met last week at a jazz club. We were both interested in the band that was playing and struck up a conversation. We had a nice evening."

"Chad, is Janice's friend the girl you were telling me about?" Paul bellowed. "This is crazy! This is the best small world story I've ever encountered."

"I can't believe it myself. I'm dumbfounded." Charles managed to utter meekly from behind a timid expression.

"Well Gette, since you already know Chad, let me complete the introductions by introducing you to Paul. Paul – Gette, Gette – Paul."

Gette sat gently next to Chad as the foursome finished their brief round of casual salutations. Janice then made it a point to have Chad recount the story of their jazz night happenstance and Gette gladly provided a few witty embellishments that had the table, including Chad, laughing in hysterics. When they finished cajoling Chad about the antics suffered at the hands of his office peers he was more than ready to turn the tables by offering up the goose-wing flapping nonsensical behavior that Paul exhibited when he captured Janice's attention. Paul began by defending his actions on the fated morn only to have Janice quickly intervene with her own off-color rendition, which was belly rolling in its comedic delivery. Within minutes the conversation no longer had to be orchestrated as the two couples swiftly reached a level of comfort that only years of close friendship, or chemistry, could muster. After a few more rounds and some appetizers they decided to dine in and ordered a variety of Angus burgers, the house specialty. When the food arrived the table fell silent as each began devouring the savory meat and homemade fries. Janice was first to break the silence when she hoisted her half-filled Corona and proposed a toast.

"To friends who moments before were strangers, to the warmth that only camaraderie can elicit, to beautiful evenings like the one that this has become." As the bottles clanked Janice leaned into Paul for a lover's kiss, a kiss with intimacy and distinction, void of unseemliness. Chad looked at Gette and saw longing in her eyes as she watched the new couple bathe themselves in each other's glow. Then she looked at Chad and both blushed instantly and smiled.

The evening continued gracefully through several forms of discourse that eventually led into problem solving the world's most difficult matters. Then, when a slight silence enveloped the table Janice abruptly interjected with "Guys should we?"

The comment puzzled Chad while the others offered only blank stares in reply. After a brief silence Gette intervened.

"Chad, I'm here because I wanted to see you again and was told that this was the only way." Gette said as she began revealing the truth of the gathering. As the story continued Chad again held the look of a deer-in-the-headlights until Gette decreed, "I'm not only glad that I agreed to come because I had a chance to meet you again, I'm glad because I now have three new friends that I know will be invaluable to me. You see, I haven't found my place in Chicago yet and until now I haven't felt at all at home here. Now I feel like I can belong to something and I'm thrilled."

"In that case can I relax and stop feeling guilty for the coercion that got you here?"

"Definitely, and by the way, my friendship with Janice IS what got me here. If we didn't become like sisters over lunch this week who knows what would've happened. In any case that's history and I hope we can all get together again soon."

"What are you doing tomorrow?" Chad asked to the delight of his comrades across the table.

Georgette agreed to see Chad the following afternoon and, because the day threatened to be perfect, decided to meet under the egg in Millennium Park. The park, which offers an amazing vista of area architecture, also invites a cast of zany locals that provide multiple levels of colorful entertainment. Sears tower, looming stoically in the background, caps the myriad architectural styles that help make Chicago famous. From the grand visage of the Art Institute to the magnificence of Pritzker Pavilion and the beaches along Lake Shore drive, every angle, position, walkway and bench is over-steeped with humankind's mastery of space.

"A great park in a great city. Chicago just wouldn't be the same without it. I wonder who had the foresight." said Chad.

"I think it evolved." Gette offered. "If I recall correctly, a lot of this land was originally owned by the Illinois Union Railroad and part of it housed a baseball stadium for the Chicago White Stockings. Sometime after the Great Chicago Fire, the land was deeded to the city of Chicago with the stipulation that there not be any commercial use and it has grown since then to its present form."

"Interesting. How do you know all that?"

"See that unique gothic style building over there? That's the Chicago Tribute. That's where I work. And when you work for the Tribute, you have to know the history of this area. It's an unwritten rule of employment, or something like that."

"So, you a reporter or something?"

"I guess so. I've been doing editorial work since I started. Mostly stuff on the community – you know – the benefit of social programs, the good works of charities, plight of the homeless – that sort of mundane thing. But just recently I was given a different assignment that's more along the lines of investigative reporting. A strange assignment – not really sure what to make of it."

"Are you allowed to discuss it or are you restricted by a 'need to know' covenant?"

"I'm not really sure, but I think I should err on the cautious side, so let's assume that my discussions are restricted, at least for now. Tell me about your work."

"I work at WorldSupplî. Ever heard of them?"

"Vaguely, I'm somewhat familiar with the name." Gette said as she was simultaneously overwhelmed by warning sirens, fireworks and schemes of knowledge extraction.

"Well, I have what everyone considers, and is I guess, the most boring job in the place. I support the technology infrastructure – systems analyst – I work on hardware, software, applications, data basing - things like that. It keeps me going but let me tell you that getting up each morning is about as much fun as pulling out your wisdom teeth."

"Believe me. I know the feeling all too well. So why don't you look for a change?"

"I don't know. It pays the bills, and still affords me time to pursue my own endeavors, so I guess it's just not painful enough yet. When it becomes more painful, perhaps a change will be in order, but I don't think I'm cut from the right cloth to make it in corporate America, so it might not matter anyway."

"What's WorldSupplî like? I mean, do you get good benefits and that sort of thing?"

"Their package is marketable. 401K, medical, dental, paid vacation, the usual perks. Used to be a nice work environment too, then some idiot got paid to improve productivity and sold the idea of cubicles to management. Now it's a rat race in a maze when before the rat race at least had some character."

"Amazing how management can lose sight of the little things; you know, throw away common sense. Too much pressure must cause a rare form of Alzheimer's that only the top brass seem to get – Brassheimers."

"Yeah, Brassheimers. We have a couple major Brassheimers. You didn't hear this from me, but WorldSupplî isn't performing as well as it should be and I don't think anyone knows why or what to do about it."

"That's a pretty strong statement from an unhappy techie. You must know more about the company than one might think, eh?"

"Sort of. I have to run batch programs a few times a week, so I see a lot of financial data. I have a knack with numbers too so it isn't hard to understand the variance reports that come my way. Variances used to be minor, but now there are some pretty big ones. Why don't we go for a walk?"

Moments later, in a deep but casual "get to know you" conversation Chad and Gette headed east toward Lake Michigan. Both found the other intelligent and witty and appropriately playful. They headed north on Lakefront Trail toward the Chicago River and then proceeded west on Riverwalk beside Wacker drive. The sights and sounds of the day were topped only by the soft, pervasive blend of virgin green carried by spring-time leaves in various stages of awakening.

They passed under Michigan Avenue and then by Trump Tower before Chad suggested that food might be in order. Gette was ready to chow and suggested Bin 36 in Marina City, just a few minutes away. By the time they arrived the sun was low in the sky and the air began to cool rapidly. Gette shivered and Chad quickly embraced her to ward off the cold. Then they were immersed in the atmosphere of Bin 36 with its famous wine flights, cheeses and small plates.

"Anything particular that interests you?" Chad said referring to the wine list.

"Not really; I tend to lean more towards reds than whites but I'm not picky or anything. How about you?"

"Same. What about an Argentinian Malbec and a small plate of cheeses to start?"

"Excellent."

Chad and Gette were laughing when the waiter presented their wine. Chad deferred the tasting to Gette then resumed their conversation with the smooth finish of the Malbec lingering beyond their words.

"So you like music." Gette offered continuing the dialog.

"Yes, it's so many things to me. Sometimes it's a needed escape from the doldrums of everyday life, other times it offers the vehicle for my creativity. I like to write, mostly riffs, rills, jingles – that sort of thing. No lyrics to speak of, the notes are poetry enough."

"Interesting. Where did you learn?"

"I played piano and guitar in high school and had some private lessons that moved me along. It wasn't until my college years that the bug to write bit and when it bit its bite was pretty hard. Sometimes I stay up most of the night toying with my notes. My penchant is more along the lines of smooth jazz and blues, but I like areas in most genres except for rap and heavy metal."

"I could tell that you were musically literate at the jazz bar by the way you listened and moved with the beat. It was fun to watch you, so intense and focused."

"If you made that observation then you must be more than just a casual listener yourself."

"I'm not really sure how to categorize my position with music. In high school I was touted as the next Madonna, having had lead roles in all the plays my last 3 years. But now I find it difficult to pursue my interest in singing and songwriting even though it's still my passion. I guess the stress of a new life in such a different environment has put a squelch on my confidence, especially considering the pounding that I take every day at the office."

"If you like to sing, you have to sing, even if it's just the church choir. Singers need to express their talents just like birds need to chirp for the coming of dawn. It's not a desire that can be repressed without negative consequences. You have to sing for me sometime."

"Ha! I'll show you mine, if you show me yours."

"Deal, but I have to get to know you better first."

Alan Chandler, at long last, had a few contiguous hours of spare time alone to review the dubious information that was mistakenly printed in the Monday morning system report. His day was one of extreme stress, having been queried in-depth on the austerity measures he would take to right the ship in the next quarter. As a result, his head was spinning from the changes he was being forced to impose and thus started his review of the numbers in a foul, foul mood. Apparently Bryan Jeffries had decided to roll up the business income statement by product line with presentations of year on year variances and actual versus budget. This was not the classical presentation that Chandler was used to, which was a roll-up by company profit center, and its newness resulted in masking areas of deficiency.

"Goddamn it! "What the fuck is Jeffries doing? This is gibberish." He spoke aloud. "Helen, get Bryan Jeffries for me. Have him come to my office."

A few minutes later Jeffries strode into Chandler's office with the look of a teenager who just lost his virginity.

"What are you smiling about? First this data gets out and is almost in circulation, now you appear before me with a grin that makes the Cheshire Cat look harmless. The company is underperforming across the board and you generate a new report that takes away my ability to analyze the situation. Explain this to me!"

"First off, Alan, I'm grinning because we just extended our deal with Walmart and they're increasing forecasts for next year. Secondly, once you get used to this report I know you will treat it as dearly as your Bible. It contains a wealth of good information. Let me show you."

Bryan sat down with his own copy and began to explain how Chandler should look at the data. Every line contained a complete allocation of overhead in it so each line represented a fully absorbed, or costed, entry. Compared to the same data from prior year each line of cost was slightly higher, always by nearly the same percent.

"If every line is off by a small amount and every line has an allocation to cover overhead then overhead has increased year on year more than the gains in volume." Chandler said with disdain. "That just can't be. Are you sure we aren't over-absorbing?"

"Believe me, I've looked into it. So have your CFO and controller. The only area of difference in our cost structure is the need to be Sarbanes-Oxley compliant and unfortunately that is a pretty big ticket."

"I thought we outsourced that?"

"We did. If you recall we instituted use of an oversight entity to confirm compliance with the new law by conducting an analysis of all transactions. We may find this a bit of overkill and cut back on the breadth of their oversight, but for now it seems prudent, especially given our government's decision to require that you sign and be held personally liable for the accuracy of the company records, and since compliance is a function that cuts across every aspect of the corporation each line takes a hit."

"This is preposterous! We're paying someone millions each year to make sure we comply with law? Isn't that a bit of overkill? Are you saying that our variances are all due to this one decision?"

"Pretty much, we've had some downward pressure on price in a few product lines, but the oversight activities are the major culprit. Everyone in industry is facing this issue, so I can't imagine that we're different than our peers."

"Well that's something we'll have confirm isn't it?"

"At least there's an explanation that's pretty concrete and defendable too."

Talk between Paul and Chad the entire next week was like two rival sparring partners each trying to knock the other down. Their demeanor had changed from obtusely melancholy to so blatantly jubilant that HR would have thought them on some really good drugs. It was so overwhelming that even Fred failed to deliver his daily banter with any pizzazz and by the end of the week simply walked by them shaking his head in disbelief.

Each were in touch with their "new found friend" on a daily basis and all so enjoyed dinner the previous Friday that they decided to plan a repeat, albeit this time at a more elegant setting. When Friday finally arrived Chad left work to get cleaned up and picked up Gette outside of her apartment; Paul did the same but went inside for an intimate moment of hugs and kisses before they returned to his car. After all had arrived and were seated their conversation resumed as if it had never ended.

"I'm so glad to be away from work for a few days." Chad celebrated. "We're nearing the end of the second quarter and the race for data is grueling. Everyone is working on special presentations to explain our current situation and what changes are forecast to mitigate shortcomings. "

"Shortcomings, that's the operative word now isn't it? Paul chimed in. "You know that report you gave me? Every invoice is being burdened with a compliance charge that gets swept into a new cost account. I haven't figured out what it is yet, but it's there and there's lots of it."

"Boys," Janice piped. "We're not going to talk shop all night are we? We're becoming the clones of our parents that we swore we never would. Let's give work a break, sip some wine, get our food ordered and discuss plans for the weekend. Sound good?"

Everyone readily agreed and glasses clinked in unison to seal the deal. As a cool rain was expected throughout Saturday some form of indoor activity was proffered most appropriate, with a trip to the latest exhibit at the Art Institute winning first prize.

They had chosen an upscale Japanese restaurant for their refreshment and made long the evening by ordering several strategically spaced small plates with Saki to fill in the gaps between courses. The warmth of their conversation was quickly heightened by the spreading radiance of their Saki laden circ systems, which changed their quiet discourse to quickened exchanges and then soft laughter to belly rolls, especially when they shared the fortunes from within their cookies.

When all were sated and the tea pots empty a rare pause ensued. The quiet caused them to emerge from their cloistered brevity to realize that only a few patrons remained. Time to ask for the damage and hit the road.

Once outside the cool air called for hasty good-byes as each couple departed for their cars. Chad strolled beside Gette and she placed her arm in his.

"That was another great evening." She said with ease. "Sorry your work week was so stressful."

"It wouldn't be stressful if things were more standardized but we seem to be modifying the way we dissect the business and the reason is not readily apparent."

"Really? What do you mean?"

"Last week I stumbled across a report that got inserted in my Monday morning run. It was weird. The information didn't make sense. It showed a bunch of variances from plan and prior year that just shouldn't be there. It's as if some general fund was being created to store money. I have no idea if it's because of forecasted issues with inventory shrinkage, or to cover some unprecedented change in our cost structure, or what. I just wish I never saw the information because now I feel compelled to understand it."

"Is that the report that Paul mentioned?"

"Not really. I shared the report with Paul and he agreed that it was weird too, so he asked me to run a special query to conduct his own assessment."

"He thinks the extra costs have to do with compliance reporting, or something like that?"

"Wow! Weren't you the active listener! I'm not sure what he was intimating, we have to get together to discuss it further."

As they neared Chad's car he opened the door for Gette and ushered her in. When he started the engine she leaned across and planted a quick kiss on his cheek. "Thanks for dinner. It was fun."

When they arrived at Gette's apartment Chad turned off the engine and faced her, but she didn't return his gaze.

"Georgette, is something wrong?"

"No, nothing is wrong. It's just that I've been enjoying your company and I don't want to blow this. I'm deciding if I want to invite you in for a nightcap, but if I do, I first need to be clear that it's not an invitation for sex or anything like that. I really like you, and because of that I need to proceed slowly. I need to know that we're both into this for the right reasons and not just because we've been lonely."

"I completely understand. I also agree with you, but I also know that every reason I can think of for being here is right, feels right. I'm comfortable around you; I'm not compelled to put on any false mannerisms or to be in any way, anything but myself."

"Okay, how about that nightcap then?"

"With your permission, my lady, absolutely!"

Chad followed Gette to her apartment standing back a few feet as they neared, fixated on her stride. She had a casual, confident gait that was definitely female without being overly hipped. Her skirt was tight across the top half of her buttocks and where it loosed, swung gently from the motion of her body with a rhythm soft, like that of a lullaby.

Her apartment was neat and clean and homey with accoutrements but not cluttered. She planned this get together and had prepared nicely for it. Already displayed on the counter was a bottle of cabernet franc and two crystal glasses which, after shedding her coat, were abruptly approached to be put to use.

"I'll get that." Chad said gently, wanting to keep mores intact.

Glasses were poured to a finger above the bevel and then they toasted their newfound friendship. "Here's to us." Gette said. "To a fine start, which, like good wine, will hopefully have a good finish as well."

"Hear hear." Chad echoed.

The next few minutes were embroiled with small talk about her apartment, how long she'd been there, where she acquired her personal things, what style of décor was her favorite, who the people were in photos placed strategically about and things of that nature. It wasn't long before their conversation again took on its casual cadence and with it, a radiant energy, an aura of compatibility, returned to embrace them. Then Chad turned to her slowly and without touching other body parts their lips met privately for the first time. It was a passionate exploratory kiss. Her lips were soft and plush like a juicy ripe peach and their contact, though controlled, was moist, warm and alluring. After a minute she gently pulled away.

"OK then, big guy. Who taught you to kiss?"

"My mother. Just kidding. I'm far from Mr. Experience. You're just so – Wow, so unbelievable, so incredible. You make me feel like nothing ever before. I can't explain it."

"You've got me in a pickle too Chad. Please sit down." Then Gette went to her stereo after which George Winston's piano playing quietly filled the backdrop of the room. "I like this song." She almost whispered. "It evokes a feeling of peace and wellbeing."

They sat in a silent embrace for a few minutes listening intently, each caught in thoughts of their own. Gette began to hum with the music just as Chad began tapping out the beat with hands and feet in perfect timing.

"I know you love to sing, Gette. Sing for me will you?"

Without a trace of embarrassment Gette got up, took a deep breath and began to sing. She picked a recent song by Natalie Cole and her rendition was superb. She had pitch and range and clarity in her voice and she could sound it out sweetly or turn it raspy like jazz or blues. It educed a heightened level of bonding in Chad and a new respect for Gette. She was a master at her craft.

"That was fantastic." Chad said emphatically.

"Thanks, but don't forget that we made a pact. Remember? If I show you mine, you have to show me yours?"

Chad thought about the afternoon with Gette when they agreed to share each other's love of music. He couldn't believe how quickly it had come to pass.

"You got it. Our next after-hours meeting will be at my place and I promise to show you mine. But please don't laugh at the meager surroundings that make up my residence."

Paul walked with Janice to his car and before entering she threw her arms around his neck and kissed him seductively on the lips. He reacted tentatively at first but a fever grew in his loins and in seconds he was erect and responding with the instincts of a male in mating season. Their kisses went from soft and mellow to groping and passionate and in that midst, with lips on lips; Janice asked Paul if he wanted to spend the night.

"Are you nuts? Of course I want to stay with you. Do bears live in the woods? Do bees live in hives? Is the Pope Catholic?"

"OK Crazy, enough with the aphorisms. Let's get going." Janice said as she slipped into his car.

Paul scooted quickly around his treasured Saab, jumped in, shut the door, buckled up, started the engine, put her in gear and sped away. A few quiet minutes later they were back at Janice's embracing with such desire that a fire alarm would have gone unnoticed.

Janice led Paul to her bedroom and began to undress him. He was instinctively called to assist, but she pushed his arms away gently as she unbuttoned his shirt and began exploring his sinewy strong torso. She found his body as appealing as she had imagined and became aroused as her tongue flitted with his nipples and her fingers toyed with the sparse but lovely grouping of chest hair above. She dropped his shirt to the floor with arms extended around his waist, acutely aware of her wetness as she massaged his back and the upper arch of his buttocks.

Paul's member, granite hard, aching with lust, and yearning to be free, almost climaxed as Janice gently rubbed it while dropping his pants. A moment later it saw the soft lights on her apartment ceiling to only go dark again as she took him warmly in her mouth. Janice worked his shaft for a brief minute with the precision of a gem cutter before urging him onto the bed. Then she straddled him for the start of his first round of foreplay.

She was wearing a shear satin blouse that exposed nothing but ample suppleness beneath a lace lined bra. Paul reached for her fullness as he loosed her buttons and Janice, with head askew, let a soft sweet sigh in response. Her breasts were not large in the massive floppy sense of breasts, but they were wide and firm and were softly outlined by a faded tan line that accentuated their perfect roundness. Her areolas were deep pink with defined edges that covered an area just smaller than a silver dollar and in the middle of each stood a beautifully protruding nipple, hard with passion, sensitive to touch, leathery tough and exceptionally pretty. Paul fondled them tenderly and before long they were both overwhelmed with the need for total nakedness.

Having shed all and thrown covers randomly asunder they lay side by side tightly embraced, groping wildly at each other's bodies, exploring oral cavities with tongues outstretched and mouths spread open. Paul moved slightly to take a nipple in his mouth and Janice moaned with pleasure as he suckled it like a baby taking his life's only nourishment. Then he nuzzled slowly southward over her belly and around her navel until he circled into her essence. She was wet with pleasure and the smell filled his nostrils with a musty sweetness so special he wanted to drink it all in. Janice was whispering for him to take her and he did. Her essence was as ready as the start of a NASCAR race which on penetration shot off in spasms of glory and shrieks of carnality.

Paul came immediately and as he did Janice squeezed his buttocks to draw him deeper. Her canal invited him to fill her with his seed and he did, again and again. When finally they rested with libidos satisfied, sudor and saliva and semen and secretions of all forms covered their exhausted bodies, filling her room with a myriad array of bouquets that spoke sexual intercourse at its finest.

The weekend flew by with weather that improved as it came to a close and by Monday the dawn awoke with shards of orange and pink amongst gentle wisps of clouds tinted with periwinkle. It was an inspirational morning despite being Monday and Gette arrived at work a bit early. She decided that her exposure to the unusual matters at WorldSupplî was sufficient to warrant further investigation and Bryan Jeffries her target.

A few google hours later she had a pretty good outline of Jeffries' life as a rambunctious young man to his current appearance as power hungry egomaniac. Her instincts, honed from years of small town scrutiny, felt certain that Jeffries was behind the circumstances at World-Supplî and set a course to prove her conjecture.

With no prior investigative experience she simply chose to start at the beginning, in a suburb of Cincinnati where Jeffries was born and grew up as an only child. It was about a four hour drive so she could rent a car after work, leave super early Tuesday morning and be in Oak Hills by ten, latest. Was she crazy or would this be the kind of self-initiative that DiGrande lauded? She decided to take her chances.

Gette spent the rest of Monday doing research and preparing for her trip. She found the high school where Jeffries graduated and had a pretty good idea of the house that he grew up in, the house where his parents presumably still lived. By close of play she mapped out the details of her Tuesday investigations, complete with directions, time line and cover story. If all went well she would leave Oak Hills in the Cincinnati rush hour and be home before mid-night.

Near dawn, just before six in the morning, she slid behind the wheel of her rented Taurus, adjusted the seat and mirrors one more time and headed south. The roads were already jammed, but were moving well nonetheless and her distance from Chicago mounted quickly. With ample time to ponder, conflicting thoughts about Chad and WorldSup-plî were quick to occupy her mind. She should have told Chad about her assignment but was not certain if that would be considered a breach of conduct with her employer. She really liked the guy, and hoped like hell that her assignment wasn't going to be a spoiler in their relationship.

Oak Hills, a sleepy suburb east of Cincinnati but inside the I-275 beltway, appeared hours later just as Gette had planned, with sufficient lead-time for some in-town driving to get acclimated and adjust her strategy, if needed. Then she decided to go to the high school.

"Excuse me." She said on arrival. "My name is Georgette Cummings and I have been hired by the class of 1974 to do a "Where are they now" book on the alumni. I was wondering if you could help me."

"I'm not sure Miss. You might have to go to the library or something, this building wasn't here in '74 and the old high school has been converted into a convalescent home. Wait here a minute, I'll get the principal."

A few minutes later the school greeter returned alone and informed Gette that the principal suggested going to the admin building where old records are kept. She handed Gette a card with the address and added that it was doubtful any records could be viewed because of privacy rules. The best bet, she said, might be to start with a copy of the year book. Gette thanked her warmly and headed to the address on her card.

There were only a handful of people in the admin office and all of them seemed to be scurrying about like rats in a maze. Gette found herself able to walk the halls unaccompanied and, much to her surprise, found a library with old school artifacts, school newspapers, trophies and other items, including a row of year books that dated back to the 1950's.

Knowing Jeffries date of birth Gette assumed him to be in the class of '74 and sat down to peruse that year's year book. The book was sectioned by grade with small photos of the 10th graders, larger ones for the juniors and even larger ones, with notables printed beneath, for the seniors. The photo of Bryan Jeffries was midway in the group of senior pics and in it his cocky posture showed a hint of smug self-righteousness. The caption beneath read "able to leap tall buildings".

Gette stared at the picture in silent amazement wondering what other shreds of enlightenment she might find inside and so, began to flip page by page from the beginning. Though interesting, because of the long hair, colorful clothing and funny clubs (like the model airplane club) nothing significant or of any importance was found until she got to the senior section. On the second page she found an impromptu photo of two boys tussling. It was apparent by the smiles that their sparing was all in fun and that they, in fact, were best friends. One of the boys was Bryan Jeffries and the other looked vaguely familiar. She stared at it for several minutes before turning the page.

Gette almost fainted when she got to the last names beginning with D. Staring at her there was the boy in the picture wrestling with Jeffries and the name below it was Matt DiGrande. An imperceptible amount of time passed staring at the picture, during which her thoughts were garbled, inconclusive, surreal. For the first time Gette truly knew what a mind felt like when swimming in a murky pool overloaded by too many tangential thoughts. In shock she closed the book with finger still holding the page, sighed briefly and then stared at the ceiling for a drop in stimuli while she simultaneously released a flood of emotions broader than the Mississippi in Plaquemines parish.

DiGrande had not been forthright. Did he pick her for this assignment because of her naiveté? What did he really want from her? Did he want her to fail? Why didn't he tell her about knowing Jeffries? What was he hiding? What was his motive? Should she confront him? What should she do now?

Gette finished leafing through the year book as she thought about her precarious situation then returned it to the shelf and departed. Her next stop was the Jeffries home, where she was determined to learn about the high school friendship from Jeffries parents. God willing, they would still be there and still be lucid.

The house was only a few miles from the admin building in a modest middle class neighborhood that, in all probability, was occupied mostly by skilled laborers than white collar professionals. The homes were tidy and clean but devoid of fancy landscaping and the Jeffries home was no different; it could just as easily been the Jones'. Gette knocked on the door and an elderly woman in a housecoat and slippers answered. From the deep wrinkles and dryish looking grey/white hair

Gette judged the woman to be in her 80's, but something in the woman's eyes told Gette that her mind still had the ability to be exercised.

"Good morning Ma'am, my name is Georgette Cummings and I'm looking for a Mr. or Mrs. Jeffries. Have I found the right home?"

"We don't get a lot of visitor's dearie, what is it that you want? People our age have to be awful careful you know. Too many bums out there trying to rip off the elderly you know."

"Oh, Mrs. Jeffries, I'm not here to sell you anything or ask you to contribute to a charity or anything like that. I've been hired by the class of '74 to put together a "Where are they now" book in anticipation of a big turnout for the 30th reunion. I just want to ask you a few questions about Bryan for the book. You know, to get something more personal."

"I never said I was Mrs. Jeffries."

"Sorry, but the twinkle in your eyes gave you away. Can I steal a few minutes of your time?"

An hour plus later Gette emerged from the Jeffries home with more information on Bryan and Matt than the Book of Knowledge. Mrs. Jeffries still had a sharp mind and was fast to recount the inseparable relationship held by the two boys. She told all sorts of stories about their exploits and how the two had displayed an uncanny, almost innate, understanding of business and a knack for making money. There was one comment that opened more doors than it closed, however, and it was this that left Gette pondering. Mrs. Jeffries, quite innocently and as if it were the normal sequence of things, told her that the boys lost contact when they went to college, after spending their graduation summer together in a rite of passage trip.

Gette left Oak Hills with mixed feelings and a bunch of open items to resolve. Her ride home was full of rumination. What to do with DiGrande, why DiGrande and Jeffries severed ties, and finally, how to deal with Chad and her assignment. One thing she knew for certain, she was coming clean with the whole group the next time they got together.

D iGrande had not a decent night of sleep since his unfortunate encounter with Jeffries and there was only one way to remedy the matter. After soaking on the bazaar nature of their exchange and the task that Bryan shoved in front of Matt he decided to complete Jeffries' black-mail-burdened request as speedily as possible. Only in that way could his life return to some semblance of normality.

The following day he set up an appointment with an international money broker with whom he had developed a strong acquaintance over many years. Matt entered the conversation on a hypothetical basis to gage the man's reaction while also exploring different possibilities for meeting Jeffries demands.

He explained to the broker his desire to set aside some money, away from the eyes of the IRS and federal government, because he was fearful of the long term economic strength of America and the ramifications of de-valuation of the dollar. He queried his acquaintance on the legality and mechanics of meeting this request and was quite surprised at the answer.

DiGrande learned that there were several grey loop holes in the system that one could exploit to launder money to foreign accounts that appeared to be legitimate when they were actually on the edge of illegality. He was also surprised by the depth of knowledge and frankness presented to him during their conversation.

"You seem to indicate that this type of occurrence is fairly common. Am I reading you correctly?"

"Yes and no. It is only common to people in high places who understand the value in using all of the tools at their disposal for financial protection. It's a small but elite group that I happen to assist from time to time."

"Do you require some form of protection for yourself? Like proof that the funds were secured legally and are untraceable? Stuff like that?"

"Not really. I only accept cash and I take ten percent off the top. Then I use my connections to get the money deposited into a numbered account. Right now Dubai has, let's call it, the most welcoming attitude towards such things."

"So if I decide to do this, I simply liquidate an asset and bring it to you in cash?"

"That's pretty much it. I just need to know when and how much and I'll get the account established. Nothing is done in writing other than to hand you a note with the bank account information, which is just like here, – ABA and routing number. There's no name on the account and you and I will be the only ones who know the numbers. What you do with it after I get the money deposited is completely up to you."

"I'll get back to you shortly. Thanks." Matt said in a relieved tone that only he could detect. Then he departed and rang Bryan to set-up a meeting for noon the following day at Humboldt Park, at the corner of Division and California.

Matt could see Bryan as he closed on Humboldt Park. "I met with a banker who shall remain nameless. You can liquidate your assets and bring the cash to me. He will put it in a numbered account in Dubai. If you want to proceed with this then I will tell him to set up the account after which I will give you the ABA and routing numbers. Once deposits are posted you can sweep them as you wish. He charges 10% off the top."

"That's a lot better than giving half of it to my girlfriend." Bryan lied. "OK, let's try it Wild Man. Get me the account information and we can begin."

"I just need to know how much and when." Matt uttered.

"I'll have to liquidate my assets somewhat slowly to avoid complication, so let's say about $300K once a week for a couple of months."

"Are you fucking kidding me? Where the hell did you get that kind of money?"

"I told you it was pretty substantial. Now do you see why I don't want it squandered by that bitch? I can't allow my luck with investments to turn into her good fortune. She doesn't deserve jack shit!" He said, furthering the lie.

"Jesus Christ." Matt spat. "You're some fuckin' piece of work Jeffries. I'll get back to you when it's ready."

Jeffries left their brief meeting with a new sense of euphoria. It was time for him to extract the money from his shell company, the money he received from invoices paid against the compliance cost account. Most of the checks from WorldSupplî had cleared and Jeffries needed to get the cash, so first he would transfer the money into another local account where he had already established the means for easy withdrawal. He would be ready when DiGrande was ready and by this time in July over $4 million dollars would be his, free and clear.

For Chad and Paul the days at WorldSuppli had never seemed longer. They stayed focused on their tasks and performed them well but always lingering beneath the surface were two externalities that each impacted the passage of time. The first and most important was the presence of their new "girls"; second was their ongoing investigation of WorldSuppli financials.

While the water cooler gossip club continued its vigil against the unsuspecting without fail, whispers about Chad and Paul had miraculously changed from chastisement to adulation, as if they were completely different people. And in a manner of speaking, they were. Much as a woman looks and acts her most radiant when pregnant so seem men who are newly in love and these guys were playing the part like Bogart after Bacall.

Wednesday afternoon Gette called Chad to see when he might be free. Her question was delivered curtly, without her normal coquettishness; it made the hair on his arms take note and his internal alarms start to sound.

"Is something wrong? You seem distant. Not yourself." He stammered nervously.

"Everything is fine. Work has been going a hundred miles an hour this week but despite that I would like the four of us to have dinner at my place tonight. I've already talked to Janice and she can make it. Can you come and can you ask Paul if he's available?"

"I can make it. Hang on a minute and I'll get Paul on the phone with us."

Less than a minute later Gette heard Paul and Chad discussing some issues with the mail server while she was being brought into the 3-way.

"Hi Gette. It's Paul. Chad just mentioned something about dinner at your place tonight. Sounds good to me. What's the occasion?"

"Nothing special really. I just need some advice and I think you guys can help. It's something I prefer to discuss in person. Janice said she would be at my place about seven if that works for you."

"Alrighty then, we'll be there with bells on."

Chad was the first to arrive, standing on her stoop promptly at seven. Gette looked a bit weary from a long day of non-stop crises and her demeanor seemed somewhat somber when she hugged Chad firmly and tucked her head into the nape of his neck. "I'm glad you're here. It's been a long day; a long week, and it's only hump day."

"You simply have the look of a tired professional, my dear, and it's beautiful on you. Turn around and let me rub some of that tension from your shoulders."

As Gette pirouetted she pulled together the strands of her hair and sent them flying over her shoulder. Her motion was smooth and effortless and Chad could feel the tightness in her muscles abate as he worked her back and neck. She let her head drop gently forward as he rubbed up and down its length and she let soft cooing sounds emanate from parsed lips in response. Nurturing Gette was the best thing Chad had done in months; it was erotic, but more, it was sym-biotic, it generated oneness.

A minute later they heard a set of unmistakable voices booming noisily and with vigor outside in the hall. Their guests had arrived and Chad opened the door.

"Nice to see you ol' chap. I just finished betting Janice that you would be late. Guess I lost. Here, a bottle of wine for the hostess." Paul bellowed while thrusting a brown paper bag toward Chad.

"Boons farm or Ripple?"

"Actually, a nice Vouvray smart ass."

After lengthy salutations and with drinks in hand everyone settled down a bit so Gette took the floor. "I didn't have time to prepare a meal so I took the liberty of ordering Sushi and some other Asian dishes from across the street. It should be delivered shortly. In the meantime I want to tell you why I asked you here."

Gette stammered for a minute before continuing. "I don't really know where to begin but the things I want to share with you seem important on many levels. They definitely impact my career but they could also impact yours and others as well. Most importantly, they could impact our friendship. That's why I felt the need to get together this way, on such short notice. I can't harbor this information any longer because I'm afraid that it could somehow hurt us- one way or the other."

The gravity with which she spoke was deaf to no-one and the room remained silent as Gette delivered her soliloquy. She started with some brief commentary on the culture at the Tribute, the rather basic nature of her assignments and her low position on the totem pole of importance and esteem. Then she gave an in-depth dissertation on her WorldSuppli assignment from DiGrande, including her most recent discoveries.

"So now you know what I know. DiGrande is using me as a pawn for some reason that I don't understand but it must be related to this guy Jeffries and that stupid report. On one level I feel outraged that he thinks of me as nothing more than a naive little girl from a small mid-west town. On another I feel scared because collectively we have the clues to something that could be really big. I don't want to involve you guys in my assignment but if I don't, and you find out about it, you'd hate me and that scares me more than anything."

Upon her conclusion Chad and Paul stared silently at each other pondering the implications of what they had just heard. Then the doorbell rang and only Janice had the wherewithal to answer it to collect their dinner.

"Sit everyone. Let's eat while we 'digest' Gette's message." She said while wielding two wonderfully piquant smelling brown bags towards the kitchen table. "I was hungry before her story. Now I'm famished."

The guys sat and opened the entrees while the girls got the table set. Then each loaded up their plates in unison, taking turns at stabbing different items from their containers as openings emerged.

Chad began. "OK, let's see. WorldSuppli is suffering from some profit shortfalls. Jeffries and Chandler came to the computer room to intercept the report that presumably identifies the sources of the problem. DiGrande is investigating WorldSuppli and has known Jeffries since they were kids, but, for reasons unknown failed to disclose this fact to Gette. And Jeffries and DiGrande lost contact with each other when they went to college. Why did DiGrande ask Gette to investigate World-Suppli now? Why didn't he tell her about his childhood relationship with Jeffries? Is he involved in some way? We need to review what we know and what we don't know so we can steer this investigation in the right direction."

Paul chimed in. "We know that there is a new cost account that is burdening every item we sell with a charge. The account has accrued a lot of money so far this year so one would assume that legitimate invoices are being received and paid that substantiate existence of the account. I'll have to conduct a query to get copies of the invoices. They may tell us something."

"I'm a banker don't forget." Janice piped up. "If you get me the details of the payments against those invoices I might be able to track the money side of this situation. You know, whose getting paid and how legitimate they are. That might tell us something too."

"Whoa! Wait just a minute." Gette yelled suddenly. "You're all ready to go storming off into an investigation without even considering the consequences. What happens if we get caught snooping around? How would I explain that to my boss? What are we going to do if something unethical or illegal is going on? Are you sure you want to risk your careers pursuing this?"

"Hell yes!" they all replied together.

"Well I'm not ready to let you. We need more time to think before we act. We need time just to make sure that any actions we take remain covert. So do me the favor of some soak time. In the interim I'll investigate the DiGrande/Jeffries bond further to see what else lies under that rock."

The group agreed to take their next steps slowly and to keep everything on the QT. They agreed to call themselves the QT Kids and to discuss the matter only with each other and only in person, to never issue any emails or otherwise leave a trace of evidence of their association in the matter. They agreed to meet again the following Wednesday to share updates and then, with decisions in place, their conversation turned to lighter matters until departing in preparation for the morning sun and their return to work.

In a matter of just two days the Jeffries account was readied for deposits and DiGrande met with Jeffries to hand him the routing numbers.

"This is supposed to be the only information you need to manage the money." Matt said handing Bryan a small note. "I didn't even look at it so you can rest assured that only you and the banker know them. OK, good-bye then."

"Wait a minute. When are you going to stop being so belligerent? I didn't want to use our past to get your support but you gave me no alternative. Lighten up Wild Man, there's nothing wrong with what you're doing. Anyway, here, I have the first deposit for you - $600 grand." Bryan said handing Matt a large duffel bag. "Please see that this gets deposited promptly."

"Anything you say Asshole." Matt replied curtly.

"I'll meet you here at noon every Monday to continue converting my assets. I was thinking that would be easiest for you. Does that work?"

"Nothing works Bri, but it's no worse than any other scenario. I just want this over as soon as possible." Matt said as he stepped backwards to retreat from their encounter. "Check the account in a few days – the money should be in there by then."

Bryan stood frozen with eyes riveted on Matt's form as it faded into the distance. A number of thoughts flooded his brain but forefront amongst them was exuberance; exuberance in the power and freedom he felt from swindling his employer; exuberance from a newfound sense of invincibility; exuberance from his cunning. He was now in complete control of his destiny and in less than four months enough money would be squirreled away in accounts all over the world that he could go back to his old ways without limit. Only this time he would roam the globe in search of rich widows and hot divorcees. They would be his next victims. They would be the targets of his control, the victims of his libido and their bank accounts the source of his expanding wealth. Bryan Jeffries, the laborer's son from a quaint Cincinnati suburb who became global playboy extraordinaire; a vision so alluring it gave him an erection that ached.

Matt got back to the Tribute too quickly for the seething to have fully subsided. He went straight to his office, shut the door and tried like hell to focus on answering messages and emails, but his angst took hold so he slumped in his chair and stared into nothingness to recover. Minutes passed in a hazy state of odd consciousness, the type of mental condition that happens with emotional overload; complicated darting thoughts with tangibility insufficient to drive actions or conclusions. Sleepiness induced by conflict avoidance. Utter frustration.

Finally, he thought that an update from Georgette on her special assignment might snap him out of limbo-land so he asked his administrator to get her on the line. A minute later his speaker came to life. "Mr. DiGrande, Ms. Cummings on line 3."

"Georgette. Do you have a few minutes? I could use an update on our project. Can you come to my office?"

Shivers of fear rose in Gette immediately as she confirmed her availability. Under the circumstances, she had no idea if she could behave normally; in any case she had no time to prepare. OK, she thought, just wing it. Expose some progress; share some ideas on the direction being taken, no specifics. She knocked on his door.

"Good afternoon Ms. Cummings. Have a seat. I know it hasn't been long since our last communication on your WorldSupplî endeavor, but please tell me, anything new?" He asked cautiously.

"Not too much new to report, I'm afraid." Gette said clearing a scratchy-dry throat in the process. "I've made further contact with some WorldSupplî employees and they are definitely a disgruntled lot, but I've nothing yet that's concrete enough to go for specifics. The undercurrent against Jeffries seems fairly prevalent, as does some rhetoric about the ineptitude of Alan Chandler, but it's pretty common for the boss to get bashed, if you know what I mean. It does seem that some negative changes coincide with the arrival of Jeffries as CTO, but it's strange though, because the CTO doesn't normally get that involved with operations, does he?"

"I guess it depends on the company and the individual. If the guy has a good grasp of systems and sound business acumen they could tap into his expertise in a number of ways. Might not be a common practice, but I'll bet it's not that unusual either."

"Well, I still need to vet things out a little further before I'm ready to give you my opinion. I have some feelers out with my contacts for more specific information, so let's see what they bring me. OK?"

"How long do you think that will take?"

"I'm not completely sure. Another week or two maybe?"

"I heard you weren't in the office on Tuesday. Everything OK?"

"Oh, yes." She stammered. "I just needed to isolate myself so I could think more clearly. I'm trying to imagine the implications of the feedback I'm expecting so I can be ready for the next step quickly. You know, staying ahead of the game so to speak."

"Makes sense to me Ms. Cummings. Thanks for the update. If anything substantial arises in the course of your investigation do not hesitate to fill me in."

"Understood. I certainly will."

J effries left the meeting with DiGrande with a renewed sense of purpose, his euphoria centered on the self-aggrandizement that comes with smooth and flawless execution of his plan. He headed back to WorldSupplî like a kid who just sneaked a cookie after being told no more. The grin on his face was plastered tight; the gait in his stride artificially accentuated. Just then his phone rang and up popped a number that he instantly recognized. Jesus, it's Mom, he thought.

"Hello. This is Bryan Jeffries."

"Oh Bryan! I don't know why you always answer the phone that way. You know it's me on the line."

"Hi Mom, how are you? How's Dad?"

"About the same as last week and the week before that, just older, that's all."

"Well, you're lucky. There are a lot of people your age that can't care for themselves, or have lost a spouse. Look on the bright side, will you?" He said, as the conversation started just like a hundred before.

"Oh I do dear. I know I'm lucky. But enough of that. I called to ask if you are coming home for the big high school re-union."

"What high school re-union?"

"Your 30 year re-union, silly. A very pretty young lady was here just this week to get information on the students in your class in preparation for the re-union. She's been hired to make a book."

"Really. That's very interesting Mom. I had no idea that it was going to be such an elaborate event. Did the girl ask any questions about me?"

"Of course. She asked if there were any funny stories or friendships that would make the book interesting. She also asked about your college years and personal tidbits that she could use to make a fun presentation of you in the book. I think it's a wonderful idea."

"Yeah, sounds great. What company does she work for?"

"Well, I forgot to ask. She showed me her card, but she was such a nice girl that I paid it no mind."

"I'd like to ask some old friends if they've been contacted. Did she leave her name? What did she look like?"

"Oooh, I'm sorry, she told me, but I don't really remember. It was unusual, I remember that. Like a boy's name or something. Maybe it was Georgie or Georgina or something like that. A very pretty girl, tall and slender with striking auburn hair. So are you coming? Will we see you?"

"I'm not sure yet Mom, but I will definitely try. Work is still crazy busy."

"All you do is work son. Take some time to smell the roses. Come see your friends from high school. Maybe Matt DiGrande will be there."

"That would be nice Mom. Tell you what; I'll mark the date on my calendar when the announcement comes out so I won't forget it. How's that?"

"That's fine sweetheart. You know we'd love to see you."

"Me too Mom. Gotta go now. Tell Dad I said hello. OK?"

"OK. Bye-bye sweetheart."

The swagger in Bryan's stride shifted like a wind filled jib luffing from an instant change in direction. He spotted a stoop and sat to ponder the input his mother had just delivered. Was this genuine or did he need to worry? He had to assume the worst to protect himself and his plans. He had to find out who this inquiring young lady was and what she was doing. Perhaps she was just doing a book for his graduating class, like his mother said, but he doubted it. She could be nothing more than an innocent reporter assigned to producing a legitimate article on him and his career, or, she could be digging into matters that would expose his scheme, and that would be totally unacceptable.

Till now Bryan had not considered the possibility of being exposed and hence had not given any thought to protecting himself or the actions that might be required to maintain the secrecy of his deception. Amazing, he thought, how impactful one phone call can be. Where minutes before he was skating on cloud nine now he had to implement command and control tactics to secure his operation. Development of a detailed plan was in order, and now.

Bryan got up and starting walking as briskly as possible back to the office. His mind was racing. How dare that fucking woman invade his life? The more he thought about it, the more his fear switched to anger and as WorldSupplî came into view, he began channeling his energy into a plan, a plan that would expose the truth of the woman and, based on the truth, how he had to deal with it because no one was going to interfere with his master plan. No one would be allowed to get in his way.

The first thing he had to do was to establish the legitimacy of the book-girl and this he determined to do by contacting the school.

"Good afternoon. My name is Tom Johnson from the Class of '74. I understand that preparations are underway for our 30th reunion. Do you know where I can find out more about it?"

"I'm sorry I have no idea. Did you google Oak Hills High School Re-unions? The internet seems to get used for these types of events quite frequently now-a-days. Perhaps that will help."

"I didn't think of that. I guess I'm just old school, so to speak. I'll give that a shot, thanks."

"It's interesting that you asked though. Just the other day a young lady stopped who was hired by your class to make some sort of book for the reunion. I've never heard of such a thing, but nothing surprises me anymore. People even have graduation parties for kindergartners, you know what I mean? Why not a book that provides updates on student's post grad lives?"

"That is a novel concept. I guess the class officers really want to throw a big bash."

"I wouldn't know about that Mr. Johnson. You'll have to ask them."

"I think I will. Thanks for your help." Bryan said as he hung up. Moments later he was searching the web for a site on his class and what he found was amazing. There was, in fact, a site dedicated to his class that was full of opportunities to share information, information that ranged from basic data to detailed descriptions of family, career, hobbies and more. While the entries were sparse this was certainly a much better way for old chums to catch up than by hiring someone to create a book. The more he thought about it, a book seemed completely impractical because the effort to amass updated information was well beyond anyone's reach. It simply was not feasible and the realization magnified Bryan's skepticism by volumes.

Fortunately an email address was provided for those caring to query about classmates and learn more about upcoming events, so Bryan setup an anonymous address and sent an inquiry. In it he asked for salient input on the upcoming event and more specifically, if a book was part of the offing. Minutes later a response kindly informed him that he had been misinformed; the only money they were spending for classmates to correspond was to be found on the website, which he was strongly urged to use.

Book-girl was a ruse; finding her was essential; finding her purpose a must. The idea that someone somewhere might be intentioned to breach Bryan's scheme made him go mad with ire and while he began to imagine wildly outlandish things he couldn't conceive how anyone might possibly have been alerted to his racket. Was she an employee of WorldSuppli? How long had he been under "surveillance"? Did Chandler suspect him of wrongdoing? The possibilities seemed endless even though the circumstances surrounding a breach were confined by his sphere of influence. There had to be a common denominator. Who would care to launch an investigation into him? It was then that the light turned on.

B etween the requirements of her normal assignment and DiGrande's request to investigate WorldSupplî downtime for Gette was scant and when the week closed she was exhausted. The only social activities she undertook were brief, and not so brief, daily conversations with Chad. Their discourse was sometimes light and teemed with witticisms and sometimes full of politics, economy, the environment. Their appetite to build a bond seemed to have no bounds and Chad, knowing how Gette was tired and stressed, arranged for dinner at his place Friday night.

Having any female in his apartment brought forward harrowing feelings of doubt and having Gette there for the first time felt more overwhelming than those dreams we all have about going to school with no clothes on. He spent every night overhauling his apartment in anticipation of the big night and it literally glistened, in fact it was so clean it smelled more like a sanitarium than an apartment. But he wasn't so lost in cleaning to forget the garnishments and picked up flowers and candles to make the table as elegant as possible. Chad was not an experienced cook and so, prepared a hearty meal of chicken fricassee, scalloped potatoes au gratin and broiled asparagus with lemon zest – a mix his mother taught him hoping he would have times like this.

Gette called on her way so Chad could meet her in the lobby. It was a nice spring evening, but still chilly enough for the steady breeze to produce beautiful facial hues in response and when Gette entered the combination of her deep bronze hair, reddened cheeks and sparkling eyes made her ever more striking. She smiled at Chad and her mirthful expression besieged him with feelings so grand that he nearly fell over.

"Good evening beautiful lady. Welcome to my humble locale. I assume that you were able to find it without event?"

"Absolutely, kind sir. Do show me your lair, if you please."

"Oh, I please all right. Follow me."

They entered the elevator; Chad pressed seven and then turned to face Gette. She sidled toward him deliberately bringing their bodies into contact and then looked up with pursed lips for their first kiss of the evening. Chad advanced steadily and with due diligence till their lips touched gently. They began to explore the sensations created by the soft moist connection, each finding the other tasty with a pleasant suppleness that begged for more. When the doors opened they were in a full embrace.

"OK young lady. You've shown me yours, now it's time for me to show you mine. Welcome."

The apartment door swung open to the discharge of a soft orange hue from lighting set to produce a romantic ambiance and Chad quickly ushered Gette inside for her first glimpse of his world. Directly to the right a galley style kitchen lay immersed in the heat and rich odors of goods baking. Past the kitchen on the far side of a bar height counter stood a wooden table neatly adorned with dishes reminiscent of the 1970's. Two candles straddling either side of a tasteful bouquet flickered softly, making dancing patterns of variegated light on the ceiling above. Behind it a modest coffee table held two glasses and a bottle of wine.

"How charming Mr. Prescott. You needn't have gone to such lengths." Gette said with a toying smile.

"Thanks, but it's nothing fancy I can assure you. A little preparation granted me by my mother, who had the fortitude to force me to learn how to cook a couple of different dishes. I hope you like chicken."

Chad laid Gette's coat across the back of his one and only couch and then poured some wine. After a quick toast to their burgeoning friendship they again found each other in a heated embrace with hearts pounding from their yearning desires. Just then the timer went off in the kitchen.

"Ooops. Gotta check on dinner." Chad said despondently. "I guess I have to work on my timing."

"Not to worry. We have all night. Can I do anything?" Gette inquired.

"Nope. Just relax and enjoy the wine." Chad said while donning a mittened hand to extract a dish of steamy potatoes.

While Chad's attention was confined to the kitchen, Gette began a methodical inspection of his living room. It was rather Spartan and unadorned. Among the scant décor were a few items of childhood memorabilia and several photos of family. The only items of prominence were his keyboards, computers and the mounds of paper that embodied his creations. She sauntered to the pile and began sifting through.

She first leafed gingerly just to gather an impression of the magnitude of his works, to size the breadbox so to speak, and then she began to look more in depth at individual pieces. What she saw was staggering. His pieces ranged from rills and jazzy melisma to entire orchestral movements, a breadth that seemed boundless. None had names or handwritten notes, none were personalized beyond the chords and bridges inked there on.

"I see you've discovered my addiction. Come and sit for dinner. We can talk about my messes later." Chad said dryly while placing food laden dishes into place on the table.

Gette hopped into her seat and sat so quickly that she failed to empty her hands, which contained several of Chad's latest works. She set them aside as Chad joined her and raised his glass. "Here's to our friendship, to the pleasure of having you as my guest, to an evening void of outside interruption."

"Cheers." Gette rang. "And bon appetite."

Their glasses clinked and they fell silent to individual thought as each began the celebration of home cooked cuisine.

"This is very good Mr. Prescott. The lady is impressed."

"Thank you. Like I said… if not for my Mother."

"Well, you'll have to tell her how thankful I am. I've had a long and stressed out week and this is just what the doctor ordered."

Their conversation flowed as easily as the wine and as gently as a meandering stream. The course it took was random and casual, filled with childhood stories and reflections of family and friends shared without reservation. Each snippet of a memory from one elicited the appearance of bygone times from the other and their volleys lasted, unbroken, well into the second bottle.

"Okay Mr. Prescott, avoidance is no longer an option. It's time to show me yours." Gette said holding the sheets of music between them.

"Dear God, now? I've been silently hoping for a reprieve. Can't this wait for another day?"

"I'm sorry Mr. Prescott but you fail to remember the pact we made. Is a promise not a thing of import in your value system? Shall I render my opinion of this evening on your hesitation to comply with our deal? In my hand rests a sample of your pieces. Tell me about them. Play them for me."

Chad took the music humbly and then rose slowly, deliberately, to setup his keyboard. A quiet minute later his system was ready and without a word he began to play. With his first note came a transformation so complete, so stark and full of contrast that it made Gette shutter. He was Schroeder in Peanuts, immersed in the splendor of his sound, captivated by its creation. He was soft, reserved and polite like Chopin. He was shining and full of incredible technique like Pollini.

Chad moved through parts of several different pieces, playing his music for over fifteen minutes before segueing into a rendition of Let It Be, at which time he looked up and smiled at Gette with an expression of glory painted over his face.

"You sir, are a genius. That was amazing stuff." Gette exclaimed with utmost respect. "You've got to think seriously about publishing."

They spent the next hour discussing his work and exploring the possible avenues for its exploitation. Gette found two pieces with exceptional beat for catchy refrains and asked if she could take them to write lyrics for, which Chad happily agreed to. Around midnight their energy was spent; dissipated like the strength of light from afar. Gette wasn't ready to stay over, but she certainly had no desire to head home either, so after an involved discussion of the fated decision, they went to bed, and hours later fell exhaustedly to sleep.

B ryan Jeffries checked his numbered account several days after his rendezvous with DiGrande and sure enough, the money was there as promised. So to seal the deal on its total disappearance Bryan initiated another transfer, this time to a small investment bank in the Caymans. His plan was now officially underway.

But the joy of it was nowhere as magnanimous as expected because the shroud of uncertainty surrounding the "book-girl" left him with a queasy, unsettled feeling from abdomen to groin. She was a dangling participle more annoying than the worst hemorrhoid and had to be clipped. Logic pointed to DiGrande as the most plausible source for her role playing as the faux reunion updater - he was the only one who had reason to probe Bryan, and his background as an investigative reporter would make the pretext simple to conjure. Because of this, Bryan reasoned that the "book-girl" was one of DiGrande's unassuming minions assigned with abstract input to learn more about Jeffries than met the public eye. It was time to confirm his conjecture, or look for another source.

On a whim Bryan opened the Tribute's website. It was an enormously sprawling thing with thousands of pages reflecting the variety of information that papers generate, but little existed on employees other than names associated with articles and photos of the most senior editorialists. While formulating a search strategy for the "book-girl" he meandered slowly through a number of sections which included sports, local, business, autos, real estate, politics and more. It was the first time he perused a newspaper website and was impressed by the detail and breadth of information it contained. No wonder circulation was down - the younger generation could stay current far more productively on-line than in hard copy.

He continued to venture into the site, thinking more about its implications on the news industry than his original purpose, when the name of an author jumped out at him like a crouched tiger pouncing on prey. Cat finds mouse, cat catches mouse. It wasn't Georgie or Georgina like his mother thought – it was Georgette, Georgette Cummings - and a simple google search on her name, which yielded information from several social websites, confirmed that Georgette was a young attractive female that fit his Mother's description.

"Jesus," he thought, "DiGrande is having me investigated. If he finds out there is no girlfriend in my life then what? Will he challenge me with that knowledge and risk exposing himself? Will he look for the source of my money? I can't afford to get rid of him – he's my conduit to safe pilferage. Should I get rid of the girl? That would certainly scare him."

Random uncontrollable problem solving scenarios began to unravel in Bryan's mind. None of them were the least bit pleasant.

P aul arrived at work on Monday ready to further the groups' investigation of the WorldSuppli financials and was quickly able to locate invoices from, and payments to, the entity charging for Sarbanes-Oxley compliance. He immediately printed one copy of each entry, exited the vendor accounts ledger system and then arranged to give them to Janice that evening.

Gette arrived on Monday in time for DiGrande's staff-bashing in the executive conference room. His meetings of late had been more lack-luster than normal, with the volume of fire and brimstone rhetoric held, for the most part, at mid-range or less. Gette presumed that his controlled demeanor was related to her assignment with WorldSuppli and the issue with Jeffries. She had to find the cause for DiGrande's failure to disclose their former friendship, but a means to secretly bridge the gap kept eluding her.

Bryan Jeffries was beside himself with rage over DiGrande's breach of their arrangement especially because, no matter how hard he wracked his brain, a scheme to wrest control of the situation seemed unattainable. One thing he did know - no matter what activity he pursued it had to be covert. No one could break the vail of concealment his plot had wrought, but how to be certain was the challenge. With no other idea in mind, and more from the mere need to engage in some form of intervention, Bryan decided first to become well acquainted with one Georgette Cummings.

Bryan had never met Georgette but he was certain she would have his face memorized, like any good reporter on a story, so when he chose to tail her it had to be in disguise. Monday was drab and misty and the thick feel of the air was just enough to give his cover an additional buffer because people were hunkered, focused on their plight with nature's nastiness, not looking outward on its beauty. So Bryan decided to follow Gette after work to gain some insight into her behaviors, to learn her patterns. The thought of spying on her was like discovering a new game, like trying a new elixir, or agreeing to fulfill a daredevil stunt. The idea rekindled his missionary zeal so completely that when he dressed like a delivery boy with faded jeans and a bland hoodie pulled completely over his head his erection had first to be dealt with.

When Gette left work slightly after five Bryan followed her leisurely, some twenty yards behind. He watched her at the bus stop deep in an animated conversation on her cell that was an obvious source of enjoyment. Her facial expressions varied from fully engaged to totally enthralled and she remained on the phone for a brief spell after boarding the bus. Bryan boarded the same bus, but he kept his distance and avoided eye contact.

Roughly twenty minutes and multiple stops later Gette exited the bus at the stop closest her apartment. Bryan exited with her but went the other direction before reversing course. How easy this is, he thought, she has no idea that she's being shadowed. He stayed with her, largely out of sight, while she went to the dry cleaners, picked up a few groceries and then headed for home. Several minutes later, thinking it safe to assume that she was in for the night, Bryan left his post and then walked the neighborhood until he was fully acquainted with its surroundings. The walk helped him to funnel his thoughts on the chess game in front of him, which pointed clearly to the investigative work he needed to accomplish, and the different moves for which readiness was now imperative.

Wednesday evening came quickly to the QT Kids whose plans, among updates on the WorldSupplî matter, involved pizza and beers at Giordano's. They met around six-thirty and were fast to be seated.

"Cheers everyone." Paul chimed when their drinks arrived. "Here's to our third encounter as couples and our first as the QT Kids."

Everyone clinked glasses, added cheers of their own and engaged in small talk to catch up with each other before the conversation got down to the business at hand. Janice led the discussion.

"Paul delivered some invoices and payment vouchers to me on Monday night from the Sarbanes-Oxley vendor. The invoices are very detailed. They are literally time sheets with names, dates, hours and individual rates. While they provide the impression of legitimacy, and very well could be, they don't have a description of work performed so it's hard to say what was done for the costs incurred. That's the easy stuff." She began.

"Then I took a look at the payment voucher. The vendor name and address is on the voucher but there isn't any information on bank routing and such, so it can only be used to search for company data. That's where things get dicey. The address is to a lock box, but not an electronic one that can be swept by their bank on receipt of payment. I think it's a physical lock box, like a PO Box. In other words, where a physical check gets deposited and then where that check gets taken to be cashed is anyone's best guess." She stopped for a sip.

"Now here's where things get really dicey. An internet search on the company reveals absolutely nothing. If it is real it has be to a privately held concern and all of the employees must work from home because there is no physical property attached to it that I could find. Smells pretty rotten from where I sit." She concluded.

Paul picked up. "If I'm hearing you correctly then someone might be getting paid for fake activity and taking it all for themselves. These are not small invoices; someone could steal millions of dollars over the course of a year."

Chad joined. "We must have contracted a third party operation to oversee our practices for compliance with Sarbanes-Oxley but the entity, whoever they are, is apparently getting paid huge sums without performing any work. Did I get that right?"

"That's what might be happening, yes, and proving it might require that we reveal what we know to senior management. That's a tricky proposition since we don't know who's involved."

"If someone gets that kind of money then that same someone also has to find a way to launder the money. Isn't that correct?" Gette asked.

"In order to protect it and to keep it away from the IRS, yes, it would have to be very carefully administered. Numbered offshore accounts – the kind of stuff you read about in fiction novels." Janice offered. "What are you getting at?"

"My investigation into WorldSuppli was authorized by DiGrande and DiGrande knows Jeffries but, according to Jeffries parents, the two have not been in touch with each other since high school. What if Jeffries contacted DiGrande with a get-rich-quick scheme and the two of them are in cahoots? I find it hard to believe, but I really don't know DiGrande that well either. On the surface he seems forthright and he has certainly maintained a stellar reputation with the public, but who knows? He wouldn't be the first Dr. Jekyll figure with a Hyde inside his being."

"In other words, no one knows that there is a connection between Jeffries and DiGrande so DiGrande can operate as the front for the money laundering side of the scheme without anyone being able to find the link. Did I get that right?" Janice asked excitedly.

"So Jeffries issues the bogus invoices, gets paid by paper check, collects the check from the lock box and gives it to DiGrande where it magically disappears. Early retirement is a pretty convincing enticement."

"If DiGrande is involved in this why would he have you investigate WorldSuppli? It doesn't make sense. Wouldn't he want the paper to stay clear of WorldSuppli as much as possible? Something here doesn't add up. There's more to this than we currently understand, so what do we do next?" Chad added.

His comment hit them all at the same time like a brick from a fourth floor ledge. Without better information it would be impossible to isolate the involved parties and their roles in orchestration of the alleged scheme. Everyone fell silent to think while they ate.

Several minutes later Gette said. "I've got to confront DiGrande with the information that I've learned. If he is involved, maybe I can stop him before it's too late. I won't divulge everything that we're pieced together; just ask him why he didn't tell me about knowing Jeffries."

"That's too risky Gette. We're talking federal charges here. If he is involved there's no telling what he'll do. There must be another way. We can't let you step into harm's way. Can we sleep on this and meet again on Friday? Maybe we need some more soak time. How about a happy hour get together to see if anyone comes up with more data or a better plan?"

Everyone readily agreed because the case for procrastination was too compelling.

Meanwhile, at the bar about forty feet away, a hooded delivery man sat sipping a beer, gazing at the foursome from behind straining, panicked eyes. Bryan couldn't believe it; he had worked like a dog for over a year developing a foolproof way to defraud the company and just as it began to yield results, there sat two WorldSupplî employees with the reporter and some other gal. Their gathering was not simply social, it had purpose and its purpose, he knew, involved him. Time to call DiGrande and kick his ass!

B ryon arranged to meet with DiGrande the next day at their rendezvous location. Bryon arrived just before Matt.

"Who the hell is Georgette Cummings and why is she investigating
me? You're behind this aren't you?" Byron yelled.

Matt was taken completely off guard. His head started reeling and
his stomach began to flip flop. "I don't know what you mean."

"Fuck you. You know exactly what I mean. That bitch is tailing me.
She went to my parent's house masquerading as a class reunion orga-
nizer. Don't fuck with me Matt or I'll bring you down."

"Listen, listen. I'll stop her. I asked her to check out WorldSupplî
before you and I had a deal. She doesn't know anything, hasn't been
able get any dirt on WorldSupplî at all so don't worry."

"There is no dirt on WorldSupplî. This transaction has nothing to
do with WorldSupplî. Why the hell did you do this? Let me be perfectly
clear. If I have problems, you have problems. You understand?"

"I do. Consider it done. I'll end her assignment this afternoon."
Matt said turning to leave.

"I mean what I say." Bryan yelled into the widening gap between
them.

Matt took some extra time returning to the office so he could figure
out a strategy to curtail Gette's assignment without raising suspicion. A
thought came to him that would make it easy so he had her paged immediately on his return.

"Ms. Cummings. Please come in. Fill me in on your little investigation if you would."

Gette was more nervous than a hound treed 'coon in the middle of
a field of cut corn. Exposed. Cornered. Defenseless.

"I, I really haven't learned much more Mr. DiGrande." She muttered sheepishly. "I keep digging and I see discrepancies, but I can't seem
to be able to nail anything down."

"Well here's the deal Georgette. In my experience if something big
is brewing it normally gets exposed all by itself. Humans like to talk, it's
in our nature. So the fact that you haven't found enough material on

WorldSupplî for a first page splash probably means that there isn't enough material. Understand?" Gette nodded and he continued.

"But that doesn't mean that your efforts are for naught. If something does come up, you've already assessed the company and its key players so we stand on terra firma to produce the best analysis in the industry, in the event that a story does emerge. Do I make sense?"

"Yes, Mr. DiGrande. That makes perfect sense."

"Good. Your investigation of WorldSupplî is aborted. Take the time to clean up your notes and get all your ducks in a row in case we need them going forward. I have another story I want you to cover, on an emerging state politician."

As Gette left his office, Matt allowed himself to feel relieved. His performance was more than adequate, convincing and sensible, as long as Gette hadn't uncovered his childhood tie to Jeffries. On one hand he was totally pissed at her for not revealing her investigation, while on the other he was pretty impressed by her ingenuity. He smiled internally, just a tad and just for moment, before turning to his next engagement.

Gette left his office spellbound. His explanation for terminating her assignment seemed credible on the surface but the myriad layers of different information made the abrupt stoppage too surreal to accept. Did he know about her trip to Oak Hills? Did he know that she uncovered his friendship with Jeffries? Was her covert association with her WorldSupplî friends no longer covert? She had to let the QT Kids know that things had changed and do it quickly.

When Bryan got back to WorldSupplî he opened the personnel files on Chad and Paul. Each in their own way seemed to be stellar employees with no reason to question the overall performance of the company or to delve into matters of Sarbanes-Oxley compliance costs because their positions had no bearing on such matters. While this observation held true, it was also true that both were sufficiently schooled and involved in the business aspects of the company to have the intellectual wherewithal to spot variances in performance if made visible. What Bryan couldn't determine was if or how that might have occurred.

Bryan also couldn't figure their connection to Georgette Cummings. She must have befriended them after DiGrande gave her the stupid assignment to check up on WorldSupplî. In any case she did, it seemed, elicit the involvement of at least two WorldSupplî employees in the process of conducting her investigation and somehow that involvement led her to him and his childhood. If she does suspect me of some wrongdoing, Bryan thought, how did she come to that conclusion and what, if anything, do my two apparent in-house nemeses know of my scheme?

DiGrande promised to terminate her investigation immediately so perhaps it was not too late, perhaps she was directed elsewhere before uncovering any dirt like DiGrande had intimated, or perhaps this ragtag group of upwardly inspired professionals was onto something. There were too many "perhaps" to assume that all was still OK so Bryan decided it imperative to put Detective Jeffries into full swing.

Besides tailing the members of this dubious foursome to further assess their group behavior, Bryan decided to start checking on the business activities of Chad and Paul by watching their Outlook transactions – from emails and events posted on their calendars to their contact lists. He also decided to run a log from the main frame system showing all reports executed over the course of the last several weeks. He hoped to see only those standard issue reports that run routinely by batch as opposed special query investigations that might indicate smoking gun activity.

It wasn't hard to generate a list of all reports created during the date range he desired but the list was pretty long so he narrowed it down using Chad and Paul's employee numbers as a search criteria. The results were obvious. Chad had issued a print request for the product line variations report on the Monday morning when Bryan and Alan Chandler took the weekend run from his hand. It was a separate, individual request that in no way could have been the copy they intended to intercept because that copy had come from a request by Jeffries himself.

His mind raced back to the moment, the moment when the two executives stormed into the print room to find Chad at the printer with his collection of weekend runs. He tried hard to recount the minutest details of that encounter but his effort was largely unsuccessful because they were too embroiled with grabbing the report and high tailing out. He did recall taking everything in Chads arms but they never looked further for additional reports in the room or in his office. He did recall Chad acting somewhat off guard, but chalked that up to nerves excited by their executive stature. Regardless, Jeffries conjectured, Chad found a special report in the Monday pile and knew it was sufficiently novel to warrant a reprint, but made no mention of it during their chance meeting.

It took no more than a few seconds to understand what Chad did with his new found treasure for staring at Bryan on the report run, like a Watusi in the middle of a Pygmy tribe, was a special query run by Paul two days later. Chad must have shared the report with Paul and Paul must have seen enough strange data in it to feel compelled to investigate further, hence the special query. Proving his conjecture required Bryan to print and study the report contents but when he tried to open it by name, nothing happened. Paul knew enough to delete the query which, Bryan concluded, was more than enough evidence of why it was done.

Son of a bitch, Bryan thought. My cat is not only out of the bag it's clawing my leg and tearing it to pieces. The stark reality caused him to pause and he leaned back slowly in his chair, pushed away from the desk and stared blankly at the ceiling, exasperated by the evidence before him. The ceiling took on a surreal floating quality with barely visible hues of pearl that danced in random patterns across it, breathing in a dauntingly flippant manner that seemed to challenge his very existence. Minutes passed with nothing more than shallow breaths to accompany him. No thought, no emotion, no visceral displays of anger, resentment or fear could be gotten. Just a hollow emptiness.

And then a credo emerged and solidified in his brain and a mantra presented itself for the taking. Containment. Focus on nothing but containment.

E xcept as couples conversing privately about their burgeoning relationships the QT Kids remained silent throughout the week, each upholding the decision to further their assessment of the WorldSupplî issue until their planned gathering on Friday. They decided to meet for burgers and such at a sports bar on Michigan where high backed booths adorning the walls would give ample privacy for their discussions. Besides, the place had over 50 brews on tap and everyone was thirsty for a hoppy IPA.

Paul and Chad arrived first, shortly after that Gette showed up and about half way through their first beers Janice made her grand entrance.

"Sorry I'm late. We had some last minute closings at the bank and I just couldn't get away."

"You're not late sweetheart. We've just started and there's plenty of time to catch up. Tell me what you want and I'll get it."

"Might as well stay local. How about a Goose Island Ten Hills Pale Ale?"

"You got it. Be right back." Paul said leaving to fetch the waitress.

Janice continued. "OK everyone. Has the discussion on World-Supplî started yet? I have some ideas to share."

Gette piped up. "We haven't started yet but I need to go first. Things have changed and we need to brainstorm why."

When Paul returned Gette continued. "Yesterday DiGrande called me into his office for an update on my WorldSupplî investigations. I told him that things didn't smell right but I haven't been able to uncover anything concrete. Then he terminated my assignment, rationalizing his decision on his experience, which has taught him that stories emerge naturally when time is spent talking to the involved parties and since nothing has turned up then nothing must exist. On the surface a neophyte like me would completely trust his rationale but unfortunately we know better. So the question before us is what happened? Why the change of heart?"

"That takes us back to our first question," Paul interjected. "If he's in cahoots with Jeffries, why did DiGrande ask you to investigate World-Supplî in the first place? It doesn't make sense."

Paul chimed in, "Didn't you say that these two guys were like broth-ers for years and then they severed ties completely at the end of their senior summer? I know that friendships grow apart when guys take off for different colleges and meet new people, but even when new connec-tions affect old relationships rarely do two best friends go cold turkey like these two did. I'm wondering if something happened between them. It wouldn't be the first time that two eighteen year olds ventured off and got into trouble. Maybe they just got sick of each other, or maybe they share some deep dark secret that resurfaced after years of being buried."

The thought caused everyone to pause and consider the implica-tions and silence abounded as each played a thousand different situa-tions in their head. Unfortunately their collective insight resulted in nothing more salient than a TV test pattern, a static unchanging flat image representing connection without transmission, a pattern with def-inition but devoid of reason.

Chad broke the raster screen, "Let's back up a minute. This whole thing started on a Monday morning several weeks ago when I discovered that strange report before Chandler and Jeffries had a chance to retrieve it from the printer. As far as I know they have no idea that I saw the report, let alone that we're questioning its content. Despite that, their behavior was edgy to say the least; Chandler seemed nervous and uptight while Jeffries played the role of supportive first mate. Come to think of it, he was more than just supportive - he seemed to be defending the data in the report as if it were more of an expectation than a surprise. Given our input on this guy from Georgette, and the dubious nature of the money being handed over to the Sarbanes-Oxley vendor, I'd say that Jef-fries is a lone wolf in this thing, stealing money from the company and trying to make it look legit."

"I think we all agree on that account Chad," Janice interrupted, "and perhaps we can assume that Chandler is just a pawn in this game as well. But that still doesn't give us a clue about the connection with DiGrande. Either DiGrande is part of the scheme or he's being forced into assisting Jeffries."

"You mean like blackmail?" Paul asked.

"Yes. Let's assume that DiGrande is being blackmailed. In order for Jeffries to have that much clout over the guy he must hold some pretty important skinny. My guess – something occurred during their summer trip in '74 that forced them to end their friendship and now Jeffries is using it to enlist DiGrande as a fence."

"Does that explain why DiGrande asked me to investigate World-Supplî?"

"I don't think so," Matt mused. "If Jeffries contacted DiGrande to blackmail him then DiGrande would do everything in his power to steer clear of WorldSupplî. But what if Jeffries contacted DiGrande under the guise of re-establishing their friendship? He could have made DiGrande nervous. Think about it, you haven't talked to your best friend from high school for decades because you share a horrible secret that you want to keep buried and then, out of the blue, he contacts you without any special reason to trigger it. Wouldn't you feel the need to find out more about this long lost buddy? Wouldn't it make sense for DiGrande to have him checked out?"

"That has to be the reason why Gette got the assignment," Paul ruminated. "That's also why DiGrande terminated it. When Jeffries twisted the knife to make DiGrande assist him, he knew that Gette's assignment could pose a major problem, that she might find out the truth and expose both of them in the process. So he had to stop her."

"If our conjecture is right then DiGrande has to be one really pissed off cat. Not directly guilty per se, but caught between a rock and a hard place. Do you think Gette should confront him?" Janice asked.

"Let's not go there right now, I have something else I have to confess first," Gette continued. "Things haven't been the same since I went to Cincinnati on my fact finding trip. I feel like I'm being watched all the time; like someone is stalking me. I have no tangible reason to feel this way, and I don't feel threatened by the WorldSupplî issue, but I can't seem to shake the feeling that I'm being tailed, and it's creepy, it's giving me the willies."

"What do you mean you feel like you're being followed? Is the investigation getting to you or has your sixth sense kicked in and you really are detecting something foreign around you?"

"I don't know, it's just a feeling that I've been getting the past couple of days. I just feel like someone is watching me. For no reason that I can discern the hair on my arms want to stand up and a chill goes through my body and when I look around I never spot anyone but I know they're there, like when you're passing a car on the highway and you look at the other driver knowing that they're already looking at you."

"Who knows that you went to Cincinnati?" Janice asked.

"Just you guys. I never told anyone."

"If someone started following you after your trip then someone knows about it and perhaps also thinks that we're onto something," Chad stated. "We have to find out if your suspicions are real and I think I know how. You and I can leave here separately. I'll go first and you follow about 15 minutes later. I'll get myself situated near your apartment building and watch you arrive to see if I can spot your stalker. Hopefully that will give us a better idea of what's going on and who, if anyone, might be behind this thing. Who knows, maybe you have a secret admirer unrelated to the WorldSuppli matter, not that that would make me feel any better."

"Whoa Tiger!" Paul chimed. "We're in this as a team. What's good for the goose is good for the gander. We're all going to leave together, go our separate ways and then rendezvous at Gette's apartment. Gette – can you stop at a grocery store or something to pass about 15 minutes while we get situated at different locations?"

The QT Kids spent the next several minutes diagramming their plans. They talked about positioning and timing and whether a photograph was needed and if so, by God, to make sure that the flash was off. They were determined to finish this matter once and for all to allow Gette to rest easier and resume her life on a more normal basis.

Their bill came and the men were kind enough to pick up the tab after a bit of contrived resistance on the part of the girls. They left with a plan in hand to seek out the truth by moving the game into their home court; to get the upper hand with an aggressive offensive position.

At the far end of the bar Bryan sat with a rigidly determined look on his face, a look that broadcast ire more prolific than a liberal's disdain of conservatives. DiGrande was not able to garner control of the situation by terminating Gette's assignment apparently because she had learned much more than she let DiGrande know. Bryan decided that he could no longer sit idly in the hope that these young minds would forego their investigation. He had to enact his plan to create the ultimate accident and put a stop to their intrusion. It was time to force a shutdown.

He watched the foursome exit the bar and then sauntered casually towards the door as they departed separately, each going their own way. He saw Gette walking quickly to the nearest bus stop and decided to follow her again, to re-confirm her routine, only this time he was finalizing his plans for executing a catastrophic calamity that involved her demise. A shame, he thought, such a pretty and motivated young lady.

When Gette got on the bus Bryan, as he did previously, entered as well. She seemed distractedly pensive as she stood grasping a strap for balance, looking around in quick bird-like twists as if searching for something lost, her actions causing Bryan concern for his cover, concern for his plan. Her behavior awakened in him the essentialness of time and the urgency with which he had to accelerate his plan so he decided that tonight he would orchestrate the final touches, to be ready when opportunity knocked.

Gette left the bus one stop before her apartment as arranged with the QT kids and proceeded slowly and as planned to the pharmacy on the corner. She glanced at the clock near the cashiers' station. In fifteen minutes it would be close to eight when she could checkout and proceed home. Fifteen minutes in a drug store is a lot of time, she thought, so she decided to browse the best seller and magazine racks after picking up some facial wash and shampoo. At the anointed time, she decided on a thriller based best-selling paperback and proceeded to the cashier's window. Several customers had checked out since her arrival, but no new customers had entered.

She paid the cashier and then hastened out of the store. Once outside she stopped to adjust her coat, purse and packages while furtively scanning the area for any untoward characters lurking in the shadows. It was dark outside but the street lights cast an uneven hue across the objects in the area with just enough brightness to see them clearly albeit through a mono-chrome overtone. Gette was not able to pinpoint anything or anyone sus-picious or otherwise misplaced, nor was she able to see any of her cohorts, as she began a deliberate saunter to her apartment building door.

Bryan watched the pharmacy from across the street and half a block east where he concealed himself behind the thick trunk of an old Oak tree. He was wondering why she took so long when finally she appeared and headed west towards her apartment. Perhaps she was waiting for a prescription to be filled, at any rate, she made a purchase which fell in line with her normal routine of running errands before holing up for the evening. He watched as she readied her things for the short trek and then, when her stride made clear her intent, he emerged in a casual lope to follow and complete the formulation of her demise.

A few steps further Gette stopped abruptly causing Bryan to make an immediate adjustment in his route. Fortunately the street was lined with boutiques so it was a simple task to feign some window shopping while Gette paused, which was apparently just to answer her phone. It was Chad. His call was arranged by the QT kids to give him the chance to trail Gette at a fixed distance. She began walking and talking, nonstop as most women so frequently do, but her discourse was just a description of her progress towards her apartment to keep Chad appropriately in tow.

"Gette, do me a favor and stop in that coffee shop on the next cor-ner," Chad whispered.

"Why? Is someone following me?"

"I don't think so, but there's a guy in a hoodie walking down the street behind you a fair ways and I want to see if he hangs around when you stop."

"OK. There's a Starbucks ahead that I go to quite frequently. I'm almost there," she said and then a few seconds later, "Going in now. I'll get a latte to go."

"That should work. Tell me when you are getting ready to leave."

When Gette entered Starbucks the man in the hoodie kept walking for little while and then did a very strange thing. He found a spot by a group of tall garbage cans and stopped there largely hidden from view, causing Chad's heart to immediately start beating like a mad man on a kettle drum. Someone was definitely following her and it was her instincts that caused him to be exposed.

Chad wasn't sure what to do, to continue trailing Gette and her stalker, to confront the man right now or to run to Gette to make sure that she was safe. The violation of her privacy and the question of her safety were driving Chad to the brink of fury when he caught his emotions to focus the bigger picture, which was a resolution to this entire matter in a permanent and lawful way.

Bryan meanwhile was relishing in the splendor of his masterful ingenuity as the final snippets of his plan came into such clarity that he could taste it over the stench from the cans. He watched as Gette left Starbucks with a steaming cup of coffee and decided then that he need not pursue her further so, when she was a sufficient distance away, he surfaced from behind his nasty cubby to back track to his car. Chad stood still momentarily in a state of utter shock before turning away from the man and heading toward a deli. The man didn't seem to take notice of Chad even though Chad tried inconspicuously to get a good look at him. His hoodie was pulled too far over his head to see any bit of his face except the gleam of white reflecting off teeth from a rye and wanton smile.

Chad was separated from Bryan by a football field when he broke out of the deli and began to hightail it to Gette. He had already told her to wait for him so it wasn't long before she was in sight and he was able to quench his anger and subdue his fears by extending a heart warmed embrace full of kisses and special hugs.

"Whoa big boy! What's gotten into you?" Gette queried with surprise.

"There was someone following you. I almost lost my mind. He stopped stalking you after you came out of Starbucks. I couldn't see his face."

Gette's jaw dropped and her face went beyond blank thinking about the fact that her intuition was spot on. "Did he see you? Is that why he stopped?" She finally eked out.

"No. I don't think so. In fact I'm almost certain he didn't know I was watching. Let's call the others and meet at your place, OK?"

A few minutes later the QT kids were seated in Gette's apartment sipping wine while discussing the stalker issue with a passion that made Romeo's love for Juliet seem a trickle to the Amazon river. Their zeal to take aggressive control of the WorldSupplî issue was now, at least temporarily, replaced with immense anger and lots of fear.

"This is crazy," Gette continued. "I'm not cut out for this stuff. Isn't there any way we can just stop this and go back to life as usual? We could all be in grave danger at this point and quite frankly it doesn't really seem worth it. I know that white collar crime is a major concern these days, but no one gets hurt by it, not like rape or murder, so why can't we just let it go?"

"I think it's too late. The guy who's following you must be from WorldSupplî and if he saw us together at dinner then he's going to want to determine if we are all involved in this and will try to find out exactly who we are and what we might know. It won't be hard for him to learn that we are WorldSupplî employees," Chad said pointing at Paul and himself. "And he probably already knows that you work for the paper and have been on assignment studying WorldSupplî. Why else would he be trailing you? He must be trying to determine if you've uncovered any dirt on WorldSupplî and how far your knowledge has spread. If this thing at WorldSupplî is as big as it seems, then this guy, or guys, must be pretty determined to see their scheme to its conclusion, and if we're dealing with someone who's totally imbalanced, then our involvement might just provide a new wrinkle of enjoyment in his already elaborate game."

"What are you saying? That his discovery of us is adding to the thrill of victory?"

"I'm no shrink so I don't know but let's just assume, whether this guy is completely insane or still somewhat sane, that he will stop at nothing to complete his theft from the company. If that's the case and he thinks that we're standing in his way then chances are he'll try to move us out of the way no matter what actions we do, or do not, undertake from this point forward."

"In other words," Janice chimed in, "We have to stop him before he stops us. Right?"

"That's my opinion."

"Mine too," Paul agreed.

After exhausting their brains about the pickle in which they found themselves, Paul and Janice departed to spend the balance of their weekend alone together. Gette closed and locked her apartment door thankful as all get out that Paul was there to comfort her. She turned to him with an immediate embrace that locked their bodies as one. Paul nosed through her hair smelling the soft sweet fragrance and feeling the smooth flow of her nape while Gette stayed coiled in his arms soaking up the reassurance of security and companionship that they proffered. They remained thus for several minutes each deep in thoughts that ranged from the evening's discovery to their discovery of each other. Gette was first to pull from the musing embrace.

"I've got something for you," she said excitedly.

"A surprise? Not sure I can take another surprise tonight, if you know what I mean."

"I think you'll be able to stomach this one. In fact, it should help us take our minds off our troubles. Wait here a minute." She said getting up quickly and with utmost eagerness. A moment later Gette returned exactly as she had departed, not carrying anything and certainly not gone long enough to use the John.

"What's up? Where's the surprise?"

She appeared incapable of controlling herself, beaming with extraordinary exuberance, like an artist ready to unveil a new masterpiece. She returned to the couch to sit with her lower legs tucked tightly under her thighs and her back soldier erect. She was quick to clear her throat and then from that posture, pulled a sheet of paper from her rear pocket and broke the silence with incredible singing. It was Chad's music and Gette's words. It was poetry with harmony. It was graceful and serene and melodic and it flowed from Gette with the softness of satin in a gentle but sturdy breeze.

Chad sat through her the debut silent and spellbound, speechless even when she was through. "Oh my God do I love you!" He finally whispered.

Chad's simple statement found its home in a recipient stunned by its impact and Gette, caught off guard in the moment, failed to utter a reply.

"I'm sorry. I definitely should not have said that. We barely know each other yet. I'm just so moved by what you just did that it just came out. I don't know what to say."

"Are you telling me that you didn't mean it?"

"No, not exactly. I do have loving feelings for you Gette. Maybe it's too early in our relationship for words like love. Maybe it's still infatuation. I didn't mean to stun you. I don't know. I've never felt this way before."

"Well, I am stunned but not for the reason you might think. I've never had feelings like this before either and while they're wonderful and exciting, they also scare me to death. Want to know why? Because I think I'm in love with you too and I don't want to go into this solo."

"Solo? Never! As long as you'll have me I'll definitely want you. As long as you want me, I'll give you my support in each and every way that I possibly can. I think about you constantly and count the minutes between our encounters like they're hours."

"Really?"

"Absolutely. For once in my life I feel like things are going to go my way. I'm happy to wake up every morning and I have a renewed sense of purpose that, I might add, has just been blown away by your song."

"Oh my God! Can this be real? You know that this set of circumstances, even without the matter of WorldSupplî looming between us, could be life changing, don't you?"

"I certainly do. A few weeks ago my routine was so predictable you could set your watch by it. Work, take-out dinner, home, write some lines, fall asleep and then start it all over again. In the process I lost my passion for creativity; could see my music suffering as a result and I was becoming sarcastic too, which is not my normal mode of conduct. Now everything is upside down and as scary as it might seem, there's no way would I change it for the world."

"Believe me; I know exactly what you mean. I was trapped too. Trapped in a rut of self-pity. Unhappy with my professional situation, alone in my personal life; feeling like a loser when I started this adventure with huge expectations. Then I bumped into you and now my life has wholly new dimensions that I can't wait to explore. But this issue with WorldSupplî is killing me. I'm being stalked? How could this be? Just when life opens new doors of friendship and camaraderie we've got this mess hanging over us like a black cloud seeded with arsenic. We have to put this to an end as soon as possible and the only way I know how is to confront DiGrande."

"Perhaps you're right. I don't have any other ideas. Just do me a favor and let the team know when you intend to talk to him so we can be ready to assist if needed."

"Then stay by your phones on Monday morning, cause I don't intend to wait."

The adrenaline rush was still in full swing when Bryan got to his car so he decided to head out for the evening in search of a lonely woman with whom to woo to bed. His favorite spot was on the north end of town between Michigan and LaSalle where dime-a-dozen office ladies drank too much in search of Mr. Right. He got there just past ten and the place was hopping. A small jazz quartet was playing acoustic in the corner while people milled about in small groups drinking over-priced lavish drinks from even more lavish glasses. He ordered a martini and began to survey the landscape.

It was too early for a pick-up. Any booze infested buzz in a girl right now was only going to light up her social zeal and listening to the incessant diatribe of a half buzzed woman was definitely not in his plans. So Bryan stayed put to swill a few stiff drinks until the body language of the ladies began to show signs of their yearning for sexual release, after drink moved south, from head to sweet spot, working its magic on their libidos.

By 11:30 Bryan had the "all-nighters" singled out and from them he singled out an attractive woman in a sleek yellow dress for victimizing. His game was on. He made eye contact with her briefly only to turn away and lean on the bar. Then he started conversing with a less attractive woman near him. He allowed his mannerisms to be showy and flirtatious. He made the conversation light hearted and witty, causing his listener to laugh with delighted animation, while casting furtive, eye-catching glances at his real target. Before long the girl in yellow held eye contact with Bryan each time he gave her one of his infamous stares.

"Excuse me," he then said somewhat softly. "I'm being beckoned by a call to the loo." And off he strode in the direction of yellow dress.

Passing her Bryan said. "I love your dress. The color adds a wonderful accent to an already beautiful lady." And he kept heading to the men's room.

"Thank you," she called in his wake. "Are you leaving?"

"No honey. Just need a break. Come on." He said holding out his hand for her to join him.

She stared at his invitation not knowing how to respond. He gestured for her come with a convincing, pleading smile; a slight twist of his head.

"Are you crazy?"

"I'm just going to the bathroom; be back in a minute and if you're still here I'd love to buy you a drink."

He took his time in the bathroom thinking she was pining for him but when he returned, she was gone. Mad as hell he went back to the bar to resume his chat with the other woman.

"So what are your plans for the evening young lady? Any interest in finding a quieter place for a more intimate discussion?"

"You mean like your place or mine?"

"Is that an invitation or are you just toying with me?"

"I don't know. I don't like it when men come on too strong."

"I wasn't the one who suggested a tryst. You were."

"That's bullshit. I was just being direct when you were skirting about your goal to get laid. I'm OK with that; everybody needs some lovin' once in a while."

"Is that what you need tonight? Some lovin'?"

"I could be talked into it if the man was kind and gentlemanly with me. I don't just sleep around; there has to be some sort of a connection first. I might be able to feel connected to you right now, I don't know."

"That sounds promising, assuming that my goal is to get laid. What if I told you that I only have sex after several dates and when the "connection" is better defined?"

"I'd say bullshit again. The girl in the yellow dress dumped you so you came back to me. That's what I think."

Bryan looked at her with darkened eyes that failed to hide all of the steaming ire inside. His ego was fine, unbruised, but his dismissal by the yellow dressed girl pissed him off to no end. He had her in his sights. He envisioned taking her violently and his groin ached with pleasure at the thought of controlling her. Now he would have to take his pleasure from a woman with lesser sexual attraction when he so badly needed a vamp. He looked at her with an uncontrollable desire to slap her silly and decided that that was exactly what he would do.

"OK then. No more games. I've been working almost non-stop for months now and need a hug. You know, someone to nestle up to, to cuddle and enjoy the warmth of skin on skin, to smell flesh and fluids intermingling."

"Is that your pick-up line?"

"No! I figured you for the type that hates pickup lines. Besides, you're obviously too smart to fall for some dumb catch phrase."

"You mean like finding a quieter place for a more intimate discussion?"

"OK – you caught me; called my bluff as they say. So now what? Are we going to be adult and satisfy each other's desires? Or are we going to succumb to society's artificial mores and go home to masturbate?"

"I think we can find a way be adult. Ready?" And with that pronouncement she began to move towards the door, with Bryan in her wake.

When they got outside she turned to him for their first touch and Bryan did not fail her. He wrapped her in his arms and kissed her greedily on her cheek and then her lips. He pressed his body to her and was pleasantly surprised at the feel of large plump breasts hidden beneath her blouse. They aroused him and he moved his hand towards them, only to be stymied en-route.

"That'll have to wait big boy. I don't get on well with PDA's if you know what I mean."

He dropped his hand and stared at her until she spoke again, "OK. Should I give you my address and meet there? I'm only about 15 minutes away, up the lake."

"I think that would be fine."

They departed after a brief kiss and headed for their cars. When Bryan arrived at her apartment the lights were on and the door was slightly ajar. He knocked softly and entered. She had some soft music playing and was in the kitchen uncorking a bottle of Chardonnay.

"Hello there. Have a seat. I'll be right with you."

A few minutes later she came to sit by his side, offering a glass of wine in the process. They completed a ceremonial clinking of the glasses, as two long held friends would on a routine reunion, and then sat sipping with an intermingling of light conversion. Bryan put his glass down and turned to an accepting upturned face. Her lips were wet with wine and anticipation and the French kissing that ensued was heated.

They moved to her bedroom where Bryan disrobed her with quick, brusque movements, like he was removing steak from a vacuum sealed package. His actions caused her to believe that a physically focused encounter was in order so she pushed him playfully and sparred with him gingerly to support his ambitious libido. Her actions simultaneously raised his ire and with it his erection, which stood pulsing on the brink of explosion. He turned her over and slapped her ass firmly but not to do harm. She winced and cried for the big boy to issue more punishment so Byran slapped again, harder. She twirled around exposing her trim pubic hair and protruding nipples. Her areolas were small and pink but her nipples were long and hard and Bryan squeezed them and twisted. She screamed in pain but it only sufficed to make him yearn for meting out more punishment so he grabbed her trimmed bush and pulled as hard as he could.

"Jesus Christ! Get out. Leave me alone. You're a maniac. Stop! Stop now! I don't want this. This is no longer consensual."

Bryan didn't hear a word. He slapped her face and manhandled her onto her belly, dragging her hips to the edge of the bed where he forced himself upon her. His member found home in a warm bath of delectable sweetness and he jammed it deep with one painful thrust. She screamed and started crying. He dug his fingers into the sides of her ample buttock and kept thrusting like a dog in heat until an explosion of semen erupted from his friend, a release welcomed like cool water on a hot forehead. He slumped forward in the relief of the moment and kissed her head as she whimpered in pain and humiliation. Bryan's ecstasy lay in his control of her, his annihilation of her self-esteem, not in the physical act itself.

He let himself out of her apartment, leaving her in a coiled heap of despair, tucked in a fetal position like she was trying to return to the womb, a gratifying sight that left Bryan alive and full of vigor. There would be no sleep this evening. The domination ritual just completed had left rivers of adrenalin coursing through his veins so he chose instead to use his verve to craft the finishing touches to his plan. Gette must die before she revealed the results of her investigation. With her gone the rest of the motley crew would recede from view and wither away like a bare flower dropped on a parched desert floor. But first he had to find a way to lure Gette into a position of susceptibility, where he, like a Praying Mantis lying in wait to snatch up its food, would put her peacefully and permanently to sleep.

G ette got to work on Monday determined to confront DiGrande
with everything the QT kids had discovered. She was able to corner him at the conclusion of their morning meeting.

"Mr. DiGrande, do you have a minute?"

"For you, of course, what's up?"

"I need to speak with you in private. There are some things I need
to fill you in on. They relate to discoveries made during my special
assignment."

Her words caused a surge of blood in DiGrande's head and an
instant increase in pressure and temperature. His life was already upside
down. Now what?

"OK Ms. Cummings. I'll have my assistant call you when I'm free."
And he turned quickly to escape before his reaction could be detected.

A few hours later Gette was in DiGrande's office with the door
closed.

"Okay Georgette, what's up?"

"I don't know where to start. There's so much. First I guess I should
tell you that I know about your past friendship with Byran Jeffries."

Matt stared at Georgette for a moment with a stunned and painful
look on his face and then said as casually as possible, "Please continue."

Gette proceeded to unload on Matt all that she knew but did not
disclose anything about the involvement of the QT kids or the fact
that she was being followed. Throughout the process Matt remained
silent and stoic, wondering if the Miami incident was part of her discovery.

At the conclusion of her disclosure Gette said, "So here's what I
think. I think Bryan Jeffries is blackmailing you for something he knows
about you from your past. I think something happened during your trip
the summer after high school graduation because you two were inseparable before and completely severed after. I think Jeffries is using you as
his patsy to launder the money he is stealing from WorldSupplî through
a bogus Sarbanes-Oxley compliance account. I think you're knee deep in
trouble and you haven't really done anything wrong; you're just a victim
of circumstance. At least, that's what I hope."

DiGrande stared at the floor and Gette started to speak again but he held up his hand and silenced her. He maintained his downcast posture for several moments with a pained expression even more palpable than the silence that enveloped them. Finally he spoke.

"Now it's my time to say 'I don't know where to start'." He paused before continuing, "Jeffries is using me to move money, and he does have a lever of sorts to force my hand, but he told me it was to protect his assets from becoming his girlfriends. Supposedly, he's terminating his relationship with her and under common law a lot of his assets would become hers and he said he didn't think that was fair. But now I know he lied to me."

He continued, "It seems that Mr. Jeffries has gone mad. At some point during his career a screw must have gotten loose and now he's apparently a psychopath. I saw some evidence of strange behavior when we were kids but it wasn't all that bad. I guess his father kept him in check."

"Kept him in check or caused him to go crazy?"

"Who knows? At least when he forced me to help him I thought it was legal, immoral yes but illegal no. Now I'm involved in a major federal offense and when he's caught I'll be implicated. This is miserable, absolutely miserable. The son-of-a-bitch new exactly what he was doing when he confronted me. I was leery from the onset, that's why I asked you to check on WorldSupplî, but never in my wildest dreams did I suspect anything like this."

"It's worse than you think. I'm being stalked by someone who's involved in this thing. That's why I came to you now. I had to rule you in or out, one way or the other because this whole mess has got to end and I'd like to still be breathing when it does."

"Jesus Christ! You've got to be kidding! You thought I was involved. Now I'm beginning to see. Jeffries comes to me with a proposition after years of absence and we renew our friendship with a get rich quick scheme. The thought has credence but my God, I would never, ever, knowingly step outside the law. You don't know me on a personal level at all; I'm the luckiest man alive; I have a great life; I've been madly in love with the same woman since the first time my eyes met hers. I would never put my wife, or my children, in jeopardy. Never!"

"OK. OK. But now you're in this mess and so am I. I can't sleep at night knowing that someone is out there that might want to harm me. I feel violated Goddamn it!"

Matt stared at Gette while her message sank in, all the way to the bottom. He had unknowingly placed her in harm's way and now he had to get her out. His secret in Miami had allowed a maniac to be unleashed and a lie involving grand larceny to be put into effect. Unfortunately Gette had learned enough from her investigation to put Jeffries scheme at risk and that could spell a disaster much worse than theft.

"His mother called to ask if he was attending the high school reunion. That's how he found out about you. That's why I stopped the assignment - so you wouldn't learn about anything that would affect his transfer of assets. But now, he must know that you've found out about his scheme and that means nothing but trouble. I got you into this mess. I've got to get you out.

"Do you think he has accomplices? Someone on the inside at WorldSupplî?"

"He might have a partner or partners, it's hard to say, but I doubt it's anyone at WorldSupplî. He would probably want to keep the involvement of insiders to a minimum, but someone on the outside to dummy invoices and collect the money, that's a definite possibility."

"Then we don't how big this is or who's following me or how to stop this and it has to stop or I'll go crazy or worse - they'll kill me. I can't take this."

"I don't know what to say. I'm so sorry. We'll work something out. I know we will. Just give me a day to think this over and I'll get back to you. I promise I'll make this right." Matt said with utmost conviction.

"I don't know what to do either, but I'm constantly thinking about it you can be damn sure of that!"

Gette got up to leave relieved on one hand that DiGrande's role in the scheme erred more on the side of innocent victim than unlawful participant; scared sober on the other that a crazed lunatic, confirmed to be stealing from WorldSupplî, had uncovered her investigation and was now working to dislodge it. God damn his mother for querying him on the re-union. She should have known that might happen. She should have covered her tracks with a disguise of sorts, but now it was too late. When she got back to her office she called Chad.

"Hi, it's me? Everything good at work this morning?"

"Yeah. A normal Monday, what about you?"

"I just had my meeting. Can we get together tonight, the four of us?"

"Of course. You know where Samali's is? About 5:30?

"No, but I'll get directions on line and yes 5:30 is fine."

"OK. I'll get the rest of the crew and we'll see you there."

"OK bye."

Their conversation was intentionally curt. They would decide their next step at Samali's where it was safe to engage in an open dialog.

Samali's was quiet when the QT kids convened at a corner table to order some wine and a mix of small plates. The tension in the air was palpable despite the easy atmosphere that made Samali's a local favorite.

Gette started the conversation. "This morning I told DiGrande what we know but made no mention of any of you so he must think I'm in this alone. You should have seen his reaction. He was blown away. There's no way he's in cahoots with Jeffries but he is being blackmailed to assist him with laundering the money."

"Did he tell you how he's being blackmailed?"

"No. Just that Jeffries has some lever over him – a lever that he confessed to when I mentioned the abrupt termination of their relationship. So it seems that we're right - something happened the summer of their high school graduation that DiGrande needs to keep secret. Why else would he agree to Jeffries demands?"

"It must be an incredible secret if he's willing to accept involvement in a federal offense."

"That's the other thing – Jeffries told him that he needed to hide the money to avoid sharing it with his common law partner, whose relationship he intends to dissolve. DiGrande only learned this morning that the money was being illegally obtained."

"Wow. Jeffries is some scumbag huh? Abuses an old friendship and lies to him in the process. He must be really pissed that his iron-clad ploy is unraveling." Paul stated emphatically.

"Nice one Paul. Why not scare more shit out of the already scared shitless?" Chad stated dejectedly.

"Sorry guys. I know everyone is scared and I don't mean to make things worse but we've got to know, like now, who's following Gette."

"Of that I am certain we are all in agreement," Janice piped up, "so let's try to make some sense of this."

She continued, "The guy following Gette is either Jeffries or a cohort and since he's followed Gette there's a good chance that he's seen us all together. And if it's someone from WorldSupplî then he'll also know that Gette has help from the inside."

Her words caused them to pause in silence. The blank stares conveyed more than any group of words could.

That same Monday was D-day for Bryan. Time to begin felling the dominos he had lined up in his plan. The first and easiest one to fall required a few minutes with Chandler to set the appropriate actions into motion and to establish an alibi of sorts. He called Chandler as the morning neared ten and asked for a quick get-together.

"No problem." Chandler replied, "I have the next twenty minutes available so stop in now if you can."

"Be right there." Jeffries retorted and promptly hung up the phone.

"How's everything going?" Bryan said as he entered, "Still having issues with the board or did our last explanation of the profit shortfall assuage their fears?"

"We're still having issues but it seems as though they've accepted the explanation for now. Of course they expect us to implement changes in our cost structure to offset the shortfall, so now I'm considering what needs to be done. It's painful, absolutely fucking painful."

"That's kind of why I'm here. There's a conference on business productivity and peer group benchmarking in Atlanta next week. I think we should attend. Not you or me but those young kids – what're their names – Paul Landau and Chad Prescott? They seem to have a handle on technology and they know our business processes so all they need to do is pick up one or two good ideas and even if they don't bridge the gap we need to fix, we'll still get payback on the investment. What do you think?"

"How can I say no? We need to do everything conceivable to get back into the top quartile in our industry. Go ahead with it and we'll hold a debriefing when they get back."

"I think the decision for them to attend should come from you rather than me. You can explain the challenges we're facing and set the stage for the type of ideas these boys should be thinking about. It will also underscore the urgency of the matter."

"I can agree to that. Consider it done." Chandler replied.

"Great. Here's the information on the conference." Jeffries said while handing Chandler a pamphlet. "I have one more thing. I'm going to conduct some research on my own. I think it makes sense to audit the way other companies are handling Sarbanes-Oxley. Perhaps I've missed something in our management of SOX."

"What do you have in mind?"

"Nothing too elaborate. I just set up a few meetings with some bankers I know from my former roles. I intend to pick their brains to see if SOX compliance can be accomplished by a different and hopefully less costly means. I set up the meetings for this week and next so our debriefing the week following can include all of the lessons learned."

"That works for me. I'll let the board know that we're moving in a few different directions to evaluate our options. Thanks. This should keep the horses from stampeding for a little while longer."

"No problem. Not to worry, we'll be the A team we were once thought to be. It's just gonna take a couple of months to get there." And Jeffries departed before more could be said.

Chandler did a quick perusal of the conference pamphlet and then asked his secretary to arrange a meeting with Chad and Paul. They came to Chandler's office just after lunch bewildered by the request. Fortunately, it didn't take long to understand that their summons was innocent of any connection to the Jeffries affair and their angst soon dissipated.

Chandler did a masterful job impressing upon them the business issue that their participation in the conference was intending to address and their immediate reaction to his colloquy was steeped with feelings of honor, but it also generated a modicum of deceit. Then the realization of their departure from Chicago, and its implications with regard to Gette's safety, loomed large, like a strong headwind in advance of a major storm. They left his office perplexed.

"What are we going to do? We have to go to the conference." Paul stated.

"We'll have to get Gette some support. Perhaps we should go see DiGrande. Give him the rundown on the complete story and demand that he get a body guard or something."

"Great idea. How do we approach him? Through Gette?"

"I doubt she'll go for that. We'll need to meet with him by ourselves."

Chad grabbed his cell phone, looked up the main number at the Tribute and dialed. "Mr. DiGrande please."

"Just one moment sir."

"Good afternoon. This is Mr. DiGrande's assistant. How may I help you?"

"My name is Chad Prescott and I would like to speak with Mr. DiGrande please."

"What is the nature of your call?"

"Please tell him that I am a friend of Georgette Cummings from WorldSupplî."

A few seconds later the line came off hold and Matt DiGrande was on the other end.

"This is Matt DiGrande. Please listen to me before you start speaking. I think I know the matter for which you are calling. Meet me at Shaw's Crab House tomorrow at 12:30 for lunch. If I'm right we have a lot to discuss; if I'm wrong you get a free lunch."

"OK Mr. DiGrande. We'll see you there." Chad said terminating the call and turning to Paul. "The guy doesn't want to talk over the phone; we're meeting him for lunch."

"Do you think we can trust him?"

"Gette decided to trust him, so I guess we should too. Besides, it's the only choice we have. Meet me in the lobby tomorrow at noon. In the mean time we should see about registering for the conference and making travel arrangements."

"Okay. I'll see ya later."

Each went their separate way thinking about the luncheon appointment and their week ahead. Chad's mind was overwhelmed to the point of dysfunction. Instead of remaining sharp and focused it felt heavy and full of mud and it left his psyche strained to the point of nausea. Paul's reaction wasn't much better but he was able to shake off enough butterflies to think about a strategy for their time with DiGrande.

Chad and Paul met in the main lobby precisely at noon, proceeded to Shaw's Crab House and arrived there several minutes early. The hostess informed them that Mr. DiGrande had already arrived and she escorted them to his table toward the rear of the establishment where, under vaulted industrial ceilings bathed by cool recessed lighting, sat a figure recognizable from his public stature. Brief salutations ensued, they took to their seats in a somewhat awkward fashion and then DiGrande spoke.

"So. You're both from WorldSupplî and you both know Georgette. Is it safe to assume that she told you about the assignment I gave her to investigate the inner workings at your company?"

"It is." Chad replied. "And we also know that the assignment was issued under false pretenses."

"That's a fairly harsh, but perhaps not undeserved criticism, young man. There were several reasons behind my decision to ask Georgette to check into WorldSupplî, but none were intended to lead where they did. Now we're at an unexpected crossroads that needs to be handled carefully and with immediacy. I would prefer to dispense of the blame and focus on a plan resolve this dilemma instead. Don't you agree?"

Paul and Chad nodded silently but made no attempt to speak so DiGrande continued.

"I'm being blackmailed. The reason I'm in a position to be blackmailed is personal. Last week Georgette allowed herself to trust me and she told me what she had learned. To that time I had no idea I was abetting criminal activity or that she was potentially in danger, but now that I know it's my responsibility to find an answer, one that's lasting; one that returns everyone involved back to their former lifestyle."

"Listen Mr. DiGrande, Gette's an amazing woman and I've come to admire her immensely. Now some fucker is stalking her and we know that a lot of money is involved so we think he'll do anything to stop her. She's not potentially in danger; we think she's being targeted to be executed. We've seen the asshole. We know the threat's real."

"You've seen him? What did he look like?"

"Nondescript. His face was hidden and he was wearing only drab oversized clothes so we don't know if it was Jeffries or some thug that he hired."

Paul continued. "To keep her safe we've been making sure that Gette's never alone but now we're slated to go together to a conference in Atlanta and she'll be alone and exposed. We can't let that happen."

"Jesus Christ." DiGrande said, exasperated. "When do you leave? When do you return? What exactly are your travel plans?"

They spent the next hour discussing the current situation and the best way to assure Gette's safety. DiGrande, as a controversial public figure, had previously run into circumstances where his opinions were detested enough to cause some weak-minded individuals to threaten his life. The Tribute responded by providing him with round-the-clock support from professional body guards so he was able, and willing, to extend that same courtesy to Gette. He promised to have a detail in place before the boys headed to Atlanta, assuring them that Gette would have the best possible safety net available.

With that immediate concern accounted for their conversation turned to the actions needed to permanently arrest the entire matter. DiGrande, overwhelmed with guilt, tried to maintain his composure while the boys vociferously emoted about the damage they wished to inflict on Jeffries and everyone else involved. Their youthful testosterone infused vigor was ushered forth with enough audacity to scare Freddy Krueger into hiding when in fact their hype was driven by an overbearing level of fear that lack of control had rendered. That notwithstanding, in the course of the discussion they devised a plan to expose Jeffries's scheme, but of necessity, their design would also open up Matts old wounds with the potential to inflict on him much personal pain.

Having accomplished what they could, they exchanged cell phone numbers and shook hands before departing.

The QT Kids met every night after work discussing the matter of the upcoming business trip and DiGrande's, now in place, body guard. They felt a little more re-assured for Gette's safety but still had no sound ploy for ending the matter with Jeffries, who seemed to disappear. Matt DiGrande was in fairly regular contact with Chad and he kept promising to bring them closure quickly but had yet to detail the means for that end to be reached. For that reason each day felt like a week and the week a full year, and when at last Friday came they felt no closer to a resolution, only further down the same road to nowhere.

Gette continued to reassure them that she would be fine but her knees kept knocking the entire time and her diminished appetite remained intact despite intense hunger. No one dared to think about good times and parties, or even quiet drinks and dinner, for the omnipresent invasion of their privacy felt greater than the weight on the shoulders of Atlas. This weekend they would simply keep to the vigil of their watch over Gette and make sure that DiGrande's protection was in place and working.

The weekend passed slowly and without any signs of the stalker. Their respite from his presence gave them cause to relax somewhat, to let the tightness in their chests to ebb slightly, to breathe with a little less effort. By Sunday evening, when all the preparations for Gette's safety were in place, everyone was exhausted. Paul and Janice headed back to Paul's apartment and Chad nestled up with Gette early, to let sleep ward off their brewing anxiety.

Monday arrived like every other Monday except Chad had to get up early to rendezvous with Paul and head to O'Hare. Chad scurried away from Gette's apartment in a state of unsettled dishevelment as Jeffries watched through binoculars from afar. The body guards were due for a shift change in the next twenty minutes or so and Bryan, whose appearance was transformed with a Hollywood style application of makeup, had already prepared to be Gette's next protector. He watched anxiously as Chad disappeared around the corner and then waited patiently to time his encounter with the night shift guy.

"Good morning." Bryan bellowed several minutes later. "Nice day. What can you tell me about our client? Any movement from within?"

"Who the fuck are you?" He inquired.

"Oh, sorry, didn't DiGrande tell you? Name's Jonathan." Bryan said extending his hand. "George needed the day off. Something personal I think."

"I better call."

"By all means please do. Here" he said handing the guard his phone, "star-two is a speed dial to DiGrande's private line. No reason he should get to sleep this morning."

The night shift guy took the phone from Bryan and stared at it with utter disinterest. "Oh never mind! I'm exhausted. Take this GD thing," He blurted while handing back the phone, "She should be out pretty soon to take the bus to work. You shouldn't have any issues."

"I think I can handle it." Bryan boasted, "My friend and I go back a long way." He said patting his side to indicate that his 'friend' was a pistol. "You go get some sleep and be back here when my shift ends." And then Bryan walked, no strutted, toward Gette's apartment with a look on his face that made the Cheshire cat seem angelic, with a sneer that made the Grinch's smile welcoming. I love it when a plan comes together, he thought gleefully to himself.

Knowing that a guard was posted outside her apartment allowed Gette to relax just enough to catch a few winks, but not to feel rested in any way. The weight of the situation was so great that even her savored morning ritual felt awkward and burdensome. As difficult as it was, she would follow the plan as promised and that meant sticking steadfastly to her predetermined routine and remaining punctual.

The weather promised no further rise in her angst as the day began with a bright sun in a dry and airy atmosphere, so with purse, PC and a light coat, she started the journey to the Tribute. Bryan was tens of yards behind her as she skipped down the stairs. His car was waiting around the corner two blocks up, where he intended to turn her envisioned abduction into his reality.

"Ms. Cummings," he stated boldly as he closed their gap, "I don't want you to be alarmed. My name is Jonathan Bryant. George had some personal issues come up overnight and is not able to make it today, so here I am instead. I hope you don't mind."

Gette stopped and stared at the man in silence with myriad random thoughts running rampant in her head. There weren't supposed to be any surprises but life is always full of unpredictable events and since this guy shared no resemblance to Jeffries her antennae did not respond with any resounding alarms. His face was wider and his body stocky. His voice husky and his posture hunched.

"I really don't have a choice now do I." She uttered nervously.

"Please don't worry ma'am. I'll just tail you as instructed."

Gette turned to resume her gate while Jeffries observed everything in their paths with utmost intensity. She would think he was employing an appropriately watchful eye, and he was, but in search of the right time to execute his abduction and not in search of her assailant. It was perfect, the focus he needed and the behavior she expected were the same but with opposite intent.

As they neared the next corner Bryan moved closer to Gette and readied the hypo full of sedative. He got within striking distance at just the right moment, pricked the hypo into Gette's neck and caught her as she slumped into a state of semi-consciousness. She went limp more than he expected and weighed more than he expected as well, so he struggled to his car, fueled only from the resistance provided by gravity and nothing more. Still, it was enough for Bryan's heart to race and his sweat to pour as his physical effort and his adrenaline combined to create the greatest sense of euphoria he had ever felt.

As he neared the car he used his key fob to pop the trunk and within seconds wrestled Gette in fetal position to the floor where she lay beautifully still with strands of hair partially covering her placidly adoring face. Bryan looked around for signs of discovery and seeing none turned back to her to stare with relish at his conquest before clicking the trunk lid closed. Part one of his plan was air bound for the conference in Atlanta and part two, the most important part, was now firmly in place and completely under his control. All of the pieces of the puzzle had been put into place; Georgette's vacation "plans" were signed, sealed and delivered so her demise would be judged the result of just another hapless vacationer doing too many drugs. The thought caused his chest to swell with manly pride and gave him an erection in the process.

He walked counterclockwise around the car as if inspecting it for dents and scratches and then jumped into drivers' seat to start the engine. It was a non-descript rental that he picked up using a fake driver's license - allowing him to be invisible, incognito, fly under the radar screen. He thrust the shifter into drive and pulled onto the road with the intention of heading south.

M att DiGrande got to work early on Monday with bags under his eyes from a restless weekend of nonstop worrying. He had to keep Gette safe until the boys returned and then they could put the collar on Jeffries. Work seemed impossible to focus on. Nothing else mattered.

Sitting in his office he could hear the clamor of his employees as they arrived and shared stories of their weekend escapades. He wasn't trying to decipher their conversations but only to confirm from the voices that Gette had arrived safely. He needed to speak to her, to rid himself of the guilt that he felt, to assure himself that their plan was going to work. Where the hell was she? She was supposed to be at work by eight and it was almost 8:30. Matt decided to head to her office. If nothing more the mere act of being in motion would suppress the butterflies in his stomach and let him clear his head. When he arrived her assistant, Meghan, was in her office lining up work materials and tending to other matters of which he knew not.

"Good morning Miss." Matt said startling Meghan. "Have you seen Georgette this morning?"

"Oh Mr. DiGrande, I wasn't expecting you. I'm sorry but no, I haven't seen her and I haven't heard from her. It's very unusual."

"OK. Thanks. When you do see her, please tell her to give me a call. I have a board meeting in a few minutes, but tell her to have my assistant interrupt if it's still underway."

"Absolutely sir." Meghan replied, wondering why Gette was a no-call no-show and why DiGrande, of all people, came to her office in person. It was too weird so she decided to make her own inquiry and called Gette's cell after he left, but to no avail. It just rang and rang until switching over to her voicemail. I wonder who Meghan is, Jeffries thought looking at the name on her phone.

Matt became so infused with the questions from the board that his brain was momentarily void of his other, most pressing, matter. When at last the meeting ended, over two hours later, it dawned on him that he still hadn't heard from Georgette and the realization instantly gave rise to an enormous jolt of dread. He quickly shut his office door and called her cell from his cell and when it rang the caller ID made Bryan giddy with anticipation.

"Hell-oo Matt." Bryan said with mock bravado.

It took a few seconds to register the implications of hearing Bryan's voice on Gette's phone. Then Matt said softly, "Where's Georgette?"

"She's fine Matt. I just need to convince her to be quiet about our affairs. That's all."

"Where are you? Let me talk to her."

"No can do amigo. This journey is all mine to control."

"You're crazy Bryan. You need professional help. Stop this insanity now and you can reverse the damage you've done. I'll help you. Just let her go."

"No can do amigo. I'm too close to the finish line and have no desire to alter my plans. I'm gonna be the world's best fucker of rich divorcees. Monte Carlo, Rome, Geneva, Rio – I've got targets located in lots of places. Superb outlets for my suave debonair and inscrutable libido. Goodbye Matt. Thanks for all your help but you never should have involved anyone else. You should have trusted me. I told you there would be consequences if you didn't. You should've listened. No loose ends Matt. No loose ends."

"Please let me talk to Gette. Don't hurt her. I'm the one to blame. Come get me if you need to but she's just an innocent kid. Leave her alone."

"I don't need to come get you Matt. I've got you already and if anything should happen to this fine woman, well, that'll just be something you'll live with the rest of your life – and a reason why you'll never forget the stupid decisions you made."

"Bryan, Goddamn it, stop this insanity." Matt started to yell, but the line went dead. He immediately redialed Gette's number and then he dialed Bryan's cell but neither phone was powered. He had lost contact and with it came unknown feelings of despair and utter inadequacy. What do I do? Call the police? And tell them what? That I helped this guy who abducted my employee steal millions of dollars from his company? That I know he has taken her but I don't know where they are or where he is going or what he is planning to do? That I was blackmailed in the process because I killed a guy in Miami a hundred years ago? Matt's mind kept swimming in ever tightening circles, forming a whirlpool that threatened to suck him under. He couldn't sit by idly and wait for things to unfold; he had to figure out Bryan's intentions; he had to get into Bryan's completely deranged mind.

Bryan had been driving for a couple of hours so he figured that Gette would regain consciousness sometime soon and decided to find a quiet place to pull over and transfer her from the truck to a seat – if she obeyed – otherwise the trunk would remain her home. He knew the area around Indianapolis pretty well and before long chose a secluded spot in Eagle Creek Park off I-65 to check-in on her. He stopped the car and listened. Birds were chirping and the sounds of maintenance crews could be heard in the distance but otherwise things were quiet, that is, no trunk monkeys as yet. Regardless, he opened the trunk slowly and with caution, not knowing whether Gette was still groggy or tightly coiled and ready to spring. As light penetrated the widening space Bryan could see that Gette was still fast asleep so he began rousting her back into her new reality with pats and gentle shoves.

"Come on girl, come on. Time to wake up. We need to get going." He said while delivering taps to her face, shoulders and arms and a minute later Gette began to stir. She was still groggy enough from the drugs to only react in a dazed and confused manner, not recognizing her surroundings or registering the situation in which she now found herself. Bryan grew impatient, slammed the trunk, returned to the driver's seat and floored the gas pedal.

Gette came to several hours later in a panic the size of Ohio and started yelling in a fright like Night of the Living Dead. At first Bryan turned up the radio to drown her out but after she continued without fail to belt out deafening shrieks he decided it was time for a face to face and stopped in a secluded spot off the highway just north of Louisville. He got out still sporting his mask in hope of having his incognito status add to the drama of the moment because he still wasn't sure if Gette had fully fathomed the severity of her dilemma.

He approached the trunk with stealth and spoke softly in his masked tone, "Georgette, quiet down. I'm going to open the trunk and let you ride in the car but only if you stop screaming and act in an appropriate manner."

"Appropriate manner? Fuck you asshole. You drug me and stick me in a trunk and talk about appropriate? Go to hell!" Gette managed to scream through the lid.

"You want to stay in that trunk or ride more comfortably? The choice is yours. Good behavior, car seat – bad behavior, trunk."

Bryan stood over the closed lid waiting for a response and after getting none continued, "OK stubborn one, I'm going to open the trunk. Come out slowly and keep quiet or I'll be forced to put you back to sleep."

Gette could hear the sound of a key in the lock and on hearing the loud click of the latch releasing she shoved her legs upward in an explosion that popped the lid open with such force that it came back down hard and bruised her shins. It was her intent to whack her assailant with the lid and make an escape, but it failed, and to make matters worse the sun was shining directly into her unadjusted eyes rendering her temporarily unable to see. Instead of knocking her abductor out and making her planned escape, she was no more capable than a blind amputee, hamstrung by loss of sight and searing leg pain.

"Goddamn you! Time to put the lights out." Bryan gasped and easily pricked her arm, for it was coiled up to shade her eyes in defiance of the sun and made for an easy target. "Nighty night sweet heart." He whispered as the darkness once again enveloped her.

The drug would keep Gette asleep for about six hours and by that time Bryan had driven south of Nashville on the way to Atlanta. The thought of passing in close proximity to Stone Mountain conjured a set of mixed emotions from the time that Bryan and Matt spent camping there back in the 70's and afterward, when each took different forks in the road. Bryan stared at the silent cell phones and then powered his up thinking he might share the moment with Matt but the numerous missed calls, all from Matt's number, made him reconsider and he powered it back down.

M att DiGrande was frantic. His security detail had let him down, Gette was now Bryan's prisoner and he was completely and utterly to blame. After the dismal call from Bryan Matt cancelled all of his meetings, abruptly left the building to find out what happened to his guards, and to seek some sort of direction to mitigate the crisis. Matt was miserable, turned upside down and wrenched inside out, ever since Bryan reentered his life with threats of exposing their past and his lies about the true nature of his money laundering scheme. His depth of despair seemed to have no end for his participation in what was now definitely grand larceny was totally out of his control and totally out of control in general.

Matt knew that he had to get hold of Chad and Paul as soon as they touched down in Atlanta because both would be checking in with Gette the moment they arrived and her failure to answer her phone would set off red flags the size of Mount Everest. They weren't due to touch down for another hour so Matt immediately called his guard.

On answering Matt received a groggy, almost imperceptible "Hello?" as a response.

"George, what the fuck? What happened? Why aren't you guarding Ms. Cummings?"

"Oh shit, Mr. Di. What time is it? I must have overslept. I feel like shit. Can't remember when I felt so bad!"

"You must've been drugged George."

"Huh? What'da mean?"

"What happened last night George?"

"Nothin' really. After I got off my shift I went to get a bite to eat and had a couple of beers. Then I went home."

"Did anyone approach you? I mean, did anyone strike up a conversation with you?"

"Come to think of it, yeah. Some suit sat down next to me. Real friendly guy. Started talking all about some whacky trip he took with a friend back in high school."

"What exactly did he say?"

"Not much. He kept talking about some night in Miami a long time ago. Must have been a doosie. He seemed to enjoy reliving the moment. Is everything OK?"

"Not at all George. Not at all. The quote "suit" that befriended you must have slipped a drug or something into your drink. He ended up as your replacement the next morning and has abducted Georgette Cummings. I have no idea where he is, but it must be Bryan Jeffries."

"But the guy didn't look a bit like Mr. J."

"I understand that George, but only Jeffries would talk about a trip to Miami from long ago. It was Jeffries alright."

"Jesus, Mr. Di. I'm so sorry. What can I do?"

"Nothing, for now, but stay available in case I need you."

Matt hung up the phone and again called Bryan. No answer. Same with Gette. He sat on a park bench to collect his thoughts, but wasn't able to bring them into focus, wasn't able to synthesize anything tangible for that matter. He bent down toward the sidewalk clasping both hands at the cusp of his neck and started to cry. I wasn't a sad cry but a cry of utter despair, of anger and fear, of contempt and dismay.

Fucking Jeffries, he thought. When and where did he go so wrong? Matt wondered how different things would have been if their trip to Florida wasn't tainted by manslaughter and flight. He wondered what would have been if they retained their friendship, perhaps it would have been better; perhaps it would have been worse, regardless, Bryan was off his rocker. It started that summer after high school when he got his first taste of independence and it apparently took years to become fully developed, but it did and now Matt had to deal with a full-fledged psychopath.

He sat still for several minutes trying to calm down, trying to control his blood pressure and lessen the pounding of his tormented heart. He could hear his blood raging through his veins like a swollen stream after a deluge and could feel the dire attempts of his brain cells trying to ease their stress induced aching. He focused every ounce of concentration on his inner self to stem the random flow of abstract thought that was overtaxing his system but gain ground he did not. The circumstance was simply too insane, obtuse to the point of losing form, inconceivable beyond all manner of rationality. Then the sound of his cell jolted him back towards reality.

"This is Matt." He said blindly.

"Mr. DiGrande, this is Chad. Is everything OK? We just landed and haven't been able to reach Gette."

""I don't know how to tell you this, but Jeffries played us for fools. He donned a mask, drugged my guard, replaced him at the morning shift and abducted Georgette. I don't know where he's going but we've got to stop him."

"Oh my God! If anything happens to Gette I won't forgive myself or you for that matter. Fuck! I'm going to be sick! Jesus H. Christ on a crutch. That crazy son-of-a-bitch. We've got to intercept him. Think, damn you. What's his plan? You've got to get into his head."

"I will. I promise I will. Stay put for the next hour while I find a solution."

"Stay put? How can I possibly remain idle? I've got to do something. I've got to save her. I love her."

"I know. It's going to be OK. He won't harm her without first making some sort of show; he'll have to do something theatrical first, something bizarre to get his time in the limelight. I know he'll be in touch with me, so be ready to move when we get the rules of the game."

"Easier said than done." Chad exasperated.

"Go to your hotel. Park your car where you can get to it quickly. Keep your phones on and charged. I'll get back in touch as soon as I can."

"This sucks. Jesus H. Christ, this sucks." Chad cried, and then hung up.

Jeffries kept driving at a quick pace but not too fast to draw the attention of troopers in the area. He was whistling to some music as his car sped through Georgia when noises could again be heard from the trunk. It couldn't be very comfortable, he thought, being cramped in a hard shelled compartment in the heat of the day. She probably had to take a piss too so maybe her level of discomfort, exacerbated by the full bladder, would keep her behavior in check – at least for a while.

He was in southern Georgia on route 75 miles from any populated land and far away from anyone with the possibility of more than an eighth grade education, so it was a simple task to toss his mask into the back seat and take the next exit for a remote place to stop.

He got out of the car, this time without a word, and opened the trunk. Gette lay there breathing heavily; her brow was wet with perspiration and her hair was mangled by the drug induced lolling that she endured for the past several hundred miles. She stared at him long with the hatred of a mother fending for the life of her infant and then slowly began to extract herself from the trunk. Bryan reached down to offer assistance and she shrugged him off like horse ridding itself of a tick.

"Don't touch me you cock sucker. I knew it was you."

"Whatever you say pretty lady."

"Why did you kidnap me? Where are you taking me? I need a bathroom."

"Some good questions, but not ones I intend to answer, and this," Bryan stated while sweeping his arms around the vista, "is your bathroom. Pee away pretty lady."

"Are you crazy?"

"Some may so think, yes, but if you want to pee you'd better go now or you'll be forced to wet yourself later."

Gette looked at Bryan's face with the loathing of a bull wanting to gore a taunting Matador and then swept the area for signs of life, help in any imaginable form, and found none.

Bryan moved to the other side of the car, "Complete your duty in the next two minutes or face the trunk and the disgrace of lying in your own piss. Your choice."

What a choice. Face the indignity of squatting on the ground like a third world peasant or endure the shame and discomfort of wetting herself. Without further hesitation she chose the former and was quick to open the flood gates.

"Very good pretty lady. Now for a repeat of the rules. Good behavior – sit in the car. Bad behavior – remain in the trunk. What'll it be?"

Gette chose not to answer or even look directly at her abductor but moved deftly instead around the front of the car and into the passenger's seat. Her cell phone lay in the console between them and she grabbed it and tried to turn it on as Matt snatched it from her still stiffened fingers.

"Let me have the honor pretty lady." Bryan said in jest as he pulled back onto the highway. "I'll just give Mr. DiGrande a little update if you don't mind."

He opened the window that displayed the most recent calls and rang DiGrande's cell. "Hello Matt. Not the voice you expected to hear is it?" Bryan said toyingly.

"Where is she Bry? Put her on the phone."

"Oh my, pretty lady, Mr. DiGrande wants to speak with you. It seems that your absence from the office has created quite a stir. Here." And he handed Gette the phone.

"Gette is that you?"

"Yes."

"Don't speak. Just answer my questions. OK?"

"Yes."

"Are you alright?"

"Depends on your definition but I'm still in one piece."

"Good. Just answer yes or no. You're in a car?"

"Yes"

"Is the sun to your left?"

"No."

"OK that means you're headed south. Is the terrain flat?"

"Yes."

"Are the trees strange looking scrubby pines?"

"Yes." Gette said to her amazement.

"OK. I think I know what's going on. Hang in there, don't rile him up and try not talk to him too much. Now..." Matt started as Bryan took control.

"Feel better ol' pal? See, I told you she's fine and in one piece."

"Bryan, wherever you are just stop at the next rest stop, let Gette go and I'll make sure that this matter ends quietly and permanently."

"It's going to end that's for sure but it just won't be as quick as you think. Goodbye ol' buddy." Bryan hollered as he disconnected and powered down her phone.

Matt immediately called Chad and Paul, "I just spoke with Gette. She's still fine, obviously terrified but fine. I was able to get enough information from her to know that they're headed south. Based on the timing my guess is that they are in southern Georgia with the goal of getting to Miami Beach. That gives us plenty of time to work on a way to intercept them and wrestle control of the situation. I'll explain more later but for now get on the first flight to Miami or Ft. Lauderdale. Leave as soon as you can but first send me your itinerary so I will know when and where to meet you."

"Miami? Why Miami? What's going on? Are you sure that's where they're headed?"

"They're going to Miami. I'll explain it all later. Just get there. I'm heading to O'Hare so text me your itineraries when you get them. Trust me. See you in Florida." And Matt hung up.

Chad and Paul grabbed their things and checked out of the hotel as hastily as possible. Paul agreed to drive to Hartsfield while Chad searched for flight options, which he was able to complete by the time they returned their rental car.

"I got us on a flight that leaves in less than 2 hours arriving in Miami at 7:45. DiGrande is getting in a little later and asked us to wait for him at the Rental Car facility."

"I've been thinking about Gette's drive down with that asshole. It should take them roughly 24 hours to get there if he drives straight through. That would put them into the area sometime tomorrow morning at the earliest so between now and then we are going to have to listen to DiGrande's pitch and agree on a plan to intercept them. I just hope that DiGrande knows what he's doing. Gette's very existence depends on it."

"Never in my life have I been as completely disheveled as I am right now. Gette is so new to me, but she's my whole life. She and I have created a bond that I hoped would last our lifetimes and now it could be stamped out within hours and I have little if any control of the outcome. I can't think. I can't breathe. Everything seems surreal, like our time is passing through some type of odd portal completely disassociated with reality. It's hard to explain."

"I understand and I'm with you every step of the way. As hard as it is, we've got to stay focused and keep a positive attitude if we want to have any chance of saving Gette."

They rode in silence the remaining minutes to Hartsfield, passed through security without ceremony and arrived at their appointed departure gate with plenty of time to spare. As is typical of rush hour at Hartsfield there were about 20 flights scheduled to depart at the same time with all of them advertising on-time departures which is a physical impossibility. Finally, an airline representative broadcast the boarding announcement of their flight and a long queue formed as the various zones were allowed entrance. By the time the normal debacle with too much carryon luggage was sorted and everyone was seated, they were past their time of departure and number 8 in line to take off. While this scenario is commonplace in Atlanta it caused their nervous anxiety to pique at unprecedented heights, so it was with pounding hearts, tapping feet and jittery hands that their flight took to the air.

Slightly under two hours later they touched down at Miami International Airport full of questions for their rendezvous with DiGrande. Silently, both were hoping that his answers would be sufficient to alleviate their fears, but doubted it because there simply was no way he could predict the movements of a madman. They deplaned in an unexpected state of remorseful quietude having already expended their energy from several emotionally laden rushes of adrenaline.

Ten minutes later they spotted DiGrande walking into the rental car area and he waved for them to join him in their quest to find the car. He didn't offer any updated information nor did he apologize or try to allay their fears. Those conversations would wait for dinner, which he had arranged at a nearby Cuban restaurant by the name of Versailles.

When they arrived and were seated Chad and Paul thought that DiGrande's selection of a restaurant was completely inappropriate because it was an airy family style place that had no ability to afford them privacy. The menu presented them with an enormous number of excellent entrée selections from various ethnicities, but it still didn't feel right for the discussion they so urgently needed. DiGrande begged them to order their meals and be patient for a few minutes before their conversation was to begin in earnest and his decision proved to be spot on for in the ensuing minutes the restaurant became intensely active with all forms of vivacious theatrical parties whose cacophony of conversation provided a noise shield from their own.

DiGrande finally began, "In the summer of 1976 Bryan Jeffries and I traveled the southeast together before heading off to college. It was the first time we were left unsupervised for any length and after a few weeks on the road the idea of independence took hold of Jeffries psyche in a bad way. Without the overbearing control of his father his natural demeanor, perhaps his real self, began to emerge and it was like witnessing Dr. Jekyll transforming into Mr. Hyde. Anyway, that's not the point of the story." Matt stopped to take a sip from his beer.

"One night he and I separated after drinking in a night club. He took a girl back to her room while I felt a chivalrous need to help protect a barmaid, who had waited on us that evening, stay safe from her estranged boyfriend, so I covertly followed her home after she left work. Her boyfriend saw me and went berserk. He was a big strong, hard drinking surfer type of guy and he immediately started beating the shit out of me, like he was trying to kill me. Fortunately at the same time Bryan happened to pass by on his way back to our hotel and saw me on the ground literally getting my brains beat out. He jumped on the guy to protect me and got the same treatment that I did. In a matter of seconds Bryan was on the ground getting bloody from head to toe. I didn't know what to do when I saw an empty magnum of cheap wine in the gutter so

I used it as a club and dusted the bottle off the back of the guy's head. The neck of the bottle broke into a sharp point and ended up piercing an artery. The next thing I knew, the guy was dead."

Chad and Paul sat still and silent as the implications of DiGrande's narrative began to gel, and then DiGrande continued, "It happened so quickly. We were scared to death. Our only thoughts were going to jail when we should have been going to college, so we left the scene as fast as we could and got out of Miami."

"That's what caused your friendship to end and what also formed the basis of Jeffries' ability to blackmail you into abetting his crime. And that's why we're here. Because you think Jeffries is so deranged that he's going to re-enact the crime with Gette as the victim," Paul said.

"Unfortunately, yes, something like that yes."

"Oh my God, he is going to kill her," Chad suddenly spurted, "This is so fucking absurd. You sent her on an assignment that you knew was dangerous. You signed her death warrant, you son-of-a-bitch."

"I was being blackmailed when I asked Gette to investigate World-Supplî, that's true, but I had no idea that the money was stolen. It was supposedly Jeffries money, money that he didn't want to lose by breaking up with his common law partner. I got duped. I believed him and I guess that made me succumb to his demands, because it was presented as an unethical activity, but not an illegal one."

"Well how do you feel now you shithead?"

"OK enough," Paul interrupted, "We have to be able to sabotage Jeffries' plan. We need a fool proof way to intercede before he does more harm to Gette. How do we do that? Where do we start?"

"If my hunch is right," DiGrande continued over dinner, "Bryan is going to take his act back to the location where we first encountered our problem. We need to go there to scout out the area so we can establish the best vantage points for full visibility. After that's decided we'll have to devise a strategy on how to communicate between us and how to intervene at the appropriate time. The last thing we need is to jump the gun and alert Bryan of our presence in a premature manner. If we do, I'm sure he'll abort his plan and flee as fast as possible, while possibly leaving Georgette in his wake. We can't afford that."

As dinner was hastily consumed they continued brainstorming the most effective strategy for stopping Bryan. Afterwards they jumped in the car and headed for Miami Beach and Penrods to visit the presumed site of the prophesized murder. When they arrived Matt needed to sit a moment to gather his thoughts and tame the butterflies that were raging in his abdomen before making the emotionally grueling trek to the scene of their so-long-ago-committed manslaughter. He had no problem recalling the route to the scene for it had played itself ad-infinitum for years in his dreams in a variety of abstract and nightmarish episodes.

Though finding the spot was an easy process knowing how Bryan would use it to safely pull off his lunatic laden plan was not so easy, for what Matt remembered as a lazy rarely used back street alley appeared now to be a more socially active location with tourists, homeless and regulars all milling randomly about. Several areas looked adequate for them to conduct surveillance of incoming activity but none really offered a means to stay hidden in the process so they were left devoid of a sound overall method from which to stymy the crazy fool.

"If he sees us," Paul began, "he'll recognize us and take off and that would be fine if Gette is with him 'cause I'm sure she'll try to slow him down. But what if he comes here by himself to scout out the area beforehand? In that case we're screwed. Since we can't hide we're going to have to disguise ourselves."

"What're we going to do?" Chad asked, "Dress up as homeless people?"

"I think we should be able to get false facial hair and sunglasses. That should be enough, it's not like he's looking for us. In fact I'll bet he's cocky as hell right now."

"Listen gents," Matt started, "It's getting late and we need some rest. We should be camouflaged and in our places by 8:00 AM at the latest. Let's go buy the stuff we need right now and then head to the hotel. Tomorrow's going to be long day."

"I'm not going to sleep a wink." Chad stated with dire exasperation.

"I doubt any of us will sleep, but we have to rest regardless."

B ryan kept a quiet vigil over Gette while he drove them from Georgia to Florida. Gette wanted to ask him a thousand questions, to play his hand with the information that she gathered during her stint as the Tribute's newest investigative reporter, but refrained from the desire based solely on the comments from DiGrande during their brief exchange. She knew there was nothing she could do at the moment anyway so she resolved to keep a clear head and be ready to capitalize on any opportunity that might emerge, when it emerged. Bryan would eventually have to stop – for gas, for food, for lodging – at some point he would give Gette a chance to scream, or run or something else.

It was getting dark and Gette could see Bryan squinting and shaking his head to keep his focus on the road and just as she was thinking that a break wouldn't be long, he exited the highway and pulled the car to a stop.

"Reach into the glove compartment and give me the hotel reservation. It's the paper on top." Bryan said abruptly.

Gette didn't know what to make of the command but complied by reaching out slowly to pop open the compartment and when she did she felt a small prick in her bicep. "You son of a ..." she started to yell as the drug enveloped her in a clouded darkened state of slumber.

"Time to get some food and rest pretty lady," Bryan whispered to no one while starting the car and heading to a fleabag hotel a few miles down the road. He paid the innkeeper in cash, headed straight for the room and then looked about the ramshackle place in amazement. The décor, even when new, was ugly at best but now it was worn, stained and outdated yet it appeared to be clean and the paper strap across the toilet seat authenticated an aura of sanitation in the otherwise stale air.

When he finished assessing his surroundings and deemed their stay secure Bryan got back into the car to find the Piggly Wiggly that he knew existed just two miles south of their current locale. It was a basic store that was lit too brightly and stocked somewhat haphazardly, but it was sufficient for his needs and would be his only stop that evening. Some chips, pre-made sandwiches, a vegetable platter, cheap bottle of wine and a few other goods were hastily acquired for their ability to satiate without any thought of their flavor or other appeal.

He filled the gas tank on the way back and when they returned, after unlocking the door, managed to quickly and secretly get Gette inside. He set her gingerly on the bed and chose not to move her further, opting instead to unpack the groceries and pour a glass of wine. He ate the meager spread in a slow autonomic fashion with the local news channel giving overly drawn-out minute-by-minute updates on the upcoming weather. The simple cadence of the local newscasters had a lulling, calming effect and within minutes of being full it brought on a crushing unavoidable drowsiness, so he secured Gette to the bed and was soon deep in sleep.

He awoke some five plus hours later feeling refreshed and was ready to get back on the road after taking a quick shower. Gette was still sleeping when he packed the car with the remaining grocery items so he dragged her into the passenger seat. Within minutes they were cruising highway 75 down the center of the state with Miami less than six hours away. Bryan was so engrossed with the favorable state of his escapade that he broke out in laughter at the idea of destroying DiGrande and vanishing into the sunset. The thought of lying on a beach in the Riviera with beautiful women swooning over him while young maidens took to his service made Bryan so giddy with anticipation that he slapped the dashboard and woke Gette up in the process.

"Good morning pretty lady," he said, though it was still dark. "There's some food on the floor by your feet. Have at it, you must be starving."

"Where are we? Where are we going?"

"That's not for you to worry. I've got everything under control."

M att stayed in one room while Chad and Paul shared another. The trauma they were managing had zapped them of all strength; had stripped them clean of every raw emotion, leaving them feeling like freshly caught gutted fish, their insides having been brutally ripped out and tossed aside like rotten food from the fridge to the garbage can. Despite all attempts to fend off the feeling of betrayal that sleep was invoking, none could withhold against their utter exhaustion and soon all were snoring.

They had agreed to meet in the hotel lobby at seven sharp to don their disguises and then take up their appointed positions at the crime scene. It was a typically sunny, humid and hot Miami Beach morning and as they exited the hotel they were blanketed by the oppressive atmosphere that beach goers thrive on. Matt was feeling confident that they would surprise Bryan and put a quick end to the matter but Chad and Paul didn't share his enthusiasm. Neither could see more than a 10% chance of success because no one had any control over the time, circumstances or actions that would be needed for success to be achieved. Their overarching fear of failure and its resultant implications were far too unimaginable to be put into words so they remained quiet, each focused on control of his own angst, control of the numerous scenarios battling endlessly in their subconscious like a writer trying to imagine the most appropriate ending to a screen play.

By eight they were in place performing their surveillance activities just as they had discussed the evening prior but this time was different in every conceivable way. This wasn't acting. This wasn't the final practice before the big playoff game. This was the real thing and with it came an unprecedented intensity that placed them all on high alert status, where every second felt like a minute and every movement a full motion picture.

The first hour passed quickly without incident and the second also passed without incident, but not so quickly. Every minute grew more difficult to bear and soon all were a nervous bundle of fidgety energy on the verge of igniting, like a match hovering above a pool of gasoline; like energy in a seeded cloud ready to cast its first bolt of lightning.

Chad stood at a corner with fixated eyes sweeping the intersection for signs of Gette; his heart racing as his adrenaline dowsed blood coursed through his veins. Under no possible scenario could he fathom continuing life without her. The improvements that her life made to his were beyond anything he ever imagined. She was his other side, what gave space depth, what gave emotion pizazz, what gave meaning relevance. The thought of her succumbing to the demise of a maniac was impossible to sort but it kept looming beneath the surface nonetheless, like a Great White toying with the ruin of a baby seal.

It was then that he spotted a car driving slowly through the stakeout and in it the unmistakable face of the lunatic that Jeffries had become. Chad stood paralyzed for a second as he gazed upon the inhuman expression of insanity held in the bottomless reflection of Bryan's dilated pupils. He could see Gette in the seat beside him just barely enough to know that something was wrong. Her face seemed expressionless, inert and her body lax, lifeless. Chad immediately speed dialed Paul and Matt but without purpose for they too had seen the car and, like Chad, were in hot pursuit.

So much time had passed since the incident in Miami that an untold level of change had occurred in the area surrounding Penrod's. Bryan was awed by several factors, first that he was able to pinpoint the spot of their altercation and second by how different that quiet little alley had become, so different that its change cast the need to pursue an alternative plan for Gette's demise.

Driving slowly through the area rekindled the adolescent emotions from their summer trip like it was happening all over again. Flirting images of their cigar sickness and failed tenting escapade and Stone Mountain flooded Bryan's thoughts with the feelings of youthful vigor and determination that was then so pervasive. It made him think of Carlo and his story of the banged up pickup that he held so dear and with the surfacing of that memory was instantly disclosed to Bryan the perfect resolve to his dilemma. That's where he would go - to Carlo's apartment complex. Surely it was still intact and without inordinate change. That's where he would off Gette. Perhaps she would fall to her untimely death from the balcony in front of the room that they rented from Carlo, but first he would have to find it.

Matt, Paul and Chad stood on the corner watching in utmost despair as Bryan drove away, northbound on Ocean Drive.

"Come on. Follow me." Matt screamed and darted westward toward Collins. "My guess is that he's turning around on Collins to head out of town. We may be able to stop him there."

"What are you thinking?" Chad bellowed.

"He needs a new location to get rid of Georgette. I think I know where he's going and if he is we should see him again because he'll have to pass us by."

Matt's brain was moving so quickly that even a Formula One would be left in the dust. He had to guess Bryan's next move and guess it now and there was only one place that made sense – Carlo's apartment complex.

"Paul, go get the car and meet us on Collins Avenue heading south. Chad and I will try to keep eye contact, if we can, for as long we can, but we have to move quickly. Here are the keys."

286

Paul took off in a shot and Matt, with Chad in tow, kept running without breaking a stride. Collins was still a block away.

Bryan knew that the general direction to Carlo's apartment complex lay southwest of South Beach but where exactly was not yet in recall, so he crossed Collins rather pensively before he decided to head south on Washington and over the causeway.

Matt and Chad got to the corner on Collins out of breath but still very much focused on finding Bryan. For several minutes that seemed like hours they scanned up and down, back and forth looking for his car. Then, just by chance, Chad thought he caught a glimpse to their west.

"I think I saw his car. It was heading south over there," Chad yelled while pointing, "a few blocks away."

"Shit! We've got to get going." Matt exclaimed as a horn behind them beeped. It was Paul.

They jumped into the car and Matt started barking orders. They had to get over the causeway quickly but also had to be ready to exit the highway the moment Matt sensed the need. Paul floored the rental with the doors still closing and they took off, albeit at the pace of the smallest engine their model provided. While it screamed and revved and gave forth what seemed like inordinate effort their gain was little, but at least they were moving and the traffic was bearable.

I remember now." Matt exclaimed. "Take the first exit when we reach the mainland and continue going straight. Stay in the right hand lane because we have to turn right, I just don't know exactly where."

Silence returned to the vehicle. All three minds remained separated in thought even though they were all sharply focused on the same objective. Matt was digging into his memory banks while scanning the area for signs of familiarity. Paul kept eyeing the road for every contingency like a bird of prey trying to spot a mouse and Chad sat still conjuring various action plans for the fated moment. Immediately on arrival he would connect his phone to 911, opening communication to local authorities.

"Paul, slow down and stay to the right. OK, OK, keep going, keep going. Now!" Matt yelled. "Take this right. This has to be the one. It's only a few blocks from here."

Paul kept moving the car at an even clip and Chad's heart was thumping so loudly he thought the car had a flat tire.

"Shit. Stop! I think we are off by a block."

Like Matt, Bryan too had difficulty remembering the apartment's location, but true to form, luck won over his vagueness and within minutes of exiting the causeway he spotted Carlos' building. An overwhelming feeling of completeness shuttered through his body like a lone wave in an otherwise still pool. His face remained calm and stoic but underneath he held a grin like the Cheshire cat; a swelling pride like a Super Bowl champ. Gette was still dazed and groggy so Bryan made for a parking spot as close to the stairs as possible. He would drag her to the second floor, administer a deadly dose of heroin and snap her neck just before she would fall to her drug addicted death. It would be ruled death by overdose from a vacationer gone awry.

Paul immediately slammed on the brakes while Matt gave new instructions. Fortunately, traffic was light and he was able to implement the Matt's reroute without much delay. A few tense minutes later Matt spotted Carlos' apartment building and as he did a dual sense of relief and fear overwhelmed him. He could see Bryan wrestling with Georgette, whose virtually lifeless figure seemed glued to his.

Chad saw Bryan too so he immediately dialed 911 and kept the connection live. Paul floored the listless engine and then slammed on the brakes as everyone piled out of the car. Bryan was at the rail getting Gette in place as he reached into his pocket to oust the syringe. The trio of saviors was running madly toward the scene – Paul bounding up the stairs while Matt and Chad made hay for the tarmac beneath. Bryan's arm shot up quickly with the killing needle to thrust it into Gette's neck and just as he did, a shot rang out from afar.

The echo of the gun blast shattered the silence and jolted everyone into a new reality like an abrupt awakening from a full-fledged night mere. At that moment Bryan slumped to the ground, and Gette, who remained steadfastly drugged, fell forward over the rail toward an open parking space below. Matt DiGrande arrived just in time to let his body break her fall and the two tumbled in a heap to the ground.

Chad arrived a millisecond later and began to assess the damage. Matt was groaning in pain and, while still listless, Gette could be heard muttering incoherently, which conferred on Chad an instant stream of tears and nonstop uncontrollable sobbing. Paul hovered over the seemingly lifeless body of Bryan and then confirmed his suspicions by checking for a pulse in the closest carotid. As he knelt there the presence of another person became evident from the shadow it cast over his immediate area and when he looked up staring solemnly back at him was an elderly Hispanic gentleman with deep piercing eyes and weathered brown skin. "I tol' the police I was gonna shoot the next bastard that came here selling drugs." Carlos said emphatically. Then Paul sat down, put his head in his hands and for the first time in years talked to God.

Thanks to Chad's phone idea a tsunami of sirens could be heard approaching the scene. It was obvious that multiple vehicles were enroute to their locale and within minutes the place was swarming with every type of public assistance employee imaginable. The cops took immediate control and then Chad begged them to let the EMT's usher aide to Gette and Matt. About twenty minutes later, and what seemed like hours, enough information had been shared with the lead detective to allow an ambulance, with Matt, Gette, Chad and a trailing cop car, passage to the nearest emergency room.

The cops had handcuffed Carlos and locked him in the back of another squad car. Lawyers would be needed to untangle this mess.

Epilogue

Matt DiGrande hired a prominent local attorney to protect his interests and to represent Carlos. Testimonies on Carlos' behalf were received from everyone and he was eventually released with a misdemeanor for illegal discharge of a firearm.

Matt suffered a sprained wrist and a couple of broken ribs and, after employing his most masterful powers of persuasion, convinced his attorney to allow him to come clean on the homicide. The circumstances of the entire event were so bizarre that the court ruled no contest by way of defense and let him go. His blond assailant from 1976 apparently had a long rap sheet and case files revealed that the authorities of the time were happy to see him get throttled.

Paul and Janice continued working in their respective companies albeit as husband and wife shortly after the Jeffries affair was put to a close. Janice remained in her position at the bank, but Paul was immediately given a shot at Bryan's old job as Chief Technology Officer. Their careers blossomed just as much as did their family.

Chad and Gette also stayed at their respective jobs but in their spare time they worked on a variety of songs. Years later, married but without kids, they became so popular making beautiful music together that both were able to forego their business careers in favor of their art.

Bryan Jeffries was buried without ceremony in his home town. His mother remained baffled by the faux reunion to her death a year later.

CPSIA information can be obtained
at www.ICGtesting.com
Printed in the USA
BVOW03s0230190717
489675BV00001B/49/P